PENGUIN BOOKS

THE GYPSIES

Jean-Paul Clébert was born in Paris in 1926. He was educated in a religious boarding-school until, in 1943, he abandoned his studies and joined the Resistance. When the war was over he took on various jobs in order to be free to continue his writing. At this period he knew Blaise Cendrars and Henry Miller and wrote under their influence.

Clébert's books always reflect the bonds between man and society; solitude and communication. His first book, *Paris insolite*, was a documentary about the tramps of Paris; his second, *La Vie sauvage*, about vagrants; his third, *Le Blockhaus*, portrayed imprisoned men. At the moment he is working on a new novel dealing with the psychology of a spy.

For the last ten years he has been living in Provence, isolated amongst the mountains with his wife, his dogs and the untamed landscape. Here he writes books on the archaeology and the prehistoric finds of the region.

D0499915

JEAN-PAUL CLÉBERT

The Gypsies

TRANSLATED BY
CHARLES DUFF

PENGUIN BOOKS

Penguin Books Ltd, Harmondsworth, Middlesex, England
Penguin Books Inc., 7110 Ambassador Road, Baltimore, Maryland 21207, U.S.A.
Penguin Books Australia Ltd, Ringwood, Victoria, Australia

—

Les Tziganes first published 1961
This translation published by Vista Books 1963
Published in Penguin Books, 1967
Reprinted 1969, 1970

—

Les Tziganes copyright © B. Arthaud, Paris, 1961
This translation copyright © Vista Books, Longacre Press Ltd, 1963

—

Made and printed in Great Britain by
Cox & Wyman Ltd,
London, Reading and Fakenham
Set in Monotype Fournier

CONTENTS

TRANSLATOR'S FOREWORD

To this English version of Jean-Paul Clébert's book I have added some footnotes of my own. The object of these supplementary notes, in general, is either to add some information of particular interest to readers in the English-speaking world; or to indicate some further source of information that will be found in English. For the same reasons I have added to the author's Bibliography one which will supplement it. The majority of the titles in my 'Supplementary Bibliography' are of important or interesting books available in English. Some of these books are classics of their kind; others contain information about British or American Gypsies. The remainder, in various languages, are either works by great modern gypsi-ologists or by other writers who have contributed something valuable or at least interesting to the subject, in one or other of its many aspects. Finally, I have deemed it advisable to add, in a supplement, some Notes containing recent information about Britain's Gypsy population, and that of the U.S.A. In regard to Britain's Gypsies, I have included some statistics provided by Mr Derek Tipler, a warm friend of Britain's Gypsies, whom he knows probably as well as any man living. My thanks are due to him.

To Miss Dora Yates and the Gypsy Lore Society, of which she has long been the very active Honorary Secretary, I am indebted for encouragement and the invaluable help in the task of making avail-able to all readers of English this fine general exposition of a puzzl-ing, often even mysterious, but always intensely interesting subject.

In at least one respect the Gypsies are unique as a people, and this is important to note: for century after century, often in extremely dangerous circumstances in some countries, they have maintained a consistent struggle for their freedom – based on a desire to live their own lives in their own way. They have shown that they can die for that freedom, rather than conform to norms other than their own. Surely they have a lesson for us in an increasingly conformist world?

London, 1963   CHARLES DUFF

LIST OF ILLUSTRATIONS

All photographs by Marcelle Vallet are © S.P.A.D.E.M., Paris 1963.

MAPS

DRAWINGS

INTRODUCTION

There are today some five or six million Gypsies wandering about the world. But we do not see them; or, rather, we do not see them except in small numbers, caravan after caravan, family after family. It is only exceptionally, and in the course of pilgrimages open to the public, that one may suddenly come upon several hundreds of them.

These five or six million Gypsies are distributed throughout our world like those rare plants which grow only in places where nature has provided a few special conditions. We find Gypsies by the sides of roads, on the outskirts of woods, and of villages where their invisible presence is attested by a notice 'No nomads' or 'No Gypsies'. Yet we rub shoulders with them in flea-markets, at travelling shows on holidays, and in the vicinity of the last travelling circuses. We even consult them on the sly. People go so far as to gaze at a group of them as on the occasion of their festival at Saintes-Maries-de-la-Mer in France (or in England on Epsom Downs; at racecourses in Britain or the United States of America).[1] Or as people formerly used to stare at the families of Pahouines from the French Congo, or at natives of Zanzibar, exhibited in cages at the 'Acclimatization Garden' in Paris. Above all else, Gypsies are feared: if the truth were known, they are not liked. When they are not openly held in contempt, the Gypsies, men and women, receive the benefit of that recurring little dose of racism which one day puts the blame for something on flashy South American adventurers, and the next on North African coloured people.[2] So it is that the Gypsies, and they alone, are held to be vagabonds, beggars, thieves and weavers of spells. Even the authorities do not succeed in regarding them as honest citizens. They forbid them to camp on the outskirts of villages; they subject them to police supervisions of which the least we can say is that they are vexatious; and incessantly they drive

1. Translator's addition in brackets.

2. In these observations the author refers particularly to France, his own country; but they apply to others. *Tr.*

them from district to district. At the same time – and this is something the public knows least about – the authorities subject these nomads to military and tax obligations. Regarded throughout their whole lives as pariahs, the Gypsies are sent on active service at twenty years of age.[1]

The little that is currently known about the Gypsies is summed up in what everyday publications – magazines, newspapers and all the bad literature on the subject – have unflaggingly repeated, unceasingly taking up the most threadbare leitmotive of a facile picturesqueness. And seldom with the least regard for truth.

The vulgarization of ethnology is such in our time that people are better informed about the manners and customs of the last thirty Alalakuf Indians than about the origins and kind of life of those Gypsies with whom we have so lightly rubbed shoulders from childhood.

The fact that 400,000 Gypsies were hanged, shot or gassed in the Nazi concentration camps, in precisely the same way as the Jews, has passed over our heads almost unnoticed. If Carmen Amaya, Django Reinhardt, the Brothers Bouglione, Yoshka Nemeth or Theo Medina in their various ways have enriched the art of the theatre, this matters little; or so it seems. In France, the pilgrimage of Saintes-Maries-de-la-Mer (at which tourists are more numerous than Gypsies) appears as a wish to revive each year the myth of the Gypsy as handsome, proud and free; a myth by which romanticism had already replaced that of the 'noble savage'. Yet, where Gypsies are concerned, the articles, newspaper reports or the pictures on television rarely reflect anything but a stubborn ignorance, a flagrant indifference.

There are profound reasons for this failure to appreciate a whole people. This book will attempt to sift out the truth, little by little. It will be seen that, at all times when people of fixed residence have regarded nomads as dangerous characters, the instability of the latter can be a menace to the stability of the former. And the Gypsies in particular were regarded as the 'sorcerers, mountebanks and thieves' of whom Beranger sang. Yet our prejudices are not alone to be blamed: the Gypsies themselves have done much in order to remain unknown to others. Living on the margin of civilization, they still make use of the means of defence suitable to people who have no

1. In these observations the author refers particularly to France, his own country; but they apply to others. *Tr.*

sense of society. Jealous of their ethnic unity, conscious of their racial originality, satisfied with their natural way of life, they refuse as far as possible to have contact with townspeople and country folk of fixed domicile. They have no wish to let us know about the less obvious features of their way of life. They systematically tell lies, thereby providing evidence of the normal, self-defence reflex on the part of a minority that has so long been exposed to the most exorbitant demands. They are ready at the same time to take upon themselves that share of malediction which men have always wanted to load upon certain of their fellow men whom they wished to treat as scapegoats.

In spite of all this, the Gypsies represent an exceptional case: they are the unique example of an ethnic whole perfectly defined, which, through space and time for more than one thousand years, and beyond the frontiers of Europe, has achieved success in a gigantic migration – without even having consented to any alteration as regards the originality and singleness of their race. Only the Jewish *diaspora*[1] can be put on a parallel with the dispersion of the Gypsies. But the Jews have integrated themselves with the civilizations of the countries through which they have gone. If they remain Jews, they nonetheless adapt themselves to the conditions of life of their new environment. The Gypsies, on the contrary, have achieved the remarkable feat of ploughing through the civilized world while continuing to conform to the rules of existence that were used by the nomads of Asia. They did so because, in their eyes, this is the only way of living that is worthy of man. For the non-Gypsy they have nothing but contempt. Their term for the non-Gypsy is *gadjo*, of which the proper meaning is 'peasant', 'farmer', with the pejorative sense of 'clod-hopper', 'yokel', or 'bumpkin'. As for themselves, they are the Lords of the Earth.

The study of this extraordinary people began in the fifteenth century, when the first bands appeared in Europe. But gypsiology (as these studies[2] are called) became a branch of ethnology only in the nineteenth century, at the time when the need for an *interior* exoticism, under the influence of romanticism, showed itself. People had before their eyes authentic examples of the 'noble

1. *Diaspora* (dispersion, dispersal). The term is often used with special reference to the 'Jewish *diaspora*', perhaps the greatest and most widely known dispersion. *Tr.*

2. Gypsiology (Gypsy studies) – these now embrace origins, linguistics, folk-lore, traditions, myths, legends, history, etc., as dealt with in this book. *Tr.*

savage', of 'uncouth fellows'. Literature and science then began to come to grips with the Gypsy problem. Innumerable books were published in which science and literature were mixed. In this way the discovery was made that the Gypsies were not '*rabouins*', messengers of the devil. Assisted by good luck, students became aware that their speech, which until then had been considered as a vulgar secret lingo or cant, copied from that of organized wandering tramps and beggars, was in reality a living language. And, through this channel of linguistics, the discovery was at last made that those men came from distant India, from which they had been driven by the great invasions of barbarians, to whom quite possibly they had refused to submit.

Learned men, following the trail, took an interest in these nomads; the area of their dispersion covered a part of Asia and the whole of Europe. And scholars appreciated the hitherto unsuspected richness that could lie hidden behind the study of an original group of people which had thus cleared its way through ten centuries and forty different countries. They began to examine systematically the manners and customs of the Gypsies, while trying to take into consideration the original elements of their way of life, and those which the nomads had borrowed from the civilizations they had come upon. This material is extremely rich. Nevertheless the result was deceptive to begin with: the conclusion drawn from it was that, apart from their tenacious unity and their ferocious refusal to be integrated, the Gypsies did not have any completely original trait. Their folk-lore, traditions, magic, practices and beliefs seemed to reflect those only of the countries which lie between India and Ireland.

This misleading conclusion did not endure. It disappeared when those interested became aware that the Gypsies justly represented an incomparable framework of folk-lore. Their migration – it conjures up a fish-bone pattern over the map of Europe – had absorbed, conveyed by vehicle, eliminated, selected, rejected and conserved the main root of universal customs and beliefs: to the point that the folk-lore of the Gypsies today represents an entrancing and exact picture of the very early Middle East and Europe.

Like caravanners who, with their bales of silk and tea, transported ideas and news, customs and manners, the Gypsies have enriched the arts of music and the dance, the travelling show, and the arts of divination; as they have also contributed to the advancement of certain artisan trades, of the forge and working in metals, horse-dealing, and the making of basic implements. In the course of these pages the reader will find enough precise examples of this for me to be content here to mention only one. It is not without humour for us to learn that it was the Gypsies who introduced butter into Spain and also the name by which the Spaniards call it: *manteca*!

Even the term 'Gypsy' demands explanation. The public has grown into the habit of abusively describing, in France for example, as *gitans*, *bohémiens*, *manouches*, *romanichels*, *boumianes* (and in other countries[1] in terms seldom lacking an element of disparagement) all those people who lead a nomad life, who live in caravans, have swarthy complexions, and whose women wear multi-coloured dresses, and who, in short, tell fortunes and live on the fringe of society. The indispensable distinction which it may well be suitable to establish within Gypsy ethnology (indicated in the supplement to the first chapter) will show how greatly the various groups differ. Physical criterions in themselves alone enable us to avoid confusion. Between the Hungarian Gypsies with coppery skins and the freckled *Sinti*, between the passionate *Gitanos* of Andalusia and the delicate Swedish beauties called *Yénische*, our eyes are much embarrassed to find points in common. The pilgrimage of Saintes-Maries-de-la-Mer could in recent years still give an idea of the variety of these types. The attentive observer could likewise at this gathering establish the fact of the diversity of dialects spoken. On a basic tongue, known as *romanī* (anglicized as 'Romany'), each group, while maintaining the original roots, has little by little created its own idiom and grafted on it not only foreign vocabularies but also its own pronunciation. Today a Kalderash Gypsy from Hungary, recognizable by his colour-splashed skirts and his necklet of sequins, would not be able to converse with an English Gypsy. This makes the longing of investigators to speak 'Gypsy' somewhat unreal.

In regard to their secret code for communication known as the *patrin*[2] which ranges from drawings traced in chalk on walls to knotting the branches of bushes, this seems to be more practically modified from one group to another, and with good reason: family secrets do not concern neighbours, even though these may also be of Gypsy stock. The customs and manners, the taboos, laws and justice, superstitions and religious beliefs – all these vary not only from one

1. See also pages 91–119 and the *Supplementary Notes* on pages 260–67. *Tr.*
2. Often called 'patteran' in English. *Tr.*

group to the next, but often even among tribes and families.

It is therefore quite impossible in such a work as this to draw up a complete statement of Gypsy folk-lore. Here I merely apply myself to the task of seeking for all the acts and doings of everyday life a common denominator which, I hope, ought to be enough to show how rich is this folk-lore, so little known to the reading public.

For, apart from those differences which I have just called to mind – and they are often capable of provoking violent renderings of accounts – all kinds of real Gypsies, by whatever name they may be known, are united in the same love of freedom, in their eternal flight from the bonds of civilization, in their vital need to live in accordance with nature's rhythm, in the desire to be their own masters, and in contempt for what we pompously call the 'consequences'.

I am black, but comely, O ye daughters of Jerusalem. Look not upon me, because I am black, because the sun hath looked upon me . . .

The Song of Songs I. 5–6.

1 · Origins

Gypsiologists are today agreed in recognizing as very probable the Indian origin of the Gypsies. But, in order to achieve this relative certainty, it has been necessary to cast aside innumerable legends, some of which must be accepted with more caution than others, and to pose many hypotheses ranging from the most praiseworthy to the most fantastic, and lastly to attempt to put in relevant order the recent data of modern ethnology. The result is still far from being satisfactory, as the reader will appreciate in the course of this book. Nevertheless, the three stages of our research will not fail to offer to the historian of virgin lands, and to the reader, the wherewithal for dreams in time and space.

LEGENDS

The origin and the earliest dispersal of the Gypsies having long remained mysterious, even to those interested in the subject, it was necessary to find the source of that fate which ceaselessly drove them forward. And, in order to do this, scholars had to fall back upon already well-established myths. And so were born the legends, springing from Gypsy and non-Gypsy sources, which took either the world of the Bible, or that of the Orient, as the cradle of this *diaspora*.

Gypsies and the Bible

The Bible provides a perennially fresh choice of elastic interpretations for whatever may be the object of research. Regarding the Gypsies, some researchers have not hesitated to see them as the cursed descendants of Cain.[1] The texts of Genesis in particular emphasize the curse put upon the brother of Abel, quite rightly

1. In the Semitic languages the word Cain means 'blacksmith', 'metal-worker'.

23

evoking the birth of a nomad people driven by the unfavourable winds of fate:

When thou tillest the ground, it shall not henceforth yield unto thee her strength; a fugitive and a vagabond shalt thou be in the earth. [Genesis IV. 12.]

... And the Lord set a mark upon Cain, lest any finding him should kill him. [Genesis IV. 15.]

We know that this famous mark, probably the *tau* (T), is not a stigma condemning its bearer to general reprobation, but a sign by which the person can be recognized as the member of a clan in which blood vengeance is carried out in a terrible way; a trait found among the Gypsies.

Genesis specifies the occupations to which the sons of Cain were to be condemned, and the reader has already been sufficiently informed of the Gypsies' trades to be able to recognize them here:

Lamech took unto him two wives: the name of the one was Adah, and the name of the other was Zillah. And Adah bare Jabal: he was the father of such as dwell in tents. . . . And his brother's name was Jubal: he was the father of all such as handle the harp and organ. And Zillah, she also bare Tubal-Cain, an instructor of every artificer in brass and iron. . . . [Genesis IV. 19–22.]

As we study the religious beliefs of the Gypsies we see the memory of this original curse reappear. But this was not enough, and it was too vague. It is in the legend of the Crucifixion that the legends have attempted to set the problem within bounds.

Several of these legends, reported in Gypsy tradition, introduce the workmen who forged the nails of the Cross. It was normal that, in the theme of the agony of Jesus, the descendants of Cain should recognize themselves in these guilty blacksmiths. The most important of these legends[1] is fairly significant in this respect. The length as well as the recitative style must be forgiven:

When the Roman jailers were given the person of Yeshua ben Miriam, whom the world later called Jesus, that they should crucify him, because he had talked ill of the Emperor of Rome, two soldiers were sent out to get four stout nails. For every man to be crucified, the soldiers were given eighty kreutzer with which to buy nails, but they first tarried

1. Transcribed by Konrad Bercovici in *The Story of the Gypsies* (New York, 1928). Quoted in *Tziganes* by F. de Ville (Brussels, 1956). (I have reproduced Bercovici's original text. *Tr.*)

24

at an inn and spent half the coppers drinking the sweet-sour wine of the Greeks then sold in Jerusalem. It was late in the afternoon when they remembered the nails again, and they had to be back in the barracks by nightfall; for early the following morning they were to crucify Yeshua ben Miriam, the Jew who had talked ill of the Emperor of Rome.... The blacksmith was an old Jew.... He stepped out from behind the forge at which he had been working, and said: 'I will not forge nails to crucify Yeshua ben Miriam.' ... Then the soldiers ran him through with their lances after setting his beard on fire.

The next blacksmith was a little farther away. It was getting on in the afternoon when they arrived there, so they told the man: 'Make us four stout nails and we shall pay you forty kreutzer for them.' But the man said: 'I can forge only four small nails for that price.' But the soldiers showed him how large they wanted the nails. The man shook his head and said: 'I cannot make them for that price.' ... Then they set his beard on fire. Frightened out of his wits, the Jew went to the forge and began to work on the nails. One of the soldiers, who tried to help at the forge, leaned forward and said: 'Make them good and strong, Jew; for at dawn we crucify Yeshua ben Miriam.' When that name was mentioned, the hand of the Jew remained poised with the hammer. The voice of the man whom the soldiers had killed ... called out faintly, as if it were only the shadow of a voice: 'Aria, do not make the nails. They are for one of our people, an innocent man.' Aria dropped the hammer beside the forge. 'I will not make the nails,' he said. ... Both soldiers, furiously, drunkenly, ran him through with their lances again and again. ... Had the soldiers not drunk forty of the eighty kreutzer, they might have returned to barracks and told what had happened, and thus saved Yeshua's life. But they were short of forty kreutzer, so they ran out of the gates of Jerusalem, where they met a Gypsy who had just pitched his tent and set up his anvil. The Romans ordered him to forge four stout nails, and put the forty kreutzer down. The Gypsy put the money in his pocket first, and then set to work. When the first nail was finished, the soldiers put it in a bag. When the Gypsy had made another nail, they put it in the bag. And when the Gypsy had made the third nail, they put it in the bag. When the Gypsy began to forge the fourth nail, one of the soldiers said: 'Thank you, Gypsy. With these nails we will crucify Yeshua ben Miriam.' He had hardly finished speaking, when the trembling voices of the three blacksmiths who had been killed began to plead with the Gypsy not to make the nails. Night was falling. The soldiers were so scared that they ran away before the Gypsy had finished forging the last nail.

The Gypsy, glad that he had put the forty pieces of copper in his pocket before he had started work, finished the fourth nail. Having finished the nail, he waited for it to grow cold. He poured water upon the hot iron but the water sizzled off, and the iron remained as hot and red as it had been when held between the tongs in the fire. So he poured some more water upon it, but the nail was glowing as if the iron was a living, bleeding body, and the blood was spurting fire. So he threw still more water on it. The water sizzled off, and the nail glowed and glowed. A wide stretch of the night-darkened desert was illuminated by the glow of that nail. Terrified, trembling, the Gypsy packed his tent upon his donkey and fled. At midnight, between two high waves of sand, tired, harassed, the lone traveller pitched his tent again. But there, at his feet, was the glowing nail, although he had left it at the gates of Jerusalem. Being close to a water-well, the Gypsy carried water the rest of the night, trying to extinguish the fire of the nail. When the last drop had been drawn out of that well, he threw sand on the hot iron, but it never ceased sizzling and glowing. Crazed with fear, the Gypsy ran farther into the desert.

Arriving at an Arab village, the blacksmith set up his tent the following morning. But the glowing nail had followed him. And then something happened. An Arab came and asked him to join and patch the iron hoop of a wheel. Quickly the Gypsy took the glowing nail and patched with it the broken joint of the iron hoop. Then he saw with his own eyes how the Arab drove off. The Arab gone, the Gypsy drove away without daring to look around. After many days, still not daring to look around, afraid to open his eyes when night fell, the Gypsy reached the city of Damascus, where he set up his forge again. Months later, a man brought him the hilt of a sword to repair. The Gypsy lit his forge. The hilt began to glow, from the iron of the nail upon the hilt. The Gypsy packed, and ran away.

And that nail always appears in the tents of the descendants of the man who forged the nails for the crucifixion of Yeshua ben Miriam. And when the nail appears, the Gypsies run. It is why they move from one place to another. It is why Yeshua ben Miriam was crucified with only three nails, his two feet being drawn together and one nail piercing them. The fourth nail wanders about from one end of the earth to another.

This legend, garnered in Macedonia some thirty years ago, where it was recited in the form of a litany around the camp-fires in the evenings, comes up in various versions among other groups of Gypsies. Thus, the Danubian nomads claim to be descendants of the miscreants who massacred the children of Bethlehem, refused help to the Virgin Mary at the time of the flight into Egypt, advised Judas to betray Jesus and, in the end, without scruple hammered out the nails of the Cross. Some Serbian Gypsies, on their part, believe that their ancestors were satisfied with stealing the fourth nail of the Cross – the motive is obscure – and their punishment was to be

26

wanderers for seven years (or seven centuries). In a tradition that runs parallel, but in which this time the nails play no part whatsoever, the Gypsies are claimed to have been Christ's guards or keepers and, having become drunk, were unable to defend Him.[1]

All these accounts doubtless reveal nothing but what is in the realm of fantasy. No text, however allusive, has yet appeared which would confirm the presence of Gypsies in Palestine during the first generations of our era. But these traditional stories, which are always held in honour among the Gypsies, show the wish of a people without ties not to be without roots. And the influences of Christianity have not failed in influencing the Gypsies to translate into biblical terms the myths of their lost origin.

Gypsies and the East

The second group of legends which refer to the origins of the Gypsies concerns that of countries which custom has long made us designate by the convenient term 'The East'. And first of all Egypt. We know that for centuries the Gypsies were called 'Egyptians'.[2] In fact, well before their officially recorded arrival in Europe in the fourteenth century, all mountebanks and travelling-showmen of the main highways found themselves dubbed 'Egyptians'. The reason for this designation has never been fully clarified. And some authors have profited by it to see the first Gypsies in the representatives of the famished-looking hordes which followed Charlemagne's armies. If the truth must be told, it is uncertain whether these 'Egyptians', known in the West before the fifteenth century, themselves claimed to come from the banks of the Nile, or whether it was that the fixed populations saw them as magicians driven out of a country that by reputation surpassed all others in this field.

In any case, the chiefs of the first groups of Gypsies who knocked at the doors in our towns took upon themselves the title of 'Dukes of Egypt'. We shall see in the chapter dealing with their history the reasons they gave for this choice; reasons which do not in any way explain an Egyptian origin. They also called themselves 'Dukes of Little Egypt', and perhaps this other title conceals the explanation. These Gypsies made their way across Germany. Now, in German

1. Tradition according to the *babilach* (chief) José Pirnay, so-called Jakoub, reputed Gypsy chief who died recently in Belgium. See F. de Ville, op. cit.

2. The English word Gypsy, as will be seen later, derives from the word Egyptian. *Tr.*

Klein-Egypten (Little-Egypt) means Egypt Minor (on old German maps Asia Minor is marked *Klein-Asien*). It is possible that in this sense Little-Egypt designates a region of Near Eastern Asia.

At all events, the Gypsies themselves, now putting aside the testimony of Genesis, base their case on the prophecy of Ezekiel: '*I shall scatter the Egyptians among the nations*'.[1]

A Russian variant of the Gypsy tradition takes into account another Egyptian origin: during the crossing of the Red Sea, when Pharaoh's troops were engulfed in the waters, a young man and a young girl miraculously escaped the catastrophe and, founding a family, became the original couple – the Adam and Eve of the Gypsies. The recurring appearance in the tradition of this myth will be seen later, and particularly the frequent use of the terms *pharaon*, *pharaona* (in Spanish *faraón*, *faraona*) in various Gypsy ceremonies.

Yet in spite of all this, the Gypsy legends which propound their Egyptian origin are few and not very explicit. More verbose and better attached to our knowledge of history are the accounts which concern the regions of Mesopotamia and the earlier Asia. Among several mythical recollections, Father Fleury, Chaplain to the Gypsies in France, has collected one which presents the *Gond Sindhu*, later called the *Sinti* in the West, a term which still designates one of the groups of Gypsies.[1] The *Gond* are known to the East of India, in Nepal and Burma, but one branch of the original people, the *Sindhu* or *Sinti*, according to the tradition turned westwards, crossed the Indian frontier, and became horse-breakers. They traded in precious stones and so were able to acquire many pack-animals and, by slow caravan journeying, reached Chaldea. There the aborigines received them favourably, for they were skilful in working bronze and gold. They taught the Chaldeans the arts of popular yoga, dangerous feats of jumping, how to walk through fire, and other spectacular exercises. In exchange, they were initiated into the local science of the stars. This happened before the time of Abraham. The *Sinti* must have remained a long time among the Chaldeans; when the patriarch left Ur, it was, so it seems, a tribe of *Sinti* who accompanied him into the Land of Canaan. When at last they arrived in Egypt, according to the same tradition, they again devoted themselves to their exhibitions before the pharaohs; and thus won the right of asylum. This sums up the myth of their Egyptian 'origin'.

1. See pp. 46–9 for the different groups of Gypsies; and Traditions, p. 159.

The *Sinti* also made an alliance with the Israelites, and even contracted marriages with them.

This legend is not above suspicion. Yet we begin to pick out in it the features which from this point onwards will characterize the Gypsies. These now begin to take familiar forms: the Gypsies are seen as public entertainers, magicians, smiths and horse-breakers.

As, at the outset of these researches, I am bent on gathering together some of the legends through which the Gypsies try to recognize themselves, I must ask for patience on the part of the most inquisitive reader of commentaries by gypsiologists, in order to give here another account, said to be by the *kako* Chaudy:[1]

After the Flood, our ancester Noah lived with his sons among whom was *Caamo* [Cham[2]], from whom we are descendents in direct line. *Caamo* mocked his father who was drunk, and his father cursed him and said that he would be a slave; we remained slaves for a long time. And the descendants of *Caamo*'s brothers, especially those of *Jafeto* [Japhet], were cruel as far as we were concerned. One of us, named *Tubalo* [Tubal-Cain], had discovered the way to smelt bronze and iron, and how to forge them. And we were compelled to work under the lash.

One day we revolted and regained our freedom; and we conquered a country named *Kaldi* [Chaldea]. This country became too small for us and our chiefs, and our wise men ordered us to separate in two bodies. The most valiant group prepared to leave for the East in the direction of India, furnished with the Ark and our collection of Sacred Books. But, before we separated, the *patrin* [the art of recognizing our road signs[3]] was taught to the hundreds of tribes; and it was predicted that the children of all the tribes should find themselves together again in some indefinite future.

Half of our people, then, emigrated towards India to which they brought out language as well as our iron and gold industries, with all our sciences. It is nevertheless necessary to note that on departure a discord had arisen among certain tribes in the caravan, and a new split occurred. While some took the route for India, the others went in the opposite direction, which led them into a country named *Chal* [Egypt]. One part continued to live in the *Kaldi*, where they made an alliance with the

1. Narrated by the chief (*kako*) Chaudy to Robert Henry, the Belgian gypsiologist, who all his life has concentrated on the problem of the Sinti, but has not yet published the outcome of his labours.

2. The Gypsy proper names have been transcribed by F. de Ville. See Bibliography, p. 269.

3. For more about the *patrin* (or 'patteran', as it is often called in English) see pp. 243–5. *Tr.*

people of the *Assiries* [Assyrians]. There were two of our kings, Pudilo and his son Romano Nirano, who took the headship of the new State. We built an immense city named *Babila* [Babylon] which we took as our capital. . . . And things went on like that until the day when *Cirusho* [Cyrus], sovereign of the people of the *Persies* [Persians], made war on us.

We had to leave the *Kaldi*: one part of our people went towards the East, the other towards the West. . . . A part of our people settled in *Pelasgii* [Ancient Greece] and on the surrounding islands. Our other brothers received authorisation to cross the country of the *Persies* and they reached India, where they found again those of our people who had left the *Kaldi* thousands of years before that. . . .

The account goes on. The Gypsies were well received by the Pelasgians, once again because of their knowledge of working in metals. With the Pelasgians they are supposed to have travelled, founded Marseille and made their way up the Rhône. But for the moment this does not concern us. It may however be added that the same tradition affirms that they built the Pyramids, by which is meant that they participated as unskilled labourers in their construction.

Without encroaching on the plan which has had to be adopted for this work, only one thing should be recorded here: according to the two traditions, the Gypsies do their utmost to identify their country of origin, whether with India or Chaldea. This hardly simplifies the problem, the distance between these two countries being appreciable, even for nomads. In the account of Father Fleury, the Gypsies came from India and emigrated into Chaldea. In Chief Chaudy's account, the contrary happens. This divergence of tradition carries with it the near certainty that the Gypsies lived in both countries and travelled from one to the other. It is furthermore remarkable that, in the legends of an almost illiterate people whose culture is exclusively traditional, we find the proper names of our own history almost unchanged.

It is from these legends, which have been unceasingly reshaped, that the first gypsiologists, before reaching from them the present meagre certainties, built their hypotheses relating to the origin of the Gypsies. They are more often than not daring hypotheses, and it will be seen that they are far more picturesque than the Gypsy legends themselves. Here the most baffling of them will be noted, yet always with the feeling that behind the most 'advanced' opinions there may be concealed some fragments of truth capable of filling in some of the gaps in this gigantic puzzle.

HYPOTHESES

For example, we do not know very much about the authority on which Vulcanius Bonaventura relied when he wrote in his book *De Litteris et Lingua Gelarum et Gothorum* (1697) that the 'Bohemians' (Gypsies) came from Nubia. Then again, strangely enough, there are authors who come upon the Gypsy legends without showing any indication of having any knowledge of them. One of these was Robert Samuel,[1] who wished to see the Gypsies as descendants of the earlier Egyptians, and he too based his speculations on his reading of the prophet Ezekiel.

Vaillant, one of the most ardent gypsiologists of the last century (he wrote *The true History of the real Bohemians*[2]), applied himself to the task of unravelling the strands of that inextricable knot resulting from the interconnexions between the legends, the accounts given in histories, and mere tittle-tattle. The result was that he believed in good faith that he could fix Phoenician and then 'Pelasgian' nationality on the Gypsies. It is, in fact, easier to become lost in his explanations than among the documents which he quotes.

For Baudrimont[3] the Gypsies were first Babylonians condemned to exodus after the destruction of their capital. The more imaginative scholars preferred to look towards Egypt, in this respect following Voltaire himself, who was of the opinion that the Bohemians were none other but degenerate descendants of the priests of Isis mixed with votaries of the Syrian goddess: 'And, as a matter of fact, when one reads in Apuleius the description of the customs and ceremonies of those priests or vagabond prophets, one cannot fail to find in them a great resemblance to the Bohemians of Europe. Their castanets and their Basque-like drums are obviously the cymbals and castanets of the priests of Isis and Syria'.[4] So much for that!

The truth is that, if the history of gypsiology had to be written,

1. *The Gypsies, their origin, continuance and destination, as clearly foretold in the Prophesies of Isaiah and Ezekiel* (London, 1836).
2. *Les Roms, histoire vraie des vrais Bohémiens* (1857).
3. *Les Bohémiens du Pays Basque* (1862).
4. Graberg: *Doutes et conjectures sur les Bohémiens et leur première apparition en Europe* (no date, but before 1817).

one would have to begin by following the tracks of this term 'Bohemians' which was applied to the Gypsies over a wide area in Europe from the fifteenth century onwards. We may put aside the opinion of Sieur Belon and of the scholar Moreri, author of the inexhaustible *Dictionary*, both of whom make this word come from the old Breton *boëm*, meaning 'to bewitch'.

The Bohemia of Europe owes its name to the Gallic (or Gaulish) *Boii* who were driven out of it by the Marcomans[1] about the time of Augustus. In the seventh century the Slavonic Czechs took Bohemia and established several small states from which Charlemagne was going to exact tribute. Some of these authentic Bohemians came to France and formed a long-lived group among the Goliards[2] and vagabond peoples who followed the Carolingian armies. In 1265 Surranus could even write these verses:

> Our army admits
> The just and unjust . . .
> Bohemians and Teutons. . . .

The name of 'Bohemians' became attached to that of the Goliards,[3] and before long the two terms meant the same. In the fifteenth century, when the first Gypsies put in an appearance on arrival from their travels in Central Europe, in colourful array not unlike that of the vagabonds, it was quite natural that this should serve to give them their name. The first written mention of the word 'Bohemian' – undoubtedly meaning 'Gypsy' – would seem to be in Pechon de Ruby's book *La Vie généreuse des Gueux, Mercelots et Boesmiens* (1596), which we shall later stress.

Yet the strangest hypothesis was that which correlated the Gypsies and the Jewish people.

Gypsies and the Jews

It is true that authors did not allow to pass unnoticed some obvious and disturbing resemblances between the Jewish *diaspora* and the

1. An old Germanic people defeated by Drusus in 9 B.C. They went to Bohemia; and invaded Italy in the time of Marcus Aurelius. *Tr.*

2. A group in the Middle Ages consisting of unfrocked priests and monks who wandered about Europe as minstrels (*jongleurs*). They came under a Bishop Golias. *Tr.*

3. On this subject see: Olga Dobiache-Rojdesvensky, *Les Poésies des Goliards* (1933): and Alexandre Vexliard, *Introduction à la sociologie du vagabondage* (1956).

Gypsy dispersion. Both bore the mark of a curse at the outset, and the two peoples saw themselves compelled to wander among other nations for an 'undetermined period' as tradition had it.

Collin de Plancy in his famous *Dictionnaire Infernal*[1] takes the bearings of this belief:

Historians made them [the Bohemians or Gypsies] – on mere conjectures – come from Assyria, from Cilesia [in south-east Asia Minor], from Nubia, Abyssinia and from Chaldea. Uncertain of their origin, Belon held that at least they were not Egyptians, for he had found records that they had been in Cairo, where they were regarded as foreigners, as they were in Europe. It was therefore more natural to believe, on the word of the Bohemians themselves, and to say with them, that they were a race of Jews who had later become mixed with Christian vagabonds. . . . Towards the middle of the fourteenth century, Europe and mainly Germany and France had been ravaged by the plague. The Jews were accused – nobody knows on what grounds – of having poisoned the wells and fountains. This accusation aroused public fury against the Jews, many of whom fled and rushed into the forests. They became reunited for greater safety, and contrived for themselves underground shelters of considerable size. It is believed that it was they who excavated those vast caverns that are still found in Germany, which the people of the country have never had any interest in searching.

Fifty years later, these outlaws or their descendants, having reason to believe that those who had so greatly hated them were dead, ventured to come out of their lairs. The Christians were then engaged in the wars of religion instigated by the Hussite heresy. To the Jews this was a favourable diversion. On the report of their spies, the hidden Jews left their caverns, without any resources, it is true, that would guarantee them against misery. But, for half a century, they had studied the arts of divination, and particularly fortune-telling by palmistry, which demands neither instrument nor apparatus nor any outlay whatever; and they well reckoned that their chiromancy would earn them some money.

First they chose for themselves a captain or chief named Zundel.[2] Then, as it was necessary for them to declare what it was that had brought them to Germany, who they were and whence they came, and that they could be questioned about their religion, in order not to expose themselves too dangerously and yet not disavow themselves, they agreed to

1. Of which the third edition, with imprimatur, appeared in 1848.
2. Another mention of this captain is apparently made by Aventin (*Zingeri, Cilices, Zigeuner-Zindl des Zigeuner König*) about 1438. Regarding this captain Zundel, note that the word *Zundel* still means in south Germany 'incendiary', 'fire-raiser'. It is permissible to attach this name to the belief which makes the Gypsies protectors against fires of houses.

say that their forefathers formerly lived in Egypt, which is true of the Jews, and that their ancestors had been driven out of their own country for not having accepted the Virgin Mary and her son Jesus. From this comes the name 'Egyptians' which was to be given to them and under which the Emperor Sigismund granted them a passport.

They had formed for themselves a slang or disguised jargon, mixed with Hebrew and bad German, which they pronounced with a foreign accent. . . . The very many Hebrew words which remained in the language of the 'Bohemians' would in itself alone be enough to betray their Jewish origin. . . .

From the moment that the new 'Egyptians' saw that they were not being driven out, they besought compassion of the Germans. In order not to appear a burden, they gave assurances that, by a particular heavenly grace which protected while punishing them,[1] the houses at which they were favourably received once would thereafter not be liable to an outbreak of fire. They also set about fortune-telling, based on a scrutiny of the face, bodily signs, and mainly on examination of the lines of the hands and fingers. They announced such fine things, and their women fortune-tellers displayed such skill and tact, that women and girls immediately treated them with goodwill.

In the meantime, the furore against the Jews having calmed down, they were again allowed into the villages and then into the towns. But there still remained bands of vagabonds who pursued their nomad life, telling the future everywhere and supplementing this profession with many knavish tricks. Soon, although the Jewish people were the kernel of these bands, they became such a mixture of diverse peoples that there was no more a dominant religion among them than there was a native country.

In this article in his *Dictionary*, Collin de Plancy expresses an opinion that was common in his time, the beginning of the nineteenth century. He mixes closely together the particular traits of the Jews with those which characterized the Gypsies. In fact, these outlaws who were condemned to take to the woods were many of them Jews, as is confirmed in the history of the persecution of this people in Germany. The lingo which they spoke 'mixed with Hebrew and bad German' could be none other than Yiddish. On the other hand, the term 'captain' (which Plancy could not have invented) has never been given to a Jewish guide or leader; for a very long time this title has been used to single out chiefs of Gypsy tribes, and from this point onwards the reader will come across it often in this book. With regard to the apprenticeship and the use of the arts of prophecy and

1. Cf. the banishment-protection myth of the sons of Cain.

divining, whereas they may be considered as characteristics of the Gypsies, they form no part of the practices of the Jewish people. Let us remember the prophetic words found in Deuteronomy:

There shall not be found among you any one that maketh his son or his daughter to pass through the fire, or that useth divination, or an observer of times, or an enchanter, or a witch. Or a charmer, or a consulter with familiar spirits, or a wizard or a necromancer. For all that do these things are an abomination unto the Lord: and because of these abominations the Lord thy God doth drive them out before thee. [Deuteronomy XVIII. 10–12.]

Other authors have tried to see the Gypsies as authentic Jews. To mention one, there is the German Wagenseil who, from 1700, based this conclusion on a physical resemblance![1] But it is not possible to-day to accept the Semitic origin of the Gypsies. All that need be emphasized is the pathetic parallel of the two dispersions, and the persecutions suffered by these two peoples.

Gypsies and the Forge

In this collating of ideas which have been expressed about the origin of the Gypsies, we shall for a moment leave the field of human geography for that of technics. Here it matters little to us that the Gypsies may have been first seen in Chaldea, Egypt or Nubia. The majority of the legends designate the Gypsies as smiths of various kinds, as workers in iron, bronze, gold and precious metals. We have seen that the traditional accounts mention Tubal-Cain as the biblical ancestor of 'all copper-smiths and iron-smiths', and that the various stories concerning the Crucifixion first refer to the making of the nails, that the *Sinti* who came to Chaldea from India were skilful workers with the chisel, that the Gypsies who claim to have migrated in an opposite direction had brought into the 'Pelasgian' world, that is, ancient Greece, the working of iron, bronze and gold. . . . Here we shall introduce another mythical account borrowed from Homer: Hephaistos (Vulcan) was one day hurled down from the sky by his father Zeus who was angry with him. 'During a whole day, said Vulcan, I rolled about in the winds and, when the sun went down, I fell on the island of Lemnos: there the *Sinti* picked me up. . . .' Without stressing the connexion between Tubal-Cain and Vulcan – the words appear to have the same etymology – we shall see that one

1. The Nazis put Gypsies and Jews together in one category for extermination. *Tr.*

35

of the principal groups of European Gypsies are the Kalderash, that is the smiths (who work in various metals).

This leads us to bring together the matter of the origin of the Gypsies and the appearance in Europe of the forge (which term here includes 'smithy' and 'smith's hearth'). After its discovery, the art of metallurgy was assimilated with the devil's occupations, the occupations of those 'possessed by devils'. The man capable of making sparks and flashes of fire shoot out by blows struck on his anvil seems at first to be endowed with magic powers, and the setting in which he works conjures up the nether regions. The number of legends relating to this subject is impressive. And if we are still ignorant of how the art of the forge came to appear in Europe,[1] we at least know how it was practised in Ancient Asia, particularly in India. For the most part it was reserved to individuals living on the fringe of society, nomads and outcasts, who were both feared and despised. 'In India, as elsewhere, a whole mythology links together the workers in iron and the various categories of giants and demons. They are all enemies of the gods.'[2] This is something which stresses the curses attaching to wandering peoples, identical with those concerning the workers in the subterranean world who dig the bowels of the earth and tame the central holocaust.

Better still, the mythologies have revealed definite connexions between the trades demanding the use of fire and the magic arts. Eliade emphasizes that 'there seems to exist, on different cultural levels (a sign of great antiquity), a close bond between the art of the smith, the occult sciences (Shamanism, magic . . .) and the arts of song, dance and poetry'.[3]

If we look at the lists of Indian castes[4] we find that several of them link together the occupation of smith and musician: the *Ghasiya*, for example, whose social rank is one of the least enviable, and who live in the north and centre of India, and the *Luri* (whom we shall meet again), nomads of Beluchistan and especially the *Asura*, who bear the name of a divinity hostile to the gods of the Aryas.[5] In

1. By the immigration of nomad peoples, according to the prehistorian Gabriel de Mortillet.
2. See Mircea Eliade, *Forgerons et alchimistes* (1959).
3. op. cit.
4. See for example Hutton, *Les Castes de l'Inde* (1949).
5. The Asura have been closely studied by Ruben in *Eisenschmiede und Daemonen in Indien* (Leiden, 1939).

regard to the last, Jules Bloch[1] recalls that they use a double bellows, worked by a man standing with a foot on each bellows. Now this instrument is still used by the Kalderash Gypsies of Romania, and, known in that country since the fifteenth century, it has left its traces across Europe as late as in the England of 1910.

It was Bataillard[2] who first studied seriously the relationship between the Gypsies and the history of the forge. But, carried away by enthusiasm, he became venturesome and in this he went too far: 'Those Gypsy smiths of the Bronze Age might have established their centre of metal-working in the region of the western Alps. From there, by trading as they roamed, they must have spread their metal-work widely among the Celts and other tribes.' In regard to this author Jules Bloch is right to speak of 'reveries' for, if the Gypsies really did bring bronze into Europe, this means that they have been settled here for about three thousand years!

A modern gypsiologist, Franz de Ville,[3] has meanwhile taken up Bataillard's thesis. 'It seems certain', he says, 'that it was the Gypsies who made bronze known in Europe' and cites the fact that some excavating along the Baltic has recently brought to light weapons and pieces of jewellery ornamented with the swastika. The swastika is known to be of Indian origin. Some Norwegian Gypsies, well before the arrival of Nazism, had a swastika tattooed on their right shoulder. At the same time, and in the same place, were discovered musical instruments in the form of long horns, called *lures*[4] and revealing an art of smelting 'of very great skill' and 'of foreign origin'. The technique used was one of wax, now lost, for which men of the bronze age used cow's udder. The decorative art peculiar to these *lures* was again found on instruments of Gypsy make. De Ville insists on affirming that 'The bronze was imported into Scandinavia by people who came from the South.' It is highly probable that it was brought there by the nomads, and that these came from southern Europe. But, were these nomads Gypsies? This remains to be demonstrated. Nevertheless, if we were to succeed in proving it, the greater part of the present data relating to the existing date for the appearance of the 'Bohemians' in Europe would have to be reconsidered.

1. Jules Bloch, *Les Tsiganes* (1953).
2. Bataillard, *De l'apparition des Bohémiens en Europe* (1844). 3. op. cit.
4. The word *lure* in the Danish sagas means the hero's horn. It is obviously permissible to relate this word with the name of the Luri.

On the other hand, according to the tradition of the Kalderash Gypsies,[1] some groups of Gypsies, who were smiths responsible for the maintenance of working stock, followed the Tartar armies on their moves from place to place. One of the legends of this group even specifies that by way of gain, they had the right to collect everything that remained in the villages after a week of pillage. At all events, this is the opinion of MacMunn: 'The Bohemians of Europe, without any doubt, followed the armies of the Huns, Tartars and Seljuks, and our own Gypsies who work in metals and grind our knives certainly sharpened swords and blades for the armies who traversed Europe in every sense.'[2]

Franz de Ville also affirms that the representatives of the ethnic group known as the *Djat*, Gypsies whom we shall soon meet again, accompanied the hordes of invaders and engaged in works of metallurgy, horse-shoeing and saddlery. He points out in this respect the possible connexion between the word *tzigane* and the word *tchegan* which means 'hammer' in Tartar. He also recalls that in the fifteenth century the Germans called the Gypsies *Tatern* (Tartars). But we find in Hutton's list of Indian castes the mention of a tribe of *Tathera*, smiths of northern India. It is normal in this field of study for us to be constantly the prey of fortuitous encounters. The works of Grousset[3] and the greater part of the documents relating to the Huns and Tartars do not, however, ever mention the Gypsies. The existence of this rearguard or camp-following remains problematical.

But this has drawn us nearer to India. The time has come for an examination of the principal data which have led modern gypsiologists to select this country as the cradle of the Gypsies.

Gypsies and India

It was not until the nineteenth century that scholars dreamed of looking beyond the Bosphorus to see whether any traces of this strange people could be found, a people whose presence in Europe defied all the laws of a still too immature science of ethnology. Furthermore it was a stroke of good luck which put them on their way. On 6 November 1763, there appeared an article in the *Gazette*

1. This tradition has been reported to me by Maximoff. (See Bibliography pp. 268–9.)
2. MacMunn, *Mœurs et coutumes des basses classes de l'Inde* (1934).
3. Réné Grousset, French orientalist and historian. Member of the French Academy, 1946. *Tr.*

de Vienne signed by a Captain Sekely de Doba. It told of a strange discovery:

While the protestant preacher Etienne Vali, of Almasch in the county of Komora, was studying at Leyden, he made the acquaintance of some Indians from the Malabar Coast, three of which people are constantly obliged to pursue their studies in that city; they cannot return to their country until they have been replaced by three others. Vali noticed that their language had many resemblances to that of the Bohemians, and he took this opportunity to write down from their dictation about a thousand words with their meanings. At the same time, they assured him that on their island there was a region or province called Czigania.[1] When Vali returned to the University, he inquired of Hungarian Gypsies about the meanings of Malabar words, which they explained to him without any difficulty.

This vocabulary was also utilized by the gypsiologists.[2] Once on this trail, marked out by linguistics, and apparently more genuine than the data hitherto examined, it was necessary to look for a human group, amid or somewhere on the Indian ant-heap, which could correspond to the Gypsies and, leaving the field of dialects, fasten once more on to that of the occupations which conformed with those chosen by the people with whom we are concerned. In this way, apart from the *Asura, Luri* and *Ghâsiya* already mentioned, there came to light[3] the *Handi Jogi*, beggars, charlatans and snake-charmers; the *Kami*, smiths and metal-workers of Nepal; the *Kasar* (or *Kaseras*), smelters of copper and metal-workers of north India; the *Korava* of the Tamil country, who are fortune-tellers, charlatans . . . and thieves; the *Lohar*, smiths from the north; the *Nat*, nomad singers, dancers and acrobats (criminals by profession, Hutton adds); the *Tathera*, metal-workers and smiths, and the *Kanjar*, a caste of 'Gypsies', mat-makers in the centre and north of the country. Finally, the *Dom*.

But of this list only the *Luri* and *Dom* have retained the attention of researchers.

1. The maps are silent about this country. Only to the south of Trebizond can a region be found with the name of 'Zigana Mountains'.
2. H. M. G. Grellmann, *Die Zigeuner* (various editions, 1719–87). The quotation is from the French ed., *Histoire des Bohémiens* (1783). See also A. Graffunder, *Ueber die Sprache der Zigeuner* (1835) and Pott (see Bibliography pp. 268–9).
3. See Hutton, op. cit., and MacMunn, op. cit.

In his *Shah Nameh* ('Book of Kings') the Persian poet Firdusi (*c*. A.D. 1000) informs us that

about the year 420 before our era, Behram Gour, a wise and beneficent prince of the Sassanide dynasty [226 B.C.–A.D. 641], realized that his poor subjects were pining away for lack of amusements. He sought a means of reviving their spirits and of providing some distraction from their hard life. With this end in mind he sent a diplomatic mission to Shankal, King of Cambodia and Maharajah of India, and begged him to choose among his subjects and send to him in Persia persons capable by their talents of alleviating the burden of existence and able to spread a charm over the monotony of work. Behram Gour soon assembled twelve thousand itinerant minstrels, men and women, assigned lands to them, supplying them with corn and livestock in order that they should have the wherewithal to live in certain areas which he would designate; and so be able to amuse his people at no cost. At the end of the first year these people had neglected agriculture, consumed the corn seed and found themselves without resources. Behram was angry and commanded that their asses and musical instruments should be taken away, and that they should roam the country and earn their livelihood by singing. As a consequence these men, the *Luri*, roamed the world to find who would employ them, taking with them dogs and wolves, and thieving night and day on their way.

In the year 940, the Arab historian Hamza confirms this account. It remained for writers on the subject to relate the *Luri* to the Gypsies. An English traveller, for example, who travelled through the Sind and Baluchistan in the last century[1] described this small tribe:

The *Loories* are a kind of vagabond people who have no fixed habitation and who, by this and many other reports, present a striking affinity with the European Gypsies. They speak a dialect of their own, have a king for each band, and a reputation as thieves and plunderers. Their favourite pastime is drinking, dancing and musick. In addition to their instruments, each troupe has half a dozen bears and monkeys, trained to do innumerable grotesque tricks. In each band there are two or three individuals who make a profession of foretelling the future by various means.

Notwithstanding the pejorative tone of this text, it is difficult not to think, in reading it, of the most familiar descriptions of our Gypsies. Another British writer[2] expresses himself less sharply, but

1. Sir Henry Pottinger, *Travels in Beloochistan and Sind* (1816).
2. Bray, *Report of the Census of Baluchistan* (1911).

40

corroborates that point of view. Hutton,[1] on his part, is more precise:

Among the tribes of Baluchistan, it is fitting to mention the humble *Luri*, wandering tinsmiths, workers of jewels in gold and silver, minstrels, musicians, midwives and common labourers. In certain respects they seem to correspond to the *Dom* people of the north of India (of whom more later), but claim to descend from the youngest son of the Prophet's uncle, and say they have come from Aleppo. They are, in fact, Gypsies, and they are particularly happy along the coast of Makran to the west of Karachi, but they are usually nomads, which seems to be one of the outstanding characteristics of the whole of Baluchistan. One third of the population, in fact, live in tents or temporary huts, and many emigrate with the seasons from one part of the country to another, and indeed from Baluchistan to the plains of the Sind and back.

The occupations enumerated by this author are precisely those which we find among the Gypsies of Europe.[2] Seasonal nomadism is also found again and again among the Gypsies. And, as will be seen a few pages further on, the importance of this localization specifies the Sind area. As for the mention of an Islamic descent, this will be dealt with later under religions.

The name *Luri* appears to have been passed on to the *Nuri*, nomads in Syria, Egypt and, today, Israel.[3] But this connexion remains problematical: for the word '*nuri*' is also the plural of the Arabic *na war*, which means the Mussulman Gypsies.

It is still a basis of linguistics that enables a correlation of the Indian caste of *Dom* and the Gypsies to be propounded. In fact, the latter are called *Lom* in Armenia, and in Syria and Persia they have the name *Dom*. (They call themselves *Rom* in Europe: but if the change of D to L is plausible, that of D to R is less so.)

Jules Bloch recalls that the tribe of *Dom* has been known in India for a long time. In a sixth-century treatise on astronomy it was associated with the adjective '*gandharva*', meaning 'musician', 'musical'. An earlier author[4] classifies the *Dom* among the oppressed:

They are perhaps the most widely spread of the outcasts. Their origin is not known, but the English are inclined to believe that they belong

1. Hutton, op. cit.
2. And in many other parts of the world, including America. *Tr.*
3. See Regensbürger, *Gypsies in the Land of Israel* in the *Journal of the Gypsy Lore Society*, vol. xxxvii, Parts 1–2 (see Bibliography p. 269).
4. MacMunn, op. cit.

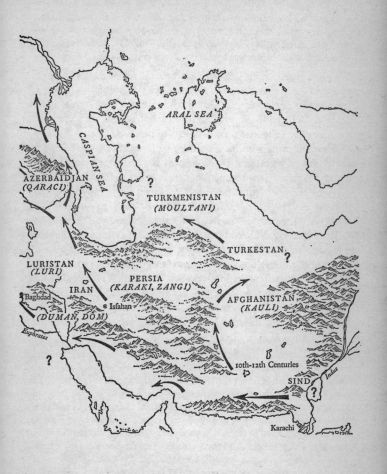

PROBABLE LINES OF THE FIRST GYPSY IMMIGRATIONS
(The names given to these people are shown in brackets)

to a race conquered by the Aryan tide, and link them vaguely with a Dravidian stock. . . . The *Dom* have a very dark skin and a primitive cast of features. . . . Their religion is a very disorderly mixture of animistic traditions too vague to enable their origin to be determined. Into this mixture they introduce divinities, and a patronage of unknown, unidentifiable saints. They venerate [also] Kâli-Ma, Mahadeo and the Ganges, but the numerous local divinities always prevail.

Without encroaching upon the chapter on religions, let it be emphasized here that the dark goddess Kâli is still worshipped by contemporary Gypsies. Yet, on the other hand, the Gypsies have a singular facility for adopting local rites and beliefs, the importance for this very religious people being 'to believe'.

These nomads who have been living (for centuries, perhaps for thousands of years) in the regions of Behar and Oudh[1] to the north act as hangmen (an occupation which again is found among the Gypsies of Central Europe). Finally, Martin Block[2] states precisely that the term *doma* comes from the Sanscrit *dom*, 'to resound', and designated the people who live by singing and music.

It is evidently dangerous to wish to establish a connexion between some Indian tribes and the Gypsies on similarities of occupation or mode of life alone. The Gypsy question does not seem to have been raised by the Indians themselves. Scholars of that country, in fact, show an awkward tendency to name *all* 'nomads' as Gypsies. Having recently cross-questioned a Bengali from Calcutta, I was able to obtain from him only the following pieces of information:

The Sanskrit word which approximately corresponds to Gypsy is *yayavar*. The equivalent Bengali word is *bede* [feminine *bedeni*]. The only tribes which can be called Gypsies are the *Vanjara*, the *Lamani*, the *Chhara* and the *Luri*. For the last two, the question here is settled. The *Vanjara* live in the neighbourhood of Bombay, in the Gujarat, the Maharashtra and Hyderabad. They are beggars and makers of trumpery objects; they live a nomad existence in groups, and use donkeys but not wagons. They sleep in tents. They may engage in magical medicine, but they are neither smiths nor mountebanks. The *Lamani* are a very handsome people with comparatively fair skins, and tattooed. Their women wear long dresses, heavy bracelets and little bells attached to their ankles. The people thereabouts believe that they come from Iran, and accuse

1. Oudh: an ancient Indian kingdom (cradle of the Aryans), now a section of the United Provinces of Agra and Oudh, capital Lucknow. *Tr.*

2. Martin Block, *Mœurs et coutumes des Tziganes* (1936). A reliable writer on the subject of Gypsies. See Bibliography pp. 268, 270.

them of kidnapping children. As for the *Chhara*, they are first and foremost thieves. A local proverb claims that a *Chhara* who is a bad pickpocket has no chance of getting married. This name *Chhara* may perhaps be related to that of the *Churari* [or *Tchurari*], which designates one of the groups of contemporary Gypsies.

It is certain that tribes of authentic Gypsies still live in India. Unfortunately a census of them has not been taken. Nevertheless, if it is not possible to describe them, it is permissible to study the clear connexion between the basic Gypsy language – *romani* – and the dialects of northern India. The patient reader will appreciate the connexions in the later chapter dealing with Gypsy languages and dialects.

Having fixed this problem in space, it is fitting that it should now be put in order in relation to time. At what moment in history did the Gypsies leave India?

The documents which specially refer to these nomads before the year A.D. 1000 are disconcerting in their scarcity. We have already read the extract from the poet Firdusi, and, on the other hand, we know that the Gypsies lived in Lower Mesopotamia from the ninth century. Thus:

Between Basra and Baghdad there was a zone of lagoons inhabited by a small tribe of Gypsy people who, continually in a state of ferment, pillaged and pestered the merchants coming from India and China. The Caliphate troops could not stamp them out. In July of A.D. 834 the Caliph Motassim, by a stroke of genius, sent against them old rebels from the marshlands of the Nile delta who had just been brought to heel and moved to Mesopotamia. These waged guerilla warfare against the Gypsies and subdued them.[1]

In spite of this fact, nothing relative is found between these two dates, or what there is must be treated with caution. One is thus reduced to suggesting that the Gypsies formed a fairly loose conglomerate of nomad tribes, dispersed over northern India and particularly in the basin of the Indus. Who were they? Where did they come from? We shall never know.

Indian history is not very explicit on the subject. In the intermixing of her ancient populations, which on first view seems incoherent, it is hardly possible to discern a race of pre-Aryan people, with very dark skins and crisp hair who led a semi-nomad life based on hunting

1. *Encyclopédie de l'Histoire*, La Pléiade, t. iii.

and harvesting. The arrival of the Aryans about 1500 B.C. probably pressed back such communities towards the least desirable areas. It was perhaps at such a moment that the *Luri, Dom* and other tribes already mentioned began to be nomads and to specialize in occupations suitable for wandering people.

One thousand years after the appearance of the Aryans, the north of India suffered from successive penetrations of Greeks, Persians, Scythians and Kusheans (the last forming an important group of nomads from the steppes of Asia). In the fifth century of our era, other nomads from the north, the Huns, invaded the country. Later came the Mussulmans.

In the midst of this incessant whirlwind the pre-Gypsy tribes (or supposedly so) felt less and less at ease. The almost general conversion of India to Islam embarrassed them far less than the attempts very probably made to settle them in one place; occupying powers seek to regularize a nomadism that is always damaging to the interests of a conquest. But, here again, we are reduced to hypotheses. Gypsiologists do not succeed in reaching agreement about the date of the Gypsies' exodus from Indian territories. It is nevertheless certain – and it is poor consolation – that the Gypsies were suddenly scattered over the East, affording us the tragic spectacle of the dispersal of a people comparable to that of the Jewish *diaspora*. And, very roughly, the year A.D. 1000 seems to place in time the beginning of an exodus which continues to this very day.[1]

SUPPLEMENT

THE VARIOUS GROUPS OF GYPSIES

Without entering into details of a 'genealogy', which proves to be highly complex (and will be dealt with in the course of this work), it is necessary to give here a list of the principal ethnic groups usually considered under the name of 'Gypsies'. These words will recur again and again in the chapters to come, and the reader should become familiar with them. This differentiation, acknowledged by gypsiologists, is itself of Gypsy origin.

There are three principal groups who assert their 'Gypsy blood':

1. Alone among gypsiologists, Fagnon and De Goeje set the date further back and drew attention to Gypsies settled in Byzantium from A.D. 855. It was Candrea who first, and relying on linguistic evidence, gave A.D. 1000 as a probable date. On this subject see: Kogaltnitcheanu, *Esquisse sur l'histoire, les mœurs et la langue des Cigains* (1837).

the Kalderash Gypsies, the *Gitanos* (*gitans* in France), and the Manush Gypsies.

The Kalderash Gypsies

The only authentic Gypsies, according to themselves, they are, first of all, smiths – tinsmiths, coppersmiths, etc. – as their name indicates (Romanian *caldera* – copper pot, boiler; Spanish *caldera* – cauldron, boiling-pan). They came fairly recently from the Balkans, then from Central Europe, and they are divided into five groups:

(a) *Lovari*, in France called 'Hungarians' – because they lived for a long time in Hungary (cf. the *Lohar* of India).

(b) *Boyhas*, who come from Transylvania and, before the 1939 World War, represented the majority of exhibitors of animals (especially in France).

(c) *Luri* (or *Luli*) who still have the name of the Indian tribe mentioned by Firdusi (p. 40).

(d) *Tschurari* (*Tchurari*, *Churari*) who live apart from the other Kalderash Gypsies.

(e) *Turco-Americans*, curiously so called because they had emigrated from Turkey to the United States of America before returning to Europe.

The Gitanos (*Gitans in France*)

These are seldom met except in Spain, Portugal, North Africa and the South of France. They differ from the Kalderash in physical appearance, dialects and customs. Among themselves they make a distinction between *Gitanos españoles*, *catalanes*, *andaluces* – Spanish, Catalan and Andalusian Gypsies.

The Manush (*les Manouches in France*)

[*Note:* John Sampson correlates the *Romanī* (Gypsy-language) word *manuš* with Sanskrit *manusa* – 'man', 'human being', and Prakrit *manusa*, and Hindi *manus* (feminine form *manusni* – woman). The terms in *romanī* are usually applied to middle-aged or elderly persons, and respectfully. It is not difficult to appreciate why a group should take such a term to describe themselves. *Tr.*]

The Manush are the traditional 'Bohemians'. Their name means 'true men' in Sanskrit. They are also called *Sinti* because of their

47

probable Indian origin, the banks of the Sind. They are divided into three sub-groups:

(a) *Valsikanès* or French Sinti. Travelling showmen and circus people.

(b) *Gaygikanès* or German (also Alsatian) Sinti. They are often confused with the *Yénisches*, European nomads who do not come within Gypsy ethnology, but live in accordance with the same traditions and same customs.

(c) *Piemontesi* or Italian Sinti. The famous Bouglione family are Piemontesi.

Outside these three big groups are the English, Irish and Scottish 'Gypsies' who resemble at one and the same time the Kalderash, the Manush and the 'Tinkers': the latter being itinerant smiths (the Irish Tinkers are also often horse-dealers), whose ethnic connexion with true Gypsy stock is uncertain.

There remain the non-Gypsy nomads, properly so called: basket-makers, chair-menders, mountebanks, jugglers or tumblers, watermen and 'travelling people' of many callings, all of whom have nothing in common with the Gypsies, apart from their mode of life. The Gypsies refer to them under the generic name *Barengré*.

These divisions are, of course, very arbitrary. Each of the above groups (excepting the *Barengré*) claims to be authentically Gypsy, and rather despises the others. Mixed marriages are rare. And, what is more, each has its own idea of discrimination. More often than not, in order to designate those whom it does not recognize as members of its own clan, it will use terms which call to mind the occupation in which those others specialize. Thus, they will speak of *Ursari* (bear-leaders) who among themselves form quite separate guilds or groupings. There are, for example:

The *Blidari*, makers of kitchen objects in wood.
The *Chivutse*, women employed as painters in the building trade to whitewash or colour-wash the fronts of houses.
The *Ciobatori*, makers of (high) boots and cobblers.
The *Costorari*, tinsmiths, tinners.
The *Ghilabari*, musicians.
The *Lautari*, musicians and makers of stringed-instruments.
The *Lingurari*, makers and merchants of wooden objects.
The *Meshteri Lacatuschi*, locksmiths.

The *Rudari*, makers of wooden objects.
The *Salahori*, masons and bricklayers.
The *Vatraschi*, agriculturists and gardeners.
The *Zlatari*, gold-washers.

This list is still incomplete. Popp Serboianu[1] lists fourteen 'Romanian' groups without exhausting the subject. But what has been given here[2] is sufficient to show the diversity of nomads who come under the term 'Gypsies'. As for the origin of each of these groups, it is extremely difficult to be precise: researches on the Gypsies as a whole have been carried up to recent years; and they still continue.

Note on the word 'Gypsy' and its equivalents

In Britain and the British Commonwealth, and in the United States of America, we now use the word Gypsy (*plural* Gypsies) and also Gipsy (Gipsies), all written with a capital letter. In this translation the form Gypsy is used throughout. The word first appeared in English in 1537 and, since then, in various spellings: Skelton, for example, used 'Gipcy'. A still earlier form was *gipsyan* (aphetic for Egyptian, from which the English word derives). *Tr.*

1. Popp Serboianu, *Les Tziganes* (1930).
2. I owe to Matéo Maximoff, the Gypsy writer, author of several monographs and novels about the life of his people, the 'groupings' at the beginning of this Supplement (see particularly his 'Principaux Groupes Tziganes en France' in *Études Tsiganes*, I, 1).

2 · History

We can very well imagine, looking at the map, the directions probably taken by the Gypsies on leaving India. The routes were, in fact, dependent on the same geographical factors as those obeyed by all the migratory peoples who, according to classical ideas, made their way towards the setting sun, attempting thereby to gain time on the duration of the day and, consequently, on death.

But the earliest wave of Gypsies (if it so be that the great departure took place at some precise moment in history) must have broken up after the first regions had been crossed, and become separated into branches that were more and more tenuous. It is therefore agreed that the Gypsies, leaving the banks of the Indus, went into, first, Afghanistan and Persia, reaching the north of the Caspian Sea to the south of the Persian Gulf. The northern group crossed Armenia, then the Caucasus, and later Russia. The southern group went up the course of the Euphrates and Tigris. But the axis of the progression again bifurcated: while part of the tribes made their way, some towards the Black Sea, others towards Syria, the main body of emigrants went deep into Asiatic Turkey. The most southern branch went along the Mediterranean through Palestine and Egypt. Very probably certain of these nomads succeeded in progressing on their way by the north coast of Africa as far as the Strait of Gibraltar and in crossing to Spain; these are our *Gitanos* – Spanish and Catalan Gypsies – but this hypothesis will be mentioned later. As for the principal group that remained in Turkey, this crossed the Bosphorus, swarmed into Greece and over the whole Balkan Peninsula. From there it discovered Central Europe. The extreme limits of the era of expansion would be, for the moment, England and Scotland. Those Gypsies who, for their part, went into Russia, it seems, reached Scandinavia.

These ordered items of historical information must be regarded with caution, based as they are on thinly scattered data and, more often than not, contradictory. It is not certain that all the peoples of which we are now about to speak are authentic Gypsies. What is more, the dates quoted overlap. It is, indeed, necessary to have recourse to written documents which do not mention the Gypsies except accidentally, and are never consistent in following the labyrinthine wanderings of this transitory people.

Nevertheless, before entering into details of this dispersion, one must take note of a disquieting detail: the Gypsies seem to have had a horror of the sea. They crossed immense deserts over and over again, yet they set foot on board ship only with the utmost repugnance. And if the Gypsies today live in the United States or in Chile, and if it was in the past imperative for English and Scottish Gypsies to risk their lives in sea travel, we do not know any seafaring Gypsies, other than fishermen.[1] For all that, water plays an important part in their rituals, as will be seen.

The Gypsies were never given a name except by the natives of the countries (the word Gypsy is not *romanī*, nor are the words *Tzigane* or *Gitano*), and the mention made of this people include the most varied names, sometimes most bizarre. They were called *Luri* in Baluchistan, and *Luli* in Iraq; *Karaki* (in which we might see the origin of the French *caraque* for *bohémien provençal* or Provençal Gypsy) and *Zangi* in Persian; *Kauli* in Afghanistan; *Cinghanés* or *Tchinganés* in Turkey and Syria; *Katsiveloï, Tsiganos* and *Atsincanoï* among the Greeks.

Linguists have clearly had great joy in building the most spectacular theses on this fact. There are fortunately some who are serious-minded. The dialects, in fact, constitute the least fragile ground on which to elaborate the history of the Gypsies. Nevertheless, the science of linguistics has laws which demand prudent application. The first of these which concerns us has been clearly stated by Martin Block:[2] 'The number of foreign words adopted by the Gypsies corresponds to the length of their sojourn in the different countries'. Under the illumination of this law, the Gypsies have remained in the Near East, Persia, and mainly in Turkey and Greece, between the tenth and the fifteenth centuries. In actual fact, their still strong basic language comprises many Greek, Turkish and Armenian words.

In the year 1100 a Georgian monk noted the arrival at Mount

---

1. Except in the Basque Country, see p. 95.
2. *Mœurs et coutumes des Tziganes* (1936).

SWEDEN
1515

FINLAND

POLAND
1509

RUSSIA
1500

Meissen
1416

LITTLE POLAND

BOHEMIA
1399

CARPATHIANS

Danube

Dniestr

Dniepr

1378
Zagreb

HUNGARY   MOLDAVIA

TRANSYLVANIA

BANAT
IN SIEBENGEBURGE

1417

BOSNIA

TEMESVAR

WALACHIA

YUGOSLAVIA

SERBIA
1348

DOBRUDJA

BULGARIA

BALKANS

Skoplia

ALBANIA

MACEDONIA

Byzantium

CORFU
1346

Modon   Nauplia

PELOPONNESUS
1378

CRETE
1322

Athos of a group of *Atsincani*, who were forthwith styled as 'sorcerers and thieves'. In 1322 a similar tribe landed on Crete; another at Corfu in 1346. This is all that is recorded in the written documents; very little it is. In order to guess how the Gypsies lived in Asia Minor, before surging into Europe, one has to be content with imagining that they had the same habits as their direct descendants, like those photographed by Professor Pittard[1] on the plains of the Balkans: a world of half-underground houses, mud huts on which they dry cakes of *teẓek*, that fuel made of straw and cow-dung, tents of woven materials lightly kept in place by stones, low, flat wagons drawn by a horse and a buffalo.[2]

APPEARANCE IN EUROPE

As early as the beginning of the fifteenth century the Gypsies had reached the Balkans. Perhaps exposed to persecutions, perhaps because their numbers had become too great (we do not know if the tide of migration continued being dispersed over the whole of ancient Mesopotamia), was it their wish to reach the wildest, and therefore the most hospitable regions for wanderers? In any case, this signifies that there was a second wave of dispersion, at least as important as the first; for, in the course of one hundred years, the Gypsies were to cover the whole of Europe.

The dates of their appearance in the various countries of Europe can now be given. These dates have been obtained by scrutiny and analysis of archives of which, in this instance, the veracity need not be doubted:

DATES OF THE APPEARANCE OF THE GYPSIES IN EUROPE

A.D. 855?	Byzantium	1378	⎰ The Peloponnese / Zagreb
1260 or 1399?	⎱ Bohemia	1414	Basle
1322?	Crete		⎰ Transylvania
1346	Corfu	1417	Moldavia
1348	Serbia		⎱ The Elbe

1. Pittard, *Les Tẓiganes ou Bohémiens* (1932).
2. Another example of this precarious mode of life is given by the *Quénites* ('Cainites') who are nomad Gypsies, smiths and horse-copers, clever in working metals, They live on the borders of Syria, are considered by the Bedouin as pariahs, and travel on foot or on donkey-back. Their name recalls that of the descendants of Cain.

A.D.	1418	Saxony, Augsburg	1447	Barcelona
	1419	France, Sisteron	1492	
	1420?	Denmark	or 1505	Scotland
	1422	Bologna, Rome	1500	Russia
	1427	Paris	1509	Poland
	1430		1515	Sweden
	or 1440?	Wales		

These dates mark the 'official' appearance of Gypsies; a fact which must be emphasized. It does not mean that in reality the Gypsies had not arrived in Europe before the authorities thought of mentioning them for the first time, before the occurrence of some local event or other with which their name was associated. Certain authors who, to tell the truth, are not very worthy of confidence, profess the belief that they were in Europe much earlier: 'The South of France was for long infested with them, and they used to attend the fair at Beaucaire from the year 1300. . . .'[1] More disturbing is the assertion of Albert Mousset:[2] 'One of the first mentions of their presence in the capital [Paris] is provided for us by the *Dit des Rues de Paris* which calls them *Logipciens* (Egyptians) and records that in the fourteenth or perhaps the thirteenth century they lived in the rue Saint-Symphorien, that is, in the neighbourhood of the present rue Valette.'

Then again, a letter from Ottokar II (King of Bohemia) to Pope Alexander IV mentions that the Hungarian Army of Bella IV numbered 1,260 of the *Gingari*, among whom there were said to be Gypsies. But, as Serboianu[3] remarks, the name of these *Gingari* is replaced by *Bulgari* in another manuscript.

Another suspect element is provided by Graberg:[4] a young Swede named Rebenius is said to prove that, from the year 1303, they had to banish the 'Bohemians' from Sweden. These nomads were designated under the name of *Vagi Garciones* (decree *De Relegatione Vagorum Garcionum*). And Graberg quotes two items from the diplomatic records of Ludwig, one of 1344 and the other of

1. H. de Galier, *Filles nobles et magiciennes* (1913).

2. In an article in the newspaper *Le Monde* (1958).

3. *Les Tziganes* (1930).

4. Graberg, *Dissertation sur les doutes et conjectures sur les Bohémiens et leur première apparition en Europe* (no date, but before 1817). (Graberg is Count Graberg af Hemsö, 1813. *Tr.*)

1394, each of them mentioning a 'street of the *Cicines* or *Zigeuner*' in Schweidenitz, which would allow us to assume the presence of Gypsies there for a rather long time. But, as the scholars have it, all this is not accepted.

The difficulty of finding one's bearings in this vast accumulation of apocryphal information springs equally from the fact that for long the 'Bohemians' – that is, real Gypsies – have been confused with nomads of every description, with public entertainers, vagabonds, tramps and wanderers who, from the Middle Ages on, overran Europe. The history of the amusement (or fun) fair, that of the various pilgrimages, and again that of vagabondage, abound in quotations which make gypsiologists dream. Thus, Freytag[1] cites among the mountebanks who came from the Holy Roman Empire to amuse the Frankish communities 'vagabond women who roamed the German countries, bold Russian women decked out in costumes of striking colours and filling the roles of dancers, singers and actresses. When they shook the Greek tambourine or the Asiatic sistrum in voluptuous poses, they became irresistible to the feudal barons; but this only made them more hateful in the eyes of grave and pious people. . . .' How can we avoid thinking, in view of such a picture, of the Esmeralda we see at our fairs?

But let us limit ourselves here to official sources only, and continue with our tabulation:

1348: Jules Bloch[2] reports the presence of *Cingarije* in Serbia: 'they are shoeing-smiths or harness-makers, and pay an annual tribute of forty horse-shoes' (unfortunately the author does not give his sources).

1378: The same author (the only one, it seems, to have found his bearings in this obscure period) discovered that at Zagreb the judicial chronicles (i.e. Law Reports of the period) record, from that year onwards, the appearance before the court of many *Cygans*, particularly butchers (an occupation that is, however, extremely rare among Gypsies today). In the same period the Venetian Governor of Nauplia in the Peloponnese confirms the local *Acingani* in the privileges already accorded by his predecessors.

1399: The Gypsies appeared in Bohemia, at all events one of them, black and a brigand, according to Jules Bloch.

1. Freytag, *Jongleurs et Histrions* (no date).
2. *Les Tsiganes* (1953).

1416: It is really between the years 1414 and 1416 that different chronicles refer to the first Gypsies in Germany. One author alone claims that they were at Hildesheim, in Lower Saxony, from 1407 on. In any case they were spoken of at Basle and in Hesse in 1414, at Meissen, near Dresden, and on the Elbe in 1416.

1417: From this date onwards the Gypsy dispersion suddenly extends over a very great part of Europe. The event marking this date is the appearance of an important troupe along the shores of the North Sea between Bremen and Hamburg. The same year, or that following, some Gypsies were recorded at about the same time in Saxony, Lower Saxony (near Hanover), in Hesse, Bavaria (at Augsburg) and up to the Swiss border. It is Hermann Croner, chronicler of Lübeck, who first evoked them, declaring definitely that these foreigners had never been seen before then.[1]

Let us pause for a moment with these Gypsies who had arrived in Germany. In spite of the suddenness of their appearance, which permits us to think that they were impelled (though whether to go or to come, who knows?), we can take it that their troupes had left the Balkans following the Danube valley, the natural route taken by Attila a thousand years earlier. The importance of the Gypsies' stopping-places on the Hungarian steppes will be appreciated. One of the principal groups succeeded in crossing the 'Metal Mountains' or Erzgebirge, or in going round by the south of the Carpathians, and reached the plains of Moldavia, next crossing the valley of the Elbe, another invasion route, coming finally right up to the sea. A second group must have been content at an earlier date to go up the course of the Danube.

Who were these Gypsies?

The chroniclers[2] say that they looked like Tartars. They were dark-skinned people who advanced in long caravans, some on foot, others on horseback, dragging with them wagons well laden with baggage, women and children. This was evidently enough for the Germans, who, still vividly remembering the invasions by Vandals, immediately gave these newcomers the name of *Tatern*, that is Tartars. And meanwhile the new arrivals introduced themselves in a very peaceful manner, claiming to be good Christians.

Hermann Croner, who describes them at considerable length, and

1. See Hampe, *Die fahrenden Leute in der deutschen Vergangenheit* (Leipzig, 1902).

2. Münster, *Cosmogonia Universala*; Hermann Croner, *Chronica*, etc.

gives the extraordinary figure of from 300 to 500 families, relates that, according to their own statements,

their infidelity to the Christian faith and their return to paganism, after a first conversion, had been the cause of their wandering life. The bishops had imposed on them the penance of continuing their adventurous course during seven years.[1] The Gypsies held and showed 'Letters of Protection' [*litteras promotorias*] from various rulers – among others from Sigismund, King of the Romans[2] – which caused them to be well received in episcopal cities, by princes, at the castles of the nobility, in closed towns [*oppidis*], by the bishops and other mitred dignitaries.

All, or nearly all the troupes of Gypsies which appeared in Europe in the fifteenth century were provided with a safe conduct. They were not the only people to have it. Since the Church, from the twelfth century onwards, had elevated charity into a virtue, and, so that there should be charity, there was need for many mendicants, many categories of wandering peoples carried on their persons letters of recommendation, genuine or faked. Such were the Goliards, the Coquillarts, the Hubins[3] in France, or the Convertis (or Converts) who showed certificates enjoining them to expiate their sins by vagabondage and by living on alms. In Germany, at the period now dealt with, such as these were the 'false hermits' or *Dobissirer*, and the 'men of God' or *Vagierer*.

The letters presented by the Gypsies, however, look fairly authentic. To forge them would have required, it seems – and in spite of the legendary cleverness of this people – a comparatively long period of residence in the country. Here is the text of one of those 'Letters of Protection', dated 1493:

We, Sigismund . . . King of Hungary, Bohemia, Dalmatia, Croatia and of other places.[4] . . . Our faithful Ladislas, Voivode[5] of the

1. The number of seven years – elsewhere seven centuries – has a strong flavour of its familiar symbolism.

2. He was in fact King of Hungary.

3. For Goliards see p. 32. *Coquillarts* and *Hubins* formed part of *Les Gueux*, the 'beggars'. For bibliography of this subject, see Vexliard, *Introduction à la sociologie du vagabondage* (1956).

4. The names of the territories listed give an idea of the geographical area within which the Gypsies were able to enjoy the immunity.

5. Voivode (chief responsible). The word occurs with very slight variations in Bulgarian, Serbian, Czech and modern Greek languages, meaning a local ruler. *Tr.*

Gypsies and others dependent on him have humbly besought Us to bear witness of our special benevolence. It has pleased Us to receive their compliant request and not to refuse them this present letter. In consequence, if the aforesaid Ladislas and his people present themselves in any place within Our Empire, town or village, we enjoin you to show your loyalty towards Us. You will protect them in every way, so that the Voivode Ladislas and the Gypsies his subjects can reside within your walls. If there should be found among them some drunken woman, if any troublesome incident should occur among them, no matter what its nature, it is Our will and formal command that the said Voivode Ladislas and he alone shall then use the right to punish and to absolve, to the exclusion of you all.

This text reveals particularly that the Gypsy Chief had taken a local name, Ladislas, in accordance with a custom among them which is never to vary, and a title, *Voivode*, borrowed from the Slav world, one which was to survive to our own times. It will be finally noted that he obtained from the king the right to exercise his full and entire jurisdiction, the Gypsies remaining in that foreign country the Chief's 'subjects'.

During this period other Gypsies had ventured far afield in Western Europe:

1419: A group presented themselves at the gates of Sisteron, on the river Durance, in France. They were given the name *Sarrasins*, (Saracens) but, in spite of this sharply pejorative appellation, proof was given of a hospitality offered to them that is quite characteristic of Provence. They received provisions and the right to camp. These were the first Gypsies known in France. Did they come from Germany, via Switzerland? We do not know, but this is probable, given the agreement of the dates.

1422: A Gypsy Chief named Michel or Michaël of Egypt led his troupe into Italy and arrived at Bologna. It is plausible to imagine that this troupe, consisting of about one hundred men, came from Germany by the Brenner Pass, following the only passable carriage way which Germanic pilgrims took when going to Venice to embark for the Holy Land.[1] Muratori[2] has fortunately preserved for us impressions of that period of residence:

Many people went very respectfully to find Duke Michael's wife to

1. For a description of that route, see Prescott, *The Journey to Jerusalem in the Fifteenth Century* (1958).
2. *Cronica di Bologna* (1749).

have their future told by her, and so in actual fact many things happened, some learning what would be their lot, none in any case returning without having their purse or some item of clothing stolen. The women of those people went through the town between six and eight o'clock, displayed their talents in the houses of the burghers, seizing everything upon which they could lay their hands. Others went into shops as if to make purchases, but in fact to steal. Throughout the whole of Bologna there was petty thieving on a vast scale. As a result of this it was proclaimed that a fine of fifty livres would be imposed on whoever engaged in any business with those foreigners, as well as excommunication. . . .

It will be noticed how the tone has changed since Sigismund's almost eulogistic recommendations.[1] But what is of most importance in this text is the appearance of excommunication. In reality it marks, in the history of the persecutions of the Gypsies, the beginning of the confusion between a 'Bohemian' and a creature of the devil.

These vagabonds [continues Muratori] are the cleverest thieves in the world. When there was nothing more to be stolen, they left for Rome. It must again be noted that there is no worse brood then these savages. Thin and black, they eat like swine. The women go about in chemises, hardly covered; they wear ear-rings and much other finery. One of them gave birth to a child in the public square, and three days later she began again to go about with the others. . . .

From Bologna, where the Gypsies stayed hardly three weeks, Duke Michael's Gypsies went on to Rome, where they succeeded in obtaining (or in forging?) letters of recommendation from the Pope himself, Martin V. Some time later a similar troupe appeared in Switzerland, led by one Michael of Egypt, and nobody could identify it with the one mentioned above.

1427: And here is a special event: the arrival of the Gypsies in Paris. *Le Journal d'un Bourgeois de Paris*, an anonymous document yet so valuable about the intimate life of the capital for the years 1405 to 1449, describes this new spectacle in full measure.

In spite of their length, it is important to quote these texts; they are the first documents to describe and comment upon this invasion of French civilization by foreign elements, a quite exceptional one because of its unwarlike nature. It was an event without precedent, which explains the care taken by the chroniclers to emphasize the

1. It is true that Muratori wrote his chronicle in the eighteenth century, at a time when it was long since the Gypsies had been given the highest consideration.

reasons given by the Gypsies themselves for their wandering life, and to connect these utterances with the body of Christian legends:

On Sunday 17 August, twelve penitents, as they said, came to Paris: there were a duke, a count and ten men, all on horseback, who said they were Christians and natives of Lower Egypt. They claimed to have formerly been Christians, and that it was only a short time ago that they had become so again under penalty of death. They explained that the Saracens had attacked them, but their faith had weakened. They had not resisted very strongly, had surrendered to the enemy, denied Our Lord, and had become Saracens again.

On this news the Emperor of Germany, the King of Poland and other Christian princes rushed upon their enemies and soon conquered them. They had hoped to remain in those countries, but the Emperor and his allies had held counsel not to allow them there without the consent of the Pope, and had sent them to Rome to see the Holy Father. They all went there, great and small, the latter with great difficulty; and they confessed their sins. The Pope deliberated with his council and gave them as penance that they should roam the earth for seven years without sleeping in a bed. For outlay he ordered that every bishop or crook-bearing abbot should give them, once and for all, ten Tours livres. He then handed them letters patent with these decisions for the prelates concerned, gave them his blessing, and they went on their way.

They had already been travelling for five years before their arrival in Paris. The common herd – a hundred or a hundred and twenty men, women and children – did not arrive until the day of the Beheading of Saint John; by order of the court, their entrance into Paris was forbidden, and they were accommodated at La Chapelle-Saint-Denise. . . .

When they were established at La Chapelle, more people had never been seen at the benediction of Lendit[1] than the crowds which came from Paris, from Saint-Denis and from the entire suburbs to see them. In truth, their children were incredibly shrewd; and the majority, indeed nearly all of them, had their ears pierced and in each wore one or two silver rings. They said this was the fashion in their country.

The men were very dark and their hair was crisp. The women were the ugliest and swarthiest one could see. They had sores on their faces[2] and black hair like a horse's tail. They were clad in *flaussaie*, a coarse old material attached to the shoulder by a thick band of cloth or cord; their only linen was an old blouse or shirt. In short, they were the poorest creatures ever seen coming to France within living memory. In spite of their poverty there were among them witches who, looking at people's hands, revealed the past and foretold the future.

1. The famous fair at which there were many mountebanks.
2. They were tattooed, it seems.

They sowed discord in many households by telling the husband 'your wife has made you cuckold', and the wife, 'your husband has deceived you'. But the worst was that, as their patter went on, either by magic, with the help of the devil, or by their dexterity, they emptied into their own purses those of their listeners. This is what was said, but I went to speak to them two or three times and I never lost a farthing and I did not see them looking at hands. Yet, as people noised reports in all directions, the news reached the Archbishop of Paris: he went to see them, bringing with him a minor brother named Petit Jacobin who, on his order, preached a fine sermon and the fortune-tellers of both sexes were excommunicated with all who had shown their hands. They then had to go away and they made for Pontoise, on the day of Our Lady, in September.[1]

The agreement of facts revealed in these two texts gives us to suppose that it is a matter of two similar troupes and perhaps of the same kind of Gypsies. The dates, in fact, correspond; since these 'Parisian' Gypsies pinpoint, in 1427, that they left Rome five years earlier.

1430: Three years later – but some writers say 1440 – some Gypsies landed in England.[2] It is not known whether they came from France or from the mouth of the Elbe (no document mentions the Netherlands at that period). Above all, we do not know how they managed to cross the English Channel. From that time onwards, and following the custom peculiar to the whole of Europe, the English called them 'Gypsies' or Egyptians. The name was to remain and in the end came to signify in English the concept of wanderer or nomad.

1447: Narciso's *Annales de Cataluña* report Gypsies at Barcelona in the month of June of this year. As these carried on their persons letters patent from the Pope, it has to be admitted that they formed part of the same group as the preceding ones; in contrast to the *Gitanos* who came from North Africa via Gibraltar.[3] But Lafuente[4] says that they did not enter Spain by the Catalan littoral until 1452.

1492: On the other side, the Gypsies arrived in Scotland in this year, unless they did so in 1502.

1. The French text of this passage was adapted by Jacques Megret.
2. See Brian Vesey-Fitzgerald, *Gypsies of Britain, an Introduction to their History* (London, 1944). He gives 22 April 1505 as the date of the first *official* reference to Gypsies in Britain, a very brief note in the accounts of the Lord Treasurer for Scotland. The note reads, '1505, Apr. 22. Item to the Egyptians be the Kinge's command VII., lib.' *Tr.*   3. See p. 50.
4. In *Los Gitanos, el flamenco y los flamencos* (Barcelona, 1955).

1500: Lastly, some other groups of Gypsies become known in Russia in this year.

Now that the Gypsies have been scattered over the whole of Europe, let us see in some detail how they behaved there and how they were received.

GYPSIES IN THE FIFTEENTH AND SIXTEENTH CENTURIES

Let us begin with France. The arrival of some 'Bohemians' coincided with the establishment of the *corporations de gueuserie*, or as we might call them in English, the 'guilds of beggars'. It is probably a chance coincidence. But the historians of the 'dangerous classes'[1] have not omitted to underline this connexion. We know that, in the period of one century, from 1356 to 1452, the Great Plague and the Hundred Years War had transformed France into a wilderness in which it was necessary 'to eat in order not to be eaten'. Law clerks and the highway robbers, having abandoned the roads or taken refuge in the still impenetrable forests, had to organize themselves in order to survive. The 'Beggars' Guild' became a veritable syndicate or sort of professional association, as one of its historians, Abel Chevalley, has well said. Conforming to the practices of society of the times, the beggars had their courts, their kings, their social divisions and classes, their territories and capitals, their system of justice, and even their own language. We are well informed about the customs of these outlaws, thanks to the proceedings at law relating to the Coquillarts. Thanks above everything to Pechon de Ruby's book, a small but important work.

In the year 1596, Jean Jullieron, a bookseller at Lyons, published *La Vie généreuse des Gueux, Mercelots et Boesmiens. . . .*[2] The author describes himself as a Breton gentleman, and takes a pseudonym (in the slang of the day, *pechon de ruby* meant 'wicked child'). He is a boy with an influential father who had broken with a good family; fearing the merited thunderbolts from an authoritarian father and,

1. Particularly Champion, *Notes pour servir à l'Histoire des classes dangereuses en France*; Sainéan, *Les Sources de l'argot ancien*; the famous *Histoire générale des larrons* by Lyonnois, which went into more than ten editions from 1623 to 1709; and Kraemer's very important thesis, *Le type du faux-mendiant dans les Vies littératures romanes. . . .*

2. This book was, in fact, published much earlier, at the beginning of the sixteenth century, perhaps at the end of the fifteenth. See Vexliard, op. cit.

with the full blast of the usual romanticism, he decided to 'live his own life'. All the same, it showed that, at ten years of age, the boy was not lacking in precocity: he got over the wall of the family manor-house and went out on the roads with a small-goods trader of his own age, one of those pedlars of whom we have learnt enough from Villon to know that they carried in their pack more rubbish than good merchandise. Sleeping in the open, and finding this life very pleasant, our little adventurer reached Le Poitou (now the *Département des Deux-Sèvres*) and had himself received as a novice in one of those organized bands that attended fairs. He took part in raids and depredations and acquired all the secrets of the 'syndicate', in particular the argot or cant lingo called *bleschien*, at that time completely incomprehensible to honest people.

Later Pechon took to wiser occupations (of which nothing is known), and wrote *La Vie généreuse*, an exemplary biography which marked the birth of picaresque literature in France. To it he added a vocabulary of *blesche*. If I say so much about this book, it is because one half of it concerns the Gypsies.

But before drawing on it, let us finish the sketch of the wandering classes of that period, for it is because of contact with them that the Gypsies were to shape their manner of life, and particularly to gain that unfortunate reputation as licensed thieves. Abel Chevalley[1] recalls the necessary dates:

1427: First appearance of the 'Bohemians' (Chevalley overlooked Sisteron).

1407–47: Regulations for the pedlars and mendicants.

1445–50: First documents on the jargon.

1445–80: Institution of the great fairs in Bas-Poitou, and at Niort, Fontenay and L'Herménault, etc.

As regards the area of activities, the 'Beggars' Organization' became concentrated around two important nuclei or 'cells': one in La Vendée and the other in the Languedoc. It was in these places that they held their 'States General' or legislative body, and it is there that we shall see tribes of Gypsies get together – up to our own times.

As for the occupation of these vagrant people, these *truands* or 'hardy beggars' (*truand* first meant one who paid tribute), it must be noted that it was not only a matter of being thieves and highwaymen. The majority of these men followed the business of pedlar. They

1. He wrote the Preface to a modern edition of *La Vie généreuse* (1927).

were itinerant packmen, the forebears of our commercial travellers. They covered great distances – from the Vendée to Lyon, for example – by roads which were not exactly safe. But they were in a position to lay the basis of a vast intelligence network. With these pedlars and packmen the real beggars known as *caymants*[1] (that is, those who made a business of receiving if not exacting charity) formed a natural alliance – and later our 'Bohemians' who brought to the community the inestimable industries of the smithy and palmistry. The three groups helped one another to prosper, but remained nonetheless independent and very jealous of their own movements. If the *blesche*, the argot of the pedlars, became mixed with the jargon of the beggars in the course of secret consultations, the *romanī* or Gypsy language remained autonomous. I have with difficulty been able to make out in Pechon's lexicon the relation between the cant word *raẓis* (priest) and the Gypsy word *rashi* (meaning the same). Nobody, I think, has yet studied the possible connexions between the argots of that period and the *romanī* dialects.[2] Auguste Vitu[3] alone records that a certain vocabulary 'descended from Slav languages was no doubt introduced by the Egyptians or "Bohemians" into the French jargon on which they have left traces here and there of their language, the *romanī*, in the form of words from Sanskrit, Persian and Indian languages'. On the other hand, Armand Ziwès[4] has discovered in a copy of *La Vie généreuse*[5] a manuscript Latin-*romanī* glossary which seems to have been transcribed in the eighteenth century by some owner of the volume.

Here now is Pechon de Ruby's text:

When I left my baggage I went to find a Captain of Egyptians who was in the outlying part of Nantes, a man who had a fine troupe of Egyptians or Bohemians, and presented myself to him: he received me with open arms, promising to teach me good things; with which I was very pleased. He gave me the name Afourette.

When they wished to leave the place where they lived, they went in the opposite direction from it, and travelled half a league in a contrary sense, then setting out the right way. They have the best and most

1. Compare the French *quémander*, to beg (from door to door).
2. Except Francisque Michel in *Études de philologie comparée sur l'argot et les idiomes analogues parlés en Europe et en Asie* (1856). Michel has greatly exaggerated the *romanī* part.
3. In *Jargon et Jobelin . . . avec un Dictionnaire analytique du jargon* (1889).
4. In *Le jargon de François Villon* (1946).
5. Preserved in the Bibliothèque Nationale, Paris (cote Li, 64B).

reliable maps on which are marked all the towns, villages and rivers, the houses of the gentry and others, and arrange among themselves a meeting-place, with ten days in between at twenty leagues from where they set out. The Captain allocates to each of the oldest men three households to escort there, taking their own short cut, and finding the rendezvous: and as for those remaining who are well mounted and armed, he sends them with a good Almanac in which are all the fairs of the world, changing accoutrements and horses.

When they stay in some important village, it is always with the permission of the noblemen or of the most outstanding men of the places: their place is in some barn or inhabited dwelling. The Captain gives them quarters there and, to each family group, its corner aside. They take very little from the place where they are living, but in the neighbouring parishes they play havoc, pillaging and picking locks everywhere: and should they find any sum of money, they notify it to the Captain and promptly go away to ten leagues from there. They make counterfeit money industriously, and they play all kinds of gambling games, buy all sorts of horses whatever vice they may have, provided their money is accepted.

When they acquire provisions they give pledges in good money on the first occasion, because of the lack of confidence in them: but when they are ready to move on they always acquire something and leave some false coin, taking good money with them, and goodbye! At the time of harvest, if they find the doors closed they open them with all their pick-locks and steal linen, cloaks, money and any other item of furniture, and render an account of everything to the Captain who takes his right share. They also render account of everything they win at gaming, except what they earn by fortune-telling. They tie up dogs very successfully, and cope extremely well with any vice a horse may have.

When they know of some prosperous merchant who is passing through the country, they disguise themselves and catch him, and usually do this near some gentry: then, changing their accoutrement they shoe their horses the wrong way round and put padding on the horse-shoes, fearing that they might be heard going away.

One day of festivity in a little village near Moulins the people were celebrating the marriage of a very rich peasant: some of the villagers began to gamble with our companions, and lost money. While some of ours played, their women stole; and in truth found booty to the value of five hundred crowns, as much from the guests as from several others. We were discovered because of four francs lost by a young merchant who was dancing at a wedding-party and had locked his house and strong boxes. The peasants flung themselves on our boxes and we on their portmanteaux and heads, and they on our backs with blows of their swords and daggers, and we stabbed them with knives, so that we gave them a good thrashing. These peasants went to the Governor of Moulins and complained. He, having heard their story, sent twenty-five cavalrymen with body armour, and fifty harquebus men to go against us. One of our women who was in Moulins gave us warning of this and we had to cross a river, which handicapped us. Our Captain went ahead at a quick trot and left a man to watch half a league behind, giving him instructions that, as soon as he should find out anything, he should warn us of the number in pursuit of us. This he did. The Captain gave orders as follows: All were commanded to get off their horses, and the men were to feign being crippled or wounded; and he commanded two women to let themselves fall off their horses and pretend to be half dead. One of these women had given birth to a child two days before, she and the child were covered with blood, and so she put it between her legs. Captain Charles blooded the mouths of his horses and daubed his children and people with blood to make a proper deception. Charles appeared before the local gentry, covered with blood; and these, moved by pity as they looked at the peasants, felt more inclined to charge them than us. Some had their arms on their neck, their legs on the pommel of their saddle, and our Colonel did not fail to demonstrate that he was in the right: to such good effect that they left us, and we spurred our horses. After their retreat, it is sure, all our people were well and we went away to feed our horses at ten leagues from there. Since then I have passed through that place, and I swear to you that this incident is remembered to this day by the people who live there.

Pechon de Ruby's text stops here, and this is a pity. The author does not seem to have lived long enough to offer, according to his resolution, 'a more useful book, which will be a compilation of chiromancy, with many fine practices and illustrations of the baton or wand of the Bohemians, by which one can make oneself capable of becoming an expert contriver'.

The Bohemian's stick or rod is also that of the organized beggars (*Gueux*), the principal utensil of the *Mercelots*. For all that, this stick 'with two ends', one thick, the other thin, served them more for driving away dogs, and killing domestic and other edible birds such as pheasants and partridges, than for walking. They also used it during the ceremonies of taking the oath administered by the 'Grand Coesre'[1] or 'Great Chief'. Among the useful purposes learnt by the *pechon* (apprentice robber) are the various tricks with the stick such as the 'feigned raising', the 'rake', the '*quigehabin*' (for deceiving dogs), the 'bracelet', the 'back one', the 'curb', all of which, the

[1]. Pronounced Couère.

author says, can be understood only from experience. In the chapter dealing with the divinatory arts it will be seen what the 'stick' or magic wand, the instrument of the mountebanks and jugglers, also meant for the Gypsies.

While awaiting the discovery of that 'more useful work' in some underground gallery of a library, the first work by Pechon de Ruby, apart from its value as a guide to chronology, informs us that, from the fifteenth century, the Gypsies knew France very well (they made detailed maps and almanacs indicating the fairs). They lived in tribes under the leadership of a chief (but each family had its own camp-fire), they paid tribute to their chief, and they were coiners, horse-copers, gamesters and fortune-tellers. If their way of life closely resembled that of the organized robbers, their occupations, if not all their activities, were different.

Documents such as the *Journal d'un Bourgeois de Paris* or the *Vie généreuse* are clearly exceptional, and we possess very few items indeed of information regarding the movements of bands of Gypsies in fifteenth-century France. It would be necessary to search too many archives, and too often without result.[1] We do know, however, that in 1447 the city of Orléans witnessed the arrival under its walls of twenty families of 'Saracens'. Six years later an item of news richer in information can be pin-pointed:

Several Egyptians, commonly called 'Saracens', who had been staying in the town of Courtésol [near Châlons-sur-Marne] arrived at the entrance of the town [of La Cheppe] with the intention of staying there. Among them were several who carried javelins, spears and other military trappings. And they did their utmost in words to indicate that they wished to stay in that town, both the first arrivals, who were about ten or twelve, and several others of their party who came afterwards: altogether between sixty or eighty people. A number of townsfolk collected together on their arrival, and some of them took the boar-spears, pikes and other staves which they take with them when they go out into the fields; and others took bows. . . . It was remembered [of the Bohemians] that not so long before, those, or others like them, had stayed there, men, women and children, and had done many bad things there, such as stealing food, money, purses, items of furniture and all the portable things they could find.[2]

1. Nevertheless, to this thankless task De Vaux de Foletier has devoted himself for years. See *Études Tsiganes*, op. cit.

2. This account is recorded by J. Bloch (op. cit.) in particular. According to Martin Block, these Gypsies were led by a certain Martin de la Barre ('Martin of the Rod').

In this incident and in the battle which followed these censures an 'Egyptian' was killed and his assassin was granted a royal reprieve.

No trace of this first band which pillaged La Cheppe can be found, but this story must date well before 1450. It is absolutely impossible, from such items of information, to try to establish even an approximate map of the wanderings of the Gypsies of that period. On the other hand, it is well realized that the French people were beginning to be on their guard against all the outrageous tricks that could be played on them by those foreigners. And the names given to the strangers accurately translate this fear into words.

NAMES GIVEN TO THE GYPSIES

It has been seen that the terms most commonly used by the non-Gypsies for Gypsies were 'Egyptians' and 'Bohemians'. That of 'Saracens' had a vogue almost as great, but more limited in time. If the memory of the Mussulman invaders began to fade, it was nevertheless normal for French people, especially in the south, to recognize in those new visitors some physical characteristics which unfavourably recalled the 'Saracens' of a former era. It was in the same spirit that some documents, quite rare ones it is true, designated the Gypsies under the name 'Moors' (*Mores*); and a theory was even formulated in the nineteenth century to the effect that the word *Rom*[1] was the anagram of *More*. But the term 'Saracen' is worth considering. It appears, in fact, to have been *caraque*, the word by which the people in Provence singled out the Gypsies. *Caraque* is not Provençal, although Fourvières' Dictionary gives *caracaio* for 'Gypsy' and *caraco* for *gitan* (*gitano*). The peasants of Lower Provence still maintain that the Gypsies are called *caracaio* because they use it for calling fowl (*caraco* also means 'cock', and the English term 'cock-a-doodle-doo' is *cocorico* in French). The truth is that the word comes from very much further back. It was under the appellation *Karaki* (or *Karaghi*) that the Persians first mentioned the Gypsies.[2] And here we have what takes us to the Saracens:

At the beginning of the Middle Ages, *Saracaenus* (in Greek *Sarakenos*)

1. The Gypsy word used to describe themselves, *Rom*, is used in three senses: (a) to mean 'Gypsy'; (b) to mean 'man'; (c) to mean 'husband'. The feminine form *romni* is commonly used for 'wife'. Adjective *romano*, adverb *romanes*. *Tr*.

2. According to Jules Bloch, some Gypsies in Azerbaïdzhan are still known by the name *Qaraki*, a word which in Turkish means 'beggar'.

was used to designate any citizen of the Republic of Characen (*Chârakainê*), a country situated at the delta of the River Tigris. . . . This people professed Sabeism or 'Zabeism'. . . . Rightly considered as a sect of this religion, the Mahometans of the Middle Ages were called *Saracaeni* by the Byzantines and their disciples, the Christians of the west. . . . The western peoples of the crusades clearly distinguished a *Saracaenus*, a Mahometan of the older kind, from a Mussulman, that is a Turk. Later, when the 'religious' type of medieval Mahometan disappeared, the word which specially designated him was forgotten: and this is why we transcribe Saracaenus as Saracen, a word with a spelling as blurred as the meaning.[1]

Then again, *kara* (in Tartar meaning 'black' and by extension 'tribute paying') is a root common to all the languages of the Near East, one which succeeded in reaching Central Europe. Just think of these towns: Karachi in Pakistan, Karak in Syria, Carakalu in Romania. . . . The linguistic evolution *Sarakenos–Saracin–Caraque* thus seems to be confirmed.

If the people of Provence chose to call the Gypsies the *Caraques*, the inhabitants of the Pyrenees preferred the variant *Caracos* (or *Carracos*). In the nineteenth century this word meant the Gypsy (*gitan*) wrestlers who gave displays in the public squares. Henri Rolland[2] describes them and at the same time places for us the psychological climate of his period in relation to the Gypsies:

The *carraco* forms part of that great unknown family, thinly scattered over all parts of the globe, condemned to a wandering and nomad life, wild in spite of the civilization which surrounds them. The Pyrenees area rejects this scum [*sic*] into the Southern provinces. At each festival these *gitanos* come the day before to set up their bivouacs at the entrance to the town, and next day they are found wrestling for all they are worth. The lure of a few pieces of silver always makes them enter the lists with professional wrestlers (*michommes*): then there is great entertainment for the spectators. In fact the *carracos* – a term of abuse which also means 'thief' as it does 'Bohemian' – are at this moment the destitute and despised race which the cruel humour of the people has always required of them to make passive playthings of themselves. The *carraco* then is the involuntary wag, the pariah, the pain-sufferer of the multitude. People laugh at his frantic exploits, at his brown body, his slender limbs like those of the Arab. . . .

1. Azy Mazahéri, *La Vie quotidienne des Musulmans au Moyen Age* (1951).
2. In a collective and romantic work, *Les Français peints par eux-mêmes* (no date).

I lay stress on this quotation because the existence of these wrestlers has not previously been mentioned in Gypsy folk-lore.

From the sixteenth century onwards the Gypsies became known in popular French as the *Rabouins*. In the Middle Ages this word meant the devil himself, and it is not difficult to find a learned etymology for the word: in the Semitic languages, in Armenian, and particularly in Syriac, *rabb* means 'master'. Hebrew has made *rabbi*, a man learned in the Jewish law. And throughout the Middle Ages the Jewish rabbis were readily accused of having commerce with demons and black magic. In the seventeenth century it went as far as inventing a Saint Rabboni[1] whose special talent was to calm jealous husbands. It was only at the beginning of the nineteenth century that the word *rabouin* disappeared from our glossaries of cant and slang.

Each French patois had its way of naming the Gypsies. The people of the old province of Saintonge (capital Saintes) called them the *Beurdindins*. Burgundy called them the *Camps-Volants* ('flying camps') clearly because of their nomadism. Their quite early appearance in the Basque Country earned them the nickname *Biscayans*. The Spanish Basque province of Viscaya had in fact the privilege of giving birth to generations of brigands, and Vidocq (the adventurer who became Chief of the Paris Police) was to use this term later for thieves and robbers in general.

One may still, for the historical period, call attention to the two appellations *Mirlifiches* and *Cascarrots*. The first concerned, to begin with, the Gypsies, and then in the nineteenth century all public entertainers. Timmermans[2] says that the comic turns of travelling showmen and mountebanks are '*mirifiques*': but he makes the word *Merlifiche* come from *merlin*, meaning 'leg' (and not the axe) and limits its usage to '*pilonneurs*' who were mendicants and specialists in the use of the false leg made of wood (*pilon*). From all the evidence, *mirlifiche* is based on *mirabilia* (marvellous) like *mirifique*, and *mirliflore* (meaning respectively 'mirific' or 'wonderful', and 'a young man who works wonders' or 'gives pleasure').

As for *Cascarrot*, this may be a corruption of *caraco*. However, in the dictionaries of nineteenth-century argot one finds: *cascaret* (miserable) and *cascara* (skin, peel). The connexion is not impossible. In any case the *Cascarrotes* are attested in an interesting way in the Basque Country:

1. Rhodes, *The Satanic Mass* (1956).
2. *Dictionnaire étymologique* (1903).

. . . between Bayonne and Saint-Jean-de-Luz one sometimes meets a troupe of young women going at a running pace and carrying baskets on their heads; they wear a silk kerchief round their heads, their necks are bare or have only a flowing neck-tie; compact of figure, they wear a red skirt raised the length of two hands, and their legs are bare; their eyes are black and their skin is well bronzed. Who are they? Are these the daughters of some ancient or wandering race, Bohemians, Saracens or Moorish?[1]

The author cannot give the answer. But the name itself leaves no doubt: it must refer to the *Gitanes* (and not to Gypsies in the sense of our differentiation, for these would not be bare-legged).

In the Vendée the Gypsies were called *Calourets*. Pierre Barkan,[2] who has gleaned this term, in fact rarely used, very rightly makes it derive from the Gypsy word *kaloré* (dark-skinned, swarthy). This author also cites the name *Coquet*, exclusively used in the region of Luçon. It is possible, in my opinion, that there may be in it some confusion with the *Cagots* or lepers of ancient France whose name became *caqueux, cagous, caquins, cahets* . . . according to the provinces.

There still remains the word *Romanichel* which has never ceased to be current for more than three hundred years, and in the whole of France. It is, in fact, a word of the Gypsy language – *romanitchal* – which means 'son of Rom'. But there again the scholars have delighted in closely examining this long mysterious word. One of them, for example,[3] firmly believing in the Egyptian origin of the Gypsies, made it derive from a Coptic expression, *romi-chal*, 'man of Egypt'! Romanichel was quickly abridged by our slang specialists into *romano*, and we meet it again in the nineteenth century, from the pen of Vidocq, as *romagnols*, hidden treasures which the 'Bohemians' claim to reveal.

Outside of France the names given to the Gypsies are invested with the same freakish variety. England alone has been content with 'Gypsy' (Egyptian), a word which has always predominated but of which the accepted meanings are slightly modified to apply at one and the same time to the true Gypsy, the sorcerer (or wizard), the swarthy, and to the 'female gad-about'. Furthermore, the English

1. In *Le Magasin Pittoresque*, year 1861.
2. In *Études Isiganes*, October 1958.
3. Lespinasse, *Les Bohémiens du Pays Basque* (1863).

invented[1] 'Gypsyism' and 'Gypsying' to designate the various activities of the 'Bohemian life', and 'Gypsy party', a picnic in the open air. Another etymologist[2] has considerably racked his brains to make this word Gypsy come from the town of Gabes (in Tunisia), which is regarded, he says, as an insult to some places on the Mediterranean coast.

For the rest of Europe, the term Gypsy has the following equivalents: *Tchinghanié* (Turkey), *Tsigani* (Bulgaria), *Tigani* (Romania), *Ciganyok* (Hungary), *Zingari* (Italy), *Zigeuner* (Germany), *Cigonas* (Lithuania), *Zincali* (Spain), *Ciganos* (Portugal), and for the classification of Gypsies in France now, see page 47. The success of this name (with its variations), used ever since the beginning of the Gypsy peregrinations in Europe, is unequalled except in the failure of the researches into its etymology. Popp Serboianu's dictionary, which relates to the dialects of Walachia, does give *tsigano* (small), but the expression seems to be primarily Walachian.

According to Martin Block, some Georgian writers formerly spoke of '*Atsincani* sorcerers'; this indeed is the most plausible origin. And it is a linguist signing himself Etnonymus[3] who best faces this problem:

The *Romanichels* have inherited in this the name of a Christian heretical sect of the Byzantine Empire – the *Athinganes*, to which the orthodox attributed magical practices similar to those which the Bohemians (Gypsies) favoured. The *Athinganes*, more Manichaeans than true Christians, were characterized by many interdictions concerning bodily defilements, and their ritual manias were the origin of their name at Byzantium, where the Greek word *athigganein* (not to touch) could be recognized, and popular pronunciation had already corrupted it into *atsinganein* by the time the first of the wandering tribes arrived in Asia Minor.

To finish with the word *tzigane*, let us note that in the eighteenth century the Germans transformed their equivalent word *Zigeuner* into *Zieh-Gauner*, meaning 'pickpocket', which is not devoid of some pungency.

As for the 'Egyptian' origin of the Gypsies, an idea which long

1. Refer to the *Oxford English Dictionary* or to the latest edition of Webster for many examples of the use of the word Gypsy, its derivative and compounds. *Tr.*

2. In *Le Magasin Pittoresque*, year 1872.

3. In the review *Vie et Langage*, November 1957.

persisted, this has given birth to many terms: *Egiftos* in Greece, *Evgit* in Albania, *Gyptenaers* in Holland; and so forth. From this same belief also comes in several European countries the word Pharaoh (*Pharaon* in French) to designate tribal chiefs or their wives: *Pharo, Farao, Faraona*. . . . Let us add, as a matter of curiosity, that Faro was also one of the cheating games to which the mountebanks of the seventeenth century devoted themselves.

The list of the others terms by which the Gypsies were designated across Europe is a very long one. Here we must be satisfied to call to mind: 'Assyrians' and 'Ethopians' in England; 'Pagans' in Bavaria and the Low Countries; 'Wanderers' in Arab countries; 'Ismaelites' in Hungary and Romania; 'Philistines' in Poland; and 'Tartars' in Germany. We can see well enough from these examples that the idea of foreigner or that of heretic has most often predominated in the choice of epithets.

Now that we have passed in review the names given by Europeans to Gypsies, let us see how these in turn call us. Such names are far less prolix. As the Jews have the word *goï*, the Gypsies have *gadjo* (pronounced *gaujo*; feminine *gadji*, plural *gadjé*), which means 'peasant', 'countryman', 'serf', which suffices to stress the sedentary, 'clod-hopper' aspect which they denigrate in us.

We may now resume the history of the presence of Gypsies in our civilization.

GYPSIES AND THE 'DANGEROUS CLASSES'

We have seen that the arrival of the Gypsies in France coincided with the first appearance in that country of the 'organized beggars', *les Gueux*. It is difficult to conceive the exact measure of Gypsy collaboration in this nation-wide movement. According to several historians, the Gypsies would have made a separate group. This opinion does not deter its authors from automatically putting the 'Bohemians' among the 'dangerous classes', the expression favoured in courses of sociology. Auguste Vitu[1] divides the organized beggars into these groups: (a) soldiers (*beroards, gaudins*); (b) mercers and *mercelots*;[2] (c) mendicants (people of the Grand Coesre, of the Kingdom of Thunes . . .); (d) Bohemians or Egyptians; (e) thieves and robbers, properly so called. Although this classification is rather

1. op. cit.
2. *Mercelots*, lesser mercers.

74

arbitrary, it is certainly a matter of a hierarchy of groups, each one self-governing, each with its own self-respect. In principle they had nothing in common but the same mode of life and the same way of using among themselves a secret argot or cant lingo such as that known as '*blèche*'. Yet although not many *romaní* terms are found in these argots, the word *blèche* alone, which used to make subscribers to the *Intermédiaire des Chercheurs et des Curieux* turn pale, seems to evoke a Gypsy origin. *Blas*, *blac*, *blacque* and *blachois* designated the *Valaques* (Walacians) for the medieval chroniclers Villehardouin and Henri de Valenciennes. ... The poem 'Arthur and Merlin' mentions '*the king of Hungri and of the Blaske*'.

Vitu, who notes the agreements in the evidence, asks the question: did many of the pedlars come from Walachia? He does not know the answer. We know for certain that, at least, this country sent to the rest of Europe a strong contingent of Gypsies.

Nobody, I believe, has yet asked whether François Villon, the vagrant French poet, had been acquainted with the Gypsies. This is, nevertheless, plausible. The dates agree well enough: Villon left Paris to wander in the provinces and to associate with the organized beggars in the year 1455. He resumed his vagrancy from 1456 to 1461, this being well after the first mention (1438) of an organization of brigands. It is not known whether he joined the famous Coquillarts. Yet it is possible that he may have met them without joining their ranks. These Coquillarts, to the number of about a thousand, ravaged Burgundy in 1453. The legal proceedings against the most unlucky of them began at Dijon two years later. According to Armand Ziwès:[1] 'Villon was initiated into the secrets and the vocabulary of the "Coquille", which was none other than the jobelin jargon which he used for rhyming the so-called *ballades* of Stockholm.'

Now certain words in these slang poems of Villon have a curiously Gypsy appearance. For example the expression *la vergne cygault* (ballades IX and XI). We know that *vergne* means 'town', but *cygault* has remained rather a mystery. Vitu translates it 'hypothetically' by 'Bohemian':

This *vergne cygault* where the strange society [of beggars] met is evidently the fairground, the centre of activity of the beggars and Gypsies, who therefore called it the 'Gypsies' town', just as the American Gypsies now call New York 'Rommeville' with the same

1. op. cit.

meaning, from *romano*, which is the name of the *ẓingaro* dialect.

In clearer terms, *cygault* actually recalls *cigain*, akin to *tẓigane*, the French word for Gypsy.

On the other hand, Villon sings in his *Ballade des Femmes de Paris:*

. . . Et sont très bonnes caquetieres	*. . . And very good cacklers are*
Allemandes et Pruciennes	*German and Prussian women*
Soient Grecques Egipciennes	*Be they Greek Egyptian women*
De Hongrie ou d'autres pays	*From Hungary or other countries*
Espaignolles ou Cathelennes	*Spanish or Catalan women*
Il n'est bon bec que de Paris	*There's no good tongue but one*
	from Paris[1]

In the text of this extract I have not inserted punctuation marks, for the very good reason that they do not exist in the manuscript at the Royal Library, Stockholm. Now, everything is in that comma which later editors generally place after the word *Egipciennes*; which, in my opinion, falsifies the sense. The text must read '*Egipciennes de Hongrie ou d'autres pays*', in English: 'Egyptians of Hungary or of other countries'. That is, Gypsies who had come from Hungary or elsewhere. For 'Hungary' to be found following 'Egyptians' is already sufficiently disturbing. But that 'Hungary' should be the only country in the whole of this piece of verse that is quoted non-adjectively seems to me convincing.

Lastly one can amuse oneself by comparing ballade XI, published by Vitu, with the adventure of the Captain of Gypsies as related by Pechon de Ruby: it is the same story. It therefore seems very probable that Villon knew the Gypsies and that he was the first in France to have sung of them.

Thus, from the fifteenth century onwards the Gypsies formed a part of the so-called dangerous classes. The *General Inventory of the History of Thieves*[2] declares that 'to be considered as an outstanding robber, it was necessary to have passed through (or graduated from) the "Beggars Republic"; to know all the tricks and wiles and activities of the Gypsies; to be acquainted with the various groups within that organization – Mercelots, Blèches, Cagnarts, Bribantins, Biscayans and other such rabble who have begun to make their way here and there among the people'.

1. Literal translation. *Tr.*
2. *L'Inventaire Général de l'Histoire des Larrons.*

This was the beginning of the persecutions from which the Gypsy people have not nearly freed themselves. It was also the logical consequence of a kind of life incompatible with the rules of an essentially proprietary society. At first the Gypsies were condemned on moral grounds. Agrippa of Nettesheim, a German philosopher, medical doctor and alchemist who led a very lively existence and associated with Gypsies, says that they '. . . lead a vagabond existence everywhere on earth, they camp outside towns, in the fields and at crossroads, and there set up their huts and tents, depending for a living on highway robbery, stealing, deceiving and barter, amusing people with fortune-telling, purporting to tell the future by palmistry and other impostures. . . .'[1] This man, chronicler of Charles V (who was himself an astrologer, but affected not to recognize the Gypsy 'science'), nicely adds regarding their nomadism: 'They like to beg from door to door, get bored with their homes, seek out strangers, and the local citizens flee.'

From the beginning of their stay in France, the 'Bohemians' have had a bone to pick with the Law, as this gloomy story testifies. It was one of the first relating to them, and is recorded by another official historian, this time of Charles VII, Jean Chartier:

In the year 1499 were judged and sentenced . . . two knaves or beggars and a woman of theirs, to be hanged and strangled, and for them were set up wooden gallows, the better to make known their case which was bad and heinous. One gallows was erected outside the Porte Saint-Jacques and on it one of the men was hanged; and the other gallows was put outside the Porte Saint-Denis, on which the other man was hanged, a hurdy-gurdy player, and with him the aforesaid woman, whom he vilified although they were moreoever both married [*sic*]. . . . A great number of people went there from all parts, especially women and girls, for it was a great novelty to see a woman hanged in France, because at that time this was not seen within this kingdom. The said woman was hanged all dishevelled, clad in a long robe with a rope round her two legs and bound together above the knees. Some people said that she had asked as a favour to be executed in this way, the custom of her country being so in such a case.

This rope attests a sense of modesty to which that period does not accustom us (let us remember the execution of Joan of Arc, who was exhibited completely naked to the eyes of the crowd). The author of the *Journal d'un Bourgeois de Paris* also does not fail to give an

1. *Paradoxes sur l'incertitude des sciences* (c. 1540).

account of this exceptional spectacle, and states precisely that these thieves formed part of a band having an elected king and queen, emphasizing the fact that it was unquestionably a matter of Gypsies.

GYPSIES AND WITCHCRAFT

In actual fact, the participation of Gypsies in the innumerable incidents of organized banditry seems to have been very slight, and this notwithstanding various reports of a nature identical with that which has just been given. The greatest misfortune suffered by the Gypsies was to see themselves even more closely identified with those engaged in witchcraft.

Continuing a tradition that was already very considerable in France, the fifteenth century witnessed the appalling 'witch-hunting manias' of the Queyras district of Lorraine (1456) and of the Vauderie d'Arras, etc.[1] But, from the second half of this century onwards, people began to perceive that those engaged in sorcery must be identified with the social rebels. This happened, for example, in 1460, in the case of Jehan de Taincture of Tournai.[2] People of fixed residence, however, at one and the same time suspicious and credulous, regarded all those of itinerant occupations who had no settled abode and came from distant countries as possessed of the evil eye: shepherds (then semi-nomads), pedlars, smiths and mountebanks; and those who lived a more or less mysterious life, outside the villages, in the depths of the forests: woodcutters, poachers, and 'splitters' (as the nomads who made staves for casks were called). Every stranger was suspect, all the more so if he had a swarthy face, wore rings in his ears, lived in 'wheeled houses', and spoke a language which was obviously not a Christian one. Already in the fourteenth century the poet Eustache Deschamps was associating together in a group:

> Wizards, witches and diviners
> Knaves, horse-copers
> Saracens, Jews, convicted thieves,
> Debauchees, rakes and ribalds. . . .

These 'Saracens' are certainly Gypsies. It must be admitted that they were engaged in occupations which people had learnt to mistrust: they were horse-dealers, mountebanks, exhibitors of perform-

1. There is a very full bibliography on this subject.
2. See Jean Palou, *La Sorcellerie* (1957).

ing animals, smiths, fortune-tellers and quack consultants about everything – all of them liable to excommunication.

From the early Middle Ages, in fact, the tumblers, performers of spectacular feats, snake-swallowers and other open-air artisans ran very heavy risks of ending their careers in the jail dungeon. If the ventriloquists, for example, had out-and-out success at fairs, they also sooner or later ended with a sentence of hard labour. A woman named Cécile who produced a turn of this kind at Lisbon, in the middle of the sixteenth century, possessed (says Collin de Plancy) 'the art of using her voice in so many ways that at one moment she made it come from her elbow, at another from her foot, and the next from her belly. She entered into conversation with an invisible being whom she called "Pierre-Jean" and he replied to all her questions. This woman ventriloquist was reputed to be a witch and banished.'

The same author – he wrote in the middle of the nineteenth century – definitely states that 'in the villages, conjurers still have the name of being wizards'. As for the showmen who exhibited performing animals – monkeys, bears, horses or dogs – they too risked the thunderbolts of the ecclesiastical authority.[1] Every innocent nanny-goat, to content ourselves here with this example, quickly became suspect when a buffoon took it into his head to make her perform tricks. Collin de Plancy, since we are turning over the pages of his book, says again in regard to those animals who ended their turn by going round the audience holding in their teeth a bowl for contributions: 'Who is there who does not clearly see that these goats were men or women and thus transmuted or disguised demons'. Victor Hugo has not in the least exaggerated in creating his Esmeralda.

And yet those fair-green shows were extremely common in the society of that period. On the miniatures of the *Legend of Saint-Denis* (1307) there is already a bear-leader giving a show on the banks of the Seine. At the beginning of the seventeenth century Boguet nevertheless wrote in his *Discours des Sorciers*: 'It was good to hunt down our comedians and minstrels, considering that most of them are wizards and magicians having no other objective but to empty our purses and corrupt us'; which is nothing but white magic.

1. Gerson, however, in his *Traité de l'avarice* (beginning of the fourteenth century) declares that: 'The flute-players, minstrels and such people are not in a state of mortal sin so long as their acts do not contain anything immoral'.

Closer to black magic were the professions of astrology and palmistry to which the Gypsies had recourse. Besides, at that time the first worked, so to speak, in harness with the second. Casters of horoscopes enjoyed great popularity at the end of the Middle Ages, and kings were not above giving them board at their courts. The Gypsies profited by this. Did they not come from mysterious Asia as bearers of secrets in occultism, easy to market?

As for chiromancy (as palmistry was called), this was regarded as a very suspect science up to the fifteenth century, or considered as an aspect of charlatanism. But from that period onwards it had great success. The first serious works written on this 'para-science', translated from Italian, appeared between 1520 and 1534. The Gypsies also were able to turn to account this coincidence in time. In the end these nomads were regarded more or less as healers. Closer to nature, which their vagabond life made them use to full advantage, they did in fact know the secrets of herbal remedies, the recipes for elixirs and drugs, and made no mistake about turning them into money. All this could only confirm the peasants in their opinion about the Gypsy sorcerers.

What is more, in order to support life in a world of settled inhabitants, in which the Gypsies had no place, the latter must needs dupe the natives, the *gadjé*. Tallemant des Réaux records in his *Historiettes* that

... a Gypsy stole a sheep near Roye in Picardy and wished to sell it for a hundred sous to a butcher, who refused to pay so much. The butcher went away, whereupon the Gypsy took the sheep from a sack in which he had put it, and instead put one of his little boys. Then he ran after the butcher and said: 'Give me so much more and you'll have the sack as well'. The butcher paid and went off. On arriving home he opened the sack and was highly astonished when he saw come out of it a little boy, who, losing no time, seized the sack and fled taking it with him. . . .

When all is said, this was simple enough: but the peasant mentality of the period was easily stretched to see in this a feat of witchcraft.

Many similar examples are scattered throughout the law reports in which the boundary between the rational and the demoniac is not clearly defined.

A judgement dated 1445 (then the very beginning of the Gypsies' stay in France) sentenced two Gypsy men and one Gypsy woman to be burned at the stake for having taught a certain Gilles Maldétour how to make a potion which gave the appearance of death to those who drank it. This happened near the small market town of Lusignan, towards Poitiers, already famous for the exploits of the fairy Mélusine.[1] In Boguet's *Discours des Sorciers* one reads of a trait of character that is even more easily likened to the practices of magic:

A Gypsy sorcerer used to change boots made of hay into pigs and sold them as such, always warning the buyer beforehand not in any circumstances to wash these animals. But a person who acquired the Gypsy's product, not having followed this advice, instead of seeing pigs saw hay boots floating on the water.

As will be sufficiently seen in this book, if the Gypsies have known very well how to utilize the everyday working methods common among ordinary people, they have also up to a point influenced the art of eastern magic. Thus, to take only Lorraine, attention can be called to many legal documents attesting that in the sixteenth and seventeenth centuries 'Egyptians' and the 'Saracens' travelled through the duchy, and devoted themselves to the occupations of supranormal therapeutics, to the techniques of divination and of the occult sciences. Then they met the diviner-healers of Lorraine and did not neglect to exchange with them formulas for ways of divining. Some even claimed to be able to track down sorcerers and protect the public from their spells. According to Delacambre[2] '... an Egyptian woman, to disclose a treasure hidden in the house of a woman diviner of Ginfosse, made a hole at a certain part of the kitchen, and put holy water into it as she began to say the Lord's Prayer, and telling her that the money would come out of it little by little; a fortnight passed, and her prediction proved fruitless. She likewise taught the apprentice magician to throw stones into the water when crossing bridges, in order to protect herself from dizziness attributed to an "evil spell".' And the author adds that 'it was Saracens who initiated a woman healer of Saint-Blaise-de-Moyenmoutiers into the use of toad-amulets for the treatment of cattle'.[3]

1. A detailed but slightly romanticized account of this matter was published in the *Musée des Familles* (1835).
2. *Le Concepte de sorcellerie dans le duché de Lorraine aux 16e et 17e siècles*, fasc. iii (Nancy, 1951).
3. In the chapter dealing with magical zoology the importance of these amulets will be seen.

One point on which it is interesting to study the relations between the Gypsies and the sorcerers is that relating to the Sabbath.[1]

It is known that all accounts of witches claiming to keep the Sabbath are in remarkable agreement. There is always the same means of transport, the same place, the same setting, and often the same scene. It is evident that the overstimulated imagination of the poor women could have recourse only to a collective basis of beliefs, duly confirmed by public rumour. In fact, they invented nothing: they were content under torture to repeat what they had already heard. The interrogations were, moreover, carried out in such a way that the accused were never asked to give any reply except 'yes' and 'no' to the interchangeable questions that had to be 'proved'.

The classical description of the Sabbath is in everyone's mind; it is not necessary to describe it again. But I may be allowed to emphasize those elements of the ceremony which are not at all imaginary and are in my opinion only the transposition of very ordinary scenes, certainly much exaggerated.

Bergier in his *Dictionnaire de théologie* was the first to remark that

what maintained popular credulity were the accounts given by some timorous people who, finding themselves astray in the forests, took for the Sabbath the fires lit by woodcutters or charcoal-burners, or who, having fallen asleep, in fear, believed they heard the voice of the Sabbath by which their imagination had been stirred.

It will be agreed that it is not far-fetched to put Gypsies in the place of woodcutters, and the classical tableau of the Sabbath becomes clear once again.

In fact, it was as a rule held at crossroads, on the outskirts of woods or in glades: that is, in deserted or remote places where the nomads, driven out of urban areas, could halt in peace. The diabolical feast, which is regularly described in terms of orgies, can very well be nothing but one of those riotous meals in which the Gypsies indulge after a long day of caravanning, at which wine, song, music and

1. The author is not referring to the Jewish Sabbath or to the 'Lord's Day' of the Christians, but to what in medieval times was called the 'witches' Sabbath'. This may be described as a midnight meeting of demons, sorcerers and witches, presided over by the devil, and supposed to have been held annually as an orgy or festival. *Tr.*

dances play an important part. Is it astonishing that peasants, deeply imbued with the superstitions of the period, when going past these nocturnal woodland banquets, should identify those dark-skinned half-seen beings as instruments of Satan? A nanny-goat can pass for a buck if only because, tame and wise-looking, she stands erect crowned with some piece of trumpery. Would not a dancing bear, or a trained monkey seem from a distance to be a perfect Beelzebub?

The examples of such a correlation could be multiplied. If we are content here with that of animals, it is possible to parallel the theme of the he-goat with certain Gypsy ceremonies, supposing, of course, that some peasants were present at them. In fact (again I rely on Collin de Plancy):

... in the province of Limburg during the last century [the eighteenth] there were still many Gypsies and bandits to celebrate the Sabbath. Their initiation took place at a lonely crossroads where there was a tumble-down hut which people called the 'He-goats Chapel'. He who was being received as a wizard was made drunk, then put astride a wooden he-goat which was shaken with the help of a pivot.

Now, among the Tinkers, the nomads of Ireland, there is found a rather similar ceremony which is perpetuated to this day. Once a year these nomads erect a wooden tower and put a living he-goat at the top.[1]

Music alone would encourage the relationship between the Gypsies and sorcerers. In his celebrated *Tableau de l'Inconstance des Mauvais Anges*, published in 1613, De Lancre makes it clear that those present at the Sabbath used to dance, 'with violins, trumpets and tambourines which produced great harmony; and at the said gatherings there is extreme pleasure and rejoicing. ...' Funck-Brentano, describing the Sabbaths of Labourd said that at them there were added 'Moorish dances, animated or languorous, amorous, or obscene, in which girls trained for this, *la Murgui* and *la Lisalda* simulated and parodied the most tantalizing things. These dances,

1. The author's description seems to refer to the well-known 'Puck Fair' that is held every summer at Killorglin in County Kerry. But the 'crowning of the goat' is not exclusively a matter of the Tinkers; some say that it is a pagan survival, though its origin is uncertain. The Roman Catholic Church frowns on it. Crowds of people flock to Killorglin for the event, which is celebrated in three days of jollification, with a fair amount of drinking, music and dancing in the streets. It is a very 'Irish' event altogether; and much enjoyed by tourists. *Tr.*

so it was said, were the only attraction among the Basques which made everybody rush to the Sabbath; women, girls and widows in great numbers.' It will be hard to blame me for wishing to compare them with the classic dances of the *Gitanes* which still seem to strangers to be the most exact representation of sensual pleasure. Collin de Plancy, for his part, pin-points this extraordinary fact:

There are three oscillations [or swings]: the first is called the 'Gypsy swing' ... these dances are performed to the sound of a small tambourine, a flute, a violin or some other instrument which is struck with a stick; this is the only Sabbath music; however, some sorcerers have asserted that no concerts in the world are better played.

As a matter of sheer curiosity, and remembering that at this period the Gypsies were treated as *rabouins*, that is, as instruments of the devil, I will record that Bochart, in his *History of the animals mentioned in Scripture*, published in London in 1663, gives the Leviathan the unexpected name of 'Zigana'!

It would also be necessary, though it would delay us too long, to compare the cookery involved in the Sabbath with that of the Gypsies. It is known that witches had the habit of stewing the most improbable mixtures. And if any peasant woman were to lift the lid of a Gypsy pot and discover there, among other bizarre ingredients, hedgehogs cooking in a spiced stock, this would only prove to her that she was seeing with horror a diabolical brew. These witches, moreover, returning home from the Sabbath, would not fail to relate that they had 'drunk tympanon', 'drunk tambourine', 'eaten cymbal'. They would understand by tympanon a goatskin bottle that served at the same time for a drum and a soup-tureen, by tambourine also a goatskin bottle, and by cymbal the copper cauldron used for cooking soup.[1] This incongruous relationship of musical instruments with cooking utensils deserves to be studied, especially as it is already found in the Mysteries of Eleusis.[2]

Gypsies and the Fairies

In studying the connexions between the Gypsies and sorcerers, I have wondered whether the stereotyped picture of the fairy does not owe something to these nomads.

It is known that the fairies, who came from the forests of Brittany

1. See Leloyer, *Histoires des spectres et des apparitions*. ...
2. Eleusis, a small town north-west of ancient Athens. The Temple of Demeter there was famous for the 'Mysteries' celebrated in it. *Tr.*

in France and from ancient Germany, often appeared not only in popular beliefs but also in medieval romances, and did not disdain to mix themselves intimately in the affairs of men; for some illustrious personages, such as Godefroy de Bouillon and the Plantagenets, gained distinction by including them on the lowest branches of their genealogical trees. Until the eighteenth century the fairies, contrary to their sisters who enchanted the storytellers Perrault and Madame d'Aulnoye, had a quite human appearance, and it is only the eccentricity of their ways of behaving which makes them beings apart.

Margaret Murray,[1] who relies on authentic documents and does not omit to indicate her sources, amply describes the life, manners and customs of these fairies, male and female, with whom the waste lands and heaths of England and Scotland seem to be invaded. The details which this author provides ought not to allow historians of the Gypsy people to remain indifferent. 'It is not rare', she first says, 'to meet in documents of the Middle Ages, or a little later, descriptions of fairies based on eye-witness accounts. ... In Ayrshire (for example), Bessie Dunlop saw eight of their women and four men: the men were dressed as gentlemen, the women were wrapped in rugs and seemed very well-behaved.'

The very human reality of these fairies is not left in the slightest doubt when the author makes clear that 'these fairies were not the little flower-like elves with gossamer wings of the Virgin in stories for children: they were creatures of flesh and blood; they caused indescribable fear and horror among the rich middle-class people of the cities. ...' And we remember that in nearly all the trials for witchcraft, between that of Joan of Arc and those at the end of the seventeenth century, the proof of dealings with fairies automatically brought with it the sentence of hard labour.

The human reality of these fairies being tacitly accepted, one will agree that the picture of their mode of life suddenly makes one think of the Gypsies. In fact,

the fairy people lived in the wild and uncultivated areas of the country; the reason for this was not necessarily that the immigrants had driven them back there, but rather the fact that, in their beginning, they devoted themselves only to cattle-raising and knew nothing of agriculture. In the woods, where they were rarely met, they preferred the waste parts and heaths where their cattle found grazing. Like some wild tribes in

1. In *The Witches' God* (1958). (The quotations are re-translated from the French. *Tr.*)

India, they fled before the stranger, being quick runners and so clever at concealing themselves that one hardly saw them even if they should wish to show themselves. Their dwellings had the form of bee-hives made of stones or interlaced willow-rods or turf. It seems that, in the first fine days of their existence, the fairy people left the houses and spent the whole summer in the open air. The Asiatic tribes live in identical conditions.

It is possible in this single paragraph to call special attention to several elements peculiar to the Gypsy way of life. Nowhere in her book does Margaret Murray appear to suspect the possibility of this connexion, and here she describes the nomad life, the winter camps, the round huts (which still retain this form on the banks of the Caspian Sea, in the Caucasus, in Macedonia . . .), the weaving with willow rods. The only contradictory point is the mention of cattle: even though the Gypsies in their peregrinations are always followed by an imposing troop of horses, donkeys, mules, goats and . . . bears.

A little further on, Murray underlines the fact that 'the official records of the law courts, like folklore, paint a picture of the fairies which irresistibly calls to mind man of the neolithic or bronze age settled in Western Europe', that is of short stature and mat complexion, 'which perhaps explains the name "Brownie" applied to one of these beneficent spirits'. This mat complexion is not the attribute of prehistoric man only; it is also that of the Gypsies. And this name Brownie calls to mind the habit of naming the Gypsies in terms of the colour of their skin. Thus Shakespeare himself, to personify the fantastic being in *The Tempest*, chose to call him Caliban; this is – did he know it? – the Gypsy word *kaliben*, which means 'blackness'.

Murray tells us that those early people formed communities, each having at its head a chief. Another author[1] notes this fact in the Irish provinces, adding that the queen's importance seemed to indicate that she was the real chief and that the king, except during a period of war, played a background role. Now we know that, from the first years of their stay in Europe, the Gypsies lived in closed tribes and that, if each tribe was officially led by a chief, it was a woman, true to the race and aged, who governed this matriarchal-type society in a more or less occult way.

As for the clothes worn by the fairies, Margaret Murray gives us

1. W. Wilde, *Ancient Cures, Charms and Usages of Ireland* (1890).

information quite as evocative: 'The women wear dresses of lively colours in which blue, black, green and red dominate, fabrics embroidered with gold, little wreaths of pearls. . . .' How could one fail to recognize the classical Gypsy woman with her multicoloured skirts, loaded with jewels (not always trumpery)? And again: 'The women allow their hair to fall over their shoulders, which heightens their beauty when young; but the long tangled locks of the old women are the object of horrified comments by the "mortals" who see them. The noble lady-fairies cover their hair with a veil or hood.' Now, among the European Gypsies, only the young girls wear their head uncovered and their hair loose. The married women have the right to wear the traditional kerchief.

I shall not weary the reader any longer with this avalanche of quotations. Clearly they must be regarded with caution; they point to nothing less than still one more unexplored channel of gypsiology. A final reflection: could we not consider that the credulous in times long ago saw a striking analogy between the fortune-telling of the Gypsies and the prophecies of the fairies over cradles?

Fairies or sorcerers, the Gypsies from then onwards were to suffer the repressions of a society in which their place was far from being regarded with a benevolent eye.

GYPSIES AND REPRESSIONS

In France, as in the rest of Europe outside the Balkans, the Gypsies were looked upon in a bad light from the moment of their presence. One remembers that in Paris the first act of the bishop, in 1427, was to excommunicate them and drive them out. Only Provence, that particularly hospitable country, treated them at first as pilgrims and went so far as to give them provisions. Elsewhere they were blamed for thefts, exactions and dupery. They were accused of engaging in black magic, of living by their wits, but above all of being foreigners. In the accounts of the Provost of Paris, in the fifteenth century, details are found of the severe physical punishment of a young girl who had consulted a Gypsy woman about the probable hour at which her father would die. It is true that the event took place at the time indicated, which in itself did not make it less suspect.

The first official repression in France is dated 1539. The Parliament of Paris records an expulsion order against the Gypsies. In

1560 the States General of Orléans called upon 'all those impostors known by the name of Bohemians or Egyptians to leave the Kingdom under penalty of the galleys'.

It is quite evident that these orders, like the majority of those which were to follow, viewed the Gypsies as beggars and vagabonds and not in terms of a racial minority. These edicts merely followed the attempts at 'social purification' undertaken since the Middle Ages. Vagabondage, that is, wandering about without recognized domicile or occupation, had officially become an offence in 1350. For more than four centuries, until 1789, the enactments designated as vagabonds not only those wanderers who had no occupation but also wandering scholars, itinerant extractors of teeth, sellers of theriac (an antidote for snake-bite), surgeons, players of the game of tourniquet (akin to modern roulette), marionette showmen, singers of laments, prowlers after girls, etc.[1] To this list is added only the word Gypsy.

If it was necessary to await this date to see the Gypsies appearing in the beggars' pandemonium, this is not proof of a sudden virulence on the part of François I. It is because the authorities had other fish to fry. It was first of all necessary to rebuild the ruins of the Hundred Years War. Until that could be done, nobody bothered very much about castigating vagabondage, since this was in a chronic state. The Gypsies were overlooked in the vast crowd of wanderers in the post-war period. In Germany the repression began much earlier; and in Switzerland also.

That punishment of the galleys, of which the sixteenth century suddenly flourished the threat, has also a paradoxical aspect. At that time there were too many men for the galleys and not enough galleys. Consequently it was found more convenient to open prisons, and to send those so condemned to be hanged elsewhere. The first Gypsies, like the vagabonds, were therefore the delinquents most often sentenced to the most expeditious punishments, and to those least embarrassing for the public authorities: the pillory, the strappado, and the cutting off of ears.

In 1607 Henry IV of France renewed the arrest and expulsion orders against the Gypsies. But this did not prevent the good king a year later from commanding that Gypsy dancers be brought before him: only, he found that three of these women smelt rather strongly, and sent them away.

1. See Vexliard, op. cit.

Under Louis XIII Parliament repeated its edict of 1539, specifying that the Gypsies would have a respite of two months to leave France, and of two hours to leave Paris. It will be agreed that the situation of these nomads, sentenced in their status as wanderers, and compelled by the law to move on as best if not as quickly as they could, was, to say the least, difficult. Where did the authorities wish them to go? The Basque country came in for a great number, but the rest could merely make a pretence of a prompt departure, only to be found again at the other end of the town or city, very slightly disguised.

In 1660 Louis XIV promulgated a law regulating the carrying of arms

in order that foreigners and strangers who come from the countryside with firearms shall not misuse them. . . . In order that, above all, the open country shall be safe and the main highways rendered free and safe for the freedom of commerce and travellers, [it was ordered that] those who are called Bohemians or Egyptians, or others of their following, shall leave the Kingdom within one month, under penalty of the galleys or other corporal punishment.[1]

Until that date, however, the measures of expulsion had only small effect. There were always Gypsies in France and, it seems, more and more of them. The same Louis XIV then ordered, in 1682, that a declaration be published with the Gypsies specially in view, and this was the first time that these people became in France the object of prosecutions as a minority group. This declaration is particularly interesting, because it gives the tone of so-called public opinion on the nomads:

. . . Some cares which the Kings our predecessors have taken to purge their Estates of vagabonds and people called Gypsies, having enjoined by their Enactments the Provosts and Magistrates and other Judges to send the said Gypsies to the galleys *without other form of trial*; nevertheless it has been impossible to drive these thieves entirely out of the Kingdom because of the protection they have at all times found and which they still find daily among the Gentry and Lords Justiciaries who give them refuge in their castles and houses notwithstanding the decrees of Parliaments which expressly forbade them on penalty of privation of their rights and discretionary fine; this disorder being common in the majority of the provinces of our Kingdom. . . . At these prosecutions we call upon our Bailiffs and Seneschals . . . to arrest and cause to be arrested all those who are called Bohemians or Egyptians, their women and children and others

1. See *Code de chasses* . . . (Paris, 1720).

of their following; to secure the men to the convicts' chain, to be led to our galleys and to serve there *in perpetuity*. And in regard to the women and girls, we order them to be shaven on the first occasion that they are found leading the life of Gypsies and that the children unfit to serve on our galleys be taken to the nearest poor-house to be fed and brought up like the other children who are shut up there. And lest the said women continue to roam about and live like Bohemians, to have them flogged and banished out of the Kingdom, all this without any other form of trial. . . . We forbid all Gentry to give refuge in their castles and houses to the said Gypsies and their women: in case of contravention it is our will that the said Gentlemen be deprived of their rights, that their fiefs be reunited to our Domaine, even though there be extraordinary proceedings against them so that they be punished by a greater penalty if the case should arise.[1]

This was becoming serious. The decree was immediately applied in all its harshness. It is recorded in local history hardly a month after its promulgation that four Gypsy women were arrested at Toulouse and had their heads shaved.[2]

The enactment of Louis XIV furthermore reveals another important fact: the hospitality, whether from self-interest or not, of which a good number of gentlemen gave proof in regard to the Gypsies, and this in spite of the law. A Seigneur de Florensac, a Marquis de Morangiès, a Sieur de Fontgival are cited in the records as having granted their protection to these wanderers. To tell the truth, the gentry took on what they wanted; the men were employed in various kinds of work, and the women danced and were employed as ferry-women. There were even Gypsy soldiers attached to the defences of certain castles.

This new edict, it seems, had no more effect than the ones preceding. The number of Gypsies who rowed for the King is not known, while the chronicles, continuing to attribute to the Gypsies all kinds of exactions, thereby attested to their presence in the Kingdom. In 1740 the enactment was again renewed but this time the toning down is appreciable. Gypsies were no longer called upon to vacate places, but to find some settled occupation, 'to take jobs, to put themselves in a fit condition to serve in them, or to go to work cultivating the land, or engage in other kinds of work or in trades of which they are capable'. Banishment, in actual practice, was revealed to be impossible; for the very good reason that the adjacent

1. E. de Fréminville, *Dictionnaire ou Traité de Police Générale* (1775).
2. De Foletier in *Études Tsiganes*, January 1957.

countries, victims of the same problem, rejected without pity these new disorderly elements. Cultivating the land, obviously, yielded no good result. It was a blunder; the nomad life is not spent at gardening without a very thorough social transformation. All the same, it must be recognized that Louis XIV had the merit of making the first attempt to give the nomads a settled way of life.

This, on the whole, was the attitude of the authorities towards the Gypsies. Let us now see how these people behaved.

GYPSIES IN FRANCE UNDER THE OLD RÉGIME

By abstracting parish and notarial registers one can, up to a point, mark out the passage of many Gypsies through the countrysides of France. And, by skilful cross-checking, an idea of their way of life can be formed. This work[1] has up to now been directed only on the Poitou and Anjou regions. Nevertheless, the example of these two, where the presence of Gypsies is very often attested, will suffice to provide a rough sketch of the circumstances in which the nomads lived.

It is the collections of certificates of baptism and death which permit the first recognition of Gypsy elements in French civilization. The first baptism registered is that of an 'Egyptian' named Pierre, in the Commune of Jarze in Maine-et-Loire. His godfather and godmother were a married couple named Girard, non-Gypsies. This mention, the first of a long series, is essential because it reveals the conversion to Catholicism of a child, the issue of a family apparently without any 'official' religion. These conversions later multiplied. The fact that the godparents were not Gypsies is also very revealing; it is possible that this qualification was demanded by the Church. In any case, it is certain that the Gypsies would know from time to time how to take advantage of what would serve the ends in which they were interested. What is more, godparents were often persons of high rank, sometimes Lords.

The names given to the children already showed a habit that would be common among all the Gypsies in Europe: the adoption of a local first (or Christian) name. These names, noted by de Foletier earlier

1. It is to M. de Foletier in *Études Tsiganes*, 1956 and 1958, that we owe the greater part of these researches. I have not been able to take account of an essential article by this author, *Chevauchées et passades des capitaines bohémiens* ... which appeared in *Connaissance du Monde* in November 1960.

than 1536, are characteristic: Perrine, daughter of Georges Mal-donnois and of Renée Delgadde; Pierre de la Haye; Claude, daughter of Pierre Gabriel and Marie Valliene. . . . The fact that the father and mother do not have the same surname does not mean that they were not married, by civil or religious ceremony. In fact, on one of these certificates, we find mention of the decease of one René, 'son of Jean Charles, captain of a company of Egyptians, and of [Miss] Marie de la Prade, his wife'.

This inventory informs us not only of the existence of marriages of 'Bohemians', but of Gypsies and non-Gypsies. For example, that of 'Jean Martin, an Ethiopian by nation, a widower who took for wife Marie Tuffier, natural daughter of the defunct master François de Broc, a living knight, Lord of Broc and Echmire', and this was still in Maine-et-Loire, in 1650.

Finally, some death certificates mention Christian burial places granted to Gypsies, and even masses celebrated for them.

Some of the same old documents enable us to give a brief description of these Gypsies. Their physical appearance is, of course, familiar to us. Let us recall their entry into Paris, described by the *Bourgeois de Paris* ('the men were very dark, their hair crisp. The women were the ugliest that one could see, and their hair black like a horse's tail'.) Certainly the picture is not flattering. It is in accordance with the taste of the period. All the texts, moreover, agree in emphasizing the sun-tanned complexion of the nomads. People had not seen such evil-looking faces since the Saracen invasions.

For every dress they wore the women had 'a piece of old material attached to the shoulder by a thick piece of cloth or rope; their only linen was an old loose skirt and an old chemise'. The Chronicle of Bologna depicts them as going about 'in their chemise, hardly covered'. Already the Gypsy women were wearing the ample dresses in which we know them and they did not mind exposing a rich bosom when suckling a child. Their sense of modesty, which has not changed, is in fact related to the legs and not to the breasts.

As for the men, they did not disdain fairly garish costumes in lively colours, in which red and green abounded. In reality they did not have a costume peculiar to their 'nation' but had borrowed the fashion of the Hungarians and Romanians. Unacquainted with this origin of the Gypsies' clothes, the people of France were astonished to see them so bedizened, covered with gold and jewellery.

But what is most striking in the old engravings is the warlike array in which the men rigged themselves out: swords, long guns, and even silver helmets. It is enough to examine the extraordinary sequence of Gypsies by Jacques Callot[1] to measure the distance between the nomads of that period and those of today, at least in regard to their accoutrement. With such arms and baggage 'were those people not brave messengers – who went wandering through foreign countries', says the famous engraver. His Gypsies have a greater resemblance to the vagabond hordes of freed soldiers than to the *romanichels* of our main roads. And we need not cast doubt on the accuracy of Callot, who, in the early years of the seventeenth century, left his family after the manner of Pechon de Ruby to travel with them from Lucerne to Florence.

The equipment of 'those poor beggars full of fortunes' differed again from that of our contemporaries on one specific point: the absence of covered wagons. Callot's Gypsies were content with uncovered wagons, drawn by horses, donkeys or even by bullocks. They slept under a tent, and had done so probably since their departure from India. Sometimes they used dogs to draw light vehicles, the donkeys carrying the tent and complete equipment of the perfect nomad. It seems that the invention of the wheeled wagon was due to their being much with travelling circuses and mountebanks in Europe, people who already possessed circus vehicles at the time when strolling comedians of the *Roman Comique* still had a wagon 'yoked to four skinny bullocks led by a brood-mare'.

The various occupations to which the Gypsies had recourse having hardly varied in France since the Old Régime, it is useless to enlarge on this subject. The reader is referred to the chapters which follow. It is, however, necessary to mention here certain occupations which have now disappeared. From the fifteenth century, for example, many Gypsies became engaged as mercenaries in different armies. Tallemant des Réaux calls to mind in one of his *Historiettes* the company of a Captain Jean-Charles, four hundred men strong, all Gypsies, who accompanied Henry IV (1589) and gave him lively satisfaction. De Foletier[2] has discovered that, towards 1690, some Gypsies were serving in Germany with the troops of His Majesty. He has also noted that the guard at the castle of the Cosse-Brissac was entrusted to Gypsies, whose loyalty never failed. In 1667, Pierre Durois, a spy in the service of the French king, was instructed

1. See illustration No. 17.
2. *Études Tsiganes*, January 1957.

to make a secret evaluation of the military forces of Prussia and Austria. In order to make his way unnoticed he had the idea of mixing with a troupe of Gypsies, who willingly accepted him. He remained in their company for about six years. They were tortured and kept in prison for nine years. The Gypsies never betrayed their protégé.

From this time onwards the Gypsies became a familiar part of the world of French people. If the word *bohème* (Gypsy) is still sometimes an insult ('in 1696, a butcher's wife at Cannes attacked in front of the Seneschal's Court a customer who was alleged to have called her a beggar and a Gypsy'[1]) it acquired its patent of nobility in compensation. When Molière in 1664 produced his play *Mariage forcé*, Louis XIV himself appeared on the stage dressed as a Gypsy woman (female roles were then played by men). Two 'Egyptian women', in fact, appeared in scene VI and one of them said to Sganarelle: 'You need only give us your hand with the cross in it' (meaning a piece of money marked with a cross). In the *Fourberies de Scapin*, played for the first time in 1671, Molière put on the stage a girl named Zerbinette, previously kidnapped by some Gypsies. In *L'Étourdi*, Célie is the slave of Trufaldin to whom the Gypsies had pledged her. 'Those fellows rarely pass for good people', says Molière, whom one would not on that account accuse of racism. Finally, in the *Pastorale comique*, he again makes an 'Egyptian woman' appear who dances and sings to the sound of *guacares* and *nacaires*, which are little drums. Molière here gives us a good example of that 'saracination' of the Gypsies: the Turkish influences appearing in that period probably harbour traces of other Gypsies from operetta.[2]

The Gypsy women of the *Mariage forcé* have Basque drums. This type of drum is the tambourine, with only one skin surface and provided with little bells – the classical accompaniment of the Gypsy dance. In spite of its name, the instrument does not appear to be of Basque origin. It seems, on the contrary, that it was the Gypsies who brought it from Persia.

Gypsies in the Basque Country

This detail leads us to the circumstances of the Gypsies in the Basque

1. De Foletier, op. cit.
2. In Vovard's *Les Turqueries dans la littérature française* (1960) none are mentioned.

country; these have taken on a complexion peculiar enough to be worthy of a separate heading.

It has been seen that the Gypsies of this region were called *Biscayans*, from the name of the Spanish province. There was a considerable number of them, because of the expulsion orders under Louis XIII and Louis XIV which had caused an exodus towards Navarre. However, the custom of this country was not very much more hospitable to the Gypsies than the rest of the Kingdom. At regular intervals the native population was assembled to the sound of the tocsin to set about hunting down the nomads, and the capture of each wanderer gave the right to a bonus. As for the Gypsy women and children, these were so severely harassed, says the author of a regulation dated 1708, that in the end they did not reappear. It is true that, between 1530 and 1730, armed bands infested the roads and went into the villages spreading disorder and fear, even to the point of committing murder. The French Revolution of 1789 ought to have caused a serious diversion in favour of the Gypsies. But the depredations having continued – and they were always attributed to the nomads – the First Consul was obliged to intervene. The effect of a prefectoral decree of Frimaire, year XI (1802) was that all Gypsies in the Basque country were caught up in a vast police net and taken to French seaports to be transported to the colonies. Only the war at sea prevented the completion of this plan. After a long period of detention, and as it was not known what to do about them, they were set at liberty.[1]

Brigandage had not been stopped by this swoop, for there is record of a band, commanded by one Bidart, which functioned until 1825. Lespinasse reports that, at the time when he wrote his book (about 1860), forty Gypsy families were living at Ciboure and at Saint-Jean-de-Luz, where they were engaged in fishing and coastal sailing. These, and I have already emphasized the fact, are the only Gypsies known to have become sailors. The other Gypsies of the Basque Country were basket-makers and grooms.

These accounts of repression, the only documents we possess regarding the Gypsies of the Basque Country, cover a misunderstanding: the unmistakable confusion between the Gypsies and the *Cagots*. The latter, whom eighteenth-century authors[2] record as 'the unfortunate residue of the soldiers of Alaric or of the Saracens',

1. Lespinasse, *Les Bohémiens du Pays Basque* (1863).
2. For example, Ramond de Carbonnières.

have not found their historian.[1] The term *cagot* was then a synonym for 'leper'. These wretched people were relegated to places far from towns and reduced to such suspect occupations as that of charcoal-burner, woodcutter, rope-maker; they were obliged to wear a red helmet marked with a duck's foot, and sentenced to go bare-footed; they were forbidden to marry except among themselves. A special place was reserved for them in the churches where they had to take holy water with the aid of a stick. They sold talismans, foretold the future and cast spells. In France they even represented the pariah type, and they also formed organized bands. It is perhaps not stretching a point to relate the name *cagot* with *cagou*, the third category in the hierarchy of fifteenth-century beggars.

Thus, the identity of the way of life, the more or less 'culpable' occupations to which society condemned these two groups of 'outcasts' because of their mutual resemblance, caused *Cagots* and Gypsies to be confused: and it is very difficult, in reading the texts, to define the position of the Gypsies.

GYPSIES IN THE REST OF EUROPE DURING THEIR PAST

In order to study the situation of the Gypsies in the rest of Europe during the period of their history, the simplest way is to take up, broadly and without entering into details, the courses they followed in their migrations.

Gypsies in the Balkans

Jules Bloch says that, in regard to the Balkans, generally speaking the Gypsies did not have any history (which in no sense means that they have been perfectly happy there). This remark must more accurately be applied to the south-east of the peninsula where the nomads, in fact, moved about more easily, and where persecutions were far less severe than in Central Europe. This privileged situation was largely due to the fact that the native inhabitants were themselves also of Asiatic origin, and because the Ottoman invasion brought into those regions an 'Asianism' that was benevolent towards the Gypsies, their nomadism and their way of life. So it is that, naturally, documents and accounts are missing in regard to Bulgaria and the old Turkish province of Roumelia that is now a part of Bulgaria.

1. Except Francisque Michel, whose work *Histoire des races maudites de la France et de l'Espagne* is rather suspect.

But once the Danube was crossed, and the Gypsies were on this side of the River Prut, the provinces of Moldavia and Walachia (the present Romania) were less welcoming. These were countries of Latin culture, and it must be added that six centuries of successive invasions – of Huns, Arabs, Tartars and Slavs – did not militate in favour of the new hordes, however peace-loving they might appear to be. At the beginning of their peregrinations in Europe, the Gypsies went through these countries without meeting too many difficulties. But these quickly became more numerous at the very time when the vast estates of the boyards were growing wild for lack of man-power to work them. No better excuse was necessary for the great Moldo-Walachian landowners to stop the passage of this army of 'unemployed' people, and immediately turn them into serfs: that is, into slaves. The beginning of Gypsy slavery is generally dated to the seventeenth century.[1] However, a Romanian gypsiologist[2] has found a curious document dated 1541, signed by the Voivode Sigile, authorizing that a Gypsy slave named Greaca, who had fled with his children, be sought out, captured and put back to work.

In any case, the Gypsies belonged body and chattels to the great lords, the hospidars or war chiefs and the Voivodes or landowners, both of whom had rights of life and death. 'Thus was born', says Maximoff, 'a new race of Gypsies of impure blood.' Impure or not, those Gypsies were to experience almost inhuman conditions. They received no wage and, as for food, they had the right only to a small portion of *mamaliga* or Indian corn porridge, helped out with some sunflower seeds. They were flogged naked, iron hooks were fixed in their necks to punish them and prevent them from sleeping.

Some Gypsies, gold-washers and bear-trainers, belonged to the State. The clergy also had their own Gypsy slaves. As there was a substantial account outstanding, it justified this shameful practice by having recourse to the old myth of the curse: the Gypsies massacred the children of Bethlehem, forged the nails of the Cross and were cursed by Christ, etc. Finally, some specially favoured rich

1. See Matéo Maximoff, *Tsiganes, Wanderndes Volk auf endloser Strasse* (Zürich, 1959). This Gypsy author is descended from the Kalderash chiefs of this region. See also Bibliography pp. 269 and 271.

2. Hadjeu, quoted by Serboianu, op. cit.

people had in their service Gypsy domestics, coachmen, cooks or valets. . . .[1]

Here is a description by an anonymous author of the middle of the nineteenth century:[2]

Their clothing consisted of a shirt of coarse material which they wore until it rotted. Rain did the work of household washing. The children went about completely naked. In winter they covered themselves with some odd pieces of discarded cloth: old clothing, old bedspreads, old carpets, everything was good in their eyes. As for a dwelling-place, they did not even bother to think about this. They slept everywhere. In the morning the lord's *vatave* or bailiff, carefully wrapped in his furs and whip in hand, mustered them to allocate their tasks for the day. It was a heartbreaking sight: a stinking collection of gaunt, half-naked, shivering creatures who came from the stables, kitchens, open sheds, from all directions. The bailiff, generally a harsh and inflexible man, struck them as much for his own pleasure as to give proof of his zeal. Such was still, in 1852, the fate of the Gypsies belonging to the boyards.

Matéo Maximoff[3] describes the slave-markets where the Gypsies, exhibited on a platform, were sold by public auction in groups or whole families. There were also convict prisons in which Gypsies guilty of rebellion or refusing to obey, and indeed of very simple little offences, used to work as gold-washers in camps situated at the foot of mountains. So long as they did not attempt to escape, they were compelled to remain completely naked in the ice-cold torrents of water. They slept in miserable wooden huts which were never warmed, and the lashes of the whip rained on the shoulders of those surviving in this almost concentration-camp régime.

Justice, in fact, belonged to their masters. 'There did not exist any tribunals, properly so called. The voivodes and the boyards', says Maximoff, 'judged and punished those who infringed the law in the territories dependent on them. There was no appeal against a sentence; and only a prince could intervene. But, as punishments followed immediately on the sentence, there was no time to appeal to such a person.'

Sometimes, in spite of this, determined Gypsies succeeded in escaping and reached the mountains of Transylvania, got into Hungary or, more often, joined outlawed Gypsies. The latter,

1. Vaillant, *Les Roms, histoire vraie des vrais Bohémiens* (1857).
2. In *Magasin Pittoresque*, 1862.
3. In *Le Prix de la Liberté* (1947).

among whom were the fierce *Netotsi*, Gypsy 'Men of the Woods', were not in fact very numerous, and it was this which best protected them. From the beginning of their slavery, they decided to flee and live like wild beasts in the almost inaccessible secondary chain of mountains which separate Romania from Hungary, forming there an under-cover resistance movement (like the *maquis* in France during World War II). Cut off in the midst of this jungle, they ran little risk, because the Romanian soldiers had no desire to venture into that maze of forests and rocks in which no law of civilization applied. It was only when they went down towards the plain in search of supplies that, from time to time, they came against government troops. Then the skirmishes left a considerable number of dead, from both sides. Sheltered in caves from which they had driven out the bears, the Gypsies were likewise victims of the weather in a climate that is particularly harsh. Scurvy was rife among them. But sometimes they were helped and given provisions by peasants or woodcutters hostile to the repressive régime, or kindly healers would look after them.

This situation changed only in the nineteenth century. In 1830 and 1835, the constitutional statutes of Moldavia and Walachia defined the status of the slave: he was not a man but a person who, with his patrimony and family, was dependent on another. Marriages between Gypsies and non-Gypsies remained strictly prohibited. However, a master could free a slave, who was then permitted to build his own house. But the Gypsies who were given their freedom had been too long servants or serfs to become farmers, even for themselves. The majority of them preferred to devote themselves to nomadic working-class occupations. They were then subjected to taxation. What is most extraordinary is that the government used Gypsies as collectors of taxes from other Gypsies, their racial brothers. In this regard, let us note that in a part of the Balkans that was then of the Ottoman Empire – now Albania and Greece – the Christian Gypsies used to pay more in the way of taxes than Mussulman Gypsies. And if these last were hit by capitation dues and onerous taxes, it was because they were 'schismatics'.[1]

The liberated slaves still represented only a weak minority as against, for example, the four thousand families which belonged to the State. Nevertheless, public opinion began to develop and to regard the Gypsies with less unfavourable eyes. As the Romannian

1. See *Journal of the Gypsy Lore Society*, vol. xxxviii.

people themselves had first suffered from the cruelties of the nobility, they began to have compassion for the slaves of Gypsy origin. It was two voivodes who took the matter in hand and succeeded in having the abolition of slavery proclaimed. Both had the same name: Ghyka – that of a very ancient and famous Moldo-Walachian family. Alexander Ghyka began his campaign in 1837. Thanks to his efforts, a Bill was introduced in the Moldavian Assembly in 1844 with the object of emancipating at least the Gypsy slaves of the clergy. Yet the latter were powerful enough to cause the Bill to be rejected. It was only in 1855 that Gregory Alexander Ghyka succeeded in achieving the liberation of the two hundred thousand Gypsies[1] in Romania. But this liberation had cost dearly: a revolt,[2] one savagely suppressed, had been necessary; yet it tipped the balance on the side of the Gypsies.

The State decreed a complete amnesty for the outlaws and at the same time gave Romanian nationality to the Gypsies. Some of the *Netotsi*, however, who had become sceptical because of long years of oppression, refused to leave their places of refuge. The others grouped themselves in tribes (*vatrachi*) under the leadership of *vatafs* and separated into 'sedentaries', that is, those with fixed residences; and nomads. They first settled down in the outlying parts and suburbs of the big towns, following their traditional occupations. Such were the *Oursari* (or Boyhas), exhibitors of bears and performing animals, makers of bone combs, crochet-hooks, rope; the Kalderash, tinsmiths and coppersmiths, makers of (sauce-) pans, pails and buckets and all metal utensils; the *Sastrari* or workers in iron; the *Anatori*, tinsmiths or tin-platers who had come recently from Turkey; the *Kastari*, woodworkers, makers of agricultural and domestic tools and utensils; the *Grastari*, horse-copers and farriers; the *Taiari*, lock- and boltsmiths; the *Laoutari*, musicians. . . .[3]

As for the nomads, they spread throughout the whole of Romania, or crossed the frontier in a westerly direction. They mostly followed the same occupations as the 'sedentaries', but some of them would form a seasonal company for work on the land. The women, of course, pursued their profitable careers as sorceresses, healers and fortune-tellers.

1. The figure has been slightly challenged, but would not be less.
2. Subject of Maximoff's book *Le Prix de la Liberté*.
3. These last were semi-nomads.

The most numerous group of these nomads chose Russia as their new fatherland. They arrived there in thousands round about the year 1860, fleeing from a country which held too many bad recollections for them of humiliations and deaths. Still two more groups were formed: the *Miyeyesti* and the *Yonesti*. There are two distinct ways in which Gypsy communities are named: tribes either have the name of the chief (the *Yonesti* being the tribe of the chief Yono); or a name designating the principal occupation (thus, the *Oursari*, or exhibitors of bears).

The *Miyeyesti* devoted themselves to trading or hawking. They bought things in the large towns and went into the countryside to attend markets and engage in door-to-door selling. The *Yonesti* who belonged to the Kalderash group of copper- and tinsmiths, were naturally tinsmiths, dancers and musicians. In 1910 Maximoff's grandfather became chief of the two clans, and had to divide them again as they were too prolific. Their children dispersed throughout the whole of Europe. One group reached Sweden where it is known by the name of *Taikoni*; the others reached Spain, France, Italy, Portugal and England. These, taken together, are: the *Belkesti, Zigeresti, Tchoukouresti, Trinkilesti, Laidakesti, Boumboulesti, Zeregoui* and *Palesti*, etc.[1]

Gypsies in Hungary

In Hungary and in Transylvania the Gypsies also experienced slavery, and this in the fifteenth century. But their conditions appear to have been less horrible than in Moldo-Walachia. They belonged to the sovereign, who undertook to share them out to the whole country. In 1476 Mathias Corvin, King of Hungary, authorized the city of Sibiu (Hermannstadt) to make use of the 'Egyptians' established on the outskirts. Twenty years later, Ladislas VI made himself protector of a group of blacksmiths, twenty-five tents of them known as the *Poligari*, who made weapons, particularly for the Bishop of Pecs. In 1514, those same Gypsies were ordered by the Palatine, John of Szapolya (who had jurisdiction exclusive of the royal court), to forge instruments of torture to be used for the punishment of Dosa, leader of the peasant rebellion. They accepted: much to their own misfortune. Some time later the Lord of Czernabo, an enemy of Szapolya, had them imprisoned and impaled alive.

In spite of a situation plainly less tragic than that in Romania, the

1. Maximoff, *Wanderndes Volk auf endloser Strasse* (1959).

Gypsies of Hungary were exposed to intermittent attacks of governmental harshness, and indeed to popular anger, which led to worse excesses. Under the pretext, never proved, that the Gypsies committed unspeakably heinous crimes – the abduction of children, rape, cannibalism – the authorities tried to find the most spectacular means of punishing them. In Bohemia their left ear was cut off if they dared even to appear in the country, and then the right ear if the crime were repeated, finally the head – if they were caught a third time. In 1782 the Hungarians accused them of cannibalism; forty-one Gypsies, men and women, were hanged, beheaded, broken on the wheel or quartered. According to the indictment they were alleged to have devoured (cooked or smoked!) some forty-four people. The Hungarian soldiers entrusted with the punitive expedition drove the Gypsies into dangerous swamps where they drowned to the last man. Tradition says that it is there the origin of their phobia for wet places must be sought.

From 1761, however, Maria Theresa, then Queen of Hungary and Bohemia, undertook to settle them. She began by naming them Neo-Hungarians or 'new settlers', finding the term Gypsy insulting. She prohibited them from sleeping in tents and engaging in certain occupations with which they were familiar, such as that of horse-dealing, electing their own chiefs, using their own language, and getting married if they had not the means to support a family. The men were pressed into military service and the children compelled to attend schools.

This attempt was doomed to failure. If, in fact, it proved that Maria Theresa had very good feelings, it also showed a complete lack of understanding in regard to Gypsies and their way of life, and consequently of their aspirations. Furthermore, the means employed did not bear witness to the utmost mildness. An intelligent woman who travelled through Central Europe in the nineteenth century has left us in her *Voyage en Hongrie* heart-rending pictures of the application of this policy:

On one terrible day for this race of people which is still remembered with horror, handcarts escorted by pickets of soldiers appeared in all parts of Hungary where there were Gypsies and took away the children, including those just weaned, and young married couples still wearing their wedding finery. The despair of these unfortunate people cannot be described: the parents dragged themselves on the ground before the soldiers, and clung to the vehicles which were carrying away their children. . . . Beaten off with blows from batons and rifle-butts, and not being able to follow the wagons on which had been heaped pell-mell all that was dearest in the world to them – their little children – some immediately committed suicide. The use of these vigorous measures was hardly calculated to convince *Zigains* of the excellence of the morality preached to them, and was not of a nature to inspire in them consciousness of the superiority of the institutions which the authorities wished to impose on them. This act of violence remained sterile, and in spite of Maria Theresa's edicts and those of her successor, Joseph II, there are still *Zigains*: that is, they are still nomads and thieves corrupted to such a degree that the imagination refuses to acknowledge it. But one may add that serious and truly religious measures have never been applied with good results to the education of this people. . . .

Twenty years after Maria Theresa's attempt, a new prosecution was brought against the Gypsies. They were once again accused of cannibalism; and forty-five of them were sentenced to death on this charge. Joseph II, Maria Theresa's successor, was able to establish the fact that no proof whatever had been produced. This particularly horrible judicial error merely illustrated a commonplace calumny. All Central Europe, during the period when vampires played havoc in literature, was groaning with many stories of this kind. The most astounding is that of a contemporary author, often quoted in these pages, one who cannot be doubted for the serious nature of his works, that is, Popp Serboianu. He asserts in a hateful way that this cannibalism on the part of the Gypsies is in no sense a legend. According to him, Gypsies are alleged to have eaten the bodies of Hungarian soldiers in 1920. He cites in support of his allegation the prosecution at Prague in 1929, where twenty-one Gypsies were convicted of having committed twelve murders followed by cannibalism, without emphasizing that it was a matter of the *Netotsi*, pillaging and degenerate Gypsies, who are descendants of members of the first Transylvanian 'resistance movement' (who lived like wild beasts – see page 99).

The Gypsies were likewise scattered in the east of the Balkans. In Bosnia, in 1565, they made iron and stone cannon-balls for Mustapha *Pasha* who was besieging the town of Crupa.

Before leaving that part of Europe (and at the risk of infringing on the later chapter devoted to tribal organization), we must be quite clear about the role of the voivodes. Generally speaking, the voivode was a local nobleman, a non-Gypsy. Yet it did happen that, in

Hungary, and notably in Transylvania, he was a Gypsy and then regarded as a voivode of lower rank, but delegated and responsible for the families placed under his jurisdiction. Some of these Gypsy voivodes administered as many as several hundred families. They had the right, Jules Bloch says, to the sceptre, to silver buttons, a great prismatic goblet, the whip and a beard – spectacular attributes of the chiefs of tribes. Marriage outside the clan was permitted to them. It is only the memory of them which is passed down to us as the type of 'Gypsy baron', so long inveterate in popular literature.

Gypsies in Russia

Known in Russia since the year 1500, the Gypsies enjoyed a relatively peaceful existence there. Catherine the Great gave them a status of their own and made them the slaves of the Crown; but she did not persecute them. Nevertheless in 1759, for some obscure reason, entry into the city of St Petersburg was forbidden to them. Some musicians and female dancers lived there by themselves and more or less clandestinely. The Russians, even among the most aristocratic, did not disdain to marry these dancers.[1]

In the south of the country Gypsy peasants are recorded for a very long time, in the Crimea, Ukraine and on the banks of the Black Sea. Documents note the fact of the establishment, on the banks of the Kuban in the Caucasus, of a people of mysterious origins. In Bessarabia[2] the government wished to make Gypsies lead a settled life, and for this purpose created colonies at Kair and at Faraonov. I have not found any details of this enterprise, but it is disquieting to my mind that these two 'prefabricated' towns have names that are dear to the Gypsy tradition, evoking Cairo and the Pharaoh: that is, Egypt. This attempt to settle them failed, it seems, for the good reason that the officials appointed to make the arrangements quite simply pocketed the funds they collected for the purpose.

We have hardly any information about the circumstances of the Gypsies in Russia during the early period of their history there. We know more about their doings and exploits in the nineteenth century. It is again on Maximoff,[3] since his parents also lived this exemplary life, that I rely for information regarding this period. Before 1900 the Gypsies camped on the outskirts of Moscow in miserable hovels,

1. This has also happened elsewhere – in Spain, for example. *Tr.*
2. See Martin Block, op. cit.
3. In his novel *Savina* (1948). See Bibliography, p. 269.

veritable ghettos of wooden huts, patched-up tents and rickety wagons in which they squatted during the six months of winter. The fact is that they went almost unnoticed among the swarm of people who then lived in Moscow's suburban areas. The artisans among them found easy openings for work in the many factories which were beginning to grow up like mushrooms. Yet, in spite of apparent poverty, it was not rare, Maximoff says in *Savina*, for these encampments to conceal wealth and even astonishing fortunes: 'Cataclysms, wars or revolutions – nothing can stop the forward march of the Gypsies. Floods, earthquakes or political upheavals have no importance for them when it is a matter of ordering their personal affairs'. So it was that, when the Russian Revolution broke out, an important group of Gypsies continued to travel quietly, making their way towards Siberia, and from there perhaps to China.

Another group, of which Maximoff's tribe, the *Tchoukouresti*, formed part, decided to reach western Europe. The situation, in fact, became precarious all the same. Notwithstanding their voluntary ignorance of events, the Gypsies could no longer either play their music, or dance, or sing in the cafés, cabarets or *traktir* (inns). They had to fall back on their artisan occupations which at one time they had been able to abandon. They did so in order to be able to take to the road again, for this never fails to call the Gypsy. The journey of the *Tchoukouresti* was to last more than a year.

Gypsies in Germany

It has been seen that the Gypsies had arrived in Germany in the first years of the fifteenth century, introducing themselves there as pilgrims. So long as the Germans believed that their dispersion was explained by religious reasons, their stay was uneventful. The tribal chiefs, who took on themselves the showy titles of dukes (*Herzöge*), princes (*Fürsten*) and counts (*Grafen*) displayed a measure of pomp which deluded the people. The latter did not have enough imagination, it seems, to suspect these travellers of more prosaic motives for being on the roads.

This golden age lasted for nearly half a century. The old prejudices then again took the upper hand. The halo did not stand up for long against the sensational number of thefts, acts of scrounging and deceit, and swindles of every kind which marked the passage of these pilgrims. And, just as easily as the Germans had taken them for heroic religious crusaders, they now put them in the less enviable category of diabolical creatures. At the same time they began to fear the Gypsies; at least to fear their vengeance and above all their evil spells. A peasant or a burgher who insulted a Gypsy could be certain soon afterwards to see his farm or his house go up in flames. To the Gypsies were attributed the epidemics and scourges of nature, such as, for example, a gigantic invasion of the fields by mice. The fact that the Gypsy women told fortunes did not help to remove from the religious spirit of the people the fact that the women were witches.[1]

From that time onwards, the chroniclers did not omit to record (as Sebastian Münster did in his *Cosmographie*) the existence of Gypsies who were 'underdeveloped, black, ugly, dirty and thieves'. Aventinus, Del Rio and even others readily considered them as a plague which now covered the whole of Europe.

It was some time before the measures taken against the Gypsies were comprehensive: in 1463 the town of Bamberg in Bavaria offered them the sum of seven livres 'gratuity' as the price for their departure. Meanwhile the situation grew gradually worse. Hostile decrees became more and more numerous and more categorical. In 1482 the Margrave Albrecht von Brandenburg expressly prohibited the Gypsies from settling in any little town or market in his jurisdiction. The Diet of Speyer (1489) decided purely and simply that they should be expelled from the Rhineland and the Palatinate, regarding them as 'traitors to Christian countries'. In 1500 the Recess of the Deputation of the Empire at Augsburg prohibited 'the granting of support or escort to the people called *Zigeuner* and allowing them to go about in the country'. The Germanisches Museum of Nuremberg contains an enactment passed by the State of Swabia: the local lord, who did not obey the orders for expulsion and the interdict against employing Gypsies, was sentenced to pay for the damage which 'must' result from their presence.

Three months were given to the undesirables to leave the country. As, of course, they did nothing about it, the repressions began. Gypsies were declared to be outlaws. Even the clergy, who saw these people as strayed though very black sheep, lined up on the side of the authorities. The native inhabitants were given the right to fire at sight on Gypsies who persisted in crossing their path, even though they should in exceptional instances be provided with a passport. At Dresden two Gypsies were drowned in the river, without any

1. Hampe, op. cit.

other legal formality. The Prince Elector of Mainz even flattered himself for having put to death all the male Gypsies in his region, and for flogging and branding with iron their women and children.

The eighteenth century saw a recrudescence of coercion, and one can only admire the fatalism of the Gypsies who persisted in living in Germany as if there were nothing to it. In 1724, in the Margraviat of Beyreuth, fifteen Gypsy women aged from 15 to 98 (say the documents!) were hanged in a single day. Martin Block puts on record the highly characteristic text of an enactment promulgated at Aix-la-Chapelle (Aachen) in 1728:

Already for a long time it has been established that on our territory as in neighbouring countries the Gypsies, united in bands and armed, as well as all kinds of vagabond people without masters, commit robberies. . . . In consequence whereof, in order to root out this brood of rascals, we have decided that if anybody should by surprise come upon such Gypsies, armed rogues and groups and vagabond bands, information thereof shall be given to us immediately in order that the necessary militia be sent against them for their repression. Protection shall be asked of the said militia called upon for their repression, and their pursuit shall be carried out with zeal to the sound of bells [*sic*]. In the event of surprise, whether the Gypsies resist or not, these people shall be put to death. Nevertheless, those who are taken by surprise and who do not counter-attack may be granted at most half an hour, to go on their knees and beg of the Almighty, if they so wish, pardon for their sins and to prepare for death. . . .

At crossroads, where today is set up[1] the too well known board with the notice 'Prohibited to Nomads', gallows and gibbets were erected which a written notice explained as 'punishment for riff-raff, rogues and Gypsies'. But the authorities, having noticed that these last could not read, took care to add drawings in colours representing punishments with the lash, and hanging.

The Aix-la-Chapelle law fundamentally put Gypsies and highway robbers in the same bag. In actual fact, in Germany as in France and in most other countries, the Gypsies rubbed shoulders with the 'dangerous' classes. Their survival, as we saw, depended on these relationships. In a society in which they were regarded as pariahs, it was very necessary for them to resort to the 'trades' of vagabond-age, and to mix closely with the *Dobissierer* (false hermits) and the *Vagierer* (tramps called 'men of God'). The Thirty Years War had

1. In France and some other countries. *Tr.*

already let loose on the whole of Germany entire hordes of well organized bandits, with arms and baggage, who lived on the country. Naturally, the Gypsies were caught up in this wave. Some of them, however, preferred official banditry and joined the ranks of Wallenstein when he raised his army of one hundred thousand *leudes*, free men who became mercenaries in his service.

However, throughout these successive turmoils, some Gypsy groups succeeded in putting the authorities on the wrong trail; and passed unnoticed. Some of them took to a settled existence. Others could move about almost freely: exhibitors of bears, for example, for the simple reason that this occupation had long been taken in Germany by Hungarian and Polish mountebanks, who were left to their own devices, and in circumstances in which Gypsies had no trouble in disguising themselves.

In Germany there appeared a group of nomads called *Yénische* whose racial attachment to Gypsy stock presents a problem that has not been completely solved even to this day. They are nomads who follow a life almost like that of other Gypsies, but their folk-lore and traditions are extremely poor. One can, however, make out several beliefs that are typically Gypsy: fear of the *mulo* or vampire, for example. According to Arnold, who has recently made a study of them:[1]

Gypsies of pure race separated themself from the *Yénische*, who were issue of a mixture of unsettled white people (vagabonds) and Gypsies, probably at the end of the eighteenth century, because the people of the mixed race were not observing Gypsy laws and customs. In this way was formed, beside the Gypsies, a second type of nomads, the *Yénische*, which explains the hatred existing between these two groups.

The reader will see that their dialect is mentioned in the chapter given to means of expression. In it is found some Yiddish vocabulary, but one cannot on that account regard the *Yénische* as Jews.

Gypsies in Poland

The Gypsies had reached the northern part of the continent in the period of their great European migrations. They went through Poland, where at first the Diets, one after another throughout the sixteenth century, tried to banish them. However, at the end of the eighteenth century, the government changed its opinion in regard

1. Dr H. Arnold, *Vaganten, Komoedianten, Fieranten u. Briganten* (Stuttgart, 1958).

to them and began on the contrary to increase the signs of clemency. And so it was that the Gypsies were able to establish themselves peacefully in the country, to the point that their children attended schools.

The Baltic countries, especially Lithuania, likewise kept them, giving proof of definite understanding in regard to them. The frontiers of Lithuania at that time, as is known, reached, or very nearly reached, the banks of the Black Sea, beyond the Ukraine. Thus, in the sixteenth century, the Gypsies had no frontiers to cross in order to reach the Baltic. We saw a little earlier that if Franz de Ville sees in this exodus towards distant Scandinavia the origin of a trade in amber, it is perhaps simpler to regard the arrival of the Gypsies in Latvia as the logical result of a migration which came from Southern Europe. In any case, the Gypsies were numerous in the Baltic countries from the sixteenth century onwards.

Gypsies in Scandinavia

From there, naturally, and by way of Karelia, they reached the Scandinavian peninsula. In Sweden their expulsion was ordered in 1727, but this did not prevent them from remaining there and taking root.

Finland and Norway will detain us longer. The first of these countries in fact constituted for the Gypsies a veritable *finis terrae*; not only did geography compel them to turn west and go down southwards again, but the climate they came up against was strange and hostile. One had to be a Laplander to venture upon a nomad life in such a world. However, the Gypsies met the indigenous inhabitants, then known by the name of Finns (or *Finner* in German, probably from *fen* = marshland, bog, or fen), but called *Chud(s)* by the Russians, that is, wizards (Russian *chudodei* = miracle worker). Those Finns had in fact the reputation of engaging in mysterious ceremonies of a character visibly devilish, in the course of which they fell into an ecstasy. It is now known that these practices were of a Shamanist order.[1] I dwell a little on this human group because the Gypsies had close and fruitful contacts with it, and they are at the same time confused with it.

1. Shamanism: the primitive religion of certain peoples of north-eastern Siberia. The good and evil of life are brought about by spirits which could be influenced only by Shamans (priests). It was founded on the cult of nature and the supernatural. *Tr.*

Among the various names which they give to the Gypsies (*Tater*, 'Tartars'; *Omstreifer*, 'prowlers'; *Reisender*, 'travellers'), the Scandinavians really prefer that of *Fant*, a term which derives like *Finn* from *fen*. The Finns already had a very bad reputation, since in 1699 the Chancellor Rosenkrantz[1] called them the most pernicious scourge. They were accused, apart from engaging in sorcery, of destroying game, setting fire to forests, or being spies (in whose service? We do not know). Bishop Pontopiddan[2] treats them bluntly as barbarous pillagers. So much and so far that the authorities dealt very severely with these nomads who shamelessly crossed the frontiers, and so that the relations of these Finns with their neighbours developed a tone of open hostility.

Now it so happens that their way of living and that of the Gypsies showed many similarities. The Finns and the Fants, 'this hated and despised race',[3] were likened to one another. The confusion was further aggravated in Norway by the fact that the Finns had arrived in that country about the year 1600; that is, at the time when the Gypsy emigration was in full force. They had left the Duchy of Finland when civil wars had set by the ears the partisans of King Sigismund and those of the future Charles IX. The latter allocated to them as their territory the immense forests which Swedish agriculturists did not know how to utilize. And there the Finns mixed closely with the Gypsy Fants.

It is clear that, for the peasants of that period, Finnish Shamanist séances and Gypsy festivities showed hardly any differences. Common to both was the use of bears and the tambourine, their dancing, the camp-fire and the ritual cauldron, etc. The gypsiologist Thillhagen[4] has shown how the Gypsies and Finns, these two groups of people, differing ethnically and culturally from the Swedish people, have shared the reputation of being gifted with supernatural powers and, by virtue of this, were at one and the same time feared and consulted. In reality, these Gypsies must be more exactly *Polatchis*, members of the last clan to come from Poland, as their name would indicate.

1. In *Relation sur l'Etat de Norvège* (1699).
2. In *Histoire naturelle de la Norvège*.
3. See Eilert Sundt, *Rapports sur les Fants ou vagabonds de la Norvège* (Christiana, 1850).
4. In *Folkig Läkekonst* (Stockholm, 1958). See also the works of Kristfrid Ganander, an ethnologist of the eighteenth century, whose work remains in manuscript and is not easily accessible.

Let us now follow the Gypsies in Britain. They may have landed there in 1430, or in 1440. These dates seem to indicate that it was the same wave which had broken over the whole of Europe. But how the Gypsies crossed the North Sea or the English Channel is not known; maritime archives are silent on this subject. Notwithstanding their phobia for the sea, these wanderers must have achieved the crossing in ordinary transport vessels. But did they take with them their arms and baggage? It may have been that they passed unnoticed among a crowd of immigrants. It is also thought that they contemplated sailing from the Dutch ports. But the matter remains uncertain.

In any event, they immediately dispersed in the British Isles: to Wales, Ireland and Scotland, as well as England. Again the authorities reacted violently. As early as 1441 an enactment against them was made public. A hundred years later Henry VIII took severe measures to meet them. But the palm for severity goes to Queen Elizabeth I, who accused them, among other misdeeds, of hiding priests and emissaries of Rome.[1] In 1563 she commanded them to leave the country within three months, under penalty of death.

In the seventeenth century, nevertheless, the Gypsies were still present and very much alive, as usual; and they regained their freedom. And from then onwards they found a hospitable land in the British Isles. They settled down comfortably, faithfully conserving their traditions, grouping themselves in tribes, and continued to elect chiefs. One of these 'kings', James Bosvill (or Boswell) was buried at Doncaster, and until 1820, his family went each year to empty a pot of light ale on his grave.[2]

The Gypsies of Wales were the most faithful to old traditions, so much so that they are almost the only ones in the world to use the *romani* language in a state of purity, including grammar and syntax.[3] The others, in accordance with custom, took on local names: they became Smiths, Grays, Hernes and Boswells ... in Scotland they adopted the generic name of Faa.

It is worth noting in regard to this, that in the whole field of their dispersion, the Gypsies have always chosen very simple local names, generally the commonest. But one may query whether some of these

1. See Fréchet, *George Borrow* ... (1956).
2. Jules Bloch, op. cit.
3. John Sampson, *The Dialect of the Gypsies of Wales* (1926).

names, especially in Germany and Britain, have not been chosen in terms of their occupational meaning. Thus, the Smiths *were* smiths (blacksmiths, tinsmiths, coppersmiths); and the Zieglers in Germany were brick-makers (in the Balkans the Gypsies had for long the monopoly of making earthenware bricks). As for the Boswells,[1] the name of one of the best known tribes in England, although Boswell is an old English name, one can see in it the form *bosh-well*; *bosh*, in the argot of the vagabonds and Gypsies, means the violin and the art of playing it.[2]

All, or nearly all these Gypsies in Britain[3] are wanderers (some people call them 'travellers', though many of those referred to as travellers are not pure Gypsies) and they live in tents. They are smiths, quack vets, horse-dealers and -copers (descendants of some of these may become jockeys), tinners and tinsmiths, clothes-peg makers and so forth. The women, for a certainty, go in for the arts of telling the future and find fair game in misguided feather-brained innocents.

At fairs and fêtes the men could be seen clad in long black cloaks, plush waistcoats, velvet riding-breeches and top-boots. The women wore plumed turbans, coloured shawls, satin dresses and black shoes.[4]

According to Fréchet, author of an excellent biography of the astonishing Borrow, whom we shall meet later, these clans had little to do with one another. The Faas and the Smiths spoke English, and these only had particular traditions, mixed little with the *gadjé* and had their dead buried secretly in secluded, unexpected places. They probably belonged to the group of Kalderash called *Anglezuri*. All of these authentic Gypsies met other nomads whose origin has not been satisfactorily established. Such were the *Koramengré*, whose name in Gypsy means colporteurs or hawkers. Such, especially, were the Tinkers.

The Tinkers (or 'Tinklers' in Scotland) pose a problem that is at present unsolved. This name is related to the roots *tik* and *tin'k* and even to *tsink*, onomatopoeic terms relating to the forge and the noise of hammer on anvil. Modern English has the word 'tinker' (tinman)

1. Very enlightening and up-to-date on English Gypsies is Brian Vesey-Fitzgerald's *Gypsies of Britain* (1944, 1946). See Bibliography, p. 273.

2. Partridge, *Dictionary of the Underworld* (London, 1950).

3. See also 'Supplementary Notes', pp. 260–67.

4. Fréchet, op. cit.

and 'to tinker' (= to patch up; to botch). In the old cant lingo of the very lowest class a 'tinker' was an apprentice or 'botcher'. In the United States he is the assistant or mate of a safe-driller.[1] Finally, it is possible to suggest a linguistic relationship between *tink* and *athingané*, the Gypsy of the Eastern Mediterranean.

Whatever may be its origin, the term 'tinker' designates generically the itinerant smiths and tinmen of the British Isles who live in similar conditions to those of the Gypsies. But are those people for that reason Gypsies? Professor Rehfish of the Department of Social Anthropology, University of Edinburgh, who has at present in preparation a thesis on the 'Tinkers', has called attention to the fact that, in seven hundred words of their vocabulary, about ten per cent of the terms are strictly Gypsy. But this is not adequate proof. The tinkers call themselves 'travellers' and aborigines. They only very rarely marry Gypsies – and they hate hedgehog, a favourite dish of the latter.

Apart from the *Koramengré* and tinkers, other nomads have in England led the 'Gypsy life'. There were Irish who, after the terrible famines of 1845–47, came to wander about Wales and live by the same expedients as the Gypsies, from working as tinsmiths, horse-copers and fortune-tellers to housebreaking and burglary.

Let us leave these northern countries to take up the Gypsy groups who, having left Romania and Hungary, continued on their way westwards. They crossed the Burgenland province of Austria, a little territory on the borders of Hungary, in which some families who are now 'sedentaries' established themselves. In 1701 Austria outlawed the Gypsies. From 1514 they were banished from Swiss territory. The manner in which they introduced themselves into Italy has been briefly seen. The documents are not very explicit in regard to their occupations and their unpleasant encounters with the authorities. We do know, however, that Pope Pius V brutally drove them out of the domains of the Church in 1568.

Gypsies in Spain

Spain constitutes a much more important stage on the road of gypsiology. The reader will remember that the *Annales de Cataluña* record the presence of Gypsies in Barcelona in 1447. This is very much a matter of European Gypsies (and not of *Gitanos* who had come from North Africa), since they were bearers of papal letters.

1. Partridge, *Dictionary of the Underworld* (London, 1950).

However, a modern author[1] does not make them appear on the Catalan littoral until 1452.

Be this as it may, there were Gypsies in Spain in the second half of the fifteenth century. But here again we run up against the problem of where to make distinctions between groups. Were those first Gypsies *Gitanos*? I repeat that in this book the term 'Gypsies' designates the Gypsy people as a whole, including *Gitanos* and other *Romanichels*, and not exclusively the group defined on page 47. This likewise poses the question of the origin of the *Gitanos* and their migration across Africa.

The *Gitanos* in fact differ considerably from the Gypsies, and the two groups find it difficult to tolerate one another. Their dialects are so different from each other as to be mutually incomprehensible. The *Gitanos* speak an idiom based on *romaní* and known as *caló*. It is well embellished with Spanish words but does not harbour a single Germanic term. *Gitanos* and Gypsies have hardly any physical resemblance either. As for manners and customs, it will be seen later in what way these differ.

The origin of the *Gitanos*, like that of the Gypsies, has caused much ink to flow and given rise to ethnological caprices. The thesis most in vogue, until the nineteenth-century researches, would have them be descendants of the Guanches, who themselves were the last survivors of Atlantis. Blaise Cendrars, who, all his life and on the most sympathetic terms, associated with Gypsies, stood by this view, but rather as a wayfaring poet than as a scholar, if truth be told:

I maintain that they are a people who originated in the Canary Islands, that they are the ancient Guanches. I must not be the only one of this opinion. Dr Capistan, Director of the Museum (of Natural History, Paris), the man who devoted his life to studying the Guanche civilization, the last people of Atlantis, was almost convinced of this.

The Guanches have stirred the curiosity of scholars for a long time. Their origin is indeed extremely mysterious. They lived in caverns dug out of the earth, and were shepherds who spoke a Berber dialect. They had a typical dance, which the Spaniards brought to their country. The only feature, however, which seems to connect Guanches and Gypsies is the common phobia for the sea. In fact, the former, although excellent swimmers (which is not the case with

1. Lafuente, op. cit.

the latter), were ignorant of navigation at a time when all the Mediterranean peoples had for long been braving the high seas. According to Devigne, biographer of Jean de Béthencourt (the Norman navigator and colonizer of the Canaries, who died in 1425), king of those islands, this strange exception was the result of a religious taboo. But a possible relationship between the Guanches and the Gypsies remains highly problematical.

Straining the hypothesis still further, the late Marquis de Baroncelli, an intimate friend of many *Gitans* in Provence, drew attention to striking analogies between these *Gitans* and the American Indians, Sioux and Iroquois. Before the Second World War he had invited Colonel Cody (better known by the name of Buffalo Bill) to come with him on Gypsy pilgrimages among Gypsies of the Camargue:

The most unexpected incident in the adventure was the resemblance in type, colour and ways of behaviour which Colonel Cody and his host discovered between the redskins and the *Gitans*. Furthermore, many words in their respective languages are the same, and they are both fire-worshippers[?]. Hence, the strong presumptions that they may be issues of a common racial stock. They support the hypothesis of a race of nomads with dark red skins, who travelled towards the setting sun, and whom the sinking of Atlantis broke up in either the Stone or the Bronze Age. Their survivors from the catastrophe on the eastern side would be the fellaheen who surged into Egypt, the *Gitans* who gather together each year in the Camargue on the day when the sun is at its highest above the horizon, and the Basques who, like the Iroquois, wear feathers to bewail their lost liberty at the foot of the tree of Guernica. . . .[1]

This is something which at least has poetic fragrance. The gypsiologists for their part are now agreed in recognizing a common origin for *Gitans* and Gypsies. The two groups left India. But, whereas the second penetrated into Europe via the Balkans, the first followed the southern coast of the Mediterranean, by way of Egypt and North Africa. The length of the road covered, without any possible contact, would suffice to explain the differences between them. Popp Serboianu pinpoints that: 'To this last group would belong the Nubian and Egyptian Gypsies – the *Ragari*, *Elebj* and *Muri* – who were found on the island of Crete in 1422 by Simeon Simeonis'. On his part, de Ville says that he is 'certain that some wandering tribes (Gypsies) have been going into Egypt from the

1. Jean des Vallières, *Le Chevalier de Camargue*, 1956.

earliest times and that they had even advanced further southwards down to the Sudan, where Gypsies are still found today. In very early times also, certain of these tribes left Egypt to go across the North of Africa and make their way into Spain.'[1]

All this seems very reasonable and could explain why a traveller meeting *Gitanos* in Spain in 1540 was able to converse with them in vernacular Greek.[2] But where can we find clear traces of the presence of Gypsies in Africa? Outside of Egypt itself, they are recorded in Ethiopia, the Sudan, Mauritania and North Africa. But it seems that in these places nobody has studied them. Here again we are reduced to hypotheses.

However it may have happened, we must admit that the *Gitanos* arrived in Spain via Africa. The Spaniards quickly gave them the name of '*Gitanos*', a term which is probably a distortion of '*Egyptanos*'; and this time the nomads really had come from Egypt. But, as fantasy is still very strong in this ethnological field, I do not resist the temptation to ponder over an improbable but curious ethnology: Tanger (Tangier in English) by way of which the future *Gitanos* were compelled to pass, was formerly called Tingis, and found itself capital of '*Tingitan* Mauritania'. Its inhabitants still bear the name of *Tingitanos*.

We do not know the date on which the Gypsies crossed the Strait of Gibraltar. Perhaps, by a mere coincidence difficult to admit, this was at the same time as European Gypsies crossed the Pyrenees going southwards. We do not know this either. Where and when did the meeting of the two groups take place? This also is not known. The difficulty in the 'African' thesis is still further increased because of the fact that the Spanish documents never speak of *two* different groups of nomads. They mention simply *Gitanos*. In my opinion, it is impossible for the two dates to agree. We remember that the northern Gypsies arrived at Barcelona in 1447 (or strictly speaking in 1452). The arrival of the southern *Gitanos* could only have happened earlier. The *Gitanerías* or *Gitano* colonies in the South of the peninsula seem to have been established at an earlier date than those of the North: the Sierra Nevada mountains must have given shelter to the first tribes, and the *Gitano* colonies of Andalusia at Grenada, Cadiz and Seville have been attested 'at all times'.

In regard to Portugal, the references are still more cautious. For

1. F. de Ville, *Tziganes* (Brussels, 1956).
2. Jules Bloch, op. cit.

myself, I have found only the account by a João Baptista Venturo, member of an ecclesiastical delegation on a mission to Portugal in 1571, in the province of Alemtejo, alluding to village dances with '*Ciganos* mixing in them'.[1] It may be inferred from this that these *Gitanos* had been there for some time. *A priori*, nothing could have prevented them from going from Andalusia to Portugal in the sixteenth, or even the fifteenth century.

Let us now see what were the circumstances of these *Gitanos* in Spain. History repeats itself with little variation. A pragmatic sanction, as early as 1499, ordered the banishment of those without any recognized occupation. An edict of 1528 revived this order and threatened vagabond *Gitanos* with the galleys. Thirty years later, Philip II wished to compel them to abandon their wild life (*vida montaraz*) and settle in small towns and villages. From this period date the city colonies of *Gitanos*; in reserved neighbourhoods quite near the Jewish ghettoes. And the end of the sixteenth century was marked by a revival of these measures. In the next century, these legal proceedings took an ugly turn to become real persecutions.[2]

In the Iberian Peninsula the *Gitanos* really seem to multiply like the rabbits in Australia. A Gypsy chief who roamed through Aragon and Castile found himself at the head of eight hundred men living on the country. It was necessary to send the military after them; and it was no slight matter to disperse this band. That happened in 1618. Two years later, four *Gitanos* were captured and eagerness was shown in submitting them to interrogation 'without having to reproach them for any thing other than having been made *Rommuni* [Gypsies] by God'.[3] Under torture the unfortunate people admitted everything the authorities wanted of them, that is that they had killed and eaten one of their own people in the forest of Gamas, and had done the same thing to a Franciscan monk. A sentence of death shortened their punishment.

The *Gitanos* then made an extremely bad reputation for themselves. A decision of the Cortes (legislative assembly) in 1610 called to mind the 'great and pitiable complaints in regard to *Gitanos*, men and women. . . .' These recriminations became such that Philip IV decided to strike a heavy blow. It took the form of the edict of 1633, which stated:

1. Vatican MSS.
2. Lafuente, op. cit.
3. Serboianu, op. cit.

Considering that the *Roms* are not *Gitanos* either by origin or by nature, but Spaniards, and in order to lead them away from their baleful habits, no longer to dress as they do, and to forget their language: that they be taken from their places of habitation, separated from one another, with express prohibition to come together publicly or in secret, forbidden to remember either their name or their apparel, or their ways in dances or otherwise, under penalty of three years of banishment. . . .

Beginning from the principle that wherever the crime is the product of the 'mass', it is the mass which must be punished (these are the terms used by the king), the doctors of the law multiplied their counsels. The *Gitanos* passed officially into the ranks of false Christians, thieves, diviners, visionaries, poisoners of cattle, spies and traitors. And – just as the Moors had been driven out, who were 'infinitely more numerous but perhaps less dangerous' – so would the *Gitanos* be driven out.[1]

In 1692, Charles II forbade the *Gitanos* to live in villages of less than one thousand hearths. He likewise prohibited them from carrying arms and engaging in any occupation other than agriculture. By a still more severe edict, published three years later, and containing no less than thirty-nine articles, this king prohibited them particularly from being smiths and possessing horses; he hardly granted them the right to have a mule or an ass for work in the fields. Those who left the villages would be punished with six years in the galleys. A document known in Madrid in 1705 shows that the roads and small towns were 'infested' with bands of *Gitanos* who gave the peasants neither rest nor surety. The *corregidores* (local magistrates) and other agents of justice were authorized to open fire on them as 'public bandits' in the event that they should refuse to surrender their arms. They could be pursued even into the churches *de refugio*, then inviolable and open to all criminals, including parricides.[2]

It was only in 1783, in the reign of Charles III, that a more liberal policy was to emancipate the Gypsies from their condition as pariahs. Wishing to imitate Maria Theresa, the king called them 'neo-Castilians'. If he was still forbidding them to use their own language and to change their places of living by wandering about the country, he did succeed in settling a great number. These then returned to their traditional trades, to which they added new

1. Serboianu, op. cit.
2. Davillier, *Voyage en Espagne* (1864).

occupations inspired by Spanish civilization: that of bullfighting, eating-house keeper, shoeblack, cattle-drover, slaughter-man in the abattoirs. . . .

Meanwhile, during the period of successive banishments, some of the *Gitanos* had for the moment forgotten their phobia for the sea, and embarked for South America.[1] There they founded colonies in Brazil, Peru and Chile.

GYPSIES IN THE NINETEENTH CENTURY

The presence of the Gypsies in nineteenth-century Europe introduces a double interest: their participation once again in the misdeeds of the 'dangerous' classes; and the mirage they caused, by the very fact of their being pariahs, to the new sensibility and to romanticism.

The period was in fact to witness in France a revival of organized banditry which transformed the countryside into hide-outs for cut-throats, where the roads were unsafe after nightfall, and the peasants did not open their doors without a gun in their hands. A whole literature popularized the exploits of the *Chauffeurs du Nord*, as they were nicknamed, and those of Normandy.[2] Going from place to place in wandering troupes with mysterious itineraries, using only a secret argot, planning their operations with attention to every little detail, these brigands inevitably came upon Gypsies. And, whether they liked to or not, the Gypsies had to lend them a strong helping hand. Their perfect knowledge of isolated places and of local resources made them, in fact, very valuable intelligence agents for the robbers. So it was that the famous Salembier, leader of the *Chauffeurs du Nord*, made use of the talents of two notorious Romanichels: the Duchess and Mother Caron.

Vidocq, in his *Vraies Mémoires*, in his *Chauffeurs* and in his *Voleurs*,[3] gives many instances of the misdeeds in which the Gypsies took part. He himself used to associate with these people before he became a policeman, and had 'palled up' with a man called Christian, a famous Gypsy, member of a band which was playing havoc in Flanders. This Gypsy devoted himself to the profession of quack

1. See Oliveira China, *Os Ciganos do Brasil* (São Paulo, 1936). For the United States of America, see 'Supplementary Notes' pp. 263–7.

2. *Chauffeurs*, 'firemen', here meaning those who perpetrated acts of arson and incendiarism.

3. Vidocq's *Memoirs*, etc., have appeared in English.

healer, treating animals as well as people. Thanks to Vidocq, we know that the Gypsies of this 'corporation' took care, in order to increase their practice, to distribute in the feeding-troughs the most fantastic drugs. 'This powder immediately makes animals sick. Then they are brought to be cured. In this the Gypsies no doubt succeeded'. Most of these 'healers', again Vidocq tells us, disguised themselves as Dutch horse-copers and their women as Zeeland peasants.

Whether as a robber or as a police officer, Vidocq never harboured any very friendly feelings towards the Gypsies. Although he knew them better than anybody, he was in this respect in tune with public opinion of that time. For him a Gypsy was automatically a criminal. As for the authorities, they clearly went further. A passage in the *Memoirs* of Canler, Head of the Paris Sûreté from 1820, takes Vidocq's descriptions word for word, but also makes the point about the moral credit accorded to the Gypsies of that period:

Now that I have explained what the Paris robbers were, it remains for me to say a few words about two other kinds of people who were no less predacious, no less clever and no less dangerous. The first exploit the whole of Europe, and are called *romanichels*. Women, girls, sons-in-law, daughters-in-law, uncles and aunts travel in all countries like alien merchants under the leadership of the father or, to put it better, of the patriarch of the family These robbers live outside of the society through which they go, taking from the country in which they live neither the language, customs nor manners, having only one aim: robbery; having only one adviser: the most active guile, the most cautious prudence; only one law: the will of the head of the family.

With morals of an utter simplicity, unions are formed between male and female cousins, brother-in-law and sister-in-law, and sometimes between brother and sister in accordance with pure inclination, passing caprice or the burning desire of the moment. A young girl who went to look for a husband or lover outside her family, or who should make the acquaintance of some foreign robber, would at that very instant be pitilessly driven from the fold like a black and rebellious sheep.

Each one, in accordance with his talents and capacity, must cooperate in the main occupation of the family. Men rob by cunning methods or by housebreaking, by scaling walls or with skeleton keys. The women prepare the way for such robberies by introducing themselves into houses under pretext of offering second-hand goods, but in reality to collect information, to become acquainted with the people of the house and afterwards pass on their observations to those individuals deputed to perpetrate the robbery. Furthermore, they practise their trade at the houses of priests and rich farmers, and by a cunning trick[1] (described later), with a skill and dexterity that are prodigious. Finally, the children, girls and boys, under the eye and instruction of their parents, begin their apprenticeship in this baleful way of living very early. In short, the *romanichels* can be compared with those ancient families of Gypsies who go all over the world, living by depredations and their wits: but they have on their predecessors the advantage of making a sham of a profession which, without being real, seems at least to be able to assure them of, it is true, a precarious but adequate existence.

When driven by some dominating circumstances, and the safety of the family makes it imperative for them to separate for a short time, or when they wish to exploit several provinces at the same time, they make an appointment for a definite day on a fair-green. And, to evade all suspicion, they go there one by one like some poor members of a travelling show, or like honest merchants from foreign parts. But, in their tents, in those frail canvas shelters, how many plots have been hatched against other people's property, how many misdeeds have been premeditated, what crimes have been concerted, studied and brought to maturity!

I have just said that the women of this caste [*sic*] devote themselves to thieving by a 'cunning trick', but since the death of the too famous Travaglioni, who was its shrewdest, cleverest and most adroit practitioner, this kind of theft no longer exists in Paris. The term is no longer applied to thefts of diamonds and jewels which was dealt with in the article regarding the Israelite thieves. Here is the manner of procedure.

The trickster would introduce himself to a merchant, a manufacturer or any shopkeeper, to buy an option with a small deposit on such-and-such an old coin of such-and-such a date, or some foreign items, and thus whet the greed of the merchant who, nearly always, promptly accepted this profitable offer, and deposited on his counter several bags of silver, opening them to look for the pieces asked for. The trickster helped him in this quest and, in order to inspire more confidence, pulled up his sleeves and removed his gloves. Bad luck then struck the too confident seller if he should turn his head for one moment, for if this expected distraction should last even a second, a certain number of coins were swallowed up into the thief's pocket, and this movement was so quick that nobody could be aware of it.

To finish with the *romanichels*, I shall add only one particular detail: when one of them should fall into the hands of justice, their whole organized body devotes itself to freeing him. Promises are given, necessary steps and threats by the men follow, and then tears and irresistible wheedlings on the part of the women; all are set working, and it is rare that, among these efforts, one is not found which will bring about the escape of the person imprisoned.

1. Known in France as *le Vol à la carre*. *Tr.*

The great thing in the nineteenth century was to accuse the Gypsies of the theft of children, making of this the standard type of 'bogey-men' with which unbearable brats were threatened. At all times the people suspected of sorcery were proved guilty of kidnapping children to serve in their holocaust at the time of human sacrifices or, more prosaically, to bring them up in the art of begging, or again by breaking their limbs to transform them into unbeatable acrobats. This, in actual fact, was what happened in India. It was also why the imagination of that credulous nineteenth century gave excessive importance to it, to the point of making it one of the leitmotives of the popular novel of the end of the century. For, if it was found amusing that Figaro was carried off by the 'Gypsies', people read with emotion in the *Magasin pittoresque* of the year 1861 this incredible description:

In the middle of the band is seated the chief, with his brown skin and sinister face, giving a grimacing smile to the pink-white stolen child who sits weeping on his hard knees. Swarthy women, fortune-tellers, companions of these professional bandits, joyfully welcome the little creature and hasten like fairies to the cradle of a prince: one will teach him songs and dances, another will train him to play the tambourine or the harp; this one promises to initiate him in the mysteries of palmistry or in the art of turning up infallible cards; that one will give him a present of a black fowl and a toad, accomplice and oracle of horoscopes. The child will be a female mountebank or witch, a male thief, or will cast spells.

This systematic association of Gypsies with rascals occurs even in French dictionaries. In one of the most representative[1] of them, the article on *Bohémien* – on 'Gypsy' that is – confines itself to associating the Gypsies with 'all sorts of mountebanks, beggars and other people without either profession or fixed residence, who wander about the countryside and whose presence too often causes anxiety to those who live on farms or in isolated houses'.

Here, finally, is the typical picture of the Gypsy woman as conceived by authors, and then by the public, at that period. All the stock phrases are mustered in it, and it is indeed in these clichés that we are interested here:

Old Gypsy women represent the perfect model of the stereotype witch with hooked nails, dirty grey and dishevelled hair protruding like

1. *Dictionnaire Universel de la Vie Pratique à la Ville et à la Campagne* (1882).

a horse's tail from a sordid turban, her eyes dull, with the grin of a wild beast, and clothes in rags and tatters. Do you see this horrible witch bending over the stove? Her eyes are fixed on the smoke escaping from a torch which she has prepared from a mixture of cypress, emblem of welcome, of cedar, which conjures up evil spirits, and of incense in honour of beneficent deities. It is a day of festivity, and the cake made of white of egg, which plays so great a role in witchcraft, stimulates the decision of the wise gods, Turkish and Christian; for the Gypsy believes in everything, in Mahomet and in Christ, and above all in those good fairies who tell us happy stories and of favourable things to happen.

The women, with matt complexion, bedecked with necklaces, letting loose their hair, reflecting a blue colour like the wing of a crow and escaping from a kerchief of golden material tied round the head, anxiously follow the direction taken by the smoke which quickly drifts towards some blades of wheat fixed between two beams. Everyone holds his breath. And only the old crone over her stove pronounces some magical words.

If the bent straw inclines towards the torch without catching fire, that is a sign of good luck. But if it is swallowed up in the column of smoke and turns down as far as the flame and burns – oh, then, that is something calamitous. The cake made of white of egg is thrown away and ill fortune follows. Those present, their stomachs empty and their minds full of hallucinations, make haste to flee from the accursed house.[1]

GYPSIES AND ROMANTICISM

These various elements in the stereotyped portrait of the Gypsy have all been used in the literature of the romantic movement, giving proof of a little poetry, if not of real understanding. Romanticism discovered the myth of the child of Bohemia, the eternal wanderer. The poets of the romantic movement, from their homes and their own narrow world, have sung with a nostalgia inspired by the nomadic life. The love of freedom, the reaction against the monotony and routine, the taste for novelty, for the unexpected, and for risk,[2] inveigled not only authentic vagabond intellectuals, but the majority of studious writers into the quest of a new inner world.

In France there were Nodier, Richepin, Hugo, Nerval, Merimée, Gautier and Baudelaire . . . who dreamed of setting out at the mercy of the roads, behind wheeled wagons, and sharing in the life of the Gypsies. Victor Hugo, in creating his Gypsy girl Esmeralda from

1. Neukomm, *Les Bohémiens chez eux* (1898).
2. As Max Sorre has shown in *Les Migrations des peuples* (1955).

documents which are themselves very romantic, nonetheless released the Gypsy woman from the curses which the people had so long imputed to her. Merimée, in forming the first Carmen from an indestructible line of spurious Gypsies, sincerely did his best to communicate something of the accused race's splendour. But Théophile Gautier remains the author whose sincere love of the Gypsies most carried him away. His *Voyage en Espagne*, published in 1840, represents a remarkable effort of understanding, and a manifest care for truth to which writers had not made us accustomed. If the Gypsies are the least romantic people in nineteenth-century French literature, they are certainly the most human. Admirably assisted by Gustave Doré's talent, Gautier has left us a very arresting picture of the *Gitanos* of the Monte Sagrado:

Their swarthy complexion brings out the clarity of their oriental eyes, which are tempered by I do not know what mysterious sadness, like the memory of an absent motherland and of a fallen grandeur. Their lips, rather thick, strongly coloured, recall the bloom of African lips. The small forehead and aquiline nose show the common origin of *Gitanos* and the Gypsies of Walachia and Bohemia. . . . Nearly all of them have such a natural majesty in their carriage, and freedom in their bearing, and they look so well when squatting on their haunches that, in spite of rags, dirt and poverty, they seem to be conscious of the antiquity and purity of their race, free from any mixture. . . .

Natural characteristics thus become one of the essential themes of the romantic myth, and behind the still reticent vocabulary of Gautier was already appearing the erotic objective which the poets would choose: the uncivilized fierce girl with brown skin, burning eyes, scorning all make-up and affectation, whose beauty shines by the lustre of her flesh. In France it was the period in which it was good form to have a dark-skinned mistress, and to paint young beggar-girls whose rags permitted the treasures of their delicate flesh to be perceived.

As for Baudelaire, although he preferred his negress to the *Gitanes*, he was not less susceptible to the Gypsy myth. His poem[1] will be remembered:

> The prophetic tribe with burning eyes
> Took the road yesterday, carrying the children

1. *Bohémiens en voyage* ('Gypsies Travelling'?). The above is a literal translation into plain prose. *Tr.*

On its back, or giving to their fierce appetites
The ever ready treasure of pendent breasts.

The men go on foot bearing their sparkling weapons
Along by the wagons in which their families huddle;
Scanning the sky with eyes dulled
By the sad regret for missing chimeras.

From the depths of his sandy retreat the cricket
Watches them pass, redoubles his song;
Cybele, who loves them, redoubles her ventures,
Makes water flow from the cliff to flower the desert
Before these travellers, for whom is opened
The familiar empire of future darkness.

The poem is far from being the best ever written on the Gypsies. On the other hand, a writer whom some regard as a minor one, I mean Richepin, has been able to put into his novel *Miarka, the Girl with the Bear,* however like a popular serial story it may be, more original and especially more accurate characteristics of the world of these people. Behind the rather naïve fiction, in this book appears a knowledge and understanding of the life of these wanderers that is indeed rare in romantic literature. In these pages an ethnologist will find something worth while.

In England, the great precentor of the Gypsies is a remarkable and still little known personage, George Borrow.[1] It is to him that the Gypsies owe a great part of their success in romantic literature. It was he who made fashionable the rather out-of-date but charming formula: the Gypsy is the cuckoo of society, of whom everybody speaks ill but without whom the world would be sad.[2]

Borrow, who led so exemplary a picaresque life that many picaresque heroes could well envy him, applied himself to describing the customs of the Spanish *Gitanos,* the *Zincali,* as they were then called, and did so with great love and sympathetic consideration. In 1817 (he was then only fourteen years of age), he loitered about those parts of Norwich frequented by wanderers, Italian barometer-makers and Gypsy horse-dealers. On Mousehold Heath he mixed with the Gypsies in their camps, and found that he was granted the rare privilege of being allowed into their tents. These Gypsies were

1. Little known in France, that is; yet in 1956 René Fréchet published an excellent biography, *George Borrow.*

2. See Borrow's *The Romany Rye,* Chapter IX, for this reference to the cuckoo. *Tr.*

the Smiths: they spoke English, took local names, but among themselves conversed only in *romaní*. His presence being tolerated, the young Borrow decided to live with them in the hillside dens. He learnt their dialect and browned his face with walnut-stain, the better to pass unnoticed. At sixteen years of age he was studying Welsh, Scandinavian, Arabic and Hebrew. Seized by intellectual voracity, he was able to read the Talmud in the original a year later.

In 1825 he left London to make a journey on foot across England. He bought a light cart and donkey and became an itinerant tinsmith, but at first had some disagreements with Gypsies who were jealous of this unexpected competition. He fell in love with a handsome solitary Gypsy woman, who took him for mad; to seduce her, he recited the full conjugation of the verb 'to love' in Armenian!

Abandoning himself to the joys of open-air work as a tinsmith, Borrow made his way across France and southern Europe. It was then that he discovered the only congenial occupation in which he could become engaged: selling Bibles from door to door. This enabled him to go as far as Russia, and to live for five years in the Iberian Peninsula. At last in 1841 he published *The Zincali*,[1] a work of capital importance on the psychology of the Spanish *Gitanos*. In later books[1] he continued to devote himself to the Gypsy problem, but in a more literary way. Borrow's work is important, not merely because of the passion with which it was received in England, but also because of the impetus which it gave to the gypsiology dawning at that time. Although in fact a considerable number of writers, from Shakespeare to Walter Scott, had taken notice of the Gypsies, it was only as setting for operetta, or strictly in opera, without caring for anything but the picturesque.

In Spain the romantic vogue of the merry Gypsy does not date from the nineteenth century. In fact, although '*gitanismo*' – the Gypsy cult – was flourishing in the 1830s, particularly in Andalusia (to the point that some monks composed poems in *caló*, the dialect of the Spanish Gypsies), one has to go back to the period of Cervantes to find the golden age of the Gypsy hero. In his Exemplary Novel *La Gitanilla* ('the little Gypsy girl'), Cervantes has recourse to the *Gitanos* on which to hang his love for the free life, and his way of confronting reality in all its aspects, even the most daring. He makes his heroine say: 'The spirit of the Gypsy people follows another

1. See Bibliography, p. 270, which gives titles and dates.

course than that of other races. It always goes further than the number of their years. There is no such thing as a Gypsy blockhead, or a silly Gypsy girl. To follow the Gypsy way of life is to show oneself as prudent, astute and a liar. Consequently they use their tricks at every turn and don't allow themselves to get all rusty.' Nevertheless, Cervantes insists on the very personal notion of property which characterizes the Gypsies, and does this so that we dare not reproach him: 'It seems that the Gypsies, men and women, are on earth only to be thieves. They are born of robber fathers, brought up for thieving, educate themselves for it, and end up nicely as full-blown thieves. The liking for knavish tricks and for knavery itself are mishaps which only death itself cures.' This quality is indeed the attribute of rascals, with the humour indispensable to those who live by their wits. Recent researches[1] have disclosed that an aunt of Cervantes was a *gitana* by birth.

In Germany the romantic Gypsies made their appearance in the works of Grimmelshausen (*Simplicius Simplicissimus*), of Moscherosch, Reuter, and Achim von Arnim. It is not possible here to list the Gypsy characters in the whole of German literature; nor those in Russian literature. I shall be satisfied with calling to mind Achim von Arnim's novel *Isabella of Egypt*, one of the most representative works of the Gypsy cult in Germany.

This story tells of the love of the young *Zigeunerin* and the Archduke Charles, the future Charles V. In reality, Isabella is only the daughter of a Gypsy father; her mother was a Dutch noblewoman who was only too susceptible to the advances of a 'Duke' Michael of Egypt (that very one who is mentioned in the chronicles). At the end of this long short story, Isabella becomes queen of the 'Egyptians', and in an ecstasy sees the future of her people. The novel *Isabella of Egypt* is dated 1811. But, as early as 1805, Achim von Arnim had begun to interest himself in the Gypsies; he had been able to meet important groups of them and some engaging Gypsy personalities during the war with France (1806–7). He had praised them in a dissertation on popular poetry, even presenting them as gallant soldiers, and good medical doctors (which is not without piquancy). Then he had discovered Grellman's work (*Historischer Versuch über die Zigeuner*) which had appeared at Leipzig in 1783. Reading this book was to him a revelation of nearly

1. Walter Starkie, *Cervantes and the Gypsies* (1960). See also Bibliography, pp. 272–3.

everything which the gypsiology of the period could teach, and to a slight degree modified his opinions about these nomad people. What most struck him was the legend (then persistently circulated both by Grellmann and by the Gypsies themselves) according to which these people were condemned to wander about the earth for not having aided the Holy Family. Von Arnim decided to give them an important place in his work, but by transforming that myth of the curse into a theme of redemption. Whereupon he invented the prophecy which concludes *Isabella of Egypt*: that one day the Gypsies would again find their motherland, led by the son of a Gypsy princess and a powerful sovereign.[1]

With the exception of Borrow, not one of these writers really knew the Gypsy state of life. Their description of this people is restricted to popular beliefs and, for the best informed of them, to works published by the pioneer gypsiologists. This myth of the romantic Gypsy, nevertheless, continues on its grotesque course, which future garrison-societies will have great difficulty in stopping.

1. See de Guignard's preface to Achim von Arnim's *Isabella von Aegypten* (1950).

1. Type of Indian Gypsy. Gypsies are still numerous in India, and their primitive way of life is familiar to us because of the tribes which came to Europe.

2–4. Various Gypsy types: Left, a Spanish *Gitana*.

3. French *Manouche* from the Lyons area.

4. French *Gitan*, probably from North Africa.

5–6. Gypsy costumes. During their migration, many Gypsies adopted the costumes and customs of the various countries where they went: 19th-century travellers were astonished to meet Balkan musicians (above), or Turkish smiths (below), whose appearance called to mind the more distant East.

7. Roumanian Gypsies in traditional dress.

8. Roumanian Gypsy. Today the traditionalist Roumanian Gypsies jealously conserve the way of dress which their ancestors borrowed from the peasants. Their head-dress and way of wearing the hair, like 'Men of the Woods', was described in early 19th-century documents.

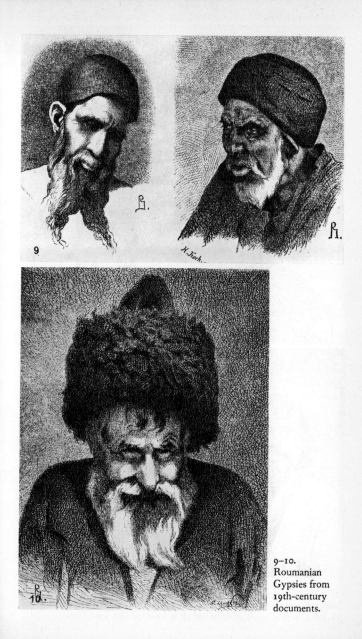

9–10.
Roumanian
Gypsies from
19th-century
documents.

11–12. Gypsy types. Three of the great variety to be met in Europe during the romantic age of travel. They could sometimes be taken for Jews and, in fact, many of them had close contacts with local Jews.

13. Moldo-Walachian driver. The Danube region, formerly known as
Moldavia-Walachia, or Moldo-Walacia, was a very important Gypsy centre.
They still borrow local customs there, such as the costume of this Gypsy
wagon or caravan driver of the 18th century.

14. Fortune-telling. Gypsies were known in Western Europe in the 15th century, when they were already engaged in palmistry and divination, feared but much sought after.

15. Literature and Gypsy myth. In his *Roman Comique*, Scarron makes his hero Ragotin and Captain Charles meet. Charles, a chief of the 'Bohemians', did in fact exist.

16. The Three German Gypsies. Romantic poetry, especially in Germany, has sung of the Gypsies, heroes of a life free from all constraint and close to nature. Thus has Lenau immortalized the *Drei Zigeuner*.

Au bout du comte ils treuuent pour desiun
Qu'ils sont venuz d'Aegipte ace [...]

17. 17th-century Gypsies – engraving by Jacques Callot (d. 1635). In the
17th century, nobody understood the Gypsies better than the French painter
and engraver, Jacques Callot. He is known to have lived with them. His
engravings have the precision of ethnographic documents.

18–19. Gypsy wagons, tents and camps.

20–21. Though the dispersion of the Gypsies lasted for some thousand years, it maintained a constant nature. The heavy-wheeled wagons of Walachia, drawn by oxen, were later replaced by caravans; but their tents, pitched on the outskirts of the great Ottoman Empire fairs, are still being used on the banks of the Danube (see overleaf).

22. Spanish Gypsies. In Spain the journey continues. Here the Gitanos adopted the Mediterranean donkey, an admirable means of transport for less fortunate wanderers.

3 · Occupations

CHOICE OF OCCUPATIONS

With a few variations, the Gypsies are first and foremost smiths and workers in metals, musicians and mountebanks, horse-copers and dealers, exhibitors of animals and fortune-tellers. These occupations will duly be dealt with in detail. But here and now it must be stated that there is a definite continuity in the way the Gypsies choose their occupations, which seem far removed from one another. One question insistently arises: why have the Gypsies at all times and everywhere been smiths, musicians and horse-copers?

Let us go back to India. The system of castes, and its strict occupational divisions, formerly condemned the pariahs and outcasts to keep to occupations which were distasteful to the upper castes, because of religious taboos, economic balance or, quite simply, as a matter of taste. If we take for reference the list of curses and occupational prohibitions contained in the collection of the Laws of Manu,[1] which dates from the first century before Jesus Christ, it will be seen that the Gypsies have followed precisely those occupations that were cursed by Manu.

It is necessary, say the Laws, to beware of 'those who engage in disgraceful occupations, those who practise the trade of mountebank' (VIII, 102); to do away with 'thieves who publicly show themselves', that is, 'falsifiers, players [of games of chance], fortune-tellers, chiromancers' (IX, 258–259); to avoid carefully 'a man who trains elephants, bulls, horses or camels, and a professional astrologer ...' (III, 162); 'a breeder of dogs that are trained to perform for entertainment' (III, 164); 'a professional dancer' (III, 155). 'Gaming [literally, dice], singing, dancing, instrumental music and unnecessary journeys [sic] are the five most abhorred vices' (VII, 47). 'Trading in horses, cows or wagons renders families vile' (III, 64).

1. *Manava Dharma Sastra* or 'Laws of Manu', translated into French by Loiseleur-Deslongchamps (no date).

'A Brahman could not receive food from a smith (even from a) goldsmith or silversmith . . .' (IV, 215), etc.

In fact, from the time of Maurya – the fourth to the second centuries B.C. – the occupations of actor, juggler and acrobat, etc. were regarded as 'unproductive' and on this account were banned by a society already divided into close guilds and corporations;[1] which, moreover, in no way impeded the development of these professions. Yet those who were engaged in them inevitably found themselves driven into the ranks of the untouchables. Such were the *Sarvades*, fortune-tellers, who carried on their back a particular kind of drum with one head; and in their pocket, I dare say, astrological almanacs. Also the *Tamasha-Wallah* (in Persian 'showmen'), sleight of hand men, trainers of bears and monkeys, nomad packmen.[2] Also the *Ghasis*, musicians, whose women sold cures clandestinely, and probably drugs for abortion. Finally the Gypsies who accepted this 'accursed and necessary' part.

But all the occupations hit by the interdict of Manu were not adopted by the Gypsies. It must be stated immediately that they chose those which were suitable for a particular form of nomadism: migrations and invasions. It was necessary, for example, that the Mongol hordes, Tartars or others, should arrange to be accompanied by people capable of forging weapons, shoeing horses, caring for animals, repairing vehicles and amusing the soldiers; they needed smiths, farriers, healers, musicians, dancing women. . . .

Another explanation of the choice of occupation made by the Gypsies is of a more subtle kind: this is a matter of the relationship divulged by modern ethnologists and mythologists between the arts of the forge, and of music and magic. In the section on the Gypsies and the forge, it has been seen (page 36) how Mircea Eliade, for example, has seized on this link. A Mongol poem exalts the smiths in these terms:

> . . . Powerful is the magic of the forge,
> Admirable are the marvels
> Of your powerful bellows.
> Oh ye nine white smiths of Boshinjoj,
> On your nine white horses,
> The spark from your forge is supreme.[3]

1. See Panikkar, *Histoire d'Inde* (1958).
2. MacMunn, *Mœurs et coutumes des basses classes de l'Inde* (1934).
3. Lambert, *Trésor de la poésie universelle* (1959).

One would never come to an end of mentioning all the examples there are of smiths as magicians. There were the famous *Dactyli* of Mount Ida who were workers in iron at the same time as they were reputed to be mountebanks and healers.[1] So also the Kalderash, Gypsy smiths and workers in metals, who first taught their women the arts of sorcery and chiromancy. In our own time in Poitou, the cauldron-maker is said to be a carrier of *drouines*, a word in the local patois which means at one and the same time 'cauldron' and 'witch'.[2] In the Balkan countries the peasants have more confidence in the Gypsy blacksmiths than in veterinary surgeons; they prefer the former for treatment of their cattle.

Even shoeing-smiths are implicated in this connexion, since they profit from both the prestige of the blacksmith and from the symbolism which has crystallized round the horse, a psycho-ceremonial animal.[3] The horse-coper or dealer is also linked to this tradition, and it may be useful to note that in ancient China the initiates for distinction had the title of 'horse-trader'.[4] As for the exhibitor of bears (or, as we shall call him from now, the 'bear-leader'), it would not be far wrong to put him on a parallel with the indigenes of the little Shamanist tribes who had to solemnize rites in the cult of this totemistic animal. But let us stop here to consider more prosaically how the various occupations of the Gypsies are practised.

GYPSY BLACKSMITHS AND WORKERS IN METALS

We must first of all keep in mind, in accordance with their distinctive functions, the various kinds of smiths and metal-workers: the (black) smith who works with a hammer and at the forge (as well as the one who works 'cold', that is, without the help of fire); the tinsmith or coppersmith who works in sheet-metal or copper, riveted or hammered out (work to which may nowadays be added, for some Gypsies, the same operations on an industrial scale); the 'tinner' or plater who covers objects with tin-plating or any other inoxidizable metal (many are content to re-tin or re-plate such objects); the silversmith who embosses or engraves pieces of jewellery; the

1. Alleau, *Aspects de l'alchimie traditionelle* (1957).
2. Boutellier, *Sorciers et jeteurs de sort* (1958); *Chamanisme et guérison magique* (1950).
3. Eliade, *Forgerons et alchimistes* (1959).
4. Duchaussoy, *Le Bestiaire divin ou la Symbolique des animaux* (1958).

modern tinplater; the maker of edge-tools and other implements; the enameller; the gold-washer who collects alluvial gold from rivers; and the coiner, the man who makes false coins. The highly skilled metal-working craftsman, in fact, who has taken an important place in Gypsy industry.

The Gypsies were conspicuous as smiths as soon as they appeared in our civilization. The cauldron-makers of Corfu are remembered and the shoeing-smiths who have been known in Serbia since the fourteenth century. Jules Bloch even pinpoints the fact that 'the link between India and Greece was made by the cauldron-makers, the *Gaodari* of Astarabad, south of the Caspian, and the Gypsies of the Khorassan (north-east of Iran), who were chain-menders and, at the same time, makers of combs and sieves'.

It was indeed in India that the Gypsies learnt how to work in metals. As Eliade reminds us, the beginning of so-called industrial metallurgy (that is, using terrestrial iron, and no longer iron from meteors) can be fixed at some time between the years 1200–1000 B.C., and its cradle was situated in the Armenian Mountains. 'It was from there that the secret of fusion spread across the Near East, along the Mediterranean and to Central Europe.'

In India the primitive tribes of Gypsy smiths at first worked with extremely rudimentary resources. Following the examples of the *Rasa-Bediya*,[1] who to this day make the bauble-jewellery of the poor Mussulmans, they used three stones as a hearth, a bellows worked with the toes, and wood-charcoal as fuel. This was likewise the technique of the nomad smiths of Central Asia who followed the Tartar armies in their campaigns. So it was that old Djartchi'oudai, the personal blacksmith of Genghis Khan, carried his bellows on his back.[2] And so it was the Gypsies astonished the people of Central Europe with the diminutiveness of their working-equipment. In the nineteenth century this precarious set of tools had hardly progressed in evolution; witness the following report which appeared in 1859 in the *Journal des Demoiselles*: a Gypsy 'is repairing old pots and goes from door to door with a portable forge to ask for work. One stone serves him as an anvil, and he has two bellows, two pincers, a file, a vice, a hammer, all roughly made by himself; these are the only tools he uses. He works at his little forge, sitting on the ground with

1. Perhaps in the region of Chota Nagpur, an ancient mining region where the *Asur* were themselves well-known smiths.

2. See Grousset, *Le Conquérant du Monde* (1944).

legs crossed, while the women and children work the bellows'.

It is not so much the poverty of this stone anvil which astonishes us. Evidently it weighed less than one of cast-iron, but it was far more fragile. Martin Block had described the same set of Gypsy tools, but in Romania and well into the twentieth century:

The anvil is about eight inches long and three wide; it is half sunk into the ground. By way of bellows a goatskin is used, the hair inside, the legs furnished with wooden pegs. A specially contrived slit at the top to open and shut assured the functioning of this instrument. The compressed air escaped through the pipe which took it through one of the wooden pegs to the foot of the goatskin. Formerly a hole was made for the fire and in there the pipe-end of the bellows was placed. Today the blacksmith works on flat ground and makes the air-pipes pass through an earthenware device about five inches high. The man works sitting 'like our tailors', say the documents of 1496. He holds the bellows in his left hand and the pincers or small tongs gripping the object being forged in his right. This immemorial picture has not changed; our ancestors saw it over five hundred years ago. The bellows has remained exactly the same as it was in Asia Minor, from which it may well have been brought by the Gypsies.

With this very limited working stock the Gypsies succeeded (and still succeed) in making a considerable number of articles for domestic and agricultural use – from needles for sewing sacks to Dutch ovens. In Eastern and Central Europe, the Gypsy smiths are itinerant during the greater part of the year, but they spend the winter on the outskirts of villages, where they make their camps of tents and wheeled wagons, or sometimes they rent houses or hut-ments. As for the shoeing-smiths and locksmiths,[1] their trade has compelled them mostly to abandon the road and become sedentary. There are few Romanian villages, for example, which do not have their Gypsy smith with his forge. Some of them even have a 'Gypsy Street'.

The European Gypsy tin-platers seem to have come from Turkey, where their stay was no doubt of long duration. Yet their dialect contains, apart from many Turkish words, many Armenian terms. These Gypsies, the *Costorari*, are known by their very strict observance of the laws and customs of their people.

Wlislocki[2] describes the primitive means employed by the Gypsy

1. The *Ferari, Potcovari, Mesteri-Lacatuchi*. . . .
2. *Vom Wandernden Zigeunervolke* (Hamburg, 1890).

gold-washers in the rivers of Hungary and Romania: a long grooved plank is plunged into the river facing the current, and the grooves retain sand and grit which are emptied into an open trough; there the particles of gold are collected with the aid of a ball of clay. At any rate, this is the technique of the *Zlatari*, *Aurari* or *Rudari* Gypsies.

It is often other Gypsy smiths who take on the work of turning this gold into jewellery. Let us still note that some of these *Zlatari*, paradoxically deprived of work after the abolition of slavery, were to become counterfeiters and coiners. They were evidently very clever and found nothing wrong about taking full advantage of the Romanian peasants who, according to an old tradition, simply loved necklets made of coins.

In western Europe, particularly in France, it is the same Gypsies who work in metals, as English and French folk-lore attest. Indeed, at least in France, their guilds were organized and powerful enough to prohibit this foreign competition. In the eighteenth century, for example, royal enactments regulated the conditions of those working as tin- and coppersmiths and as makers of kitchen utensils. An edict of 1735 declared that it was forbidden 'under penalty of fifty livres fine, for pedlars to hawk tin or coppersmiths' work in the Auvergne country and to all others, without qualification, to take to their own place of residence pieces to be plated and repaired': they were permitted only 'to plate and repair them at the doors and in the houses of the particular people to whom the said pieces belong'.[1]

This order had a double effect: on the one hand, it prevented the Gypsies from settling as artisan-smiths (even if they were likely to want to), and, on the other, it offered them the possibility of engaging in an officially approved kind of work without thereby breaking with their nomad circumstances. Very quickly the work done by the itinerant tinsmith, coppersmith and metal-plater tacitly became a Gypsy monopoly, and remained so until the recent advent of mass-produced goods.

Among other Gypsy craftsmen in metallurgy may be mentioned the tin-platers (Western Europe), the makers of cast-iron spoons (Hungary and Romania), of hoppers for mills (France), etc. But the appearance of machine-made articles very quickly eliminated these occupations. Although wandering smiths are still to be found in French villages, the Gypsies are now obliged to yield to the exi-

1. *Dictionnaire ou Traité de la Police générale des villes, bourgs, paroisses* ... (Paris, 1775).

gencies of industrial civilization: some have become specialists in boiler-making, a trade in which they are highly appreciated as the only workers capable of enduring the exceptionally arduous conditions in the repairing of factory boilers (in the region of Grenoble, for example). However, even these retain an element of nomadism, since they do this work only to order, as they are summoned from one town to the next by their employers, and continue to live in caravans. Others, especially among the young ones, find outlets in garages, where they are very skilled in repairing motor-vehicles. Finally, it must be recorded that the French Army readily trusts them with the plating of its war material.

GYPSY HORSE-TRADERS

The Gypsies follow the cult of the horse, like all the peoples of central and western Asia. The importance of this animal in the mythology of the East is known, and the highly important role it played in the historical and economic connexions between Asia and Europe. The great migrations and invasions were equestrian. In that world of nomads, which was Asia on the move, the horse, at first a royal ornament, became a vital factor for the warriors. It was thanks to their cavalry that the Arabs were able to advance as far as Poitiers in France, and Marco Polo records that the Great Khan of the Mongols had a postal service of three hundred horses strong.

The part played by the horse in Gypsy rites will be seen later, but, without waiting any longer, it is fitting to emphasize now the striking parallels between the beliefs of the Gypsies and those of other Asiatic peoples in regard to this animal. According to Bernard, the Gypsies never say: 'I hope that you will live happily', but: 'May your horses live long'.[1] Like the reindeer in Scandinavian civilizations, the horse is pre-eminently a funerary and psycho-ceremonial animal, for the Gypsies as well as for the whole of the Shamanist groups.[2] At this point only two peculiar aspects of this problem will be dwelt upon: the ritual burial of the horse; and the injunction against eating its meat.

It would be wearisome to list the peoples among whom the horse acts as a funerary element, whether by way of sacrifice or in a more

1. In *Mœurs de Bohémiens de Moldavie et de Valachie* (1869).
2. See Mircea Eliade's studies, already quoted; Malten, *Das Pferd im Totenglauben* (Berlin, 1914); and Durand, *Les Structures anthropologiques de l'Imaginaire*, (1960).

commonplace form by its presence only. Several Indian tribes, in particular the *Bhil*, represent their dead as on horseback.[1] These rites have come as far west as France: at the funeral of Phillipe de Rouvre in 1363, the dead man's horses were led to the altar.[2] Documents are lacking which would inform us how long the Gypsies continued this ritual. Nevertheless, oral tradition of Central European groups takes account of the fact. It is verified in regard to a primitive Gypsy tribe, that of the *Zyghes* (whom Strabo describes under the name of *Sigynnes*) who, after leaving Iran, dispersed as far as the Danube. Alexandre Bertrand, who associated with them in the Caucasus in 1885, ends the account of a funeral ceremony thus:[3]

After the burial of the corpse, for several days at the dinner hour the deceased man's horse was saddled and the order given to the servant to lead it to the new grave, and there to call the deceased three times by his name, to invite him to dinner.

This making of the horse into a sacred animal has passed into dietary ritual: it is strictly forbidden to eat horseflesh, under penalty of becoming mad – a taboo found not only among most of the people of Altaic culture, but likewise among the Irish and English. Christianity itself formerly excommunicated those who transgressed this interdict. Some groups of Gypsies, especially the *Gitanos*, do not observe this law; to such a point do they ignore it that, in the south of France (at Beziers, Saint-Gilles-du-Gard . . .), one finds horseflesh butchers' shops kept by *Gitans*; and Gypsy horse-knackers are on record.[4]

It is always the horse that is the Gypsy's best friend (he has no great affection for the dog). The Gypsy treats his mount, if I may say so, 'as man to man'. He knows his horse admirably and shows himself to be an excellent veterinary surgeon. He is also, of course, a past-master in the art of concealing the animals' defects, as the reader will learn. The Russian gypsiologist Barannikov has been able to write that 'to employ oneself with the horse is the noblest profession and only occupation worthy of a Gypsy'. The poorest tribes in Central Europe, the *Cerhari* and the *Masari*, are accustomed to assert that a Gypsy without a horse is not a Gypsy.

Martin Block maintains that the Gypsies did not begin to be horse-

1. See Mayani *Les Hyksos et le Monde de la Bible* (1956).
2. Duchaussoy, op. cit.
3. See the section on Funeral Rites, p. 230.
4. *Études Tsiganes*, April 1959.

dealers before they had arrived at the plains of Hungary. This is possible, but it has not been proved. It is, in fact, difficult to believe that the Gypsies formerly living on the borders of the Sind country were ignorant of the methods of capturing wild horses, and breeding them, which were used among the Mongols and particularly in the region of Djend, on the Syr-Daria.[1] In any case, there again, documents are lacking.

It is curious to find that, in spite of his love for the horse, the Gypsy is generally a very poor horseman. For him the horse is essentially a draft or pack animal, or one for barter. He is before everything a horse-dealer (*maquignon* in French). Let us note in passing that the etymology of the French word is very doubtful. Dauzat[2] makes it derive from the Dutch *makelaer*, a broker (relating to the German *machen*, to do or make?). Speaking for myself, I see in it a deformation of the old French thieves' cant word *maquier* that we find in Villon and used by the malefactors of the fifteenth century. This in modern French is *maquiller* which means 'to make up a face' or 'to fake a picture'. The exact meaning of *maquignon* is 'he who fakes' or 'makes up' horses in order to sell them. For this is really the true business of the Gypsies, who are not content just to buy and re-sell the animals. Their greatest art and their reputation consists in 'putting right' the beasts which they show at fairs.

It would require a whole volume to list the artifices used by the Gypsies for this purpose. The question has been studied in detail for Hungary by the gypsiologist Kamill Erdös, and from him I borrow the following examples.[3] Thus, the *Lovari* excite the horse by pricking him with a hedgehog before showing him in the market-place. If they have time before the fair is held, they shake pebbles in a pail under the animal's nose until the moment comes when it is almost crazy. At the time of sale, it is enough for the Gypsy to show the pail to the horse, even from a distance, and then the animal will begin to prance like a spirited cavalry charger. In order to make him look mettlesome and hold his tail nicely, the Hungarian Gypsy puts a piece of ginger into his anus, and, to rejuvenate a sorry old nag, the practice is to bore holes in its teeth and fill them with rosemary. To make a horse's breathing good for a short time, he is fed with

1. See Rousselot, *Genghis Khan* (1959).
2. In *Dictionnaire étymologique* (1938).
3. *Gypsy Horse-Dealers in Hungary*, *J.G.L.S.* XXXVIII, 1–2. See Bibliography.

solanacæ (henbane) mixed with (elder-?) berries. For one who is not a veterinary surgeon, it is difficult to differentiate in the list of Gypsy nostrums between the function of sympathetic magic and that of the official pharmacopoeia. Thus, to cause a horse to urinate, he is made to eat a fistful of grass mixed with paprika. If the animal is constipated, they make him drink salted meat-juice.

In any case, a horse entrusted to Gypsies for a time comes from their hands unrecognizable. And what is most surprising is that the peasants of Central Europe, where horse-faking is now strictly prohibited, continue for preference to go to the Gypsies for the purchase of their horses. Those peasants also recognize, in spite of the almost certainty of trickery, the innate knowledge of horses which these nomads have. In actual practice, the Gypsy horse-dealers act more and more as simple intermediaries (*censar*) and the peasants readily give them a commission (*mita*) because they are the only dealers who know the current state of the market, the animals available, the trade prices, the breeds of horses in demand, and this not only in the prospective region but far beyond its boundaries. They have in fact a remarkable information system, one which is permanently functioning. The transactions in which they become involved are certainly not exempt from obscure machinations in which the peasant is not capable of putting up a struggle. Often a horse that has been bought in apparently perfect condition turns out after some days to be a wretched old screw; the drugs and dopings have ceased to produce their effect. But, as for finding the Gypsy who has sold the beast – there is no question of that. In the eyes of the countrymen, Gypsies have the deplorable quality of all looking alike, and the law of silence is taken much more seriously among them than in our social surroundings. It even happens that the Gypsy who has sold a 'Rosinante' will follow it wherever it goes, and buy it back, in order once again to change it into a frisky mare.

On the other hand, the sale of horses, at least in Central Europe, takes place at special horse-fairs which evidently end in more or less prolonged gatherings in the taverns where other Gypsies are singing and dancing. The Gypsy horse-dealers quickly win back at gambling the money paid to a peasant as the price of his horse. Hazards common enough in business! It is very rare that the Gypsies will buy horses from one another, or sell them to other Gypsies. Knowing too well what lies beneath the surface of this trading, not one of them will do this kind of business. If there should nevertheless happen to be a transaction, it is never accompanied by any promise whatever, and is embellished with protestations of good faith as long as litanies.

Without on this account cutting into the province of Gypsy beliefs, it must be noted here that this horse business is accompanied in most tribes (particularly the *Lovari* of Walachia) by strict rituals which nothing in the world would cause to be overlooked. The preparations for setting out for the market are the object of special precautions: no money must leave the wagon or caravan; eating is not permitted (sometimes throughout the duration of the fair); women are forbidden to pass in front of the wagon; when the latter moves off, a piece of bread or girdle-cake is thrown on to it; if a rabbit or a cat crosses the road, this is a sign that business will be bad, etc.[1]

In these pages I have dwelt on the horse-copers of Central Europe, but similar characteristics are recorded in the Ukraine, Finland, England, Scotland, Ireland and even in Chile. However, the trade is on the way to dying out and the Gypsies have now been guided by a very logical transfer of interest to the new means of transport: the automobile. They became dealers in second-hand vehicles and 'breakers' who sell the metal parts of old cars, etc. Their hereditary gifts for faking easily find material on which to function in this occupation.

Let us finally mention that, in England, the love of horses (which, moreover, came from the Islamic Orient) gave birth (at Chester) in 1511 to the first horse-races. The turf remained an exclusively British sport until the nineteenth century, and England is the only country in the world to record some Gypsy jockeys – a small number of them, it must be admitted.

GYPSY BEAR-LEADERS

After the horse, the bear is the second totemistic animal of the Gypsies. As will be seen, it is a familiar figure in their folk-lore and magic.

Professor Vukanovic, who has made a close study of the bear-leaders (*Ursuari* in *romanī*, *oursiers* in French, both meaning 'bear-men', or 'bear-leaders' as gypsiologists usually call them) in the

1. For further details, see Kamill Erdös, op. cit.; and *Magie des Tzigane hongrois*, Review *Psyché*, No. 116.

Balkan peninsula,[1] recounts a curious legend still current among the nail-makers of the Aleksinak region in Siberia: a young virgin (*detarbandji*) became pregnant without ever having had any amorous relations. Horrified by this misfortune, she decided to drown herself. But a man suddenly surged from the water and told her not to be frightened by that pregnancy, for she would give birth to an animal capable of working like a man. And the young girl gave birth to a bear. The Gypsies of her tribe consented to bring up the animal and they taught it to dance and do innumerable tricks. After that, all the Gypsies became exhibitors of bears. (An identical legend, honoured by the same Gypsies, attributes to the monkey a similar miraculous birth.)

This belief could easily be connected with certain animistic myths of Asiatic peoples. One finds, for example, in the mythology of the *Dolganes* of Siberia, the mention of a woman giving birth to two reindeer, animals which also help man in his work. Mircea Eliade, who calls attention to this among other facts, connects it with the old cult of the Mother of Animals, which is found again as far away as the Caucasus and in Armenia, linked to the ancient matriarchy which Gypsy societies have inherited.

But this is not the place to suggest a 'bear civilization' in the same way as one speaks of a reindeer civilization. Let us limit ourselves, and draw attention merely to the bear festivals among the *Ostiaks* that are accompanied by dances consisting of 'a sort of body-twisting and shaking of the limbs, mostly the arms, movements of which the meaning is today incomprehensible but seem to resemble a kind of display or the motions of an attack'.[2] And there are the *Orotches* of the River Tumen who, like the *Oroks* of Sakhalin, capture young bear cubs, rear them up, and walk them through the villages before sacrificing them in the arena.[3] It is not far from the mark to see in the training of bears by the Gypsies a commonplace derivation for this 'bear ceremonialism'.

It is indeed not easy to see any direct line of consanguinity between the Gypsy bear-leaders of Western Asia and those of Eastern Europe. It may be that, blinded by an excessive mass of facts, we do not see a simpler truth: just as they discovered horses in the Hun-

1. *Gypsy Bear-leaders in the Balkan peninsula, J.G.L.S.* xxxviii, 3–4.
2. Karjalainen, *Jugralaisten uskonto* – in Finnish (1918).
3. Uno Harva, *Représentations religieuses des peuples altaïques* (1959).

garian steppes, so it is not hard to believe that the Gypsies may have found bears in the Sub-Carpathian Mountains.[1] It was in fact in the Balkans that, as early as the Middle Ages, Gypsy bear-leaders were noticed by the ancestors of the Albanian *Veliqui*, belonging to the tribe of *Berishi*.[2] Some gypsiologists are more inclined to believe that these bear-leaders, known by the name of *Oursari*, are the descendants of Gypsies who came from Turkey, the *Zapari*, who, according to Paspati, wintered near the villages, worked at shoeing horses, and wandered during the rest of the year exhibiting bears and monkeys.

In any case, the territory most preferred by the Gypsy bear-leaders remains the Balkan Peninsula – up to our own time. They are all nomads, but their nomadism has taken a particular form. It was indeed long the custom for the women and children to remain in camp, from which the men left in little groups, of from two to five, for the roads to show their animals. During the bad season, or when bears were lacking, they returned to the camp and devoted themselves to their forges and shoeing of horses.

To obtain these bears, the Balkan Gypsies generally have recourse to non-Gypsy hunters who make an occupation of beating the mountains that are rich in big game. All the same, there are groups of Gypsies who are themselves hunters. The bear-hunt, evidently a collective effort, lays claim, apart from great skill, to a deep knowledge of the magical rites associated with hunting; and once again these rites are not unrelated to the traditions of Siberia and upper Asia. And the women, especially those indisposed, must not in any circumstances go near to the hunters before their departure.

In the East of Serbia the hunters bring in front of the bear's den a cake made of maize, and quite hot. When the animal comes out of its hiding-place, attracted by the aroma, the Gypsies begin to withdraw slowly, taking the cake; and the bear follows. As the men and the beast reach a good distance from the grotto, one of the Gypsies remains hidden, goes into the lair and takes away the little cubs. In the Carpathians the cake is replaced by a beehive, which is suspended from the highest branch of a tree, not far from the den. Hanging by a strong rope under the beehive is a barrel full of water. Finally, at the foot of the tree are planted some sharp-pointed spears;

1. Non-Gypsy bear-leaders have been recorded in all Europe well before the appearance of the Gypsies.
2. Vukanovic, op. cit.

and the hunters conceal themselves. The bear comes prowling round the tree, then he climbs it and, as he goes up, he comes upon the barrel of water which he tries to push aside. The barrel is balanced like a punching-ball. The bear again pushes it with more and more force until the moment comes when the barrel hits him and he loses his balance. He then falls on the spears and is transfixed. Finally, in other Balkan regions the Gypsies use a bowl of plum alcohol to make the animal drunk and send him to sleep. Once captured, the bears have their teeth pulled out with pincers. The young are then led to the camp for a cruel course of training. Without knowing that they are using the Pavlov technique, the Gypsy *Oursari* make the animal walk on a sheet of hot metal, with a stick well in sight, and to the sound of a drum. The reflex which makes the bear perform, on the mere appearance of these two instruments, is quickly acquired. He is then made to nod or wag his head, to advance as steps are counted, and even to mount a bicycle or motor-cycle. Once trained, the bears are led away for public display by the men (never by the women – another old taboo).

But this trade of the itinerant bear-leader is beginning to disappear. Before the Second World War, many of us were still able to see these showmen by the Pyrenees. Most of them have changed their occupation or, if fortune has smiled on them, they have entered the realm of the circus.

There is one curious point to which I must return, as it relates to the religion of the Gypsy bear-leaders in the Balkans. As one will see, the Gypsies in general have a great capacity for adapting themselves, and easily submit to the rules of religion observed in the countries where they live, or are crossing. In the Balkan Peninsula, which was so long under Turkish domination, the bear-leaders practised two religions: they were Mahometans in public and Christians in private, this opportunist position not impeding them, moreover, from going back to their ancient Gypsy beliefs.

The Turkish occupation likewise influenced the way the Gypsies dressed. So it was that, in 1896, a French traveller,[1] who was exploring the district around Eleusis in Greece, met a troupe of 'Gypsies' who were going to Thebes and were leading a bear on a chain:

At the head of them marched a solid, cheery fellow with a swarthy almost black skin and wearing a red fez, who over his colourful rags was carrying a most improbable pile of instruments: the drum for making

1. De Launay, *D'Athènes à Delphes* (1896).

the bear dance, the beggar's double sack, a goatskin bottle, a stick or baton, daggers festooned over his sleeve, a powder-flask of beaten silver, and some pistols. There were urchins with big black eyes, long hair and red skull-caps. Women were riding on donkeys, others were carrying burdens on their backs, and there were three bears. Half-naked infants lay in baskets slung on the donkey's sides; an ass's colt carried bundles of firewood. . . .

I have long wondered why most of the tame bears are honoured with the name of Martin, not only in France but also in the countries of Central and Eastern Europe, as is emphasized in the intoned sing-song of the Balkan bear-leaders:

> Ajde malo, Martine, da poigraš, de, de, de. . . .
> (Dance a little, Martin, come now, go on, go on. . . .)

Now I have just found, rather by chance, the passage which follows from a communication from Professor Gomoiu on the folk-lore of the Balkan countries:[1]

In some Romanian provinces the people celebrate the *Martini*, which are days consecrated to the god Mars. In the course of these festivities the sick are brought to a position where they are placed to be trodden under the feet of tame bears. The custom is a Romanian importation. But, in other provinces, the festivals are called *Lucines*, a word that has come from the Croats and Slavs. Elsewhere, the use of the fat and the scorched hair of the bear is mentioned in Pliny, but this is practised as well as the trampling under bear's feet by all the mountain peoples of the Balkans where bears are found, and where the terms *Lucines* and *Martini* are unknown. It is from this last term that we get the name Martin, which is given to these 'plantigrade' animals (that is, which walk on the soles of their feet).

The bear is not, of course, the only animal which the Gypsies have trained for show purposes. In Central Europe, and especially in the Near East, exhibitors of monkeys are still numerous. In Western Europe it is the goat which has had greatest success. At the present time only a few little provincial troupes remain to keep alive these popular amusements. The beautiful Zorka of the Kostich family, tamers and trainers of wild animals for generations, still excites crowds on the outskirts of Lyons with her tigress 'Marguerite'.

The Gypsies have learnt how to tame lions, tigers and panthers since they have been in contact with the circus world. Every year

1. *Xe Congrès international d'histoire de la médecine*, Toledo, 1935.

during the period when the *'fêtes foraines'* are held, Paris sees the famous Lambert menagerie. As for the famous Bouglione family, these are representatives of the old tribe of Italian *Sinti*.

MUSIC AND DANCING

The earliest known Gypsies, the reader will remember, are the ten thousand *Luri* musicians which King Sankal sent to charm the ears of his son-in-law, Behram Gour. These *Luri*, says the poet Firdusi, were expert lute players. The term lute (old French *leüt*, thirteenth century) is borrowed from the Arabic *al'oud* (literally 'of wood', 'wooden') through the intermediary of old Provençal *laut*. 'Lute' is *der Laut* in German and I think we must see in it the origin of the name *Laoutari* (or *Lautari*) for those Gypsies who were essentially musicians (one of the most famous Gypsy violinists of Moldavia was named Barbu Laoutaru). Without any doubt, this musical instrument comes from the East. It appears in many Indian and Persian miniatures; but it is not certain that it was the Gypsies who brought it across the Bosphorus.

The majority of the musicians who play in public, from Persia to Egypt, are in our own times still Gypsies, according to Jules Bloch. But of this we lack details. It was only when they arrived on the Hungarian plains that the Gypsies really achieved their reputation as virtuosi in this field.

Here we must face the difficult problem of what is called Gypsy music. For more than a century scholars have hesitated to assume the responsibility of admitting the right of either Hungarians or Gypsies to claim this music as their own. The partisans of the two hypotheses are not short of good arguments, as will be seen.

Those who believe in Gypsy priority have on their side ancient documents which, at one period when the chroniclers did not breathe a word about other musicians, clearly recorded the presence in Hungary of Gypsy musicians of such high reputation that they were invited to play before the nobles and lords. The official Registers of Accounts of Queen Beatrice of Aragon, wife of Mathias Corvin (end of the fifteenth century), inform us that this queen already had Gypsy musicians in her service.[1] These frequently visited the castles and were soon at every festival. Every great lord wished to have his own orchestra. Prince Ulman had as his protégé a

1. Haraszti, *Histoire de la musique* (1956).

23–24. Palavers with the Chief and round the fire. The Gypsies of Roumania gladly lead a simple life, perhaps a primitive one, but at all events human.

25

25. Gypsy girls bring wood for the fire. Eternal camping obviously demands many duties; but the smiles and pleasant looks of these French Gypsy girls (*Manouches*) do justice to the presumption of immortality, too often attached to this kind of existence.

26

26. Russian Gypsy chief of the 19th century. In 19th-century Russia the Gypsy chiefs reigned majestically over the destinies of thousands of wanderers who were fiercely attached to their traditions.

27. Itinerant tinsmith in Southern Spain. The number of trades in which the Gypsies are engaged is limited to some crafts that change little outwardly. This Gitano carries his outfit with him. On roads such as those of Spain he meets with little competition.

28. Gypsy with performing goat. Victor Hugo's Gypsy girl, Esmeralda, is disappearing. Public amusement on roadsides no longer 'pays'. However, at Lyons the Kostich tribe of the Bohias group, from the Banat region (Danube), still successfully show the tricks of their she-goat Marguerite.

29. Bear-leader of South-East Europe. There are still many Gypsy bear-leaders in South-East Europe. Roumania is the favourite country of these traditional *Ursari*, as bears can still be caught in the Carpathian Mountains.

30. Central European tinsmiths. In Central Europe, other Gypsy smiths use the same tools and equipment as the Spanish smith (plate 27). But these nomads know the comfort of tent and wagon or caravan.

31. Zorka Kostich, the beautiful equestrienne. This Gypsy girl is a circus rider who performs in the tradition of the authentic nomad horsemen: bare-backed and bare-footed.

32. Shamanist with tambourine rhythms the dance. To provide the rhythm for Zorka's dance there is only one Gypsy instrument: the big one-faced tambourine, used from time immemorial by Shamanist peoples.

33. The cithara. From India the Gypsies brought the cithara, for them a magnificent and nostalgic instrument. If the Gypsies have no authentic art of their own, one must admit that they are incomparable *virtuosi* in the interpretation of, for example, popular music. Painting also has its Gypsy interpreters, such as Torino Ziegler, whose face reflects the nobility of the Spanish *picaros*.

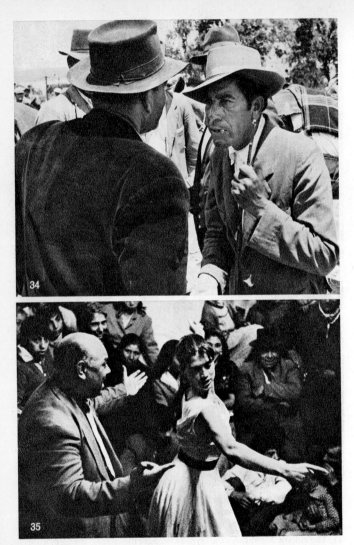

34–35. Expressive hands. Hands, like words, are used to express feelings.
These Catalan horse-dealers have a reputation for being hard nuts to crack.
The Carlos tribe of Barcelona Gypsies have some of the best women dancers.
At fetes and pilgrimages there are serious but enthusiastic contests in which
singers and dancers of the big tribes of Southern France compete against one
another.

36. La Chunga, Spanish Gypsy dancer, now an international star, began by
dancing for her tribe at the cave-dwellings of Sacro-Monte. Her dance is
lascivious only for our too civilized eyes. In actual fact she recaptures the
movements of the sacred dances of India, inspired by Vedic songs.

37. Zanko, a chief of the Kalderash, reigns over Gypsies, both nomads and 'semi-sedentaries', in the region of Lyons-Villeurbanne. The Kalderash Gypsies have a particularly rich and respected tradition. Zanko is over eighty, and has travelled the world.

38. The 'phuri dai', or wise old woman, is the female representative of the tribal chief. Her power is occult and considerable. This one, of the great family of 'Hungarians', has all the majesty of an authentic queen; and is aware of the fact.

39

39. Election of a voivode, or tribal chief of Roumanian Gypsies resident in France. The ritual announcement.

40. The new voivode enthroned. Though merely a chair, the 'throne' loses nothing of its symbolical value. The voivode is separated from his 'subjects' by a chain.

41. The blood oath. By the veins of the left wrists the blood of the old and new voivodes is mingled. This is a very old ceremony, and always held to be sacred.

42. Serenade for a Gypsy archbishop. Whatever may be their 'official' religion, all Gypsies have an ardent faith. The great pilgrimages, and Lourdes recently, attract thousands of the faithful who come from all parts. In 1959 the Archbishop of Bombay, their racial brother, came to greet them. In his honour the Doerrs, *virtuosi* musicians, surpassed themselves.

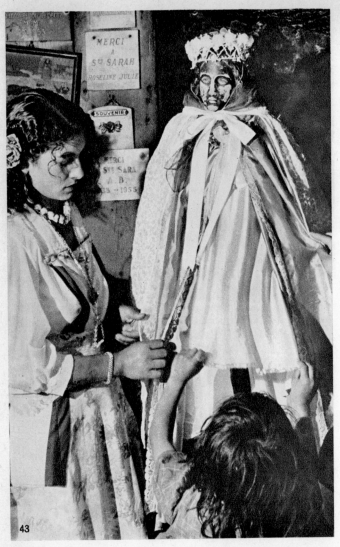

43. Sara, the Black Virgin. At Saintes-Maries-de-la Mer, in the south of France, a Gypsy of the Carlos tribe fulfils the ritual touching of the clothing of the patron saint of the Gypsies.

virtuoso named Karman. From the seventeenth century, at the courts of great lords as well as at village dances, it was Gypsies who accompanied the singing of *kuruc* (songs) with their cymbalums, pipes and violins. Thanks to these extremely popular rhythmic chants, such Gypsies as Michel Varna and his granddaughter Panna Cinka became famous throughout Europe.[1]

Not only did the Gypsies lead the way in great processions and other celebrations, but they were even invited to lead armies into battle, violins in front. At the end of the eighteenth century they made a speciality of playing the *verbunkos*, the famous dance of the recruiting-sergeants with which these sergeants embellished their delicate undertaking. Gypsy violins, cymbals and bass instruments made the eyes of recruits sparkle with the deeds of a war conducted in conditions of elegance.

Characterized by a very short step, with sharpened rhythm, this dance was composed in two parts: one of them slow, of indomitable hautiness; the other, impetuous and of bouncing gaiety. Hussars and Gypsies enlivened the melody and the pace, supported by the clicking of heels and the rattle of spurs.[2]

The *verbunkos* marked the renaissance of Hungarian music and, at the same time, made a Gypsy tribal chief illustrious: Jean Bihari, of whom Liszt would speak with emotion.

Liszt is here the great defender of Gypsy originality. Gypsiologist before writing this, he describes, in his *Gypsies and their Music in Hungary*,[3] what a golden age the eighteenth century was for Gypsy music, and quite definitely says that 'it is to the fortuitious meeting of the two races, Magyar and Gypsy, that we owe this branch of the art called Gypsy music'.

Liszt is supported in this opinion by one of his latest biographers, Claude Rostand,[4] who gives a precise judgement on this problem: speaking of the *Rhapsodies* he says that

they are in no way Hungarian, but Gypsy in their own right, as are the famous *Dances* of Brahms. But Liszt did not know this. In his time authentic Magyar music was almost entirely lost; at least it survived only in the depth of some parts of the country. At all events, the fact is

1. Vigué–Gergely, *La Musique hongroise* (1959).
2. Haraszti, *Histoire de la musique* (1956).
3. Published at Leipzig in 1881.
4. Rostand, *Liszt* (1960).

that only at the beginning of the twentieth century were two such musicians as Bela Bartok and Zoltan Kodaly to appear – to prove the case to us, by exhuming those melodies and rhythms that are authentically Hungarian. Their charms are profoundly different from those of the Gypsy music from which Liszt fostered his *Rhapsodies* and the style of these. Let us note, in order to be exact, that all Hungarian musical influence is not completely banished from Gypsy music; in particular, it often calls upon the Hungarian pentatonic scale to the extent with which the Gypsies partly assimilated certain local particularisms of the countries in which they lived. But that is all. And if the intervals are similar to those of Hungarian music of Magyar origin, neither its melodies or rhythms or especially its instrumental style, which is essentially sober, are found in it – which is far from being the case with Gypsy music.

Against Liszt's opinion is that of some modern musicologists and, up to a point, of the gypsiologists themselves. Vigué and Gergely, historians of music, remark that what is habitually taken for Gypsy music is only music that is 'deceptive to the point of having been regarded as belonging to the national patrimony by the Hungarians themselves'. And the gypsiologist Jules Bloch affirms that 'the Hungarian peasantry were in possession of their musical folk-lore some centuries before the entry of the Gypsies into Europe'.

This problem of the originality of Gypsy music in Hungary is, fundamentally, badly stated. It seems that the two elements, Hungarian and Gypsy, in fact blend together even outside historical chronology. It is forgotten, in particular, that the ethnic group called Finno-Ugrian which gave birth to the Hungarian people had itself an Ural-Altaic origin. So it is that therefore the original characteristics of non-Gypsy Hungarian music present evident agreement with those of Turkish, Mongol, or, let us say, more generally with Asiatic music. And that we have been able to find, for example, in the very old basis of Hungarian folk-lore some funeral chants whose kinship with the 'bear-chants' and the Shamanist epics of the Ugrians seems indisputable.[1]

To regard the Gypsies as simple adaptors, even though gifted with great virtuosity, would therefore be unjust if one really considers that they found in the folk-lore of the Hungarian plains the musical elements which had already struck the ears of their ancestors.

This problem of musicology must not obliterate the extreme importance of music in Gypsy life. Whatever his occupation may be.

1. Vigué–Gergely, op. cit.

the Gypsy knows how to play the violin, and cannot live without this instrument. Gypsy legends have not failed to relate the miraculous origin of the violin. Among those recorded by Wlislocki, here are two that are particularly original:

There lived formerly in a forest a young girl, with her father, mother and her four brothers. The beautiful Mara was in love with a foreigner (a non-Gypsy) and, in spite of her beauty and powers of seduction, she did not succeed in attracting the glances of the brave *gadjo*. Whereupon she had recourse to the Devil. The latter, only too willing, promised to help her, but on condition that she betrayed her four brothers to him. Of these he made four strings, and of the father a sound-box, and next her mother, of whom he made a bow. From the five souls that were sold was born the violin. Mara learnt to play it, and the music soon fascinated the hunter who no longer resisted the beautiful girl's charms. But the Devil, always dissatisfied, suddenly reappeared and carried them both off. Only the violin remained on the ground abandoned. One day a poor Gypsy who was passing picked it up, began to caress it, and set out from village to village bringing laughter and tears.

In another forest, and at another period, there lived a married woman who could not have children. By chance she met an old musician who advised her to make a hole in a gourd, put milk into it and then boil the liquid. The operation succeeded. Nine months later the woman gave birth to a fine boy. At twenty years of age, this boy became an orphan and decided to roam over the world in search of good fortune. He travelled for a long time without finding it, and at last stopped in a big city. There he was assured that the king would give his daughter, a wonderfully beautiful girl, to the man who succeeded in doing what nobody had ever yet done. The young Gypsy presented himself at the court, and found the courage to ask the king what he must do in order to win his daughter. Furious at this audacity, the king immediately had him thrown in prison. But, in his dungeon, the hero had a visit from the *Mautya*, the queen of the fairies and protector of the poor and disinherited.[1] To console him, the *Mautya* showed him a box and a very small stick. Then she said to him: pull out some of my hairs and stretch them on the box. In this way the first violin was made. The youth then asked the favour of being once again presented to the king and, by good luck, his request was granted. Thanks to his new instrument, the Gypsy at one and the same time made His Majesty laugh and weep, something in which no man had ever before succeeded. And he obtained the hand of the girl at the same time as a success which was never again denied.

Very many Central European Gypsy songs express a veritable

1. There exists a *Mautia* sorceress in Albanian folk-lore.

veneration for the violin. Here is one that has likewise been noted by Wlislocki:[1]

Na janav ko dad m'ro has,	*I have never known my father,*
niko mallen mange has;	*And I lack friends;*
Miro gule dai merdyas,	*My mother is long dead,*
Pirani man pregelyas;	*And my loved one departed angry;*
Uva tu, oh hegedive,	*You only, oh my violin,*
Tut sal minding pash mange. . . .	*Accompany me in the world. . . .*
The m're vodyi man dukhal,	*Let my heart break with grief,*
Posici cuces tu sal,	*I hear no money in my pocket,*
Papel ma bashavav,	*I play a song on my violin,*
Paletunes pashlyovav. . . .	*And silence hunger and grief. . . .*
M'ra shatrako hin duy malla	*My violin has two pals*
Mange, pera, vodyi cavlya;	*Who eat my very marrow,*
Kamaviben te piben	*Love and Hunger they're called*
Taysa hin pash bash bashapen. . . .	*And accompany me, a musician. . . .*

In regard to the violin, mention must be made of the criminal industry favoured among the Gypsies in Germany: the clever transformation of a commonplace instrument into an 'authentic' Stradivarius. This faking is no longer in fashion, but a fair number of collectors have allowed themselves to be duped by it, for the Gypsy craftsman carried the delicacy of his work to the point of sticking inside the box a label showing the origin of the instrument. The review *Problèmes* has given details of this piece of faking.

Of course, the violin is not the only instrument dear to Gypsy musicians, who have adopted a good number. But, one observes with astonishment that these instruments are never 'for sale'. I have not found any explanation of the fact, but why not attribute it to the repulsion the Gypsies have for selling in all its manifestations?

In the Balkans, mainly in Bulgaria, the Gypsies have borrowed the *cobza*, a sort of lute with pizzicato string, and the *naiou* or pipes of Pan. In Romania they use the *tsimbal*, a rudimentary and portable

1. Translated into French by J.-P. Clébert.

piano. This instrument, which Liszt calls the *zymbala*, appears to be of Asiatic origin, and it seems very likely that it was the Gypsies who brought it into Southern Europe, as early as the fifteenth century. Notwithstanding its name, this instrument corresponds to our dulcimer, and not to the cymbals.

Another group of instruments greatly appreciated by the Gypsies is that of drums and tambourines. It is probable that these also come from the Orient, India. The tambourine is known to be one of the essential objects in Shamanist rituals throughout the whole of Asia. Kai Donner[1] gives a significant description of it:

> Behind the drum there is a vertical handle of wood or iron which the Shaman holds in his left hand. Horizontal metal wires or wooden splints keep in place innumerable pieces of tinkling metal, small globular bells, hand-bells, iron images representing spirits or various kinds of animals. . . .

If the handle has disappeared from the Gypsy tambourine, there remain the little bells and coloured ribbons, probable vestiges of the metallic elements in the ritual. Among the Tartars and Lapps, the two sides of the drum-skin are painted with symbolic pictures: of the horse, the sun or moon. . . . Likewise some instruments found in the hands of Gypsies have retained this imagery. In the Basque drum, or *pandero* of the Spanish Gypsies (the use of which is reserved for women), these have the portrait of their lover painted on one side of the skin and on the other a swollen heart pierced with an arrow. This tambourine is evidently not exclusively Gypsy, since it is found everywhere in Mediterranean countries. But it is remarkable that among Gypsies it should still be reserved either to women to accompany the dances, or to bear-leaders to give rhythm to the movements of the animal.

As the majority of Gypsies are illiterate and have no system of writing of their own, they cannot be other than ignorant of the use of musical scores. This is one of the major reasons for the absence of written Gypsy music during the period of their history. But it has not prevented their fame from covering the whole of Europe, and musicians such as Haydn, Beethoven, Brahms and Schubert (without again mentioning Liszt) have not hesitated to use Gypsy themes. Still more significant is the attraction they exercised on a great personality with a name famous in the history of music. It happened

1. *La Sibérie* (1946).

that one day in the mid eighteenth century, amongst a Gypsy tribe camping at the gates of Darmstadt, a young violinist attracted particular attention; his talent, according to music-lovers, was so amazing that the Bürgermeister took the trouble to question him. The mayor learnt to his great astonishment that the virtuoso was none other than Wilhelm Friedemann Bach, eldest son of Johann Sebastian. Once a teacher of mathematics and organist of Our Lady at Halle, he had left everything a few years previously to follow a tribe of Gypsy musicians. The Bürgermeister of Darmstadt offered him the position of Choirmaster, which W. F. Bach held for several years. But, seized by nostalgia in recollecting his freedom in wandering, he went back to live with his chance companions.

One fact which at first seems very strange is the resemblance between the music, songs and dances of the Gypsies of Central Europe and those of the *Gitanos* of the Iberian Peninsula. In an account of a journey in Russia dating from the last century, one could already read this:[1]

Listen to the songs of the Caucasian peoples who are today subjects of the Russians – Armenians, Georgians, Bashkirs, Khirghiz, Circassians, etc.: nothing more resembles the Arab songs still sung in Andalusia, and all the Russian music which has come from the Caucasus has maintained, like Spanish music, the characteristics of its oriental origin. Chiefly in Moscow and in the popular district of Zamoskvaretchie (beyond Moscow), one could believe oneself to be in Triana in Seville, a district on the other side of the Guadalquivir. In Moscow also live a considerable number of Gypsies. . . . They are the people's musicians, and form many troupes of singers who make trips as far as St Petersburg, where a person will invite his friends to listen to Gypsies – as if for tea and dancing. What is most striking in their national songs is the remarkable resemblance, the similarity, which is found between them and those of the Gypsies of Spain. There are slow, soft pieces of music which seem to be Andalusian *tiranas* and *polos*; others are lively, quick and sprightly like the *seguedillas* of La Mancha or the *jota* of Aragon.

This is merely an example of the bony structure in the formation of Gypsy folk-lore which I wished to stress in my Introduction.

Hungary, at one end of Europe, and Spain, at the other, are the two poles which attract Gypsy musicians. And for Manuel de Falla, it was certainly the *Gitanos*, settled on Sacro Monte at Granada since the fifteenth century, who introduced into the old Andalusian music,

1. Joanne, *Voyage dans les cinq parties du Monde* (1896).

already impregnated with Arab influences, the new element which was called *cante jondo*.

But in Spain we come up against the same problem which the originality of Gypsy music in Hungary has set us. The birth of *flamenco*, for example, has given rise to different interpretations. All we know is that this style, born in the South of Spain, was formed from popular themes which are not all of peninsular origin. Some of them were brought from abroad; so it was that, hearing the soldiers' songs on their return from Flanders, the Spaniards gave their rhythm the name *flamenco*, that is, Flemish. But many also came from Africa by the same route as that taken by the Gypsies. To sort out the Gypsies' part in these importations is extremely difficult. In accordance with the same phenomenon of osmosis found in Hungary, Spanish folk-lore and that of the Gypsies are mingled.

The guitar is inseparable from the *Gitano* musician, in the same way as the violin is from the Gypsy. But it is, as Walter Starkie says,[1] the ideal nomads' instrument. It is far from being exclusively Spanish. The Gypsy tribes of Persia, Syria and Mesopotamia,[2] who are, so to speak, the hyphen between Asiatic and Spanish music, always play instruments such as the Arab lute. ... In India, the *sitar*, which has mobile frets, and the *tambura*, which does not have these, are indeed also variations of the guitar.

Finally, let us note that, as for the castanets, they were mentioned in Spain well before the appearance of the *Gitanos*; and, in accordance with the traditions of some groups of *Gitanos*, a woman must not dance unless she accompanies herself with her bare hands.

With music, dancing is one of the earliest activities attributed to the Gypsies, and it has never ceased to be of considerable importance among them. It is more than likely that the first Gypsy dancers in India were professionals. One remembers Firdusi's description of them, and of the court of King Sankal. But it is no less probable that the origin of Gypsy dances is likewise ritual, and that in some way they represent an everyday or commonplace rendering of the sacred dances of Vedic India. One meets again, in time and space, traces of dancing with a non-religious but magical function. For example: the Gypsy women dancers called *dodolé* who, in Yugoslavia, serve by their rhythms to prevent sterility in herds of cattle. These women

1. Walter Starkie, *Histoire universelle de la musique, L'Espagne* (1958).
2. See Sinclair, 'Gypsy and oriental music' in *Journal of American folk-lore*, Boston, 1907.

have a widely beneficent role, since it is sufficient to touch them for throat maladies to disappear. The ground which they have trodden with their feet will cure us of warts and gall-stones. And in Bulgaria, Gypsy women dancers are sprinkled with water to bring rain (the dance is called the *paparuda*).

In Romania, the Gypsy women have long adopted a very ancient local dance which formerly served to create collective ecstasy: this is the 'Dance of the *Kalus*' or sticks. The word seems related to the *kalu* who was the magician-cantor of the Babylonians. The dancers are

armed with sticks and dressed in a special costume for the occasion. They have little bells and spurs on their feet. A young girl of about fifteen crosses her stick with that of the chief. A trouble-maker tries incessantly to introduce himself into the circle of dancers, but each time is repulsed. At the end, they set about a game with sticks; on an agreed signal all the sticks are placed on the ground, and then, after several round dances, they are picked up on another signal. Whoever is last to catch hold of his stick receives nine strokes on the soles of his feet. Then comes the final round. The mothers lead their children up to the leader of the dance and make them touch the poles placed there and bearing garlic or absinth: this will protect the children from illnesses. The dancers receive little presents.[1]

The exact meaning of this ritual dance is not clear. It is in any case very widespread geographically, since I have been able to be present at it in the courtyard of the Birla temple in Delhi. It exists in Hungary under the name of the 'Stick Dance', the sticks representing the old sabres with a flexible blade, and it seems natural to see in it a sham combat. In Hungary again, it is generally accompanied by the dance with spurs.[2]

In Russia the Gypsy women dancers, who became individualist professionals, had a great vogue during the tsarist régime. They were one of the most popular attractions then existing, not only in establishments where shows were put on, but also in private houses. It was considered good form among the nobility and rich *bourgeoisie* to employ one or several Gypsy women chosen for their talent and beauty. They were remunerated with gifts of gold coins which they wore on their foreheads or cheeks.

1. Martin Block, *Mœurs et coutumes des Tziganes* (1936).
2. See Ladislas Lajtha, *La Danse hongroise* (1944).

The classic turn of Gypsy women is the snake dance, which has evidently become confused with the 'belly dance'. The undulations of the hips and loins have seemed, in our western eyes, to possess an erotic character which the Gypsy woman in no way aimed to create. From the beginning of the seventeenth century in Spain, for example, Father Mariana[1] consigned to hell the *zarabandas* which are 'so lewd in words and so detestable in their movements, that they make decent people blush'. In the chapter dealing with sex, the reader will see that this lewdness exists only in our mind. As Martin Block emphasizes, the Gypsy woman, in contrast to Arab women dancers, never dances undraped.

Spanish *Gitanas* and their dancing are too well-known nowadays to need description. On the other hand, here is a nineteenth-century account which stresses the exotic taste of an epoch, and the discovery of a folk-lore then almost new:

The women dancers, with superb unselfconsciousness in their miserable rags, clicked their castanets impatiently while waiting for the guitars and tambourines which had been sent for in their nearby lairs. Soon the guitars began to twang and hum under the fingers of the vocal accompanists who intoned the strangest melodies in their falsetto nasal voices. An old *Gitana*, archetype of the witch, one of the most renowned women of Sacro Monte, was seated at the foot of a wall on which was stretched the dried skeleton of an enormous bat, an accessory which further added to her nearly satanic appearance. She armed herself with a big *pandero* or Basque drum, of which the brown skin was soon reverberating under her fingers, accompanying the tinkling of the copper strips. . . .

A tall girl with a fine figure, named La Perla, began to dance the *zorongo* with charming lissomness and grace. Her bare feet lightly touched the surface of the ground on which pebbles were strewn, as though she were dancing on a carpet. The guitars hastened the dance movement, and shouts of '*Juy! Olé! Olé! Alza!*' echoed from all directions, accompanied by enthusiastic applause and *palmeados* or hand-clapping. The *Gitanilla* moreover knew that fine silver coins would be the reward of her talent. . . .

. . . A moment later it was the turn of two little Gypsy girls of eight to ten years old, who, being jealous of their sisters' success, set about imitating them. One of them, who was barely covered with ragged garments, full of holes, described circles with her little arms and made the sound of her castanets keep in time, while the other, lifting the edge of her skirt with one hand, her knees taut and her fist on her hip, gave this

1. In *Tratado contra los juegos públicos.*

the to and fro horizontal movement called *ʒarandeo*, because it resembles that of a sieve that is shaken. . . .[1]

ARTS OF DIVINATION

While their husbands are smiths, horse-copers or musicians, the Gypsy women (and they only) usually tell fortunes. According to most of the specialists, and particularly François de la Noe,[2] women, and not only Gypsy women, have a special aptitude for palmistry. It is a feminine privilege to possess a sensitivity and a receptivity greater than those of men. 'Women think emotively and reason by feeling.'

The Gypsies not only practise chiromancy, the art of predicting the future by the hand, but also chirology which discovers from the hand 'natural predispositions and psychological tendencies'. Although both chiromancy and chirology were already favoured among the Assyrians, their origins seem to have been in India. But neither is supported by evidence until the tenth century. This date strangely reminds us of that of the probable departure of waves of Gypsies going westwards. In our western world, palmistry[3] long remained a science for initiates, but from the fifteenth century it acquired a considerable importance, one that was even disturbing in the eyes of the Church, which heaped anathema on it. In our time, if I may use the expression, it is in everybody's hands.

Those who have assiduously associated with Gypsies have realized that they never have recourse to palmistry for themselves. It remains an occupation, and is addressed exclusively to non-Gypsies, to the *gadjé*. Not that the Gypsies don't 'believe' in it, but they are superstitious enough to feel no confidence in it. Their fundamental beliefs require, as will be seen, an art of divination that is manual and digital. The fingers especially are the object of particular beliefs. But between these beliefs and applied palmistry there is a clear demarcation. We must therefore consider, on the one part,

1. Charles Davillier, *Voyage en Espagne* (1864). *Zaranda* = sieve, sifter, riddle (Sp.) *Tr.*

2. In *Le Langage de la main* (1958).

3. We have the two words 'chiromancy' and 'palmistry' in English, the first being now little used, except perhaps by the more pretentious practitioners of the art. So, from this point onwards, I propose to use the common term 'palmistry'. *Tr.*

what the hand represents symbolically for the various groups of Gypsies; and, on the other, what are the techniques of prediction by examination of the palm.

The secret meaning of the fingers among the Gypsies has been particularly studied by Wlislocki and in the review *Ciba*.[1]

The very rich folk-lore that is practically world-wide attributes to the nails, the hair and the teeth a life of their own, independent of the body: a notion whose origin must doubtless be seen in the fact that these elements continue to live, or at least do not die immediately, after the decease of the subject. To this triad the Gypsies, like some other peoples, add the fingers. A whole folk-lore that is almost inexhaustible considers them as 'beings' endowed with personality.

For the Central European Gypsies (the Kalderash . . .) the thumb is the digit of misfortune. The angle which it forms with the index finger is called the 'devil's saddle'. The left thumb plays the most important role: that of a dead person, who has been for nine days in the grave, and is removed, then has the power to give light to burglars in their expeditions and to plunge the inhabitants of the dwelling into a deep sleep. This same left thumb, this time from the corpse of a child, cures warts. Finally, when the nail of a pregnant woman changes colour or becomes covered with spots, the woman who is telling the future gives an assurance that the child which her client is carrying will be puny. (It is possible that a toxicosis of pregnancy may in actual fact be revealed by the state of the nails.)

Contrary to the thumb, the index finger is the digit of good luck. If a Gypsy should be unfortunate enough to wound this finger and one single drop of blood falls to the ground, the *Nivaschi* or 'Water Spirits' will seize him and the injured man will die of drowning. But this same blood in water is the cure for dropsy.

The middle finger is in harmony with necromancy. In fact, if a child dies lacking a middle finger, he changes into a vampire. Adults who have lost this finger will wander endlessly after death, without ever finding tranquillity. Also parents, when there are funerals, will take care to place on their chest a middle finger made of wood. By letting fall three drops of blood from the left middle finger on the nail of the right, spots will appear which clearly (?) indicate where a lost object or person will be found.

The third or ring finger has a pseudo-medical role. In a case of fever, if a red thread be put round it, 'the fever cannot go out any

1. Basle, December, 1939, an article signed G. . . .

155

more in perspiration' and the sick person will get better. (Among North American Indians, this is the health finger.)

Finally, the little finger, nicknamed the magpie (above all, a thieving bird), serves for touching objects which one would like to appropriate without opening one's purse.

It is not always easy to discover the passing of these beliefs into their practical use in palmistry. By being maleficent, the thumb becomes for the palmist, the 'master digit', probably because it is opposable to the others. The diabolical angle it forms with the index becomes a sign of will and independence. The index finger is no longer an indication of good luck but of decision. The necromantic middle finger now signifies the vocation at grips with destiny. If the third finger, the *digitus medicus* of Pliny, no longer sanctions theft, it is a mark of fancy or curiosity, which brings us to the magpie.

The Gypsies likewise use the tarot cards[1] as material support for predictions and divination. The origin of packs of cards and of the tarot set has often given rise to hypothetical connexions with the Gypsies' arts of divination. Vaillant[2] was one of the first to claim that the tarots had been introduced by the Gypsies. Later, Phillipe Encausse, better known by the name of Papus, went further and held that 'the people entrusted with transmitting occult teaching from the remotest antiquity were the Gypsies. The Gypsies had a Bible, and this Bible enabled them to live, for it allowed them to tell fortunes.' (Which did not prevent this author from describing the Gypsies as ignorant and vicious men.) Again, according to him 'Gypsies alone have the primitive game intact.' This again is the opinion of several historians; such as Chatto[3] and Boiteau d'Ambly.[4]

Jacques Bourgeat[5] (the indefatigable moving spirit of the *Courrier des Chercheurs et des Curieux*) has taken the trouble to call attention to all texts which shed light on this hypothesis. He quotes in particular the *Istoria della Città di Viterbo* by Feliciano Bussi (Rome, 1472) in which can be read this reference: 'In the year 1379 the game of

1. The tarot cards (or tarots), a pack of playing-cards consisting of seventy-eight cards that are longer and marked differently from the pack generally used in the English-speaking world. *Tr.*

2. In *Les Roms, histoire vraie des vrais Bohémiens* (1857).

3. *Facts and Speculations on the Origin and History of Playing-Cards in Europe* (London, 1848).

4. *Les cartes à jouer et la cartomancie* (1854).

5. In *Miroir de l'Histoire* (May 1958).

cards was introduced to Viterbo, coming from the country of the Saracens and called Naib among them.' Now the Gypsies were not mentioned in Italy until 1422. This difference of a few years must however suffice to destroy the authority on which attribute we owe playing cards to them. The debate, nevertheless, remains open.

In any case, the Gypsies have used tarots for a very long time as support for their divination. It is difficult to say which pack of cards was first used. Between the Egyptian tarot, in which Solomon, Moses and Judas reigned, and the Marseille tarot, whose symbols are occidental, the Gypsies have been able to make their own choice in accordance with the routes of their migrations. However, it does not look as though they had an original pack of cards of their own.

Here is the standard way of drawing the tarots, the one in common use among Gypsy fortune-tellers for the 'Great Game'.

In the centre of an imaginary triangle, point downwards, of which the upper side represents the present, the right side the past and the left side the future, a card is placed: the first card drawn at random from the pack, shuffled by the questioner (or the eighth, if the questioner is a woman). Then eleven cards are placed to the right of the triangle, from the top downwards, then eleven others to the left of the triangle, but this time from the bottom upwards, eleven cards more above the triangle from right to left. Next are placed in a circle round the triangle, beginning at the point and going upwards towards the right, three more series of eleven. This gives sixty-six cards set out. The last twelve cards not drawn are placed in a heap within the triangle under the first card. Each time the questioner turns a card to place it outside the triangle, the fortune-teller explains and comments on the cards.[1] This method is called the *Etteilla*, and is not, according to the occultists, in conformity with tradition. But with this we are not concerned here.

The other kinds of apparatus used for divination by the Gypsies are part of the universal catalogue, valid between Mesopotamia and Ireland: molten lead, a looking-glass, beans, coffee-grounds, shells (of shell-fish), bones, knives, etc. In Hungary, however, the Gypsy women-diviners still use the divining-drum, on whose skin are drawn three black and three white circles. Ordinary or kidney beans are thrown on it, and the future is deduced from the way the beans have settled. Maxime Bing sees the origin of this kind of divining in

1. For this interpretation, see Papus, *Le Tarot des Bohémiens*; Marteau, *Le Tarot de Marseille*; and Van Rihnberck, *Le Tarot*.

the drum which Hungarian rural guards used to beat when they announced news in public places. The hypothesis is tempting. We can well enough imagine the Gypsies' mental step as they digested the news 'coming from' the municipal instrument disclosing the future. But is there not here again a borrowing from the world of Shamanism?

4 · Traditions

Although it is difficult to determine exactly the border-lines of their ethnic groupings, the Gypsies nevertheless constitute a homogeneous whole. First of all in their mind, since they call themselves the *Rom*, meaning the Men, archetypes of the species, and in their eyes all who are not *Rom* are not worthy of this name. Moreover, this way of regarding humanity is common to many so-called primitive peoples. Thus there are Eskimos who call themselves the *Innuit*, and this is also 'the Men'. 'The Gypsies regard themselves as one people, notwithstanding the dispersion of their groups and the lack of uniformity in many of their customs', says Jules Bloch, adding: 'A person is Gypsy by right of birth.'

Adoption and Exclusion

Cases of adoption have been noted, not only in historical and literary texts, but in conversations with Gypsy chiefs. Recently Jacques Verrière, author of the successful song *Mon Pote le Gitan*, dedicated to the memory of Django Reinhardt, has been 'adopted' by the Reinhardt tribe (who are *Manouches*). Joseph Reinhardt, Django's brother, himself hooked the traditional golden ring to Verrière's ear. In my opinion, however, and after personal investigations, such adoptions are purely symbolic, and I do not think that Verrière was from that moment taken as a true *Manouche*, even though he has the right to the title of *phral* (brother). It would not be possible for him, for example, to marry a Gypsy woman and have a lineage with the right to the name.

Jules Bloch records details of the adoption of a man named Charles Payne by a Gypsy group in the County of Kent, England, at the beginning of this century. Having taken an active part in bringing about the cure of a young girl of the tribe, they wished to reward him. Payne asked for nothing but their friendship and hospitality.

The girl's fiancé, in accordance with custom, declared: '*Gadjo*, I owe the life of my *Rommi* to you and no money can pay for that. But no *gadjo* can share my camp and food: only brothers and sisters can do this. It's therefore necessary for you to be my brother.'

Then the chief came and summoned a member of the girl's family. They made incisions in the arms of the *gadjo* and of representatives of the two families, binding the arm of the first to that of each of the others, so as to mix their blood.[1] Then he made a little speech proclaiming the new relationship and Payne's duty to live from then on in accordance with Gypsy law, without ever revealing what he may know of what his brothers and sisters of the two families will be during their lifetime (one notes this restrictive delay). He was sworn in with the novice's oath as he touched the three chests with the point of his knife. Finally the fiancée, who had been holding his wrists, released them after giving Payne a Gypsy name and dividing in three strips the gold-coloured ribbon which bound her to her fiancé, one piece for each of the two men, and one for herself. An old woman belonging to the other family repeated more or less the same ceremony, but in a rather lighthearted tone of voice, and shared with the new Gypsy the white ribbon which had held her arm to that of the man who represented her family, making of her own piece a garter for herself.

A simple ceremony to describe, but a serious one for the interested parties, adds the author who, in 1949, considered himself released from his oath, all the participants being dead.

It is then very much a matter of temporary adoption, and I shall gladly call these adopted ones 'honorary Gypsies'; because, for an adopted *gadjo* to become really Gypsy, he must at least wed a Gypsy woman. Now marriage between Gypsy and non-Gypsy is expressly disapproved of. More often than not it brings with it exclusion from the tribe, and the outlaw no longer has the right to the name of Gypsy (whether it be man or woman who weds in an 'unrighteous' marriage). Sometimes this ostracism extends to the whole family and lineage of the guilty party.

The proscription is regarded as the most severe punishment that Gypsy justice – the *kriss* – can inflict on a member of the community. It is worse than death. This age-old excommunication, whose origin we find in the Laws of Manu, is described in all its severity by the Gypsy writer Matéo Maximoff:

It is sufficient, on the order of the tribe, for a married woman to tear from her dress a piece of cloth and throw it at the head of the *Rom* who has

---

1. For the blood marriage, see p. 212.

44. The basket-maker is at the other end of the social scale of the wanderers. Not a true Gypsy in terms of ethnography or tradition, they call him a *Barengro*. But his craft and customs are like those of other nomad peoples.

45. Basket-makers' caravan and workshop. These *Barengré* live in the same manner as Gypsies. The caravan is at the same time their dwelling, their means of transport and their workshop. But these old horse-drawn caravans are becoming rarer in most countries.

46. To be childless is a curse. Maternity is the prime anxiety of Gypsy women; and children belong to the community.

47. Preparing hedgehog stew. Gypsies know how to prepare original dishes which our customs often forbid us to taste. Such is the *niglo* or hedgehog (called *hotchi-witchi* by Gypsies in Britain).

48. 'Flying village' in the Carpathians. Tents are still the familiar habitat of nomads from the East. At the foot of the Carpathian Mountains, the 'flying villages' of the Gypsies use modern army tents as well as clever constructions of sacks and sewn rags, etc.

49. Shrine in a caravan. Gypsies have little need of altars and cathedrals to express their faith. The *iconi*, placed with veneration on the instrument-board of their lorry-caravan, are sufficient.

50. Django Reinhardt, Gypsy musician. Nomad Gypsies have no cemeteries, but families do keep the memory of the departed. In Madame Django Reinhardt's caravan is a life-sized portrait of the famous musician.

51. Mimi Rossetto, Italian *phuri dai*, is dying. When death visits the Gypsies it is particularly tragic and demands complicated rites. According to their own law they may not die inside their tent or caravan. The dying person is therefore placed outside on a mattress.

52. Death agony of Mimi Rossetto. To gain a few minutes on Destiny, a man of the tribe 'breathes' into the dying person his own vital 'flux' through the channel of some conductive object, here the wood of a chair.

53. Gypsy schoolgirls. Society must give Gypsy children the same education
as is given to non-Gypsies; often a very difficult problem. Nevertheless,
Spain has already created special schools for nomads.

54

54. Matéo Maximoff, Gypsy author, lives in France and is one of the extremely few authentic Gypsy writers. He is of the Kalderash tribe, speaks several languages and all the Gypsy dialects. His novels are valuable ethnographic documents (see Bibliography).

55. Hop-picking in Herefordshire. A seasonal occupation.

56. An encampment on Epsom Downs, where Gypsies assemble for the Derby and other big race meetings.

57

57. An English Gypsy woman, and well-known fortune-teller, Charity Fletcher.

58

58. Edwin Fletcher, Charity's husband, picking peas in Worcestershire.

59

59. Gypsy camp at the gates of Paris. While waiting for a decent solution to the problems which have arisen for them and for non-Gypsies through their presence in such conditions as these, one may ask who has more freedom: those who live in the caravans or those in the dismal buildings whose silhouettes evoke those of prisons.

60. An assembly of the tribe.

61. Norman Dodds, a Member of Parliament, being entertained by Gypsies in Darenth Wood, Kent, early in 1962, when he joined them in their defence against eviction.

been sentenced.[1] The latter then finds himself banished for evermore from all tribes. Nobody in the world, neither his wife, nor his mother, nor his children will speak to him any more. Nobody will have him at their table. If he touches an object, even one of great value, the sacred law insists that this object be destroyed or burned. For everybody, the person is worse than if he were a leper. Nobody will even have the courage to kill him in order to cut short his misfortune, for merely to go near him would risk making *marimé* [polluted, defiled] whoever has tried to do so. When he has ceased living, nobody will have anything to do with his funeral or burial, nobody will accompany him to his last resting place. Gypsies will be quick to forget the accursed individual.

Nevertheless, in some tribes the exclusion is less absolute. According to Jules Bloch, the condemned man is authorized to go on living in the camp, but he is then under compulsion to do all the unpleasant and dirty chores. 'Among the Sinti of Vienna, his glass at the inn is marked with a red ribbon so that the other Gypsies may avoid polluting themselves by using it.'

In the end there can be rehabilitation, which is settled by the council of elders of the tribe. This is then followed by a feast of reconciliation similar to that described in the chapter which deals with laws and justice.

In this custom is found the intransigence of the Indian caste system, and the tribal organization of the Gypsies can indeed be compared with that of the Indian castes. We know that the word 'caste' comes from the Portuguese word *casto*, which means 'pure', 'undefiled'. Ketkar[2] defines caste as a social group having two essential characteristics: (1) the right of membership can belong only to those who were born members of the community; (2) an inflexible law forbids marriage outside the group.

Senart[3] is one of the few authors to have explained clearly what caste is:

Let us imagine a close corporate group, one that is at least in theory strictly hereditary, and provided with some traditional and independent organization – a chief and a council, which in case of need meets in gatherings, more or less plenary; often united for the observance of certain

1. This rite is also found in some Indian tribes. 'Among the *Nagos* of Assam, it is a terrible misfortune for a man to find that he has been struck with a skirt of a woman who has been bearing children.' (Hutton, *Thugs and Dacoits*, 1921).

2. In his *History of Caste in India* (1909).

3. In *Les Castes dans l'Inde* (1927).

festivals; bound together by a common occupation and practising common customs which concern more especially marriage, food and various kinds of 'impurity' ('uncleanness'); and, finally, to assure authority in these things, fortified by a competent jurisdiction more or less widespread, but capable – with the sanction of certain penalties, above all of exclusion from the community, whether this be definitive or revocable – of making the authority of the community be effectually felt. This is, in short, how caste appears to us.

The reader will see to what extent, and with what exactness, this definition applies to the various bands of Gypsies.

Authority

The collective whole of the people called Gypsy is made up of a fairly considerable number of different groups having as social 'cement' only Gypsy law. In actual fact, there is not, nor has there ever existed a 'king' of the Gypsies. This journalistic invention must be swept away, once for all. The press regularly tells us about the election of a king or a queen of the Gypsies or of the *Gitanos*. And it is quite true that the Gypsies themselves do not fall short in fostering the legend about such ceremonies; by this they gain something. Thus, in 1930, in Poland they unjustifiably crowned one Michael as King of the Gypsies of Europe, a ceremony at which the President of the Polish Republic thought fit to be represented. In 1959, during the pilgrimage to Lourdes, a feather-brained blonde with the name Zarah cleverly represented herself as the future 'Queen of the Gypsies'. As she readily distributed hard cash among the urchins in the camp, these and many adults did not require much pressing to hail her and confer this envied title. The previous year reporters of the biggest newspapers attended the funeral of Mimi Rossetto, 'the one and only Queen of the Gypsies', who had died after some days of death-pangs at Lendinara in North Italy. It was really a case of an old Gypsy woman of the *Piemontesi* tribe, whose precise role was that of *phuri dai*, that is, wise adviser, who was highly respected by the whole tribe.[1]

When old texts describe the Gypsies who were led into Europe by dukes and counts, the authors merely employ the titles in use during their epoch. These 'dukes' and 'counts' were in fact tribal chiefs.

Indeed, each Gypsy tribe (*vitcha*), whose importance can vary

1. See p. 164.

from ten to several hundred tents or caravans (the equivalent of so many households), recognizes only the authority of a chief elected for life (the responsibility is never hereditary) because of his intelligence, strength and feeling for justice. He is nearly always a man getting on in years. His authority embraces the whole tribe. He has the right to inflict corporal punishments and to pronounce measures of exclusion. He presides over the council of elders and does not have to render accounts to anybody. Chiefs of tribes are equal among themselves; there is no hierarchy based on the importance of the tribe. It is the chiefs who decide about migrations. In principle they are the responsible persons of their group; they are likewise sometimes treasurers of the community.

Formerly in Eastern and Central Europe, where he was called *vataf*, the chief was distinguishable by a particular get-up: dishevelled hair, blue or garish clothes, open to show the bare chest; a game-bag hung from his neck and a purse-belt round his hips held up very wide trousers that were stuffed into high boots. He was the only man in the tribe to flourish metal buttons on his short jacket.[1]

Although this picturesque costume has now disappeared, the tribal chief nonetheless affects a very haughty bearing and retains the big broad buttons on his jacket as well as an enormous chain with pendants hanging from his waistcoat. But the true insignia of 'royalty' is the staff with a silver head, the last vestige of the Gypsy sceptre, which is worthy of description:[2] this sceptre, made entirely of silver, was called *bareshti rovli rupui*, that is, 'the chief's silver stick'. The head, adorned with a red tassel, had the shape of an octagonal disk (then of symbolical value). Under this tassel was engraved the *Semno* or authentic 'Sign' of the Gypsies, comprising the five ritual figures:

> The *nijako* or Battleaxe – half axe, half hammer.
> The *cham* or Sun.
> The *shion* (also *shonuto*) or Moon.
> The *netchaphoro* (also *tchalai*) or Star.
> The *trushul* or Cross.[3]

1. See the section on Clothes and Finery p. 219. Formerly in India the wearing of gold or silver ornaments was reserved to the 'twice born'.
2. As given by the Rev. Fr. Chatard in *Zanko; Traditions, coutumes et légendes des Tziganes Chalderash* (1959).
3. Perhaps a corruption of the word *cruce* (cross) from Latin to Romanian?

The reader will see later the symbolism which may be attached to these figures.[1]

Let us note, to finish with the tribal chief, that it often happens, in relations with the *gadjé* (non-Gypsies), particularly with the authorities, that he stands aside, behind a false chief, in order that the exact source of authority for the group shall not be divulged.

The elders are, of course, the old men of the tribe on whom their years confer wisdom and authority. They are addressed as *Kako*, a term of respect which really means 'uncle'.[2]

The *phuri dai* is the feminine version of the tribal chief. She is generally a very old woman, whose power, however unofficial and concealed it may be, is not less real. Her influence is exercised on women and children especially, but the council of elders, indeed the chief himself, does not disdain to take her advice in delicate matters. She is called *Bibi* or 'aunt(-ie)'. In the role of *phuri dai* very clear traces are found of the old Gypsy matriarchy.

Here again it would be easy to establish a parallel with the Indian caste system. The council of elders is quite simply the Indian *panchayet* (etymologically, this means the body consisting of five members – in practice there can be more) which meets when the internal affairs of the tribe require it. In some Indian castes the Head of the *panchayet*, to whom the Gypsy tribal chief corresponds, wore a gold ring and rode on horseback, privileges again found, though in diminished form, in the customs of the Gypsies in the past. It really seems, in fact, that only the 'dukes' and 'counts' of bands of nomads had the right to be mounted.[3] As for the gold ring which, in actual fact, is worn by Gypsies, its use and symbolism are almost universal. One need note only the relationship which it is possible to

1. However, I shall not again refer to the Battleaxe. This appeared among the voivodes of the Danube as a parade weapon and sign of authority. In all of medieval Europe, it indicated the temporal power, the judiciary, the constabulary. The Vichy Government even tried to have revived in this sense the battleaxe called *la francisque* (which was in use among the old Germanic tribes, notably the Franks. *Tr.*).

2. Regarding the ethnological importance of the uncle in kinship, and the problem of avuncular relationship, consult Lévi-Strauss, *Anthropologie structurale* (1958).

3. For this privilege, consult works on the origin and history of Chivalry, particularly Léon Gautier's *La Chevalerie* (published by Arthaud, 1959).

establish in this regard with secret societies: the old '*Compagnonnage*'[1] in France, for example.

Matriarchy

It is not easy to clarify the situation in regard to the matriarchal régime mentioned above. In any case it is certain, as Martin Block reports it, that kinship was formerly counted by lineage through the mother. Traces of this custom remain, this author says, among the Gypsies of Southern and Eastern Europe. When a man marries a woman, he 'enters' her family, and returns to his own the moment he becomes a widower. But as marriages generally occur within the same tribe, it seems that this basic matriarchy has only a secondary importance. However, among some tribes, children who are the offspring of different groups speak the mother's dialect, and not that of the father.

In actual practice, the precise nature of consanguinity, whether it be by descent through the mother or the father, is a minor question; the interesting fact is that the essential nucleus of the Gypsy organization is the family. Authority is held there by the father who, in the family, plays a role similar to that of the tribal chief. As for the woman, on the family scale she is the *phuri dai*: her power is unofficial and occult, but it is often of solid and of undeniable reality. One example will suffice to show the cohesion of a family. As Jules Bloch says, 'property belongs to the family and not to the individual'.

But the family is not limited to the father-mother couple and their children. It spreads out to include uncles, aunts and cousins. Gypsy cousinship can assume quite unexpected proportions. I was rather bewildered one day, when some Gypsy friends were introducing to me the entire population of a camp, to hear them say in front of each individual: 'this is a cousin'. In fact, the word cousin, like that of brother (*phral*) serves no more than to describe a friend, or else a distant relation. Moreover, some Gypsies honour me with this title. It is known that in 'primitive mentality' the term 'brother' plainly goes further than the narrow idea of kinship. It designates the person on whom will fall the ill done to the first person.

Jules Bloch emphasizes 'the marked fondness for marriages between cousins, the said cousins being for preference those parallel

1. *La Compagnonnage*: this was formerly a 'workers association' for men of the same occupation who helped each other to secure employment. *Tr.*

in traditionalist families and, more generally, the children of sisters in families whose lineage is through the mother; the children of brothers in others'.

Justice[1]

In regard to the respect which they have for their particular laws, the Gypsies prefer to settle their differences themselves. Not for anything in the world would they apply to the police or to official justice in the countries where they live.

The system of justice used among themselves is called the *kriss*.[2] The term first of all means 'the law in general' and next the assembly or council of elders who have the responsibility for applying this law. The matters which require the meeting of a *kriss* are clearly very varied. They concern, for example, the disputes, conflicts or clashes of interests which happen between two groups or two tribes: taking away a girl (kidnapping), brawls followed by blows and wounds (sometimes murder), jealousy or rivalry in regard to a piece of land or a business or trade, wrongs (i.e. 'torts' in English Law), injuries or insults, and the non-observance of Gypsy laws, etc.

Once a *kriss* has been decided upon, the elders hold a meeting. Women are never admitted to these deliberations except as witnesses, but the opinion of the *phuri dai* is sometimes requested.[3] Young boys can be present, but, evidently, they have no right to speak.

The president (*krisinitori*) of the *kriss* is seated on a chair, indeed on an ordinary cauldron turned upside down, which does office for a throne of justice. The members of the council squat on the ground. Witnesses walk past, one after another, and each has the right to speak freely. When the problem is difficult or ticklish, the *krisinitori* asks for the opinion of the elders and chiefs of tribe. But it is he, and he only, who decides on guilt, and then on punishment. If it is necessary for the witnesses to swear an oath, the altar of justice is

1. The term 'justice' as used here must be interpreted broadly to include not only abstract justice but Gypsy laws, procedure, sentence and penalty. *Tr.*

2. The origin of this term is unknown. In Hindi, *krishi* meant the taking advantage and making of rules relating to the sun. At the other extremity of Indian influence, the Bali *kriss* was at first a ritual dagger used in fights over personal honour. As for *Krishna*, the black god, it may be of interest to emphasize his role of mediator and avenger.

3. Among the Kalderash Gypsies the women have the right to be present at the *Kriss*; then they remain standing behind the men. (See Maximoff's novel *Savina*.)

set up; it consists of the icons of the tribes present. (In his novel *Savina*, Matéo Maximoff has described at length a ceremony of this kind. The altar he describes has dark-coloured skirts placed on the ground around a stone.) Candle-ends, kept by the women during the recent funeral, symbolize the presence of the dead.

Death is not excluded from the punishments inflicted on the guilty party. But this penalty has become rarer and rarer. Exclusion from the community and corporal punishments replace it. The latter are sometimes of exceptional violence: an eye torn out, or mutilation. The *krisinitori* may likewise arbitrate in a duel between two rivals: a duel with knives in Central Europe, with whips in the Ukraine, by boxing in England.

When an accused person has been found innocent, the *kriss* orders a banquet (*pativ*)[1] of rehabiliation. The victim of the error or some other person raises his glass in a toast to friendship and an oath of peace is sworn. He spills a little of his wine on the table. In other tribes he sings a solo account, like a popular lament, of the story of the alleged crime or offence. A woman dances, and mimes the action, while those present hum an accompaniment (a tradition of some Kalderash tribes).

With some variations in detail, the ceremony of the *kriss* is still customary among all Gypsies, even those who are integrated in our civilization. I will add that differences which, for one reason or another, have been settled by official justice are remitted for their own Gypsy trial, the *kriss* taking no account of the official trial. This loyalty to the *kriss* is one of the important factors in the cohesion of the Gypsy people. But their cohesion is even more assured by the rigid limits of the family and tribe, and by this superior authority which, if it is not decked out in the commonplace guise of a king, is nonetheless exacting and exclusive: that is to say, Gypsy Law and Tradition.

GYPSY LAW OR TRADITION

This Tradition offers various versions and includes compromises to their way of life on the part of people who are non-Gypsy nomads.[2] On the other hand, for the Gypsies themselves it dictates not only

1. A Romanian Gypsy term. Among other groups it means any (non-traditional) festivity.

2. The *Yénische*, *Barengré*, 'Basket-makers'.

their beliefs but their customs. Consequently, for convenience in the statement which follows, customs and myths in the everyday life of Gypsies will be mixed.

Let us say, nevertheless, that the Law and the Tradition cannot be compared in all respects. Gypsy Law may rightly be regarded as the collective whole of the customs (in the sense in which this is understood by elders who know them) which, from generation to generation, ordered in an immutable way the smallest acts of practical living. The Tradition is not only the formation of a complete basis of beliefs, of a 'credo' orally transmitted, and intended to order the universe as well as the taboos which result from this pseudo-revelation. It is also a 'History in legends', yet one whose myths are malleable, shifting, and adaptable to particular situations. The Persians make an important distinction between their *afsaneh*, which means story, and *tarikh*, which is history, and there is, in addition, the more subtle *dastan*: this last is, at one and the same time, both story and history – that is, a history in which the stories are being endlessly reshaped and remodified. From this, it is sure, come contradictions that, to say the least, are conspicuous, and yet they give shape to the migrations and the distinction between groups. There is, nevertheless, a comparatively uniform web throughout, and this is the denominator which I try to follow. Whatever may be the version of a story told in the camp of an evening, the Gypsies invariably exclaim at the end: *Chapité!* which means, 'It is true!'

Oral Tradition and the Absence of Writing

It is clear that the tribal chiefs do not know all the laws which make up the Law. There are too many of them. Thus there are some of the laws of Manu. For the most part, the miscellaneous laws are interpreted only by customs, the meaning or earliest need for them having been forgotten. The fact that they are transmitted orally, and that no document has recorded them has greatly altered their original purity. However this may be, one must never forget that the Law is categorical and irrefutable. This stringency counts for much in the astonishing and continual cohesion of a people that for so long has been migratory.

Finally, and it is now a commonplace, we must take into account the secrecy in which the Law is wrapped. The Gypsies are really conscious of a secular taboo which prevents them from disclosing to non-Gypsies the majority of their rituals. This, believe it or not, is not a matter of joking, intended to cover the Gypsy myth with 'mystery'. In any case it is no joke for the gypsiologists who are incessantly running into the wall of silence or, what is worse, the deliberate lie. Put the same question twenty times to Gypsies and you will get twenty different replies. This is one of the reasons why, in spite of the long sojourns I have been able to have among Gypsies, I have in this book applied myself to citing only those facts which have been recorded by standard gypsiology.

Before entering into details of Gypsy life, it is necessary to consider the problem of oral transmission and the lack of writing.

Gypsies are all explicit: 'Our language is not written. . . . This is our curse.'[1] Gypsies are regarded as illiterate. But illiterate does not mean uncultivated (that is, without intellectual or moral culture).[2] Culture, a certain form of culture, if you will, is deeply rooted in them; as will be seen. As for their reading and understanding of the world, this is not done on paper or in books; it is done on the very soil of the planet. An illiterate people is usually capable of reading, better than we can, the signs of nature, whether in meteorology, pharmacopoeia, or divination.

But where does this refusal of writing come from?

The Gypsies themselves speak of malediction. According to an account by Kalderash Gypsies reported by the Rev. P. Chatard with the title 'The End of the First World', the ancestors of the Gypsies, the *Pharavono*, led by their chief, made war on the *Horachai* (Turko-Judaeo-Christians). The *Pharavono*, having blasphemed, were swallowed into the bottom of the sea.

Only a few *Pharavunure* [that is, Gypsies] escaped. We are their sons. Ever since that misfortune we, the *Pharavunure*, no longer have any power, any country, any State, any chiefs, any Church, and any writing, for our power, our force, our chiefs and our [hand]writing were drowned in the sea for evermore.

Other legends include this loss of writing. I have not found the equivalent for what seems in reality an uncompromising taboo of Manu and some Indian castes. On the other hand, we know that the 'occultists', or, rather, those who believe in revelation, hold

1. Chatard, op. cit.
2. It is even prejudicial to read in Jules Bloch's work: 'One can hardly expect a philosophy of the universe, even in the form of mythology, of a people without culture.'

that the refusal of the thing written is necessary. Robert Amadou[1] interprets this necessity clearly:

Tradition is etymologically transmission. It is the act of delivering, of causing to reach. By extension, Tradition is what is transmitted, the deposit which is delivered. But the word Tradition has taken on a more limited meaning. This limitation applies to the manner of transmission. Whoever says Tradition says in fact oral transmission. . . . The meaning is that Tradition is not presented in the form of written texts, which deliver it complete and naked. Tradition is oral. It is not literal.

And this author recalls that it was the bad angels who taught writing to men, according to the *Book of Enoch*.

Another more realistic explanation obviously occurs: nomad peoples hardly have time to think of writing. By virtue of being wanderers they can take along with them only what is indispensable. Books would be too heavy a load. They must therefore learn everything by memory and consequently they memorize what is essential, preferably in verses that are easy to remember. Thus, the Scythians knew nothing of writing.[2]

As among other 'primitive' peoples, the transmission is more willingly made by means of stories, songs, recitations or intoned psalms in the evening, around the camp fire. In this way the children hear, for years, of the exploits in a Tradition that has many faces. And, as was formerly the case in our own civilization, on hearing tales from the nurse of Mother Goose, their conscience little by little becomes impregnated with the rules which it behoves them to follow in order to become a good Gypsy, and the mistakes which it is important to avoid.

RELIGIOUS BELIEFS

Although civilization upsets more and more the old traditions, the Gypsies remain attached to a whole cycle of religious beliefs – some of them rather nebulous – which form part of the basis of these people's organization, and of their cohesion.

Perfect self-adapters in all fields of activity, the Gypsies have

1. *L'Occultisme, esquisse d'un monde vivant* (1950).
2. A gypsiologist has, however, been found to 'discover' Gypsy handwriting. This is Decourdemanche (in *Grammaire du Tchingané ou langue des Bohémiens errants*, 1908). I give some of his examples, as a matter of curiosity, in the chapter on Languages and Means of Expression. See pp. 235–45.

known very well how to accommodate their faith to the outward requirements of the religions predominant in the countries they have gone through. So it is that they are Orthodox Church, Mussulmans or Christians. It even happens (as already noted in regard to the *Beri*, Balkan bear-leaders) that they hold a plurality of religions in Islamism and Christianity. Today, an evangelical movement succeeds, up to a point, in converting them to Protestantism.

What counts is the evidence of an intense religious faith outside of any religious persuasion. Whether they are Christians or Mussulmans (or even though they may be outside every 'official' credo), the great majority of Gypsies give proof of a strength and enthusiasm in matters of faith which astonish even priests. One has only to be present at the Lourdes prilgrimage to realize how deep and exacting this faith is.

But if they so easily adopt the outward array of our religions, the Gypsies possess above all else an accumulation of formal beliefs that very nearly constitutes a genuine mythology. Granted the secrecy attached to Gypsy Tradition, it is difficult to push one's way through the somewhat dense system of these beliefs. The tales and legends, the commentaries of the gypsiologists, and the accounts of the Gypsies themselves are often suspect. Besides, each group has more or less modified the original cycle; and this for its own practice. Consequently, the elements reported here must not be placed end to end in order to form an exact, homogeneous whole. Dogmas can overlap and even contradict one another, and the interpretation of this collection is very much subject to caution. Finally, everyone preaches for his own saint, and the Catholic priests, for example, who have been leaning towards Gypsy mythology, have been tempted to enhance chiefly that in which this mythology comes close to Christianity.

Mythology

The Gypsies believe in one God only: *o Del* (*o Devel* among some groups, *o Deloro* – a friendly diminutive form – among others). The presence of the definite article (*o*, the) will be noted: *the* God.

It seems that we have to deal with standard monotheism. *O Del* is all together: the sky (or heaven), fire, wind, rain; or rather the sky is God.[1] (But water, on the other hand, is not God – the problem of

1. *Devel* in Balkan Gypsy means both 'god' and 'sky'. In Basque Gypsy, likewise *Devla*. Compare Sanskrit *deva*: 'celestial being', 'god with form'.

water will be dealt with later.) However, the first difficulty arose when the Gypsies of the Kalderash[1] tribe affirmed that this God is not a *demiurge* or creator of the world. The earth (*phu*), that is, the universe, existed long before him; it always existed. 'It is the mother of all of us' (*amari De*) and is called *De Develeski*, the Divine Mother. In this one recognizes a trace of the primitive matriarchy. Similar myths appear among the majority of the Altaic peoples, for example the Yakuts (of Siberia) who show no interest in the creation of the earth, for the good reason that this has never needed to be created.[2]

On this uncreated Earth appeared one day (still for the Kalderash Gypsies) the God, *o Del*, more exactly the old God, the ancient God, *o pouro Del*. He was not alone. At his side suddenly loomed up and stood his usual acolyte the Devil, *o Bengh*.[3]

O Del is the principle of Good, *o Bengh* of Evil; both likewise powerful and ceaselessly contending against each other. 'These principles are not abstract, but on the contrary are materialized in the elements of nature, which constitutes for them a kind of universal church.'[4] In this there is perhaps an influence of Zoroastrian or Manichaean dualism (other elements, it will be seen, permit us to think so) and one would have to have time to study the connexions between the Gypsy myths and those of ancient Iran: it is found, for example, that the *Dev* represent in Mazdaism[5] the gods of Evil, while the heavenly doubles of the good beings are named *Fravahr* – which brings in the Gypsy term *phral*,[6] meaning 'brother'.

If the world has not been created by God, the latter, however, has created man. At least He competed with the Devil in the making of two statuettes of earth (*papusha*). The devil made them in the form of man and woman. God breathed the word into them.[7] Such was the birth of Adam and Eve, *Damo* and *Yehwah*, terms which are very close to the Hebrew. We know that this 'earthy' origin of man is

1. Chatard, op. cit.
2. Uno Harva, *Représentations religieuses des Peuples altaïques* (1959).
3. Compare the devil of the Tungus (a Mongol people of Siberia): *Buninka*.
4. Serboianu, *Les Tziganes* (1930).
5. Mazdaism: religion of the ancient Medes and Persians, which had two important principles: Good (*Ormuzd*) which created the world, and Evil (*Ariman*) which seeks to destroy the work of the Good. The struggle has to end with the defeat of *Ariman*. Tr.
6. See Mariam Mole, *La naissance du monde dans l'Iran pré-islamique* (1959).
7. Chatard, op. cit.

universal. But the fact that the Devil and God collaborated in it is a typically Manichaean feature. Ruysbrœk, a traveller of the thirteenth century, already recognized it in Central Asia.

The birth of Adam and Eve is linked in the Kalderash tradition with the presence of two non-fruit-bearing trees which sprang up beside water, one behind the man, the other behind the woman, covering both with their branches. It was on this contact that the earth became transformed into flesh. Once again this is a universal theme which makes itself felt as far afield as the tribes of northern Australia,[1] and with which is connected that of the 'Marriage of the Trees', attested among the Gypsies of Transylvania. There is an astonishing agreement between this myth and some of the Altaic legends.

These two trees are not yet those of Paradise.[2] They are a pear tree and a plum tree. *Damo* begins to eat a pear. The Serpent (*sap*) then appeared and 'seeing how the man was becoming' tried to prevent the woman from eating an apple. But *o Del* intervening, the Serpent retires and Yehwah eats the fruit.

Here biblical tradition is reversed. However, the same sexual symbolism of the fruits is again found in it: the pear arousing the man's desire, the apple that of the woman. *Damo* and *Yehwah* 'know each other'. He is satisfied, but she wishes to begin again. With God's authorization the man embraces his companion a second and then a third time. But she is still unsated. It is since then that woman has not ceased craving for love.

The traditional Gypsy accounts vary, let us repeat. A Transylvanian legend, reported by Franz de Ville, relates the birth of the first man in a more picturesque manner. One day God decided to make a man. He took a sour lime, made a statue and put it to bake in his oven. Then he went away for a walk and ended by forgetting his work. When he returned the man was burned, quite black. This was the ancestor of the Negroes. God began again but this time he was so afraid to let time slip by that he opened the oven too soon; the man was still quite pale. This was the ancestor of the Whites. God tried a third experiment, which this time succeeded; the last man was baked to a turn, well browned, a nice tan-colour. This was the ancestor of the Gypsies.

1. See Mircea Eliade, *Traité de l'histoire des religions* (1953).
2. Yakut legends on the theophanic tree seem closer to this tradition than to the Bible.

According to Zanko, it was well after the birth of *Damo* and *Yehwah* that *o Del* made *o Cham*, the Sun, and *o Shion*, the Moon, come out of the earth. Now, among the Kalmuks of Astrakhan the same chronology is found, and is explained by the fact that Adam and Eve before sinning gave off their own light. After the fall, they had lost their luminosity, and it was necessary to create two luminaries, the sun and the moon. This belief is common, according to Harva, to a great part of Asia Minor.

As against *Cham*, the sun, and *Shion*, the moon, one cannot help thinking of the corresponding Babylonian luminaries: *Shamash* and *Shin*. If Eliade emphasizes the fact that *Shamash* in the Mesopotamian pantheon has played a role inferior only to that of *Shin*, he recognizes that the former, 'patron of prophets and diviners', is in close relationship with the subterranean universe.

Wlislocki, who has studied the Central European Gypsies, reports that they believe that, at the extemity of the world, there is a hole (*hiü*) through which it is possible to enter into the bosom of the earth. By following the sun (which the Gypsy migration did in its march from East to West), this hole would be inevitably reached. The journey would have to be made thanks to two harnessed cocks (the cock, clearly a solar symbol, has an important place in the magical zoology of the Gypsies; as elsewhere, it announces the return of the sun and the end of the reign of the vampires). By that hole, entry is made into the abode of darkness. There, one would walk for two months (?) before coming upon, at the same time as light, the castle of the 'black cannibal emperor'.

This grim lord compels us to lay stress on the sun, who plays a leading role in the labyrinth of Gypsy beliefs. I have not been able to find the Gypsy name for the infernal divinity met at the end of the journey. Nevertheless, one could no doubt identify it with the Chthonian ogres in Greek mythology.

Another legend[1] (of which I borrow Jules Bloch's version) puts the sun and moon on the stage in the following way:

When there were not yet men in the world, the Sky and the Earth formed happy and harmonious domestic arrangements. They had five sons: that is, King Sun, King Moon, King Fire, King Wind and King Fog. As they grew, these sons were in perpetual discord. The Sky and the Earth contrived a hollow space between them in which to enclose their sons. Whereupon the latter became angry and decided to separate

1. Reported by Wlislocki.

from their parents, so that each of them went out into the world and made for himself a suitable dwelling-place. First King Moon attacked his mother, the Earth, and tried to separate her from the Sky; but he was too weak to succeed. Fog and Fire had the same lack of success when they uselessly attacked their father. When King Sun attacked his mother, the Earth, his parents began to totter but he did not succeed further than this. Then King Wind made a rush at his mother with all his strength and separated Sky and Earth. Whereupon the sons began to quarrel about who should stay with their mother, the Earth; and who should follow the Sky, their father. Then the Earth said to her five sons: 'You, King Sun, you, King Moon, you, King Wind – you all have attacked your mother. Begone! But you, King Fog, and you, King Fire, you have done me no harm; remain with me.' Ever since then, Sky and Earth are separated and, their five sons are in everlasting conflict.

The analysis of the myths in this legend would take us too far. It is, however, advisable to remark that those here staged are elementary divinities whose participation in the universe is least abstract. In so far as nomads are concerned, the Gypsies first retained the importance of these meteorological and climatic elements. One notes likewise that it is the Mother who makes the final decision; another trace of the primitive matriarchy.

Although a solar cult among the Gypsies is often mentioned, this is very difficult to study because precise documents are lacking. Perhaps we must infer from this absence that such a cult is less important than that of the Moon? But this is not certain. Nevertheless, on the *nijako*-staff of chiefs of tribes, one has seen that the Sun had right to second place, taking precedence over the Moon.

The lunar cult, on the contrary, is more accessible. *O Shion* is of the masculine gender (like the German *der Mond*). For if this heavenly body rules the cycles of the female sex, it has first to be considered as a luminary in the same way as the Sun. Here again it is difficult to know exactly how the Moon cult is practised. Martin Block says that he has seen some of the 'most uncouth' Gypsies take off their clothes to the Moon, bow their heads and mutter certain words. According to him, this adoration is in harmony with a matriarchal social structure which has 'remained secret', and only those Gypsies who have remained pure nomads still conform to it.

In actual fact, the Moon, especially among Gypsies, plays a pseudo-magical role in harmony with the weather. She also appeared on the *nijako* (see page 163 ff.) in the third position, represented in her first quarter; which is important. Unlike the Sun, the Moon in fact is a heavenly body whose form is not immutable. She is born, grows, decreases, and disappears. She must therefore, from the earliest periods, have regulated the measure of time. In our own lifetime, some small nomad tribes of hunters and husbandmen use only the lunar calendar.[1]

Zanko asserts that, when each new moon appears, the Kalderash Gypsies address a special prayer to her, making quite clear that they devote themselves to this rite as we, the non-Gypsies, do for ours at the beginning of each year. We are therefore confronted with a calendar rite.[2] On that occasion they say:

'Shonuto [diminutive of Shion] nevo ankliste – Tal aminghe bachtalo – Alacl'ame bivolengo – Te mukel ame bachtasa Ai sastimasa – Ai lovensa. . . .'

'The New Moon has come out – May she be lucky for us – She has found us penniless – May she leave us with [good] fortune – And with [good] health – And with money. . . .'

The Moon therefore likewise plays the role of mascot or luck-bringer.

Among the other luminaries, the stars have their importance. They were born with (or at the same time – or are?) the innumerable children of Damo and Yehwah. All men have their star in the sky. 'The myth of the Star, o Tchalai,' says Father Chatard, 'is still widespread, even among the Gitans and Manouches. A star which falls [a shooting star] is a dying man.' This is not original to the Gypsies. Nevertheless, contrary to the belief familiar to us, the Gypsies do not make a wish when one appears.

O Tchalai (star is also masculine gender) is represented on the nijako and on some Transylvanian(?) wrought objects and in the south of France in the form of a sixteen-point star or comet. Why sixteen? According to Franz de Ville, the Gypsies of Latvia claim to be the sixteenth offshoot of the Gypsy disperson. But there is no authority for believing that there were on their departure (from India) sixteen groups or tribes. The presence of the star with sixteen points, which can be seen on the sky-blue banner adorned with the effigy of Christ and the Madonna, carried by the Catholic Gypsies at the Lourdes pilgrimage, oddly enough is also again found on the armorial bearings of the lords of the Baux-en-Provence, which are

1. Eliade, Traité de l'histoire des religions (1953).
2. In most Gypsy dialects Shion also means 'month'.

'gules with a comet having sixteen silver rays'. The Baux family, which dates from the tenth century, aver that they are descended from Balthazar, the Magus king, who, according to various legends, lived on the coast of Provence. What is more, the Baux village has a chapel said to be of the *Tremaié*, that is, of the Three Marys, the Saintes-Maries-de-la-Mer (of the annual Gypsy pilgrimage in France).

For the Gypsies, still according to Franz de Ville,

the Comet, sister of the Sun, is the sign of the Chief. It recalls the Star which long ago led the Three Wise Men towards the stable in which the Child God was sleeping. The Wise Men were chiefs of wandering tribes. One of them, he of a Gypsy tribe. . . . It is, in order to perpetuate this memory, that they call themselves Sons of the Comet.

And, to quote this fragment from the work of Tikno Adjam, the Gypsy poet:

Your Royal Highness the Sun, brother of the Comet, loves his sister too much not to love his children; and moreoever God said to him: Efface yourselves before the Star which is leading them. . . .

Although in my opinion this Gypsy nationality attributed to Balthazar must be accepted with great discretion, it is nevertheless true that, in the Tradition, *o Tchalai* shows some connexion with the Star of the Magi. It is in fact also called *o Netchaphoro*. The origin of this name is not known. Yet one cannot help being struck by the Greek ending, *phore*, to carry. But *netcha* does not remind us of anything. Is it 'carrier of light'? The Gypsies translate it by 'luminous crown', 'halo of God'. 'We bow to the *Netchaphoro* in the *Reat* (nocturnal sky in contrast to diurnal sky) and we then invoke the *Sunto Del* (Holy God). We have the habit of saying "I shall cease to believe in God when I see the *Netchaphoro* fall"' (Zanko). It seems, then, that it is a matter of an apparently fixed star and not of a comet, a celestial body which, moroeever, has always been regarded rather as the announcer of catastrophe.[1]

This story of the Three Wise Men leads us to consider the connexions between Gypsy and the biblical traditions. Or rather the contributions conceded by the latter to the former. In fact, still according to Zanko, the Gypsies venerate Christ and the Virgin

1. Let us note that the star with eight rays (or points – half of sixteen) appears on the stele of Assurbanipal and designates Ishtar.

Mary. The fourth of these traditional accounts reported by Father Chatard sets the scene for

the new *De Develeski* or Divine Mother which the Gypsies today identify with *Sunto Mario*, Saint Mary or 'ancestor Mary'; *Sinpetra*, her father; the *Sunto Del*, the holy God, his Child: *Cretchuno*, Saint Joseph – here the godfather and not the adoptive father of the Child (who also has the right to that name of godfather but does not use it).

It is evident that there has been 'gypsification' of traditional names: Christ becoming *Cretchuno*. And so other personages in this chronicle: *Yacchof* (Jacob), *Abraham*, *Moïshel* (Moses). . . . It is even remarkable how the Gypsy language has conserved better than our own the original form of these names: *Moïschel* is the exact transcription of the Hebrew.

Nevertheless, we may regard as certain the purely Romanian origin of the majority of the names quoted in Zanko's tradition. And perhaps Father Chatard has not sufficiently emphasized this point. In fact, in Romanian *Cretchuno* means 'manger', 'crib', then Christmas; *Sinpetri* is the transcription of *Simpietru*, Saint Peter; *Duneria* is the Romanian name for the Danube. If time permitted, one would certainly find the same Romanian origin in the other names of the Tradition. For me there is no doubt whatever that *Rusalino* designates Jerusalem, *Bonat*, the Banat, etc., and that the Gypsies who have been living for a long time in France have conferred a mythical aspect on very ordinary places and events. The distortion of time which an oral tradition inevitably provokes is alone responsible for these obscurities. The methodical analysis of the said tradition remains to be achieved.

But all this does not make it any less nebulous. It is probable that it turns out for a certain Gypsy group, in the instance of the Kalderash of Zanko, to be confronted with a Bible which oral tradition has turned rather topsy-turvy. Legends which take into account a struggle between *Pharavono* and *Horachaï* (between Pharao and the Jews?), of a crossing of the Red Sea would be worth analysis in this sense. On the other hand, the same confusion between God and Christ is found again among Asiatic peoples such as the Yakuts.[1]

It is nevertheless remarkable that the majority of Gypsies, apart from those who are Mussulmans, have a very definite propensity for cults of the female. That of Sara is worth stopping to consider,

1. See Harva, op. cit.

because it is extremely well known in France, and because it poses the question of the Black Virgins.

Sara, the Black Virgin

There are in fact two Saras: one of the Catholic Church, and one of the Gypsies. The first, servant of the three Marys, Mary Salomé, Mary Jacobé and Mary Magdalene, is supposed to have come with her mistresses and landed at the village of Saintes-Maries-de-la-Mer. The tradition dates from the time of King René the Good (1448). This Sara did not have the right to canonization, and remains in the crypt; she is banned from the church itself. The Sara of the Gypsies must on the other hand be a *Gitane* who was living on the banks of the Rhône with her tribe, and must have greeted the three Marys when they landed.

One of our people who received the first Revelation was Sara the Kâli. She was of noble birth and was chief of her tribe on the banks of the Rhône. She knew the secrets which had been transmitted to her. Near the Rhône the tribes worked in metals and engaged in commerce. The *Rom* at that period practised a polytheistic religion, and once a year they took out on their shoulders the statue of *Ishtari* (Astarte)[1] and went into the sea to receive his benediction there. One day Sara had visions which informed her that the Saints who had been present at the death of Jesus would come, and that she must help them. Sara saw them arrive in a boat. The sea was rough, and the boat threatened to founder. Sara threw her dress on the waves, and, using it as a raft, she floated towards the Saints and helped them to reach land. The Saints baptized Sara and preached the Gospel among the *gadjé* and the *Rom*.[2]

But, before continuing, it is necessary to recall the essentials of the famous pilgrimage of Saintes-Maries-de-la-Mer. On 24 and 25 May each year, the Gypsies have become accustomed to follow this Catholic pilgrimage. For it was really the Church which first instituted the commemoration of the landing of the three Marys after King René had ordered investigations to be made. An older tradition did in fact record the landing of the three Marys, but there was no certainty in regard to the place where they touched land. The place already mentioned, with which we are dealing, was successively called Notre-Dame-de-Ratis, of the Three Marys, and Sainte-Marie-de-la-Barque; *ratis* would seem to mean a 'wooded island', from the

1. See p. 176 for reference to the Babylonian star Ishtar.
2. Franz de Ville, *Tziganes* (Brussels, 1956). Tradition of the Belgian Gypsies.

Celtic *rads* – unless it should derive from the Latin *ratis*, 'raft'. The excavations ordered by King René were successful, for underneath the choir of the primitive church (the date on which it was built is unknown) were discovered the supposed relics of the Saints. The pilgrimage, which has been recorded since the fifteenth century, was soon flourishing.

The official appearance of Sara took place a little later and in *L'Auteur de la dernière vie de M. Olier* one finds the following sentence: 'In a bronze chest were afterwards found ... various human remains which were believed to be those of Sara, a follower of the Holy Marys.' In 1521, Vincent Phillipon, in his pious little novel *La Légende des Saintes Maries Jacobé et Salomé*, records the presence of Sara, pinpointing her role: in order to come to the help of her mistresses, she went out through the Camargue collecting alms.[1] The 24 May having been chosen to honour the saints, the Gypsies (present in Arles in 1438) mingled with the pilgrimage. But at first they did not recognize Sara-la-Kâli. According to other writers, it was only in 1496 that the remains of the 'servant' were invented.

Why did the Gypsies choose Sara? Perhaps because of her unobtrusive role. Also, maybe, on account of her nickname: 'the Egyptian'. But if we keep to the Gypsy tradition which would have it that Sara was one of them and a tribal chief, we can consider the possibility of identifying her as a Black Virgin.

The name given by the Gypsies to Sara – '*la Kâli*' – means in their language both 'the black woman' and 'the Gypsy woman'. As for the name Sara, if it is, for the Church, that of Abraham's wife,[2] this is to bring together a whole series of goddess-mothers, of which there are the *Saraï* of the Caucasus, the same people who could have given their name to the biblical Sara.[3]

The Gypsy worship of Sara is extremely interesting, and especially because this is one of the few activities of theirs at which the *gadjé* can easily be present. Up to 1912, only Gypsies had the right to go inside the Church crypt. They spent a whole night among themselves there, and this vigil did not fail to be surrounded with mystery, particularly in the eyes of the Saints' priest who in that year was permitted to be present. It is known that the crypt, which is usually

1. Delage, 'Les Saintes-Maries-de-la-Mer', in a special issue of *Études Tsiganes*.

2. The Romanian peasants, to drive away a witch, shout: *Mana Sara!*

3. Mayani, *Les Hyksos et le Monde de la Bible* (1956).

flooded with seeping water, harbours three elements: on the left, as one enters, there is an old altar, the pagan altar (some say that it was for bull-sacrifice in the worship of Mithra, but of this there is no proof); in the centre there is the Christian third-century altar; and, to the right, there is the statue of Sara. The latter does not strike me as dating from before the eighteenth century. André Delage had the opportunity to examine it several times, since to him is due its restoration and conservation:

This statue, in plaster, and not in wood as has sometimes been stated, is not, however, very ancient. It is a plaster cast moulded on a body which I shall call 'standard', with a head which all the evidence shows is not on the same scale nor by the same hand as that which modelled the body. In my opinion it must have replaced a wooden statue that was much more ancient.

Of this last not a trace remains. The present statue has obviously been painted black. If it clearly shows patches on the face, this is because of continual retouchings which have little by little obliterated the paint underneath.

During the vigil the Gypsies do not (or no longer?) practise any special rites. They are content to keep watch, usually in bare feet and with the head uncovered. Some of them doze or sleep along by the walls. When present at this scene I have again experienced exactly the same mental impression which I used to have in Indian temples, where the faithful remain, by turns indifferent and deeply moved, at the very feet of the idols.

Those who arrive devote themselves to Sara in two acts of ritual: the touching and hanging up of garments. The women in particular respectfully stroke the statue or kiss the hems of her many dresses. Then they hook up clothes beside her, clothes they have brought, from a handkerchief to a silk kerchief, a slip or a bust-bodice. Sometimes it is merely a matter of torn pieces of cloth. Finally, they touch the saint with miscellaneous objects representing those absent or the sick (photographs, medals . . . or again items of clothing). In actual fact, this touching is really rubbing. The ceremonial is clearly not original. The rite of hanging up garments is known among the Dravidians of northern India who 'believe in fact that the linen and clothes of a sick person become impregnated with his malady, and that the patient will be cured if his linen is purified by contact with a sacred tree'. Hence, among them are seen trees or images covered with rags of clothing which they call *Chitraiya Bhavani*, 'Our Lady of the Rags'.[1] There exists likewise a 'Tree for Tatters' (*sinderich ogateh*) among the Kirghiz of the Sea of Aral. One could probably find other examples of this magical prophylaxis.

The second part of the Gypsy pilgrimage consists in the procession to the sea and the symbolical immersion,[2] common to all cults of the great goddesses of fecundity. The magic of immersion induced rain.[3] Clearly, to obtain rain seems less important for nomads than for sedentaries and husbandmen. Nevertheless, and even apart from the fact that the nomads need grass for their horses, the Gypsies seem to have formerly served as intermediaries in this fecundity ritual. In fact, even recently in Belgium and in the countries of Central Europe,

> The Gypsies used to take part in certain festivals of fixed date, one of them a little before Palm Sunday . . . and in periods of great drought. They went in groups outside the front of residences of rich landowners, and to the market-places . . . and there they performed their dances, all the time asking that there should be a beneficent rainfall on their crops. The spectators then went forward with receptacles full of water which they poured over the heads of the dancing women. . . .[4]

The author makes it clear that the women were thoroughly drenched. Their 'work' accomplished, they collected a piece of silver and went away to start again elsewhere.

It is evident that the symbolical immersion of Saintes-Maries-de-la-Mer is no longer intended to induce rain. The fecundity ritual (in which we have seen that even Ishtar took part) has become a blessing of the sea by a subtle adaptation of the Church. The Gypsies have followed this transformation. But, in this evolution, they have conserved the archetype of the mother-goddess and of the Black Virgin.

Ruth Partington[5] recalls that the three Marys are still honoured by Gypsies in the little village of Miguières, near Chartres, and that magical (or miraculous) cures are witnessed there. But Sara, she

1. Saillens, *Nos Vierges noires* (1945).
2. It was only in 1935 that the Church authorized this ceremony.
3. Eliade, op. cit.
4. Delage, op. cit.
5. 'More Legends of the Gypsies and the Holy Family', *J.G.L.S.* XXXVIII, 1–2.

says, has disappeared from this cult. However, in examining the works of Saillens on the Black Virgins, we see that Chartres is not only the owner of a Black Virgin dating from very ancient times, but, furthermore, that this one is Saint Anne, protectress of births and of mines (the subterranean world). Now, in a moment, will be seen the importance of Saint Anne in Gypsy demonology.

Nerval relates, in *Octavie*, his visit to a Gypsy lady from Italy in whose home sat enthroned in a well-chosen place, a black madonna. This is not a poet's reverie. Today one still discovers in some Gypsy caravans the statue of Kâli on the icon altar. Tita Parni, Matéo Maximoff's wife, has even made a fine reputation by painting and sculpting effigies of the black goddess. But a really careful study of the cult of Sara-Kâli among the Gypsies still remains to be made.

Finally, it would be necessary to compare with Sara *La Macarena*, the Virgin of the Spanish *Gitanos*. She wears symbolically seven skirts or long dresses. A Jewish tradition emphasizes the role of these two madonnas by attaching them to the doctrine of the Cabbalists of the school of Isaac the Blind, born at Beaucaire on the Rhône, who possibly contributed to this cult: Sara in the Cabbala means the 'residence in exile' and bears the name of 'Fallen Widow'.

DEMONOLOGY

Dr Maxim Bing of Budapest has for a long time studied the 'Medical Demonology of the Gypsies of Transylvania'[1] and has collected this astonishing myth whose richness demands that I reproduce it *in extenso*:

In a very remote era, the Gypsies of Transylvania relate, the queen of the Good Fairies, the *Keshalyi*, was a very beautiful girl who lived in her high rocky mountain palace. Her name was *Ana*. But, in the depths of the earth there lived the demon people, the *Loçolico*, terrestrial spirits who in the beginning had been men but whom the devil had transformed into frightful demons. Their king had fallen deeply in love with the beautiful and pure *Ana*. When he introduced himself to her, the princess was terrified by his appearance, and she repulsed him with horror. Then the *Loçolico* attacked the *Keshalyi* unawares, devoured a great number and were preparing to exterminate all of them when Princess *Ana*, to save them, agreed to marry the horrible monster, their king.

1. In the Review *Ciba* ('Démonologie médicale des Tziganes de Transylvanie').

But the princess felt such a repulsion for her husband that it was impossible for her to give herself to him. Driven to despair, the king, who was wandering about at random, came upon a golden toad . . . and this golden toad advised him to make his wife eat the brain of a magpie. Soon afterwards the queen would fall into a deep sleep, and he could then do what he wished with her. The king followed this advice and so could make love to *Ana* while she slept.

The queen duly gave birth to a demon, *Melalo*, who had the appearance of a bird with two heads and whose plumage was a dirty green colour. [*Melalo* is the most dreaded demon of the Gypsies.] With sharp claws he tears out hearts and lacerates bodies; with a blow of his wing he stuns his victim and, when the latter recovers from his swoon, he has lost his reason. He stirs up rage and frenzy, murder and rape. As he owes his birth to the brain of a magpie, those whom he has struck with madness chatter nonsensically, like the magpie.

After the birth of *Melalo*, *Ana* continued to reject her husband's advances. But when *Melalo* had grown up, he also insisted that he should be given a woman. Therefore he advised his father to cook a fish in ass's milk and then put some drops of this love-potion into the sexual organ of his wife while she was asleep, and possess her forthwith.

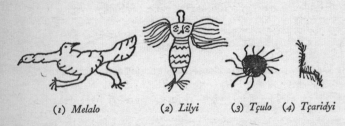

(*1*) *Melalo*   (*2*) *Lilyi*   (*3*) *Tçulo* (*4*) *Tçaridyi*

Nine days after this embrace, *Ana* gave birth to a femal demon, *Lilyi*, the Viscous. She was *Melalo*'s wife. Her body was that of a fish with a man's head, from each side of which hung nine hairs of beard or sticky filaments. When these filaments penetrated a man's body, he immediately contracted a catarrhal disease.

The king could not make love to his wife except when *Melalo* had first put her asleep with his vapours. Now *Melalo* had many children and the king was jealous of this. *Melalo*, enemy of man, wished to prevent men from multiplying. He therefore agreed to put his mother asleep, in the hope that she would bring new demons into the world, numerous enough and strong enough to destroy the human race. Whereupon, on the advice of *Melalo*, the king ate a stag-beetle and a crayfish. Then *Melalo* put *Ana* asleep and she gave birth to the demon *Tçulo*.

Tçulo, the Thick or 'Potbellied', looked like a spikey little ball of prickles. He stole into the human body, and, rolling himself up inside it, brought about violent pains in the lower belly. He specialized in torturing pregnant women. *Tçulo* persecuted even his sister *Lilyi*.

In order to rid himself of this harassing creature, *Melalo* advised his father to procreate a daughter who should be his wife. And so it was that *Tçaridyi*, the Burning One, was born. She had the body of a small worm covered with hair. When she succeeded in penetrating into the body of a man, she caused burning fevers, and especially puerperal fever to women in childbirth. *Tçulo* and his wife greatly tormented ailing people, but rarely caused their death.

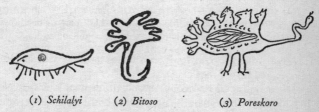

(1) Schilalyi   *(2) Bitoso*   *(3) Poreskoro*

On the instigation of *Melalo*, the king had cooked a mouse on which he had spat, and of it he prepared a soup which he gave his wife to eat. She fell ill and, while she was drinking water, a white mouse escaped from her mouth. This was *Schilalyi*, the Cold. She has a great number of little feet and causes cold fever.

But when *Schilalyi* set about molesting her brothers and sisters, *Melalo* inspired his father with the idea of eating garlic on which he had first urinated; then the king visited his wife. After which she gave birth to *Bitoso*, who became *Schilalyi*'s wife. *Bitoso*, the Faster [the one who fasts], is a little worm with several heads who induces headaches and stomachaches; he also causes loss of appetite. His numerous children provoke colics, buzzing in the ears, toothaches and cramps.

Ana had a skin eruption. *Melalo* advised her to get herself licked by mice. This she did, but one of the mice penetrated into her stomach. She gave birth to *Lolmischo*,[1] the Red Mouse. When *Lolmischo* runs on the skin of a sleeping man, that man is soon covered with eczema.

Ana was extremely unhappy to have delivered so many monsters into the world. She asked *Melalo* what she should do in order to become sterile. He suggested to her that she should have herself buried in a dungheap. She consented to do so, but a dung-beetle slipped into her body. She gave birth to *Minceskro*, who causes maladies of the blood. *Minceskro* is a female demon. She married her brother *Lolmischo*. They had

1. A male demon.

185

many children. It is they who cause small-pox, scarlatina, and measles, etc.

Finally the *Keshalyi* made *Ana*, now driven to despair, eat a cake in which they had mixed hair of the hound of hell[?], powdered snake, and cat's hair. And, when the king had visited her, she gave birth to *Poreskoro*, the most terrible of all demons. This is a hermaphrodite who can fertilize himself. He has four cat's heads and four dog's heads and his tail is a snake with forked tongue. It is he and his children who start the worst epidemics: plague, cholera, etc., as well as the most deadly parasitical diseases.

The king was so terrified of this appalling posterity that he gave *Ana* her freedom, on condition that every woman of the *Keshalyi*, on reaching the age of 999 years, should be delivered to his *Loçolico*. Ever since then *Ana* lives alone in an inaccessible castle amid high crags. She shows herself only very rarely, and only in the shape of a golden toad. . . .

This is a thrilling legend, for it deals at the same time with demonology, sex and Gypsy medicine.

For the moment we shall consider only the demonological aspect of it. And, first, what can be the significance of the names of persons in this awful story?

The queen of the fairies is called *Ana*. She is pure and beautiful. She lives on a mountain. She is the typical princess of fairy tales. And, if she gives birth to demons, this does not seem to be entirely her fault. But where did she come from?

There was among the Celts a great goddess named *Dana* or *Danu*. According to MacCullough,[1] she gave her name to the whole group of Celtic divinities, and is called their mother. She was parent of the goddess *Ana* or *Anou* whom Cormac describes as *mater deorum hibernensium* ('mother of the gods of the Hibernians'). Cormac, moreover, associates the name *Anou* with the Gaelic word *ana*, 'abundance'. It is impossible not to think of the foster-mother of the Romans, *Anna Perenna*, who herself was the *Anna Pourna* of Brahmanism. If the Celtic word *ana* means 'abundance', the Sanscrit word *anna* means 'nourishment', 'sustenance'. *Ana* or *Dana* (*dé* means 'of the goddess') is therefore a sister of all these mother-goddesses which have a name analagous to French 'mama' and to English 'mamma'; one of the names of Cybele (the Phrygian Aphrodite of Mount Ida) was *Nanna*, and, among the Germanic peoples, the beautiful *Nanna* was the wife of Balder (the Scandinavian deity). Like a Chthonian goddess, *Dana* was guardian of the dead and she must have required human sacrifices. In the folk-lore

1. *The Religion of the Ancient Celts* (Edinburgh, 1911).

of Leicestershire there is a cannibalistic Black Anna who lives in a cave.[1]

If this author did not know of the existence of the Gypsy *Ana*, one will allow that there is a strange connexion by similitude. This Celtic *Ana* from whom, what is more, the French Saint Anne derives, the Saint Anne who, at Cungin in the Aube, or Saint-Sulpice in the Dordogne, gives the rain, the Saint Anne who, notably at Chartres, is black.

It therefore seems as though we are once again dealing with the degeneracy of an archaic cult, itself already subjected to many changes in form.

Melalo, the first son of *Ana*, has a name that is typically Gypsy. It means 'dirty', 'obscene'. He is a bird with two heads. . . . As Dr Bing emphasizes:

The two-headed bird was already found among the Hittites, who brought it to Byzantium, where it became the famous heraldic bird, and then in this form passed on to the coat of arms of old Russia and to that of Austria.

Ana's second child is *Lilyi*: an analogy with the Lilith of the Bible immediately comes to mind. The Babylonians already knew the demons of night, among whom were Lilu, Lilitu and Ardat Lili.[2] This is again found in the Jewish tradition in which Lilith, the first wife of Adam, gave birth to giants and demons.[3] Classical iconography readily represents her with the appearance of a serpent-woman. Now among the Gypsies she is named 'the Viscous'. Arab translators call her *ghul*, from which there is the French *goule* and the English 'ghoul', who devours sleeping men. Furthermore, Lilith is represented among Alsatian Jews[4] on the protective amulets and talismans of the woman in confinement, and on these same talismans (known as *Scheimostafeln*) likewise appear invocations to *Sini* and *Sinsini*, deeply mysterious personages who we again find mentioned in Romanian manuscripts of the eighteenth century, and usually connected with the Greek saints *Sisynios* and *Sinsini*. Possibly it is here a matter of the *Sigynnes*, the people described by Herodotus who came from the Iran which Mayani[5] records as having

1. Saillens, op. cit.
2. Toufy Fadh, *Les songes et leur interprétation selon l'Islam* (1959).
3. See the *Jewish Encyclopaedia* under this word.
4. See the Jewish section of the Alsatian Museum, Strasbourg.
5. *Les Hyksos et le Monde de la Bible*, op. cit.

been identified with the Gypsies.[1] In this I merely indicate a relationship, and a doubtful one at that.

The other names of the demons of *Ana*'s lineage sound quite Gypsy. Thus *Lolmischo*, which means 'red mouse'. The name of the fairies, *Keshalyi*, seems to be copied from *Kachli*, 'spindle'; so, in this reappears the old connexion of fairy with spindle that is widely testified. An invocation against sterility pin-points this: *Keshalyi*, *lisperesn* ('Fairies, spin'). But this root *kesh* exists in Hebrew *kishep* (magic) and in Akkadian *kashshapu* (wizard, sorcerer).

We shall find these fairies, the *Keshalyi*, and their multiple symbolism in Gypsy rituals of everyday life and in their medicine. But they are not the only Gypsy fairies. Much more commonplace are the *Ursitory* (or Fates): Matéo Maximoff has dealt with them in his novel of that title. The *Ursitory* are three male fairies who, on the third night after birth, come down to a child and decide his future. Nobody has ever been able to see them, except the infant, the mother and the sorceress (who is called the *Drabarni* – that is, 'the herb woman'). No one can annul the life which the *Ursitory* have ordained. The belief in the *Ursitory* seems to be confined to the Gypsies of Romania.

The same symbolism of the number three, or its multiple nine, governs the manifestations of another category of fairies: the *Matiya*. So long as they are virgins they remain astonishingly young and beautiful. But, motivated by the desire to multiply, they seduce men and give themselves to them. Their male partners usually die, like humble-bees. But at the same time the *Matiya* lose their youth and beauty, in return for which they beget three pairs of twins. Though their working of havoc is limited, they must still be compared with classical ghouls.

Although the cult of the dead has a prior interest, I must at this point speak of the Gypsy vampire. He is called *Mulo* (plural *Mulé*) which means precisely 'one who is dead' (past participle of the verb *merav*, 'to die'). The vampire is, in fact, the soul of a dead person. Some groups of Gypsies differentiate between the *Mulé* and the *Suuntsé* (plural of *Sunto*, 'saint'), the first representing the spirits of men who have died accidentally, or who have merited the torments of hell, the second being spirits of new inhabitants of paradise. However, only the *Mulé* are of definite importance. It is fully

1. Or *Zyghes* of the Caucasus, already named.

understood that the Gypsies' dead become authentic *Mulé*, to the exclusion of all others. The Gypsies do not in the least fear non-Gypsy ghosts, and nothing, for example, will stop them from sleeping in a *gadjé* cemetery.

The *Mulé* live only by night. Among the Hungarian Gypsies it is enjoined not to throw muck or hot water out of the tent or caravan after sundown; the *Mulo* who was touched would take revenge immediately.[1] But the *Mulé* also live at exactly midday: the moment, in fact, when the sun is passing from East to West and marks a dead moment in time. Does not Stendhal speak of the 'dark' (or 'mysterious') hour of noon? At all events, the Spaniards are very sensitive in regard to this crucial moment. For the Gypsies, during this fleeting instant, the trees, the road, the smallest objects belong to the *Mulé*. At noon they stop travelling, as it is forbidden for them to travel after the sun goes down. Midday is the hour at which shadow does not exist; in this belief must be seen a relationship not only with the sun's 'psycho-ceremonial' role but with the problem of the Double. The *Mulo* really seems to be in effect 'Death's Double'. Zanko makes this quite clear:

the *Mulo's* 'headquarters' or point of attachment is the body of a dead man. His dwelling-place is the grave or tomb of the deceased. But he is not firmly attached to the body. Death has liberated him, and he can wander, travel, go to and from this base. He is not the corpse; he is the man himself in the form of his double.

So it is that at cock-crow the *Mulo* returns to his grave (or 'headquarters'). But he is not on this account a vampire of the classical type. If he is still capable of sexual appetite and carnal commerce, he does not suck the blood of his victims in the manner of a vulgar seducer from the Austro-Hungarian world of sensational films. The excessive bibliography devoted to the vampire prevents me from seeking the exact relationships between him and the *Mulo* of the Gypsies. Yet it is evident that throughout the whole of Central Europe the frightening importance of the vampire, one might call it the cult of the vampire, could not leave the Gypsies indifferent. Nevertheless, as Kamill Erdös has remarked, clear traces of belief in metempsychosis have been noted among the Carpathian Gypsies, and it is in the sense of the Latin *spiritus* and the Greek *pneuma* that the significance of the *Mulo* must be sought.

1. Kamill Erdös, '*Magie des Tziganes hongrois*', *Psyché*, No. 116.

How does the *Mulo* torment the living? This essentially depends on the group of Gypsies concerned. Among Zanko's Kalderash, the ghost of the dead husband would reappear in the evening and, on arriving at the camp, ask for his wife. He spends the night with her and, after all, there is nothing to prove that this is a great moment for her. In Maximoff's novels, it is in the form of a voluptuous girl that the ghost leads a good young man to suicide. Although the terrible role of the *Mulo* is regularly spoken of, I have not found a single instance of monstrous or criminal practice. As a matter of curiosity, I shall quote what can be read in regard to the *Mulo* in the *Encyclopaedia of Pallas*:

The *Mulo* is a vampire-like figure. The child born dead becomes *mulo* and grows until he attains eight years of age; only then does he enter the country of the dead. There is not a bone in his body, and his hands are without the middle finger, which he must leave in the grave. Once a year, on the anniversary of his birth, his companions boil him so that he shall regain his strength. On New Year's night the *mulé* kidnap women, whom they boil in big cauldrons so that they may shed their bones and become boneless women *mulé*.[1]

MAGIC

The reader has seen that during the past the Gypsies were automatically regarded as sorcerers. This is still so today in the majority of remote country places. There are in fact some Gypsies who are pre-eminently magicians. They are so in terms of their non-civilized way of life, as aliens, by choice of this profession, and, on the other hand, through some natural predilections. This was the case of the Jews in the Middle Ages, and of the Lapps and Finns in Northern Europe. This assignment to ethnic groups has been made by Marcel Mauss:[2] 'All unsettled tribes who live among a settled population are considered as sorcerers. This is still in our time the case with the Gypsies, and also of many wandering castes in India.'

The natural predispositions of nomads are those of people who still live in accordance with the rhythms of the seasons, plants, and elements. Their contempt for mechanical techniques has conserved intact among them senses that are now dulled in civilized man – in

1. Quoted by Kamill Erdős in *Études Tsiganes*, January 1959.
2. In *Sociologie et Anthropologie — Essai d'un théorie générale de la magie*, 1960.

the city-dweller. Uncultivated, that is not encumbered with the vast accumulation of knowledge with which we set out on life's journey, the Gypsy still knows how to look around him and draw lessons from the exterior world. Furthermore, in his capacity of pariah, his nervous potential has been considerably increased, also his susceptibility, his faculty for getting excited by daily mental pictures, and he has become (or remained) extremely sensitive to 'wavelengths' which do not reach us. So it is that he lives in an essentially magical universe.

Lehman, the sociologist, has defined magic as 'putting superstitions into practice, that is, beliefs which are neither religious nor scientific'. In the course of the present work, these superstitions will be found to be widely distributed. Here I shall note only those which are not included in the chapter on Everyday Life (page 201), or those of which there is as yet no question: particularly those relating to maleficent magic.

As there are black magic and white magic, so there are the sorcerer and the magician. The Gypsies know on the one hand the *cohani* whose acts of destruction are greatly feared, and on the other hand the *drabarni*, the herb woman (from *drab* which means grass (herb), magical plant and tobacco)[1] who renders appreciable services. It will be seen which ones.

The black magic of the Gypsies embraces the usual evil spells intended to make enemies suffer or die, or similarly their livestock. The list of these is immense. Apparatus and procedure are those of classical magic: dolls or figurines pricked with a needle in a particular place (Hungarian Gypsies) but used to the number of nine and made of stearin (melted candle); they contain the inevitable piece of clothing, and of the nail or hair of the victim. Sometimes grass is gathered at a crossroads and placed under the threshold of the tent or caravan. Less commonplace seems to be the technique which consists in watering a branch of weeping willow for nine days and pouring this water in front of the dwelling of the person who is to suffer (the weeping willow symbolizes tears).[2]

The evil eye is particularly enduring among the Gypsies, who use these terms relating to it: *iachalav*, 'to cast the evil eye', from *iach*, eye; *iachalipé*, the 'act of fascination' or 'bewitchment'; *iachalo*, 'struck by the spell'. Belief in the evil eye is partly original

1. *Darbha* in Vedic India meant 'sacred grass'.
2. Erdös, op. cit.

to the Gypsies. It is a fact that 'this superstition', which one might think is the most widespread of all, is not found in Australia, Melanesia or North America, nor in any clear form in ancient India, nor in non-Islamic modern India.[1] (However, Henry[2] uses the expression several times. In fact, the precise notion of the evil eye has never been clearly defined. One should be satisfied with not attaching this label to anything but the processes of bewitching in which the fixed look is essential.)

Among the Gypsies the rites for protection against the *iachalipé* are numerous. But most of them are intended to protect the child of tender years. So, in the whole of Central and South-East Europe, they pour his bath-water over him, making it run along the blade of a scythe. Demons could not bear the contact with iron (is this the symbolism of the metal or of its bright shine? Formerly in Provence the openings of dovecots were surrounded with faience tiles, whose glitter would prevent the approach of maladies due to demons).

Among the Carpathian Gypsies, Erdös has noted the following superstitions against the evil eye affecting a child. To the child's wrist was attached either a violin string or a piece of red string. Or his eye was licked three times, while spitting with each lick. Or again, one spat into his eye. Another technique is related to practices of divination: on the surface of water in a wash-basin are placed three glowing embers of wood and two straws. If at least one of the straws sinks to the bottom of the water, then the child is under a malign influence.

Naturally Gypsy magic uses a great number of plants, animals and minerals. It is not possible to list them all here. But let us note that the animals most often used are the toad, the snake, the weasel; and birds – the cock, peacock, pigeon and magpie. A whole volume could be written on the toad and its use in magic. The reader will remember that, in the legend of the *Keshalyi*, the toad is the adviser of the demon's king who is enabled by him to possess his wife *Ana*. And that *Ana* reappeared at the end of the story in the form of a golden toad. The toad-womb-lewdness relationship is universal, and known even in Brazilian rites. The Middle Ages, and Rome before then, saw this batrachian as a loathsome animal that was then maleficent and greedy for blood. Its form was regarded as that of a uterus turned inside out, or, as you wish, the uterus had the form of a toad.

1. Mauss, op. cit.
2. In *Magie dans l'Inde antique* (1909).

Woman's sex had the faculty of leaving the body to go on mysterious nocturnal peregrinations and to gambol in some mystical bath.[1] The batrachian then very soon appeared in the shape of a votive offering made of wood or iron. Among the Gypsies, these offerings showed, for example, a remarkable resemblance to the *Gebär-mutterkröte* (matrix toads) of Alsatian folk-lore.

The snake (*sap* in Gypsy, *sarap* in Hebrew: root in Sanskrit) gives rise each year on 15 March to a special feast of the Kalderash Gypsies, called the Feast of the Serpent. 'On that day, if anybody succeeds in killing a snake, he will be fortunate throughout the year.'[2] In maleficent philtres the snake's skin is pounded or pulverized. Some amulets of sea-urchin fossils are called snake's-eyes.

The weasel is called the *phurdini*, that is, the Blower. This very peaceable-looking animal is the Gypsies' pet aversion. The fact that a weasel 'blows' (or 'puffs') when it is afraid or angry is the origin of this repulsion. The Gypsies, in fact, have an almost morbid horror of puffs of air, and of wind. Wind, they say, is the Devil's sneezing.[3] All the nomads of the steppes fear this element, which throws their camps into confusion. The weasel's puff is a sign of ill-luck (cf. the breath of classical dragons).

When a pregnant woman sees a weasel on her path, she is sure to have a troublesome childbirth and her child is predestined to a life of afflictions. A Gypsy caravan which comes upon a weasel, especially if the animal starts to 'puff', must immediately change direction, otherwise they are sure to have difficulties with the police and authorities. This is why those who walk ahead of it put up a signal at the place: they tie a tuft of woman's hair to the nearest branch, and mark on the ground the new direction to be taken by those who follow. This ground sign consists of three parallel lines with the middle one longer than the others. When a betrothed girl sees a weasel and it threatens her by puffing, the girl must wash herself immediately in the next running water, otherwise her marriage will not be a happy one. If by chance a Gypsy should kill the weasel, the whole tribe will have bad luck for some time.[4]

Superstition surrounding the weasel is ancient and still strong. It

1. Paullini, *Du Crapaud* (Paris, 1696).
Dr Blind (in *Globus*, 1902) published the Slav and German incantations which were to compel the uterus to go back to the woman's body.
2. Chatard, op. cit.
3. The devil–wind connexion is found a little everywhere, for example in Guyenne (see Seignolle, *Le Diable dans la tradition populaire*, 1960).
4. *Ciba*, op. cit.

was already existing in Ancient Greece. In several of Aristophanes' comedies, he shows the dissolution of assemblies at Pnyx on the appearance of a weasel. This belief is found again in the Mâconnais district in France. And Theophrastus records in his *Characters*: 'When a weasel crosses the road, the superstitious person will not proceed unless another has passed it or until he himself has thrown three stones beyond the place.' Although this animal was abominated in India, it was worshipped in Egypt.

The squirrel, the *romen morga* or Gypsy cat, on the contrary, is a lucky mascot that is particularly effective in the realm of love. But the Gypsies' favourite animal is the hedgehog, the *niglo*. Yet this does not prevent both squirrel and hedgehog from being seasoned in various ways, and constituting savoury specialities in Gypsy cookery. The hedgehog was important in the whole of Iranian mythology. A docile animal, sometimes the creator of fire, sometimes of agriculture, its cult is spread throughout all the northern part of the Middle East.

As for the plants used in magical 'cookery', they are too many for all to be listed. There are, obviously, the classical herbs used by all witches and 'wise women' in Europe, and a census of them has not yet been attempted. By way of example here is a list of those plants which enter into the composition of just once recipe for abortion used among the Gypsies of Yugoslavia: aloes (wood), cloves, ginger, nutmeg (ground to powder), cheese-runnet (a rubiaceous plant popularly called *grateron* in France, 'goose-grass' in Britain), borage, sage, rue, mint (boiled for three hours as the Lord's Prayer is recited). Let us note, to be accurate, that to these plants white wine *must* be added, and that it is necessary to filter the resultant decoction for three days through an apron that has been worn by a woman.[1]

Gypsy magic evidently makes great use of amulets and talismans. (It is agreed that the object which wards off a misfortune should be called an *amulet*, and the one which brings good luck a *talisman*.) In the course of the chapters which follow, the descriptions of some of these will be given. Charms are likewise of great diversity, and range from the shells of shellfish (against the evil eye) to scoria (or slag) used in the Banat region of Temesvar. Some of them are attached by thread, like the cat's-eye, which is put on the wrist of an infant that has been baptized. Others are sewn on the inside of gar-

1. *Ciba*, op. cit.

ments. Such is the 'rose-window swastika' which has club-shaped petals turning leftwards (and not to the right like those of the better known swastika). The most curious in the collection might be the relic used by a Kalderash Gypsy (Zanko): a newspaper cutting announcing that the Pope had given his blessing to the Gypsies.

PHARMACOPOEIA AND MEDICAL MAGIC

Here I shall deal with the part of medical magic which does not come into the chapter on Everyday Life. This medical magic is considerable, as it is indebted to a nomad people whose contacts with civilization(s) have always been slight. This kind of life has furthermore immunized the Gypsies against many of our infectious diseases. Although infantile mortality is still very high among them, the survivors are remarkably sturdy. Life in the open air, and the struggle with the elements, have advantageously counter-balanced anomalous food and lack of hygiene. For all that, there is no certainty that the last two factors do not themselves contribute to their health.

Nevertheless the Gypsies are not unaware of illness and, as among all 'primitive' peoples, when it appears it seems very mysterious to them. They have had to resort again to demonology in order to explain it. This was what the inhabitants of the Mesopotamian world had done before them, because for these people the morbid agents were demons which had entered the human body. Still further back in the past, ancient India knew of the existence of these demons, such as the goddess Diarrhoea. The inexhaustible legend of the *Keshalyi* has shown us demons–illness with Sumero-Akkadian similarities: Babylon feared *Ashakku*, the tuberculosis demon, the *Akhkhazzu*, the jaundice demon, the *Labartu*, the demon of accidental abortion. . . .[1]

Through that legend of the *Keshalyi* we see that once the Gypsies realized the existence of a disease, they 'invented' a demon responsible for it, and then made use of the particular qualities and characteristics of this demon to cure the disease. There is nothing in this that is not very familiar. But it would be necessary to study the choice and invention of the demon–malady and the symbolism attaching to the combination. Gypsy knowledge of anatomy and pathogenesis are extremely rudimentary. Thus, they believe that dysentery has its seat in the heart.

1. See Contenau, *La Magie chez les Assyriens et les Babyloniens* (1947).

To make an inventory of the 'magical pharmacopoeia' of the Gypsies is also impossible. Besides, this pharmacopoeia is hardly original. The ingredients used in it are usually rotten or putrid things, excreta (saliva, urine) ... skin of snakes, mouldy bread-crumbs, stale liquid from sauerkraut, manure. ... Animals whose curative virtue is commonplace enter the composition of these remedies: bear's grease, snake flesh, carapace of beetle, not counting the famous cantharides.

Likewise unoriginal is the systematic recourse to a basic sexual symbolism. And so women's urine, menstrual blood and pubic hairs frequently enter into the composition of love-potions. In regard to sexual characteristics, also very important are the elementary factors of fecundity that are part of the magical pharmacopoeia: the moon, water, rain, the fruits of the gourd family (e.g. the gourd, melon, cucumber, etc.)[1].

All these remedies are not exceptional, far from it. The contemporary pharmacopoeias of civilized countries contain items quite as astonishing that have not yet been industrially transformed into pharmaceutical remedies. Thus, modern medicine discovers that in the old magical use of 'eyes of crayfish', that is the internal concretions of the carapace, the Gypsies are merely using the properties of phosphate and carbonate of lime.

But this use of plants or minerals is founded on the analogy, on the usual 'signature' of the magical rites. 'A plant is good for such-and-such an ailment because it has the same colour as the skin or urine in that illness, a stone will be ordered to be crushed in a potion because it more or less resembles the ailing organ.'[2]

Let us finally point out that the Gypsy pathogenic method seems to form part of the Semitic group for which the malady is caused by a divinity or a demon, while the pathogenic method of the Greek group resorts to *fatum*, to misfortune, simply, and is not personified.

As an example of the magical medicine of the Gypsies, we shall be content here to call to mind the processes calculated to cure mental illnesses. It is still the legend of the *Keshalyi* on which I shall fall back.[3] It will be remembered that *Melalo*, the most perverse of the Gypsy demons–maladies, 'stirred up rage, madness, murder and rape'. As he owes his birth to the brain of a magpie, those whom he has struck with insanity talk nonsense in their speech, like the mag-

1. See the section of Love and Love-magic, pp. 209–10.
2. Contenau, op. cit.   3. And on the Review *Ciba*, op. cit.

pie. For this reason sensible Gypsy women rub the back of the mentally deranged with the brain of a magpie whose body they bury on the bank of a river. Into the stream, before sunrise, on six days running, the women magicians on each occasion throw two cantharides, two teeth of a white dog and two frogs. If the sick person is not cured at the end of six days, he is declared incurable [sic]. Another therapy seems more rational:

For six days in succession the patient is made to take powder of cantharides, the first day a single powdered cantharis, then one daily afterwards. At the same time a waistband or sash, on which the picture of *Melalo* is embroidered in wool, is put on the invalid, next to the skin itself. The cure achieved, these waistbands are thrown away or burned.[1]

Among the Serbian Gypsies,

to cure headaches, it is necessary to go and fetch water from nine places into which first glowing charcoal embers have been thrown. But to make sure of a good cure, it is essential to embroider symbolical designs on the ailing person's clothing: cocks, roses, suns, cakes, knives, snakes or acorns. Headache is always caused by a calumny, by the evil eye or the *nagaẓa*, that is, when the person affected has walked on some object that is under a spell.[2]

Found also among the Indians of the Vedic epoch are wood cinders or glowing charcoal which are used against possession by evil spirits. And the sick person himself goes up along the stream against the current. The use of cantharides is common to too many people to require emphasis on this point.

To be recorded, finally, is the important part of music in the medical magic of the Gypsies. Music has the reputation of being able to calm nervous troubles. The invalid's parents attach a banknote to the musician's forehead to thank him. This banknote is merely the modern form of the coin which once served as an amulet for many peoples of Western Asia.[3]

WITCHCRAFT

If Gypsy women healers are still very numerous and make a fuss of

1. Bing, in the Review *Ciba*, op. cit.
2. Bernadzikovska, 'Superstitions médicales des Tziganes serbes', in the Review *Ciba*.
3. The music–magic connexion has been studied by Crook in *The Popular Religion and Folklore of Northern India* (London, 1897).

members of their own tribe as well as of non-Gypsies, the manner in which they obtain the raw material for their art is nonetheless deceptive from our point of view: in actual fact it is in pharmacies and drug stores that they buy officially recognized medicines and drugs which they resell to sick people under the guise of pseudo-magical preparations. It is natural that the results should be satisfactory.

There remains, nevertheless, an original Gypsy witchcraft (or black magic) which their old women magicians grimly defend. These women have learnt their art from childhood, being called to play this part in terms of their heredity. There is a category of them who have received their gift from the water spirits and earth spirits, the *Nivashi* and the *Psuvushi*, those demons of a particular species who have the power to join in carnal union with future witches. The sexual act takes place while the young girl is sleeping and, to be sure, without her consent. It is only when she awakes that the chosen girl realizes that from then she possesses unforeseen powers. She next must have an indefinite period in which to acquire mastery, and, while this transformation is taking place, she is bound to keep her secret. At last comes the day when, sure of herself, she announces her new vocation to the tribe, and from that moment she is treated with particular respect.

To be a witch is, in fact, regarded by the Gypsies as an exceptional favour – to the point that the rebukes which the *drabarni* might suffer before her transformation vanish of themselves. So, a very beautiful Gypsy woman of the Siebengebirge, at seventeen years of age had a hateful reputation for frivolity and, what is more, the tribe suspected her of granting favours to non-Gypsies. The whole tribe cursed her and treated her with contempt. She was called nothing but *Parni Lubni*, the White Tart. This girl then had the idea of passing herself off as a (woman) magician. One night the whole camp was roused by her strident shouting. To her companions who ran to her, she declared that a *Nivasho* had just then possessed her and, as proof, she showed traces of clogs around her tent. Then she began to utter words without end, being apparently under a spell, and fell into a trance. Naturally she was accepted as a witch and again given her real name, Ileana Darej.[1]

1. Reported by Wlislocki, *Vom Wandernden Zigeunervolke* (Hamburg, 1890).

(1) Fragment of baton-sceptre of a Central European Gypsy chief.

(2) Magic characters inscribed on an amulet.

(3) Ancient coin bearing the 'Charmer bird' and the three mysterious dots.

(4)

(6)

(7)

(5)

Amulets and Talismans of Central European Gypsies.

In our own time some non-Gypsy miracle-workers or healers are still in harmony with the Gypsies. Jean Palou, who deals with witchcraft in sociology,[1] draws my attention to the fact that, in August 1939, all Gypsies within a radius of about 135 miles had decided to move in order to attend the funeral rites of a known sorcerer at Saint-Christophe-en-Boucherie (Indre). This author also knew a sorcerer of the Berry region who gave medical attention free to Gypsies who, in return, sent him patients.

This rejection of orthodox medicine does not always work without some mishap. And I cannot avoid quoting the sad news-item recently published in the Press: at Bethisy-Saint-Pierre near Compiègne, 'in order to succour little Albert, a boy ten years old, the *Romanichels* relied on the prayers of a miracle-worker. But this thaumaturgist, a plumber, performed miracles only on Sunday' – and the child died.[2]

To wind up, I shall glean from Erdös some of the many superstitions which he has collected among the Carpathian Gypsies of the Nograd Comitat. At the present moment these beliefs are still active.

'To drive a storm away, a broom is thrown out of the door.' (The Gypsies' broom seems to be quite unrelated to that of western sorcerers. Its function is intended rather to drive away the *Cohani*: a broom is placed across the threshold for this purpose.) 'When walking alone at night, one must not turn back.' (The Gypsies do in fact fear the night-time and solitude. This fear of the dark is reflected in various legends.) 'On leaving for a long journey, put a small piece of bread in the pocket and in this way every misfortune will be avoided.' 'The parent of a person setting out on a long journey takes a little sand from any tomb on the back of the left hand and throws it over the head of the person leaving without him seeing it.'

Once again we must wait for a more fruitful all-embracing view so that a writer may apply himself to publishing a work on Gypsy folk-lore, lack of which is now most regrettable. It will be seen in the pages which follow how very much alive these superstitions still are, and the prominent part they play in the doings and exploits of everyday life among Gypsies.

1. Jean Palou, *La Sorcellerie* (1957); *La Peur dans l'Histoire* (1958).
2. Serge Maximoff in *L'Aurore*, 12 May 1960.

5 · Everyday Life

We are now going to study the manners and customs of the Gypsies, particularly in order to link them with the substratum of their beliefs. However, what is dealt with here is always a matter of separate groups of Gypsies, and what is valid for some may not be so for others. Here again I shall do my utmost to find a common denominator.

STERILITY AND FERTILITY

Sterility[1] is the greatest misfortune that can strike a Gypsy woman. Central European Gypsies attribute it to a magical cause: 'A childless woman is pitied and despised, and her situation with her husband becomes untenable, for, in the mind of the Gypsies, she has had carnal commerce with a vampire, which causes her sterility'.[2]

Fertility spells are therefore many and varied. Yet all of them overlap the old well-known symbols. 'When the moon is waxing', writes Maxim Bing in regard to the rites in force among nomads of Transylvania,[3]

the sterile woman must eat grass plucked from the grave of a mother who has died of puerperal fever. She may also gather gossamer (e.g. spiderwebs) and eat them in company with her husband. At the same time the good fairies, the *Keshalyi*, must be invoked. . . . The future mother must also drink water into which her husband has spat, or into which he has cast glowing charcoal embers. In other circumstances the husband takes an egg, makes a little hole in it at each end and blows the contents into his wife's mouth for her to eat immediately. (The possibility of conceiving by the mouth is a very ancient presumption; the symbolism of this spell is obvious.)

1. For everything relating to the Gypsy woman, a useful book is the massive work on comparative ethnology by Ploss: *Das Weib in der Natur- und Völkerkunde* (Leipzig, 1899).

2. Wlislocki, *Vom Wandernden Zigeunervolke* (Hamburg, 1890).

3. 'La Grossesse et l'accouchement chez les Tziganes', Review *Ciba*.

The fertilizing action of the moon need no longer be emphasized, and not only on women but on plants. The moon's power is therefore transmitted to grass. Puerperal fever is not regarded as an infectious disease but a clear sign of pregnancy. Gossamer in universal popular belief has been spun by a goddess; the fertility symbolism attaching to the spindle and distaff is known. (The prostitute priestesses of Aphrodite long ago used to wear a thread round their foreheads.) The invocation to the *Keshalyi* is that which was quoted earlier. '*Keshalyi*, spin, spin . . .' (on page 188).

Spit likened to semen is found again in several Indian legends, one of which relates to *Agni*[1] and, according to Contenau, in the popular expression 'He's the dead spit of his father' is seen a reminiscence of those accounts in which persons of rank are born from the spit of a god. Sometimes water emphasizes the symbolism.

The fire spell is known,[2] and likewise that of the egg, whose use in fertility rites has been studied, particularly by Mircea Eliade.[3]

There is, lastly, a custom common in India that is also known among the Transylvanian Gypsies: the marriage of trees. Childless married couples, husband and wife, each plant a different tree on the bank of a river, and the two trees are bound together. If one of them should wither away, there will be no offspring from the marriage.[4]

The extreme rarity of abortions among the Gypsies corresponds with their vital need for offspring. It will be seen, when considering the problems of chastity and betrothal, that a pregnant girl does not on that account feel obliged to 'do away with her mistake'. Love of children among the Gypsies distinctly goes beyond the idea of such a sin. But, if the women do not use methods of contraception (even in their conjugal relations), they are nevertheless acquainted with an impressive collection of philtres and rituals for abortion, which they lose no opportunity of selling to non-Gypsies. The Gypsy woman to whom appeal is made by unfortunate girls in a fair way to becoming mothers is a traditional character in popular literature. And with good reason: the 'herb woman' knows all the secrets of deliverance and the list she gives of them can seem comforting. But it is notable that these Gypsy 'midwives', apart from

1. Sacrificial fire and god of fire in Vedic religion. *Tr.*
2. See Bayard, *Le Feu* (1959).
3. In *Traité de l'histoire des religions.*
4. Frazer, *Taboo and the Perils of the Soul*, Part II of *The Golden Bough* (3rd ed., 1911).

magical means (amulets, incantations, formulas and gestures), use only a purely sympathetic pharmacopoeia (philtres, ointments, herbal teas ...) to the exclusion of the standard criminal interventions (needles and probing instruments ...). In their uncompromising refusal to 'kill in the egg', and in spite of the lure of gain, the consequence of a maternal instinct that is remarkably developed must be seen.

In order to know whether a woman is pregnant, the Gypsies of Hungary practise divination by means of grains of maize cast into a

basin or on to the divinatory drum. The way the grains settle enables foretelling of the sex of the child. This method was known long ago in Vedic India, except that the operative agent was grains of flax. In both instances the omen was inferred from the fact that either grains were touching one another, or they were not.[1] Among the Siebengebirge Gypsies of the Rhineland the woman breaks an egg into a plate without separating the yolk from the white, and then sprays it with water from her mouth. If the egg is floating on the surface next morning, it means that she is pregnant. If the white is separated from the yolk, she will give birth to a son; and a daughter if white and yolk are mixed. Here again is found the symbolism of the conjunction of fertilizing elements.

If ever a Gypsy woman is licked by a bullock, or a cricket alights on her, she must expect to be pregnant. If one evening she should see wild ducks or geese go past, she will give birth next morning. The talisman reproduced above is used by the Danube Gypsies. This is a tablet of limewood in the form of a heart. On one side nine stars, the

1. See Henry, *La Magie dans l'Inde antique* (1909).

full moon, the waning moon, and a serpent are burned on it. In a hole on the upper part is inserted a hazel-nut wrapped round with hair from the tail of an ass. If the nut falls of itself after a certain time, the bearer of the talisman will be pregnant.[1]

Another practice current throughout the whole of Central Europe consists in making water pass through a sieve. This is a very ancient fertility rite. Water is fundamentally germinative, but it is in the form of rain – in this case water from the sky and not water from the earth – that its fertilizing power is most intense. The rain symbol is met again in every ritual described by Wlislocki.

PREGNANCY AND CHILDBIRTH

When the Gypsy woman is sure that she is pregnant, she announces the fact as quickly as possible, not only to her husband but to all the women of the tribe. From that moment she is looked upon very differently: she has the right to every kind of consideration.

According to the custom in the *Kama Sutra* her women friends place within her sight pictures suggesting beauty, icons or popular prints without any sacred significance but representing gods, goddesses, princes and princesses chosen for their physical perfection. According to de Ville, these images (*iconi*) belong to the chief of the tribe, that is, to the community. They are not lent to anybody but mothers-to-be.

The same writer reports a curious custom of the Romanian and Transylvanian Gypsies: the festival of Green George, which is held on Easter Monday, or on St George's Day, 23 April. 'The evening before, pregnant woman place one of their garments under the willow tree chosen for the celebration; if they find a fallen leaf on the garment next day, they know that their confinement will be easy.' Frazer quotes analogous traditions existing in ancient India. It is probably a matter of the grafting of Christian symbolism – Saint George and the dragon – on this immemorial cult of the tree.

It has been seen earlier that the pains of women in childbirth were due only to ill-feeling on the part of the demons, *Tçulo* and *Tçaridyi*. The last, born of a crayfish, forbade the consumption of shell-fish by future mothers.[2] Yet, by a phenomenon of inversion usual in magic, women at the same time protected themselves by wearing a

1. Wlislocki, op. cit.
2. Bing, in the Review *Ciba*, op. cit.

sachet full of crayfish shells and stag-beetles (another kinship of *Tçaridyi*).

Although the Gypsy woman clearly takes so much care to protect herself against demons, she shows in compensation absolute indifference in regard to physical fatigue. She will wait right up to the last moment before stopping work and calling her near-by women friends. Yet it still often happens that she will give birth, all by herself in a corner, and sometimes standing upright with her legs apart. The powers of endurance of these women in the inclement climates of our latitudes has never ceased to astonish our doctors.

Nevertheless, normal childbirth among the Gypsies follows a strict ritual. Some time before the final labour pains, the knots in all her clothes must be cut or undone. This practice is merely an act of sympathetic magic intended to prevent the umbilical cord from becoming knotted.[1]

The only persons authorized to attend at the delivery are the mother of the woman in child-bed, and the matron of the tribe, who fulfils the office of midwife. The latter does not intervene unless the operation threatens to be tricky. Her role is half-gynaecological and half-magical. If her function is to disentangle the cord, she also prepares philtres for protection against demons. In Hungary she lights the fire in front of the tent to drive them away.

The egg symbolism reappears in childbirth rituals in various forms. When the birth is too slow, the *phuri dai* drops an egg between the legs of the woman giving birth and chants:

Anro, anro hin olkes	*The egg, the little egg is round*
Te e pera hin obles	*All is round*
Ara cavo sastovestes	*Little child, come in health*
Devla, devla, tut akharel. . . .	*God, God is calling you. . . .*

'When a woman dies in child-bed, she is buried with an egg under each arm to prevent the vampires from feeding on her milk. When the egg is bad, the milk will be dried up.'[2] Among the *Yénische* in Germany, when a woman cannot give birth to the child, they make her drink water in which three eggs have been boiled, and these eggs are afterwards eaten by her husband.[3]

These rituals are accompanied by strict taboos. Excepting in some

1. On this see Frazer, op. cit.
2. Bing, op. cit.
3. Haessler, *Enfants de la grande route* (Neuchâtel, 1955).

very recent (and, moreover, exceptional) instances, the Gypsy woman must not give birth to her child in her own dwelling: that is, in her own tent or caravan. She must go out of the camp, or at the very least, give birth under her vehicle. In some tribes (in England, for example), a special tent is pitched for the purpose if the weather is too bad. In other communities, she must produce new life near a river.

In fact, the woman in childbirth is regarded as unclean. Men, even including her husband, must not on any account go near her. According to Jules Bloch, the confinement 'is the starting point of a sort of quarantine which may last three or four weeks in England and up to six weeks in Germany'. The young mother cannot touch either kitchen utensils or food. As a rule, the period of impurity ends with the Gypsy baptism of the child; and the father must wait for this moment to see and kiss the new-born baby. Ritual uncleanliness of the confined is attested in the primitive castes in India, among whom not only is the woman unapproachable for a time, which is longer the more one moves towards the north of the continent,[1] but she must likewise be confined in a separate hut, or at least in a remote room in the house. Once the period of impurity has passed, the woman washes herself in a river, and everything she has used during the confinement is generally thrown away or destroyed.

Among the Kalderash Gypsies (?) the announcement of a birth devolves on the *phuri dai*, who goes round with a plate of water and sprinkles the tents, one after another.

BIRTH AND BAPTISM

Gypsy baptism consists, first of the usual immersion, if possible in running water, and then the conferring of a secret name. Gypsies have in fact three names: one is secret, the second is reserved for use among their racial brothers, and the third is intended to be used for the *gadjé*, and their own civil status.

The secret name is spoken by the mother in a very low voice at the moment of birth – for the first and last time. This name is, indeed, intended to deceive demons who, not knowing the true identity of the child, will have no power over it, or at least will be able to attack it only in their imprecations. According to de Ville, this secret name is, however, repeated into the child's ear when he or she attains the

1. See Hutton, *Les Castes de l'Inde* (1949).

age of puberty. Finally, according to Block, it is possible to substitute another secret name in the event of the person being cured in an exceptional way of some illness, or in the event of a twin brother having just died. It is believed that this name is more often than not an appellation with a physical, moral or totemistic significance. The father himself, to be precise, does not know the real name of the child. This invocation taboo springs from the archaic custom by which it was forbidden to name the gods by their true names – the quality of being ineffable is common to several religions of the ancient Middle East. Some belated formulas give it thus: so-and-so X ... who is called Y.... From the gods this usage passed on to mortals.[1]

Among some groups the second name is that given in baptism. It is reserved to the Gypsies themselves and must not be used in the presence of non-Gypsies. Yet it becomes more and more confused with the 'official' name, the one that has been declared to the civil authorities. In such a case the Gypsies often call themselves by a surname that is known only to people of the same tribe.

Examples of baptismal names most commonly in use among the Kalderash[2] are: for boys – *Frinkelo, Fero, Yakali, Miya, Vaya, Yerko, Chavula, Ilika, Terkari*; and for girls – *Dunicha, Tereina, Malilini, Saviya, Oraga, Tekla, Orka* (and *Savina* is the principal female character of Maximoff's novel of that name).

Gypsy baptism is extremely important. Before the double ceremony the child is 'unclean' or, rather, does not exist. And it is probably the 'impurity' of the unbaptized child that is thrown back on the mother.

Baptism takes place in the presence of a godfather and godmother (*kirvo* and *kirvi*) who are both Gypsies and whose importance is considerable. According to the tradition of Zanko, 'the godfather and godmother are the child's true parents, more so than its natural father and mother; because it is they who first touch the child at baptism and make a man of him'.

There have been some variations in Gypsy baptism. (In Turkey it is accompanied by the Mussulman rite of circumcision.) Following the official religion practised by the tribe, there is a second baptism in accordance with its ceremony, whether this be of the Catholic, Protestant, Anglican or Orthodox Greek Church.

1. See Contenau, *La Magie chez les Assyriens et les Babyloniens* (1947).
2. In the works of Maximoff, for example. See Bibliography, pp. 269, 271.

Various magical rites accompany Gypsy baptism. I have already called to mind the role played in it by the fairies. In order to drive away the evil eye, some Gypsies resort to the practice of tattooing, but this is limited to one or two spots placed near the eye. Tattooing seems formerly to have had a much more important function, in India for example. It will be mentioned again in relation to ornaments.

There is no history of baptism at puberty for Gypsy children. They do what they please with complete freedom in the camp. If slaps are too often the reward for their exploits, they are not on that account any less the darlings of the whole tribe. One will nevertheless note the almost complete absence of toys or playthings; this problem, so far as I know, has not yet been raised.

PUBERTY AND VIRGINITY

I have found no trace of puberty rites among the Gypsies, nor precise information about the average age of puberty. It is in any case certain that the more we know about Gypsies in the Middle East, the more precocious is the appearance among them of the first menstruations. Even in climates such as ours in Western Europe, Gypsy girls seem to have reached puberty before their thirteenth birthday.

Gypsiologists are not in agreement regarding the importance given to maidenhood. Martin Block says that this is the sovereign good. As for Serboianu, he asserts that Gypsy girls offer themselves to the first man who comes along. Let us settle one problem now: there is no prostitution among Gypsy women. Girls who sold themselves would be excluded automatically from the tribe. It is obviously possible in the Balkans and Spain, or at Pigalle in France, to meet prostitutes got up and masquerading as Gypsies (*Gitanes*). I do not believe that they are authentic Gypsies. At all events, if there are black sheep in this respect among the Gypsies, they are the exceptions which prove the rule.

On the other hand, girls who give themselves for love have the right to claim extenuating circumstances. Generally speaking, it is only at the time of marriage that the question of virginity ever arises. In the primitive tribal organization, as will be seen later, the absence of virginity constituted a considerable handicap in the commercial bargainings which preceded marriage. However, a girl who has 'fallen into sin', even though she may not be pregnant, must wear the traditional head-scarf of the married woman. The scarf is then knotted under the chin, whereas married women wear it on the nape of the neck. And so, in spite of everything, the unmarried girl who has sinned is publicly marked in the eyes of all Gypsies. I shall return to this later.

LOVE

Love is of very great importance to the Gypsies, who are fundamentally complete romantics. And if love somewhat defies tradition, it is the oversight most easily forgiven. But being romantics, Gypsies are nonetheless quick-blooded, and love needs to be strictly governed by laws.

Among Zanko's Kalderash Gypsies, young people have neither the right to 'keep company' nor can they themselves choose companions. When they have reached the age for marriage,

it is the father or the mother who makes to the son or daughter the proposal of a girl or young man, after having made full inquiries. Parents do not impose their will. Son or daughter say whether the match proposed pleases or does not please. When, in the end, a suitable match is found, the father indirectly gives an inkling of it to the parents of the other family, to find out whether they are agreeable. If they are, the father now takes a formal step, after which they discuss settlements; and then they celebrate the betrothal. The two young people may then meet, but only in the presence of their parents.

Nevertheless, young lovers do not waver about meeting one another in secret. If they are in harmony, all is well. But the importance here is the repertory of means used for winning the love of a young man or of an unmanageable girl. In this again magic has its word to say. The enamoured young man goes out to find the *drabarni*, the herb-woman, to obtain one of the innumerable love potions in which she is a specialist. In a novel of his, Matéo Maximoff describes one of these potions, the *farmitchi*: the boy must go near a river and pick a leaf from a tree. Then he pricks his wrist with his knife, and smears the leaf with his blood while saying his real name, turns the leaf over and repeats the operation while saying the name of the girl he loves. Finally, he throws the leaf into the river. As for the etymology of the term *farmitchi*, one hesitates between two solutions: it comes either from *fericimé*, meaning 'happy', 'lucky'; or from *pharaimata*, meaning 'pricks'.

Among Central European Gypsies, if a girl wishes for a boy's love, she makes a paste in which she puts some of the hair, saliva, blood and nails of her well-beloved. Of these she moulds a figurine which she buries at a crossroads, when the moon is at first quarter. She then urinates on the spot, repeating: 'X ... I love you. When your image shall have perished, you'll follow me as a dog follows a bitch.'

Elsewhere she adds to this paste some quince pips and drops of blood from her left-hand little finger. This paste is cooked once, and she chews it looking at the full moon and saying; 'I chew your hair, I chew my blood – from hair and blood love shall be born – a new life for us shall be born. . . .' After this, she smears one of the boy's garments with the paste in order that he shall not find peace except close to her.

In the Siebengebirge the girls believe that apple pips burnt and powdered, mixed with their menstrual blood, and given to a boy in his food, will incite him to become madly in love with her. This operation has still greater chances of success if it is done at the New Year.

Finally, the girl can take some earth from a grave with the back of her right hand and, having wrapped it in paper, put it under the boy's bed.

As for the boy, he steals three hairs from the girl and pushes them into a chink in a tree so that they may 'grow' with it from then on. To work well, the hairs are taken from the back of the girl's neck, on three occasions while she is sleeping, and the boy keeps them on his person for some time.

There remains to be mentioned the case of a girl who is lovesick but who has not yet fixed upon the boy of her choice. Erdös quotes the following ritual: on the evening of the feast of Saint Lucy she makes three little balls with flour and water, writes the names of thirteen men on thirteen bits of paper, and one by one puts these into the little balls. Then she casts these into boiling water. The first little ball which comes to the surface contains the name of the elected.

A detailed analysis of the symbols which come into these operations, however clear they may seem, would demand many pages. So also would the catalogue of points in them corresponding to those of the white magic common to all peoples.

BETROTHAL AND MARRIAGE

The customs relating to betrothal still bear the marks of old times. Thus, in Turkey the young people drink from the same cup, symbolically breaking a caste taboo of Indian origin. (In the Punjab, however, it is the contrary, and when the betrothal must be broken off for some major reason, then the interested parties are obliged to share a glass of water.[1]) In the Balkans, the girl accepts a red handkerchief from the boy. Fabrics and ribbons of this colour in fact come into many fertility and good-luck rites.

Among the Kalderash Gypsies described by Maximoff, the betrothed girl has no right either to visit or talk to the boy – even when other people are present. A gold coin is placed on her neck, and in everybody's eyes this marks her as 'promised' (*tomnimi*).

Free union is accepted in certain tribes, although love must ratify it. However, it is difficult to verify how many instances there are of couples living in marital union who have not been 'officially' married in accordance with the law of the country, but have nevertheless been married in their own Gypsy way. In actual fact, civil and religious marriages, as conceived in our society, although more and more frequent for the whole of the Gypsy peoples, never exist except to round off a ceremony that is intrinsically in the nomads' tradition. In any case, it is among the Spanish and Catalan *Gitanos* that concubinage is most easily tolerated.

Gypsy marriage assumes several forms: abduction (by force or consent); purchase; mutual consent. Marriage between members of different groups (for example, between a *Kaldera* and a *Gitano*, between *Manouche* and *Yénische...*) gives rise to complications and sometimes to special rules or regulations. The strictest law requires that a union between Gypsy and non-Gypsy automatically brings with it exclusion from the tribe. If a *gadjo* legally marries a Gypsy woman, the husband cannot in any circumstances consider himself as a neo-Gypsy. At the very most, if he should have particularly full dealings with Gypsies, and shows the (liberal) 'modern spirit', he may pride himself on the title *phral*, 'brother', and to a certain extent gain by the friendship and solidarity of the group. But the young woman is nonetheless secretly held in contempt, indeed hated. The law is less severe for the Gypsy man who marries a non-Gypsy woman. But the latter is from then on obliged to follow the Gypsy tradition, and to submit to the laws of the tribe, laws which are often applied to her in a more tyrannical manner than to Gypsy

1. See Makarius, 'Prohibition de l'inceste et interdits alimentaires', in the Review *Diogène*, 1960.

women. For example, she is absolutely forbidden to leave the camp, and she must show absolute submission to her mother-in-law.

We have seen, in regard to adoptions, the description of a ceremony of blood bond. But it really seems that the famous 'blood marriage', with ritual incisions in the wrist and the mingling of the blood of both parties, is a legend. Gypsies themselves are quite silent on the subject. It is, however, possible that the *Netotsi*, the most primitive Gypsies, may have practised it long ago.

The two ancient marriage formulas – abduction and purchase – are still conserved, but in increasingly symbolic ways. Among the *Nuri* of Asia Minor, purchase still exists in its original form. An account published by Jules Bloch lays stress on this custom:

My brother came to ask me to marry him to his uncle's daughter. We asked the father for the young girl. He replied: 'Fetch the money'. We paid over twenty pounds. The father did not want to give her for less than thirty, but we hadn't the money. Her cousin took her and made off with her. The father followed and couldn't catch him, but I offered the father twenty pounds in my brother's name. We brought and killed two goats and prepared rice with meat. The father and mother ate it until there was no more. The girl and the boy returned and showed themselves. He kissed his uncle's head and his aunt's hand, and he and his wife remained with us.

Jules Bloch adds an example just as telling, the case of a family of fortune-tellers of Greek or Balkan origin, settled in Wales in 1942.

Until recent times [said a member of this family], women without exception were bought; the price was arranged between the parents without consulting the young people. The father received as much as eight hundred pounds. This custom, which persists in the United States, is beginning to fall into disuse, because girls who get warning of what is going on threaten to run away and thus lose their commercial value.

According to Martin Block, the purchase price must be paid before the marriage. It is not until they have received it that parents announce the marriage.

Marriage by abduction with consent, or the 'run-away' marriages, of young people no longer exist among the *Sinti* and the more traditionalist Gypsies such as those of Latvia. The boy comes one evening to abduct the girl he loves, alone or with the help of a few comrades. He disappears with his belle for some while, sometimes for several weeks. Then he brings her back to her parents' camp. In general, after a pretence of violent discussion, a broadside of abuse and a ritual cuff given to the girl, the validity of the union is tacitly approved. However, so long as the indispensable marriage ceremony has not taken place, the young people must behave as an engaged couple, chastely and respectful of the traditions.

The ordinary marriage, the kind that is most usual today, implies interminable palavers between the parents who, praising the qualities of their offspring, make this pleasure last as long as possible. It is the boy's father who visits the girl's, and the latter makes a show of not knowing what it's all about, and of not being willing to part with his child for anything in the world. Once the decision has been made, it is announced to the tribe and often to neighbouring tribes. The boy is authorized to see his fiancée 'for the first time'. It is fitting that she should look as though she is deeply grieved to leave her parents.

The festivities which go with the marriage sometimes last several days, according to the wealth of the tribes concerned. In any case the nuptial feast is one of the most outstanding events of everyday life, and for it the Gypsies are capable of spending fortunes. All the nomads in the vicinity are invited. So long as the merrymakings continue, quarrels and enmities are forgotten. This is a sacred truce, one which nobody would dare to break (unless in an advanced state of drunkenness).

It is one of the prerogatives of the chief of the tribe to officiate; he fulfils the functions of priest and secular official. The ceremony itself varies according to groups. Among some, as in Britain, they are satisfied with asking the young people to clasp hands. Among Zanko's Kalderash the bridegroom must go on his knees at the feet of the chief.

What follows is an account of a recent marriage of *Gitans* in France, as reported by Jean Didier, one of the rare journalists who provides accurate information about Gypsies:

Nolli Colombar was married on Saturday. She is thirteen years of age. In accordance with ancestral rite she wed Benito Demetrio Gomez. Benito is fifteen. . . . Ramón Gomez, the married man's father, who was touring the North of France in a superb Plymouth car, had for the moment left off selling automobile accessories (he owns several businesses in Morocco) to ask Nolli's father for her hand. Her father is, more modestly, a tinsmith. This must also be a good trade, since Papa Colombar gave as a dowry the same amount of money as the ostentatious Gomez: a million francs in cash. Both sides sent out the indispensable invitations. They had to find the relatives on the highroads of Europe. This was done in a fortnight. They came from all directions, but especially from northern Italy. There were one hundred and twenty of them who met again near the Wingles bridge in the mining district of the Pas-de-Calais. This is a place reserved for Gypsies. There were so many tents and caravans there that the local gendarmes were alerted. Official minds were set at ease: the Gypsies were merely going to hold high festival.

Nolli put on her wonderfully white wedding dress and was introduced by her mother to all the guests. Only the husband was missing. The custom is that he should be 'bashful' and not show himself. Another custom has it that he must profit by this interlude to round off his education, asking wise counsels of other people and even practical explanations in the matter of conjugal happiness. Consequently, Benito Gomez did not join the guests until after midnight. In front of the brilliantly illuminated tents they danced some of the old dances of the Gypsy world – *czardas* and *flamencos* – but also modern dances, which would shock the old fairy women.

French wines had been drunk. But they had eaten *goulash*, *paprikash* and *paella*, thirty-two roast chickens, and a pig roasted on the spit. They wound up with *kolatcha* and *retechki* cakes which the old Gypsy women had kneaded with their hands. At dawn, according to custom, the Gomez father came to ask permission to bring the married girl to a tent where his son would receive her. He was granted this right. And Nolli, with a necklace of twenty gold dollars, disappeared with her young husband.

At eleven o'clock in the morning, according to the rites, they went on to the real marriage, and from now onwards were a married couple, without, however, going before the municipal magistrate; and kneeling, they received bread and salt, the symbols of bliss. The whole company continued to feast throughout the day. . . .

This description is interesting in more than one sense. First, it underlines the comparative precocity of the husband and wife; the girl, thirteen, the boy, fifteen years old. This is not an exceptional phenomenon. In Paris, in 1947, still younger children were married: at thirteen and a half and fourteen and a half years of age. Yet it seems that, in this particular case, the parents previously made sure that the future husband and wife had both reached puberty. Nevertheless, among some Gypsy groups traces remain of the marriage of children before puberty: in general, between eight to fourteen years of age. Such unions are decided upon by the parents and, for a certainty, without the consent of the interested parties. The ceremony is limited to a simple formality, and the children remain with their own families until they have reached puberty. There is never any cohabitation. At the moment of puberty (and when no unavoidable difficulties have arisen), a second ceremony seals the effective union. Yet the custom of precocious marriage is becoming extremely rare, at least among western Gypsies.

Nolli Colombar's marriage enables us to be quite definite that the 'marriage night', the carnal union, takes place between the beginning of the feast and the ceremony properly so called. This means, in some degree, that this formal ceremony consecrates the 'official' deflowering. The latter gives rise to some rites still in use. In Spain it is made known publicly and, according to Jules Bloch, 'is fulfilled by four matrons who are afterwards charged to show the result to the company present.' They take round a handkerchief stained with the blood of the young wife.[1] But sometimes, in order to save everybody's honour, it is chicken's blood, and the husband prefers to agree to this superficial demonstration. (The problems of sex will be dealt with later.)

The ceremonial elements of Gypsy marriage are, first and foremost, bread and salt, which are found among all groups of Gypsies. The chief of the tribe, sometimes the *phuri dai* (see page 164), breaks the bread in two pieces, and puts a pinch of salt on the fragments, which are given to the couple, at the same time saying: 'When you are tired of this bread and this salt, you'll be tired of one another'. The newly-married couple must exchange their portions before eating them. Among the Kalderash Gypsies the expression 'to take the bread and the salt' means to get married. This alimentary communion, symbol of wealth and prosperity, is sometimes accompanied by a shower of grains of rice afterwards thrown over the married couple by those present.

Another ritual requires whoever is officiating to pour on the heads of the husband and wife the contents of an earthenware jug or pitcher full of grains, and then break the jug by throwing it violently on the ground. He keeps the handle, while the others present share the pieces, which are regarded as lucky charms.[2] Moreover, this custom is not original to the Gypsies; it was formerly common enough, even in France:

When a woman was getting married, she limited herself – as a whole

1. The handkerchief is called *o dichlo*. The expression 'to lose one's *dichlo*' among the Gypsies in the United States means 'to lose one's virginity'.

2. Franz de Ville, *Tziganes* (Brussels, 1956).

ceremony – to breaking an earthenware vessel in front of the man whom she wished as her companion; and she respected him as her husband for as many years as the vase had been reduced to in pieces. At the end of that period, husband and wife were free to separate, or to break another earthenware vessel.[1]

Although among the Gypsies marriage is a sacrament that is dangerous to break, divorce nevertheless exists. In Wales the young wife can return to her family, and plead that she has been badly treated. She then goes before the tribal council. If this finds her to be in the wrong, her father refunds most of the purchase price. However, he keeps parts of it to compensate him for the loss of his daughter's virginity, which diminishes her market value. On the other hand, if the accusation is well founded, the father keeps both his daughter and the money.[2]

MATTERS OF SEX[3]

Gypsies, so easily regarded by non-Gypsies as a pack of outlaws and vagabonds, apply the rules of their own moral code with a severity which we would sometimes do well to envy. It is among them, at least in our western countries, that sexual moderation is most rigorously observed. Authors of picturesque literature evoke at every turn the dreadful promiscuity in the lives of Gypsy men and women, fathers and daughters, brothers and sisters. It so happens that the prohibitions which govern the sexual life of these nomads are extremely exacting.

Thus, sexual relations against nature (homosexuality, sodomy ...) are severely prohibited, even in married life. A woman who complains of being the victim of shameful practices on the part of her husband automatically obtains the annulment of her marriage, and the man risks being expelled from the tribe.

As for female prostitution, this does not exist, as I have already stated. One can hardly cite the case of young Gypsy women who, under compulsion, were made to share the beds of voivodes and

1. Collin de Plancy, *Dictionnaire Infernal* (3rd ed. 1848).
2. Jules Bloch, *Les Tsiganes* (1953).
3. *Sexualité* in the original, which is defined in the *Petit Larousse* (1962) as: 'The entirety of the special features, external or internal, shown by individuals, and determined by their sex'. *Tr.*

non-Gypsy administrators or estate managers during the period when the Gypsies were slaves in Romania.

Fidelity in marriage is also enforced in an extremely uncompromising manner. Among the Kalderash Gypsies it is rare for a man to have a mistress (*piramni*). Even before 'something happens' a certain amount of extra-conjugal looking at a woman is enough to start violent reprisals. On the other hand, confidence between husband and wife is so great that nobody takes offence on seeing a man and woman gossiping, each of them being married to another. But the Gypsy man is very jealous of his prerogatives. The smallest punishment received by a wife for adulterous gestures is a severe hiding. The commonest punishment is shaving off the hair of the guilty woman; it is cut 'clean off', and for many months she finds herself categorized as an object of shame in the eyes of the tribe. Recently a woman of the Sauzer family, who had been punished in this way, presented herself at one of the central police stations in Paris to have herself arrested under the imaginary pretext of shoplifting. What she really wanted was to get herself into jail, that is, away from the eyes of her tribe during the time when her hair would grow again decently. Of course, this custom is not specifically Gypsy; it is remembered in France, on the Liberation after the Second World War, that women accused of 'horizontal' collaboration with the occupying enemy had their hair shorn in this way. Tacitus spoke of adulterous women being similarly stigmatized among the Germanic peoples, and this spectacular sanction existed in ancient India. Girls of easy virtue suffered the same treatment in nineteenth-century Vienna.

More severe corporal punishments still exist. Mutilations, for example, of which ethnologists have recorded definite cases: an eye put out, a nose cut off, teeth broken, an ear torn off. Old Gypsy women mutilated in this way who are met in some countries have so paid for their extra-marital exploits.

In order to combat their wife's infidelity, the Gypsies rely not only on the horror inspired by such ministrations. They also have recourse to magic. Thus, the Hungarian nomads make the young wife walk barefooted on little disks of linden wood. These amulets, about two inches in diameter, have poker-work designs. On one side (illustration on the left, p. 218) there is a chain (marriage), two crosses and a circle (guilty sensual pleasure and happiness which cause falling into the hole: that is, into forgetfulness of duty), a serpent (the partner who tempted), and a square marked with four dots (the family and the strength of the hearth). On the other side (illustration on the right) there is a plant or flower (love), and two crossed sticks (the prohibition).

If this charm is not effective, the Gypsy man strings the skulls of three magpies on three stripped twigs of boxwood or rosemary tied together with red thread, and places this amulet under his wife's pillow. If her conscience is at peace, she will sleep without noticing anything strange. If, on the other hand, she is guilty of some adventure, she will reveal in her sleep the details of her misconduct. This talisman works with greater certainty if it has been buried in the grave of a child who died unbaptized, and then dipped in the menstrual blood of a woman other than the wife.[1]

The modesty of Gypsy women does not correspond exactly with the canons accepted by our women. So it is that, for them, the breasts are not sexual objects, and to expose them for men to see (when suckling an infant, for example), whether the men be Gypsies or not, does not in the least embarrass them. I have often seen (and admired) girls washing their bare breasts at a public fountain, without ever showing consciousness of the slightest lasciviousness. Their busts are well known to be very open to sight, easy to view from above by the *gadjé*, and this is a thing which just makes them laugh.

On the other hand, their legs, thighs and midriffs are very carefully concealed by their clothing. It is not merely a matter of fashion that their dresses are so long and, at least among Central European Gypsies, go down to their ankles. The dances of the *Gitanas* obviously reveal a considerable part of their legs and hips, but, and this is remarkable, only to non-Gypsies is this an erotic spectacle. These famous dances, so often described as lascivious, are not in any sense of this nature to the *Gitano* men, who are conscious only of their rhythm. The dances are sensual; they are not erotic. At least they are not so intentionally.

1. Wlislocki, op. cit.

It is probable that the first Gypsies from the banks of the Indus wore little in the way of clothing; a piece of linen or calico wound round their loins no doubt sufficed for them. In regard to the nakedness of the breasts just mentioned, I shall be permitted to recall that, in India, to be clothed above the waist was the privilege of the 'twice born' castes. Little by little the custom became extended to the Sudras,[1] but, until quite recently, even these insisted that it should remain forbidden to outcasts and untouchables.[2]

Not being able to adopt the *sari*, which was forbidden to the lower castes, the Gypsy women from India must needs use the ordinary bodice, which went under the arms and clearly outlined the bosom, which it left largely uncovered so that the breasts should be accessible to infants, and the wide pleated skirt which went down to the calf of the leg. This costume was to be retained by the Gypsy women from then onwards through the early migrations in Asia. It is only in Central Europe, and especially in Hungary, that they were to make their skirts similar to those of the peasant women, contenting themselves, however, with choosing more brightly coloured and decorative fabrics such as we see today swinging on the hips of 'Hungarian' Gypsy women in Western Europe. The absence of the *sari* has another possible explanation: it would, in fact, be a very uncomfortable garment for nomad women who were walking long distances on foot.

The number of these 'skirts' worn one over the other is sometimes impressive. Among the *Falqani* nomads of modern Iran there are seven, a ritual number: *la Macarena*, the Virgin of the Spanish *Gitanos*, also wears seven skirts and this was probably the case long ago of the Sara of Saintes-Maries-de-la-Mer. Gypsy women of the groups which came from Central Europe are today distinguished from the French *Gitans*, the *Manouches* and the Spanish *Gitanas* by the richness of these multi-coloured skirts.

It is only quite recently that the Gypsies have discovered the use of footwear. Although young girls affect the very latest in stockings and high-heeled dancing-shoes, for generations they walked barefooted after the fashion of all Eastern peoples. Moreover, in the

1. Members of the lowest of the four great Hindu castes. *Tr.*
2. Hutton, op. cit.

camps today, the moment the girls have some leisure, they lose no time about shedding their shoes.

As for the men's dress, this has taken more easily to local fashions. Men adopted more quickly than women the clothes of Central European peasants, as old documents quoted in this book bear witness.

I have already described some of the costumes formerly worn by Gypsy chiefs. In the Danube valley, to be more precise, the voivodes on feast days wore a long crimson coat which contrasted strongly with their yellow top-boots and gold spurs. They had a close-fitting, brimless lambskin head-dress and, in one hand, they held a heavy axe, symbol of their authority (again found on the *nijako*), and in the other, a whip with three leather thongs whose stroke they did not fail to inflict on adolescents guilty of some misdeed.[1]

For something still more picturesque, here is the description of a '*bourgeois*' Gypsy, a blacksmith by trade, in nineteenth-century England:

Mr Petulengro was dressed in Roman fashion, with a somewhat smartly cut sporting coat, the buttons of which were half-crowns, and a waistcoat scarlet and black, the buttons of which were spaded half-guineas; his breeches were of a stuff half-velveteen, half-corduroy, the cords exceeding broad. He had leggings of buff cloth, furred at the bottom, and upon his feet were highlows. Under his left arm was a long black whalebone riding-whip, with a red lash, and an immense silver knob. Upon his head was a hat with a high peak, somewhat of the kind which the Spaniards call *calanes*,[2] so much in favour with the bravos of Seville and Madrid. Now, when I have added that Mr Petulengro had on a very fine white holland shirt, I think I have described his array. Mrs Petulengro – I beg pardon for not having spoken of her first – was also arrayed very much in the Roman fashion. Her hair, which was exceedingly black and lustrous, fell in braids on either side of her head. In her ears were rings, with long drops of gold. Round her neck was a string of what seemed very much like large pearls, somewhat tarnished, however, and apparently of considerable antiquity.[3]

Not without some *naïveté*, the Gypsies have always had a weakness for military or domestic uniforms. Their love of metal buttons,

1. Neukomm, *Les Bohémiens chez eux* (1898).

2. Of a type then worn by the Spanish working-class men, with the rim turned up against the crown. *Tr.*

3. Quoted by Fréchet in his *George Borrow*. The passage is from Borrow's *The Romany Rye*, Chapter VI.

Brandenburgs, and fake decorations has caused them to adopt throughout Europe unusual costumes when we think of the rank or status which these were supposed to represent. Vivid colours – yellow, red and green – are particularly attractive to them. So, one need no longer be astonished at the usual get-up of the Gypsy violinist in the night-club.

It is remarkable that all these costumes for men and women are not of Gypsy manufacture. They are always bought, new or second-hand, for no Gypsy woman would deign to spin or weave. The children go about almost naked, as long as their age and the climate permit.

Gypsy love of finery extends into the domain of jewellery. One could go into long raptures about the number and variety of the adornments which the women and even the men are capable of wearing in their everyday life: necklaces made of coins, jewelled rings on every finger (and sometimes on the toes), bracelets extending to well above the elbow, or worn on the ankles, watches with alberts worn crossed, or enormous ear-rings. This travelling treasure (for it is rarely 'imitation' jewellery) springs from Indian custom which required that, while the man was working outside the home, the woman kept on her person all the family savings. It may occur to us, in regard to this need to exhibit wealth, to ask whether the nomad could not find a better safe than his or her own body? It is curious to find that the heavy necklets and necklaces of sequins, of which the women are so proud, comprise gold and silver coins that are now very old and come from every western European country. Numismatists would make some fine discoveries here. But, apart from their intrinsic value, some of these jewels act as amulets.

A more original adornment is tattooing. Originally this was purely magical, and served not only as a means of defence against the evil eye, maledictions, demons and vampires; it also assumed a 'medical' function to the point that some writers have seen in its use a trite popularization of acupuncture.[1] In the Balkans, the babies are tattooed by their mothers. More often than not, a few imperceptible marks, placed symmetrically close round the eyes, are sufficient to drive away evil spells and maladies.

Then tattooing became an adornment, particularly among the

1. A system of therapeutics (common in Chinese medicine) based on pricking the surface of the skin with needles in order to stimulate nerve centres. *Tr.*

nomad Gypsies of the Iranian Fars (the *Kolis*) and among the half-sedentary bear-leaders of the Balkans. Although it sometimes extends to the cheeks, chin and forehead, it never appears on the body – in contrast to the custom among sailors and other lovers of western tattooing. It is always geometrical. A Gypsy would never allow himself to be tattooed with evocative designs, or those of an erotic or obscene nature.

Martin Block has described the process (he notes that in Persia the women have a monopoly of this art):

Three or nine sharp needles, made by the Gypsies themselves, are tied together in a cluster, but not before first having had the appropriate formula spoken over them; nothing relating to magic is ever done in silence. Then the woman practitioner takes the set of needles, presses the points into the patient's cheek, and begins her work as *'pointilliste'* at the chosen place, until the blood spurts. She then plunges the needles into a liquid prepared beforehand; and continues the operation. The subject does not allow the slightest grimace to betray the pain, which is really torture. It is remarkable that the wound does not cause inflammation. It seems that the liquid used prevents this. Even in ancient times the evil eye was warded off with a mixture of charcoal soot, mineral oil, child's urine and plum alcohol. German superstition also attributed this practice to witches; in any case, the mixture is a natural disinfectant. For a Gypsy it stands to reason that the person tattooed will allow three days to pass without washing the sore. When it has healed, a blue stain has taken its place. The objective has been achieved.[1]

HABITAT AND MEANS OF TRANSPORT

The Gypsies have three kinds of dwelling; that of the 'sedentary' or settled Gypsies, which may take many forms; that of the nomads – the tent or caravan (wheeled-wagon); and finally, that of the semi-nomads, who settle somewhere for the winter.

More and more of the sedentaries are leaving the camps at the gates of towns, to settle in houses and premises of *gadjé*. Unfortunately they still live in them in such numbers that the accommodation mostly continues to look like interiors of overcrowded caravans. Furthermore, their ancestral nomadism, and their mentality as human beings too long harassed, impels them to replace furniture by suitcases and similar portable receptacles – always giving the

1. Block, *Mœurs et coutumes des Tziganes* (1936).

impression that they have just moved or are about to move – and causes them to suffer from claustrophobia.

The first Gypsies in history travelled on foot. Four-wheeled wagons and caravans only came later. The sole luxury at first was the purchase of little donkeys on whose backs the wanderers put their baskets of provisions and the children. This was the mode of transport used by the Gypsies who came from Asia to Europe, and also of the *Gitanos* of Catalonia who, in the fifteenth century, crossed the Pyrenees to come and settle in France (where they are called *Gitans*); and also of the many itinerant groups who dispersed over Northern Europe.

The richest, however, on leaving the Indian world, could treat themselves to heavy wagons with solid wheels, drawn by those oxen with huge, widely-spread horns which had long been the only beasts of burden that could be used in the jungles and marshlands on the south side of the Caspian Sea. The wagon with four or six wheels, divided into two or three compartments and covered with a hood of thick felt, was the transport vehicle of the Scythians; a veritable travelling house. It is found again in the Kuban and in Cappadocia.

In these conditions the problem of habitat was solved: when night came the wheeled wagons were halted and the families packed themselves into them as well as they could amid the bundles and utensils. The travellers settled down to sleep on heaps of rugs, fabrics and carpets. Obviously the cooking was done outside, but in bad weather they made tea in the samovar inside.

These wagons became lighter and lighter – the solid wheels were succeeded by wheels with spokes – and eventually reached Central Europe. The ox was replaced by the horse as soon as the Danubian plains were reached. These are the modified wagon-teams which were painted by Jacques Callot.

Then the wheeled wagons became caravans. Nobody knows where and when the change was made from one to the other. According to Martin Block, it was on their arrival in Western Europe that the Gypsies adopted the light vehicles used by travelling showmen. Jules Bloch is definite that the new vehicle was still a novelty in England in 1833. Horse-drawn caravans are still numerous, although they are rapidly giving way to the elaborate caravans used in modern camping. Those who are most attached to the traditional Gypsy caravans are not, moreover, the real Gypsies but the *Barengré*, non-Gypsy basket-makers who work on roadsides and in village markets. These still have vehicles twenty years old, recognizable by their decorations of carved wood on windows and door. The caravans of wagon style have two unequal pairs of wheels, and the Gypsy term for them, *vurdon*, has become *verdine*. Comfort is evidently reduced to the strictly necessary. A stove which burns wood or a coal-burning range, a table, some chests and the inevitable pile of eiderdown quilts, feather beds, and bedclothes are all pushed in a heap at the end of the caravan during the day. Underneath the vehicle are packing-cases secured by chains which contain their tools and buckets, emergency food for the horses, and the hen-coops.

In our time caravan furniture has lost in the picturesque what it has gained in the practical. Interiors are often so neat and clean that one could 'eat off the floor'. The radio sets, the curtains on the windows and the bright furniture make them very acceptable homes. The Gypsies have rediscovered the characteristic cleanliness of that other nomadism: of inland water transport, of the canal boats and barges.

The very luxurious motor-caravans of some carnival operators or owners of travelling circuses are now worth fortunes. As for the vehicles, they compete with one another in length and width and chromium plate. The secondhand 'Americans' (as they are called on the continent of Europe) which consume twenty litres per hundred kilometres but can house two big families are part of contemporary Gypsy folk-lore.

However, before reaching this stage, Gypsies experienced less enviable housing conditions. The sedentaries and half-sedentaries from Asia Minor and Eastern Europe have long been content with squalid shacks. The reader has been told of the conditions in which Gypsy slaves and serfs lived. The tent itself was already a step forward. In point of fact, the most primitive Gypsy habitat was a simple hole dug in the earth. It is found mentioned in Pakistan.

Troglodyte Gypsies still exist in the starkest regions. These are sedentaries who, as in Asiatic Turkey, occupy whole villages. In Transylvania the *Rudari* (basket-makers and makers of wooden tools), who are counted among the poorest Gypsies and are called 'Men of the Woods', are satisfied with half-underground habitations, covered with earth but going below the level of the soil. Interlaced branches prevent them from caving in. Only the pipe from a stove emerges from the hole in the earth. The interior is as tiny as the old hiding-places used by woodcutters and charcoal burners of former times. A man could hardly stand up in these *Rudari* 'manholes', and the atmosphere in them is about as pure as in an Eskimo igloo. The walls holding up the habitat are faced with roughly squared wood or pieces of old earthenware. Martin Block has visited and described these manholes:

A wood fire crackles and burns on the hearth arranged on the beaten soil, to the right against the partition wall; above there is a chimney-pipe, which may be round or square, formed of sticks joined together, which seems to be falling to pieces. The cauldron hangs from a wooden peg planted slantwise in the clay ceiling, or on a chain which comes from the chimney-pipe. A wooden camp bed, about a foot and a half high, has a mat made of rushes or reeds. Some fowls have become accustomed to the fire which is always burning, and peck grains of fallen maize even up to the edge of the fire. A vast receptacle made of the bark of cherry-tree or plum-tree serves to hold the maize flour acquired by barter from the people of the country.

Other Gypsies use caves and the natural shelters of the Carpathian Mountains and Balkans. These are semi-nomadic bear-hunters and bear-leaders. In some Gypsy villages in Walachia, after being freed from slavery, the inhabitants became (wretched) husbandmen. They dug dwellings half-underground, but rising above ground near to little granaries on piles for storing their meagre harvests. The roofs of these dwellings were made of dried grasses and rushes reinforced with mud.

The most famous troglodyte Gypsies are, of course, those of Spain, and their way of existing has been raised to the level of a profitable tourist industry. The biggest troglodyte village in the world is to the east of Granada, in the suburb of Albaicín. From the nineteenth century onwards, travellers, and particularly English people, have visited it and brought back romantic descriptions:

One would believe it to be an enormous collection of ants' nests. It is just as if the valley, once filled with a deposit four yards deep of very dry red soil, had been denuded by a flood in an irregular way so as to remain dotted with pointed heights and holes. Among these extra-ordinary imitations of mountains, the Gypsies have dug out their windowless residences which, apart from the door, are airless and without any other ventilation but the chimney, which is built of dry stones and goes through the soil of the ceiling. To the spectator, the whole quarter seems to be a big field in which a crop of chimneys is growing. Nothing else can be seen, except the doors of the nearest dwellings. In these terrible hovels, close together in hundreds and thousands live the Gypsies, men, women, and children cheek by jowl, with their fowls and donkeys.[1-2]

Today, thanks to the lucrative returns which accrue from the tourist trade, the caves at Granada are clean and tidy, the walls are regularly lime-washed, and the *Gitanos* amass small fortunes 'acting the Gypsy' in front of the cameras. But it seems that we must go back for the origin of these troglodyte dwellings to the troubled periods during which Jews, *Gitanos* and Spaniards sought refuge in the natural caverns of the region against their common enemy, the Moors.

Between the 'manhole' and the caravan, the tent is one of the essential characteristics of nomads. It represents astonishing diversities. Jules Bloch recalls that in Albania around 1860 one still saw 'wood cabins covered with bark set on wheels and drawn by a team of from ten to twelve oxen, while the whole family followed their habitation on foot'. The crudest tents consisted of two stakes placed upright against a bush, and against the stakes the wanderers were content to throw a piece of canvas. The material used would vary in accordance with local resources: goatskins, mats made of rushes or reeds, branches of trees, sacking and so on. One understands why the Gypsies call the wind 'the devil's sneezing'!

Martin Block, who has made the best study of the problem of the Gypsy habitat in Eastern Europe, singles out three characteristic types of tent: the high and pointed; the low and squat; and the semi-circular. 'The first is found only among the really nomad Gypsies and those who repair cauldrons. The itinerant blacksmiths and the bear-leaders camp in the other two kinds of tent.'

The tent is sometimes called *tsaro* (in Romanian *tsara*, encampment), sometimes *chera* (pronounced either *tchera* or *kera*). It is interesting to compare with this term the words *gher*, *ghir*, which among the Mongol peoples designate the round tent of felt or skin. The connexion is not only possible but probable. But the problem of the links between these small tribes and the Gypsies has still to be studied.[3]

1. Cross, *Easter in Andalucia* (1902). (The passage quoted has been translated from the French. *Tr.*)

2. Less famous, but perhaps more interesting, are the Gypsy cave-dwellers of the Barrio de Santiago at Guadix. These Gypsies have not yet (1963) been contaminated by the tourist traffic. *Tr.*

3. Furthermore, *Kher* in Breton and Gaelic also means 'house'.

On the other hand, the use of tents made of tree-bark among the Balkan *Rudari* has been noted, recalling perhaps the identical habitations of the Yakuts of Siberia.

FOOD AND COOKERY

The Gypsies seem to have been originally a people of gatherers and collectors. Not being hunters, fishermen or husbandmen, they must have been content at first with natural products gathered from nature: berries, mushrooms, roots, wild fruits, small mammals and rodents, snakes and molluscs . . . all being sprinkled with fresh water before use.

With the beginning of the migrations, the changes took place with settled populations and the Gypsies then began to use cereals and leguminous plants. But for a long time their activity was limited to what we call poaching. Being very clever in this, they quite soon knew how to use traps, snares and springes, their own being more ingenious than those of the native inhabitants. It is to the Gypsies that we owe the invention of baits for line fishing. They were the first, about one hundred and fifty years ago, to make artificial baits such as those little wooden fish decorated with tufts of coloured feathers in the middle of which hooks are concealed. As for the Gypsies of Britain, they invented the artificial fly for trout fishing. In the end they knew how to make allegedly magical baits, 'Magic nutmeg' or, more modern, the 'Radio-active ball'; these are generally made with gums of resinous plants whose attraction for fish was already known in Persia, or stones were coated with sweet-smelling oils.

This activity of collecting natural products is certainly the origin of the systematic thieving practised by the Gypsies. In point of fact, the concept of theft is, strictly speaking, *gadji*, non-Gypsy. Accustomed to collecting what they found in the way of comestibles on their journeying, the nomads are not conscious of stealing the property of others. Who are 'others', if not the Creator? The fruits of the earth belong to all men. It is not absurd to claim that when a Gypsy comes upon a domestic fowl wandering on the road or along by a hedge, in seizing it he is only repeating the ancestral exploit of the *Sammlervölker*. Obviously, in contact with our civilizations based on property, the Gypsy has well understood that his act has become reprehensible. But it is remarkable that the term *ciorav* (pronounced *tchourav* and passed on to French argot in the form *chouraver*) means 'to take' and, by extension only, 'to steal'. *Ciora* in Gypsy means 'magpie'; and this says everything.

The berries, mushrooms, herbs (nettles, for example), the vegetables growing wild, and small animals still to this day play a prominent part in the confection of Gypsy soups and stews. If meat is greatly appreciated, its consumption is the object of strict taboos: the flesh of the horse, dog and cat are very strictly forbidden. On the other hand, Gypsies greatly esteem game and fowl. Long ago they acquired particular techniques for obtaining these choice dishes. Some of them see nothing unseemly in eating meat that has gone bad. Those of Central Europe and the Middle East seem even to prefer it to fresh meat. Travellers have reported instances in which this form of food looked just like carrion. And the poorest Gypsies, who catch fowls on the approaches to farms, begin by carefully burying their catch to avert suspicion, and return to take it away only several days later.

One of the dishes peculiar to Gypsies is the hedgehog, the *niglo* (in English Gypsy *hotchi-witchi*: *Tr*.). It has its place in the festal meal, the marriage banquet, for example. Among the ways of preparing it, the most picturesque (and perhaps the best) consists in roasting it slowly in an earthenware oven sunk in the ground. The animal is enclosed in clay and placed on flat stones made white hot. When it is cooked, the prickles remain attached to the clay crust, and the hedgehog is served wrapped in big leaves. The entrails are not thrown away until the last moment. It is, in fact, a delectable dish.

The Gypsies use little spicing and very little salt. The only condiment they appreciate is wild garlic. Among some groups, however, the knowledge of medicinal herbs has made it possible for them to improve the flavour of their soups. Generally the meal consists of a single dish: a thick soup with many ingredients and as fatty as possible. (The reader will note that the so-called 'Gypsy' dishes recommended in exotic restaurants have nothing whatever to do with Gypsy food, and are merely adaptations of Russian, Serbian, Romanian, Ukrainian and Jewish cookery.)

The ordinary drink is, of course, clear water. The Gypsies drink little wine, and then only at a festal meal. Rather than wine, they often prefer beer. Nevertheless, on some ceremonial occasions they are capable of drinking enormous quantities of alcohol, like the Russians. Those who come from Central Europe have acquired the tea habit;

and they drink it boiling hot. They have, furthermore, their own particular manner of consuming it. The boiling-hot liquid is poured little by little into the saucer, and they lap it up very noisily. When the cup is empty, it is placed lying sideways on the saucer to indicate that they do not want any more. Otherwise they leave it standing upright.

Gypsies do not eat much bread (*manro*), but they consume large quantities of maize cake (*ankrusté*), perfumed with coriander seed and cumin (among the Kalderash).[1]

Tobacco, on the other hand, is one of their favourite pleasures. Women, and children down to infancy, smoke cigarettes like seasoned campaigners. As for the old women, they draw all the livelong day on roughly fashioned pipes. The most luxurious of their pipes have a thin copper band. As they do not always have tobacco at their disposal, they do not mind using herbs and dried leaves ground up. The stronger the mixture, the more it is appreciated. Besides, the word *drab*, which usually designates tobacco, means firstly 'grass' or 'herb'. In addition, they carefully collect tobacco juice and still use the expression, 'to drink tobacco' for 'to smoke'. It is often the case that, from assuaging their hunger with tobacco, the nomads acquired the habit of smoking so much.

HYGIENE

Gypsies feel a particular aversion to water, at least in regard to its extra-culinary use. Excepting among the young people of today, they hate washing themselves. Soap is practically unknown to them. This is one of the characteristics of nomad civilizations. Being very scarce in deserts and steppes, water was at first reserved for quenching the thirst of their animals, and that of the men afterwards. Only a strict minimum was used for cooking. To divert a little of this precious liquid to wash some linen, or for toilet purposes, would be considered a crime. So it was that the Mongols never washed themselves. A strict taboo was made an edict by Genghis Khan; to disobey the prohibition meant a sentence of death.

The Scythians likewise used an unguent or salve to clean their skin, but only from time to time. And the Gypsies of Asia Minor have kept to the use of a folded leaf of the jujube tree, which serves

1. Cumin: a small plant bearing aromatic seed-like fruit used in medicine and cookery. The liqueur *Kummel* is made from it. *Tr.*

them as soap. But this rejection of water for toilet purposes has consequences other than relative physical uncleanliness. The Gypsies began to hate water in general, whether as rain or sea. One may well imagine that rain is the scourge of their caravans. As for the sea, they have so strong an aversion to it that very few examples of Gypsy fishermen are known, and these have already been noted. In any case, there are no Gypsy sailors. Camps are always carefully set up on perfectly dry pieces of land. It is only the non-Gypsy *Barengré* (basket-makers) who settle near rivers or pools where they find reeds.

The phobia for water, when it is not for drinking, has become so deeply rooted that a Gypsy said to me one day: 'If I give myself a wash, I no longer feel the man'. One suddenly thinks of that remark of Gaston Bachelard: 'Psycho-analytically, cleanliness is a [form of] dirtiness'.

DEATH AND FUNERAL RITES

A Gypsy does not die in his bed. Like so many other peoples, like the Eskimos who go out far from sight of others to die on the snow, only as proof of their final act of impropriety would Gypsies render up their soul in tent or caravan. No more than birth may death pollute the home, even a temporary one. So it is that the women give birth outside, and the old men, in their last extremity, are moved out in front of the tent or caravan. As a rule even the person at death's door must be taken out by a 'concealed door', whether this be by the rear end of the tent, or by a hole made in the wall of the mud hut. Obviously the use of the caravan has destroyed this rite. During the death-pangs of Mimi Rossetto, *phuri dai* of the *Piemontesi* Gypsies, the members of her family had taken her from her bed and placed her lying on a mattress on the ground outside.

The funeral wake begins before death[1] in candlelight and to the sound of lamentations. But generally the witnesses are content to wait without showing too much emotion; which is not shown outwardly until after the death. Those present continue to chat, smoke, and even drink, beside the dying person.

The corpse of the deceased is washed in salt water (Gypsies of

1. Not to be confused with the Irish wake, which is watching the corpse after death and before the funeral, when grief is often accompanied by merrymaking. The Irish wake is a Celtic pagan survival. *Tr.*

Britain), and is then dressed in new clothes, often in great number (five skirts for a woman).[1] Among the Kalderash, the dead person's toilet is made, if I may dare say so, during life. Thus the dying man has the satisfaction of seeing himself well clothed for the great journey.[2]

On the announcement of death, the whole tribe begins to weep and cry out, even yell. Men and women whimper and cry bitterly showing much sorrow; and there is no reason to believe that their grief is feigned. Among some groups, the loud lamentations continue long into the night, and then change to rhythmic chanting. Their faces are literally contorted with suffering. Even the children wail as though they have been thrashed.

The shrouding takes place some time after death, sometimes three days afterwards, but the body is placed in a coffin, hands crossed on the chest or along by the body (Christian Gypsies of the Balkans). The English and Scottish Gypsies place the jewellery of the deceased and some gold coins in the coffin. According to Jules Bloch, with them are also placed some objects useful for the journey to the next world: fork and spoon, violin. . . . Formerly, among the Spanish *Gitanos*, his guitar or mandolin was placed in the arms of the dead man. Then a member of his family accused himself in a loud voice of having committed all the deceased's sins and challenged him: 'Play, and if I have done wrong, may your music turn me deaf; if I have done right, do not move and I shall receive absolution.'

Before burial in the Balkans the dead person is carried on a bier and exhibited at crossroads or street corners.[3] In Romania and Russia, he is moved without a pall, this being used only in Western Europe.

Burial has several forms. Christian and Mussulman influences have evidently been at play. If the Gypsy is a Catholic, the burial takes place in conformity with Church rites, but the details remain typically Gypsy. Thus, in addition to the handfuls of earth thrown on the coffin, sometimes coins or banknotes are thrown. The sprinkling is done by hand; the aspergillum is not used. In England this assumes an unexpected feature: the water is replaced by beer. On the grave of the famous Boswell, a Gypsy chief who died in 1820 at Doncaster,

1. Jules Bloch, op. cit.
2. F. de Ville, op. cit.
3. Martin Block, op. cit.

those present poured a jug of mulled ale. This act was repeated for several years, on the occasion of each pilgrimage to the cemetery. In Eastern Europe the witnesses drink wine round the grave of the deceased, with the toast: '*Te avel angla ei (Parni), ei sev le (Feroski)*': 'In honour of (Parni), daughter of (Fero)'.[1]

Jules Bloch gives a rather astonishing description of the funeral of a Gypsy woman who died in London in 1911:

> . . . Before lowering the coffin, a small hole was made in it beside where the left foot would be. With this may be compared a Romanian custom in which two holes are made beside the head, for breathing according to some, and others say in order to hear the lamentations better. Once the coffin had been lowered, the chief poured some rum on the said coffin, tasted the rum himself, and passed round the bottle.

Usually musicians play their instruments during the lowering into the grave. Sometimes during the transfer to the cemetery, one of the parents distributes money to the witnesses, especially to the children. Among some groups children do not attend funerals.

To make sure that death has really occurred, the Kalderash Gypsies in Paris and Sweden (?) pierce the heart of the deceased with a long needle. This is an ordinary rite for protection against ghosts or *mulé* which we have called to mind.

In bygone days, chiefly in Central Europe, the real funeral rites of a Gypsy chief took on a more symbolical character: the corpse was placed in a caravan painted white, with the intent that he should be made to do the journey of his migration in reverse. This clearly could last a very long time, when a frontier or several frontiers had to be crossed. The shrouding took place in the greatest secrecy, and no non-Gypsy could be present.

Another custom that has vanished, which, it seems, is based on nothing but suspect accounts, would have it that the dead person was committed to the course of a river. The German writer Achim von Arnim in his story *Isabella of Egypt* has used the Gypsy funeral rites (but his sources must be checked) and reports that, when a Gypsy was hanged, his companions came to take down his body during the night, and left it to be moved by the current of a small stream 'in order that he should go to find his own people'. It is at least certain, among the tribes of Asia Minor, that after someone had died, a young girl discreetly went out alone to the bank of a river and

1. Maximoff: in his novel *Les Ursitory*. See Bibliography, pp. 269, 271.

committed to the current a little plank on which were placed the vessels from which those present had drunk and a lighted candle. This tradition seems to be of Indian origin.

Some Gypsies break the dead person's little finger before he is put in the grave, and with red thread attach to it a piece of silver. This is in the tradition of Charon's obolus.

After the burial, it is necessary to part company with the clothes and personal belongings of the deceased. Those which can go from the chute on the caravan are thrown away, burned, or ... sold. In any case, no member of the tribe can inherit any of them. It is possible for the sacrifice of his horses to be part of this custom. Obviously, to burn a caravan is an enormous sacrifice. In the majority of cases the Gypsies are content to make it over to some member of another tribe or to a scrap-iron merchant. The last concession that would be acceptable would be to repaint it completely before using it again as a habitation.

There remains the matter of protecting oneself against the possible return of the deceased in the form of a ghost, a vampire or a *mulo* (see Demonology, page 183). The Hungarian Gypsies place on the grave a thorn-bush, which is supposed to prevent the dead from coming out. In Greece a heavy stone (often confused with an ordinary tombstone) fulfils this function. In England, Ireland and Scotland the rites are still stranger: it is forbidden to comb the hair, to wash oneself or to make up for a considerable period.

One would have to be able to compare these customs with European and Middle-Eastern folk-lore. By way of example, here is a connexion that can be established between the Gypsy rites in Spain and those of Wales. In Spain, as the reader has just seen, a member of the family makes his self-criticism at the grave; the Welsh have their 'sin eater'. This is generally some poor devil in the parish who, on condition of payment in food, takes on himself all the unexpiated sins of the deceased.[1]

The Gypsies do not have the cult of cemeteries. Once the burial is finished, the place of burial is practically forgotten. Only the Sinti go regularly to the grave of their departed, and that on All Saints Day; but nomadism and peregrinations often prevent this visit. When it does take place, the Gypsies eat and drink near the grave, taking care to scatter food and drink on it.

1. See, on this subject, de Maricourt, 'Superstitions de Pays de Galles', in *Mémoires de la Société d'Anthropologie de Paris* (1889).

Let us mention lastly the Gypsy funeral chants, which include some of their most beautiful poems. They are improvised and never repeated. This ephemeral character confers great value on them; but how is one to write down those intoned chants in a bass voice which sing to the repose of the dead person and vaunt his virtues?

6 · Language and Means of Expression

GYPSY LANGUAGE

The Gypsy language, properly so called, or 'basic Gypsy', is the *romani* (or *romanes*); from *rom*, 'man'. A century of gypsiology has proved that this language is of Indian origin. More than half of its fundamental vocabulary is connected with groups of languages or dialects still spoken today in northern India: in the Indu-Ganges basin and the north-west of the Deccan. It is known that these dialects are all derived from one mother tongue, now non-existing except by reconstruction, and of which Sanskrit is one of its most important branches. Among these dialects are Hindi, Gujarati, Marathi and Cashmiri; and *romanes* is one of them. According to Pierre Meile, Professor of Modern Oriental Languages at the National School of Oriental Languages,[1] Gypsy has a grammar and vocabulary which cannot be explained except by Sanskrit. 'Its fundamental vocabulary is fairly close to that of Hindi. And this kinship . . . is clear and palpable because it is very close.'

It is usual to give, by way of example, a list of the first cardinal numbers:

	Hindi	Romanian Gypsy	Greek Gypsy	Armenian Gypsy	Syrian Gypsy
1	ek	ék	yek	yaku	yoka
2	do	dui	dui	dui	di
3	tin	trin	trin	t'rin	taran
4	car	chtar	(i)star	ch'tar	star
5	pansh	pansh	pansh'	bensh'	punj

Here are some examples, picked at random from those given by Jules Bloch, of *romani* words and their Hindi equivalents:

Gypsy	Hindi	English
yakh	akh	*eye*
yag	ag	*fire*

1. In France. See the Review *Études Tsiganes*, April 1955.

Gypsy	Hindi	English
kalo	kala	*black*
ker	kar	*to do, make*
khil	ghi	*butter*
kin	kin	*to buy*
amaro	amara	*our*

The sentence is constructed in the same way in Gypsy and Hindi. Franz de Ville gives the following example:[1]

> *Gypsy*: dja, dik kon tchalavedo o vurdo.
> *Hindi*: dja, dekh kon tchalaya dvar ko.
> English: Go and see who's knocking at the door.

Conjugations of verbs and declensions of nouns etc. closely follow the Hindi pattern. The feminine ending *-i*, for example, is found in both: Gypsy *kali* is Hindi *kali*, both meaning 'black'.

A 'basic' grammar and vocabulary of Gypsy has still to be established in French.[2] The only one in French[3] relates only the dialects spoken in Romania by the *Lovari*, *Oursari* and *Tchurari* groups and must not be taken too literally.

If *romanī* is to be unquestionably classified in the family of northern Indian languages mentioned, it nonetheless includes a non-Indian vocabulary of very wide range. Being in fact essentially a language of wanderers, it has served as a vehicle for a large number of words gleaned in the countries that were crossed or in which the Gypsies remained. So it is that it has been possible to recognize a large number of Iranian roots. And 'There are reasons to suppose that the Gypsy populations have lived for some time in Afghanistan, during a period in that region when the Indian language had not yet withdrawn, as it did afterwards, when pressed towards India by Iranian.'[4]

The second language which strongly contributed to enrich *romanī* was medieval Greek. The words have hardly changed, most of them even not at all. Thus *drom* (road), *kokalo* (leg), *forco* (town),

1. In the example given, the Gypsy word *vurdon* (caravan) has replaced the word 'door'.
2. We are more fortunate in English with John Sampson's great work on the dialect of the Welsh Gypsies (*see* Bibliography). This dialect preserves the rich inflexional system of 'deep' *romanī* in a state of great purity. *Tr.*
3. Serboianu, *Les Tziganes* (1930).
4. Meile, op. cit.

octo (eight). .... It is furthermore probable that it was from the Greeks who lived in Asia Minor that the Gypsies picked up this vocabulary, rather than in the Peninsula itself. It is remarkable how these Greek words still persist in all the dialects spoken by Gypsies in Western Europe, even as far as Wales.

Romanī likewise includes Armenian terms: *grast* (horse), *bov* (stove), *kotor* (piece); Ossetic (the famous *vurdon*, wheeled wagon, caravan); Kurdish; and even Ukranian (*kurve*, whore). So much for borrowings from the East. From the time of their first arrival in Europe, the Gypsies have steadily assimilated many terms from Romanian, Hungarian, Russian, Slav, German, Serbian and Polish. .....

The methodical detection of these borrowings has allowed us to form more accurate ideas of the migration routes. Thus, the language of the Gypsies of Finland contains Swedish words, but not Russian; they would therefore have reached Finland via the West. On the other hand, these linguistic 'spottings' cause a little confusion in regard to trails when someone ascertains, for example, that the Gypsy dialect of northern Russia has elements from Greek, Romanian, Serbian, Hungarian, German and Polish. A map of the migrations, to be accurate, would very much resemble a skein of yarn impossible to disentangle.

What is most curious is the constancy of some of these contributions to the language. For example, in the dialects furthest removed from their 'native country' – that of Wales – the same Greek, Iranian, Armenian and other terms are found.

On to this 'basic' *romanī*, which practically no Gypsy any longer speaks in its purity, many idioms become engrafted. To establish frontiers between them appears to be useless. Their many variations fluctuate greatly; they depend on the groups of Gypsies. Within the same country difficulties do not fail to arise. It is enough for the visitor to listen attentively to the Gypsies around him, during the annual pilgrimage to Saintes-Maries-de-la-Mer, to appreciate for himself a diversity in pronunciation sufficient to dishearten anyone. My personal experience has been that, some years ago, having painfully learnt to form a few schoolbook phrases such as *latchi rat'* ('good evening' or 'good night'), I noticed that nine times out of ten this simple phrase, acquired from some Gypsies said to be 'Hungarian', was incomprehensible to the ears of their caravan neighbours. In spite of the unmistakable good will of my listeners,

I never succeeded in making out whether I ought to have said *latcho ghes* or *latcho dives* in order to wish them good day. One cannot but admire gypsiologists like the Abbé Barthélémy, the *Ioschka* of the Gypsies, who, sailing cheerfully from one dialect to another, succeeds in making himself understood in all the *verdines* or caravans.

It is even difficult to estimate the exact number of these Gypsy dialects. The principal ones are Armenian Gypsy (spoken in Transcaucasia), Finnish, Hungarian, German, and Welsh Gypsy, the dialects of English Gypsy, Catalan Gypsy and Andalusian Gypsy. Finally, the *Yénisch* merits a particular mention. It does not belong to the *romaní* group of languages: the *Yénische* people are not regarded as Gypsies. It is a way of expression derived from German *Rotwelsch*,[1] but remarkably influenced by Yiddish; although, it must be repeated, the *Yénische* are *not* Jews. The presence of Yiddish words in *Yénisch*, nevertheless, has had the curious result of introducing some Hebrew terms into the Gypsy dialects of Germany.

The Spanish *Gitanos*, for their part, although they remember little of the *romaní*, have evolved for themselves a rather original dialect: the *Caló* (a word of which the root is *kala*, 'black'), and of which the peculiarity, already emphasized, is not to harbour a single term derived from German. On the other hand, over two thousand Arabic words or words deriving from Arabic are found in it. This confirms the passage of the *Gitanos* to Spain via North Africa. Whatever its origin may be, the *Caló* has left many traces in everyday Spanish.[2] Lafuente has picked out among other important contributions the following: *gacho* (lover) and its feminine *gachi* (girl friend, mistress), *gili* (fool), *sandunga* (elegance, gracefulness), *chunga* (joke, fun, merriment; 'La Chunga' – 'the merry girl' – is the name of a ravishing *gitana* dancer who now tours the world), *najarse* (to go out, away) from the Gypsy world *natchav*, *cate* (blow, slap), *mangante* (beggar, vagabond), *camelar* (to court), *canguelo* (fear, funk), *ful* (false), *fulero* (trickster), *acharar* (to annoy, make jealous), *terne* (bully, 'bravo'), etc.

In Portugal the *caló* became *calão*, a dialect with the same structure

1. *Rotwelsch*: not a language properly speaking, but a made-up 'lingo' or jargon, like the sort of gibberish used by thieves and other lawbreakers in many countries. *Tr.*

2. See Carlos Claveria, *Estudios sobre los gitanismos del Español* (Madrid, 1951). See also Bibliography, p. 272, for Rebolledo. *Tr.*

as that of the Spanish *Gitanos*; but obviously including many Portuguese terms.[1]

If the Gypsy dialects have abundantly adopted the vocabularies of the countries they went through, they have also contributed in some degree to the enrichment of European languages. Obviously it is the secret slang of evildoers which has drawn most profit from Gypsy sources. But we know that this slang easily advances to the rank of accepted popular language and then, with the help of snobbery, integrates itself in everyday speech. Some *romanī* contributions to Spanish have been noted. English has inherited various terms such as: pal (from *phral*, brother) and cosh ('stick', from *krash*). We also know that Caliban, Shakespeare's fantastic hero, is the Gypsy name for 'darkness', 'blackness': *kaliben*.

The contributions from Gypsy to French were chiefly made in the nineteenth century, whether in their purity or appreciably distorted. The list is a long one. If some words of *romanī* origin, which were part of the slang vocabulary during the Balzac period, have since then disappeared, there are others more durable that are now in current use without the public suspecting their 'bohemian' origin. Thus, the word *bath* (popular term for 'excellent', 'fine' as in *c'est bath!* 'that's fine') is pure *romanī*; *bakht* means 'luck', usually 'good luck'. A toast is proposed saying: *bakht to ke!* or '(good) luck be on you'. This is the *baraka* of the Arabs which, formerly in India, carried with it a more subtle meaning of 'devout abandon, almost loving surrender to the supreme divinity, the *bhakti*', according to Louis Renou.

The philologist Esnault has noted some twenty to thirty words used in popular French speech which can be linked with *romanī* without fear of error. Thus: *berge* ('year' from *bers*); *surin* ('knife' from *tchuri*); *rupin* ('rich' from *rup*, 'money' as in the Indian 'rupee'); *ouste* (an exclamation, as in *allons, ouste!* 'Come, let's go!' or 'Let's get a move on!' from *uste!* Get up!); and *costaud* ('strong', 'strapping', 'hefty', from *kusto*, strong).

The most closely reserved argot of modern malefactors in France has these terms: *chouraver*, 'to rob', 'steal', from *tchurav*; *lové*, 'money', 'dibs', from *lové*, money; *michet* and *micheton* (a prostitute's

1. Just as the manuscript of this book was being delivered, I received the long-awaited work by S. Wolf: *Grosses Wörterbuch der Zigeunersprache, Wortschatz deutscher u. anderer Zigeunerdialekte* (Mannheim, 1961). Unfortunately I was unable to make use of it.

client, and 'victim of a bad blow, misfortune' derivatives of *mishto*, good); *natchaver*, 'to run away', 'escape' (and perhaps the expression *mettre les adjas*); *choucard*, 'beautiful', from *shuchar*; *trac*, 'fear', from *trach*; and finally the expression '*tchao!*' 'good-bye' or 'au revoir' (*ciao* in Italian) from *tcheav*, 'to go'.

What is more, the usual ending of Gypsy verbs (-*av*) which is found in *natchaver* and *chouraver* has set a fashion, for in argot again we find *mengave*, 'begging', 'mendicity'. Finally, those who use slang and who have had contacts with Gypsies have adopted some terms known in the 'milieu', such as: *gail*, horse; *ẓoumine*, soup; and *verdine*, the caravan used by itinerants.

HANDWRITING

It has been noted that the Gypsies were not acquainted with the use of handwriting, and the reasons for this lack I have tried to explain.

Nevertheless, there was a gypsiologist, J.-A. Decourdemanche, who published a *Grammar of Gypsy or the Language of the Wandering Bohemians*,[1] at the end of which he gives a Gypsy alphabet. The reader will see for himself that this system of writing is not without interest. At all events, it is inconceivable that a linguist whose works were authoritative in their time should have invented every single thing in it. This alphabet tallies, up to a point, with the group of runes used for old Hungarian and old Turkish, of which definite examples will be found in the latest work of Ernst Doblhofer.[2]

According to Decourdemanche, the Gypsy alphabet consists of twenty-three characters, of which five are vowels and eighteen are consonants. It has three forms, each depending upon who uses it: (1) the children's alphabet (*c'avorengera kripta*); (2) the alphabet of old men (elders) and of the dead (*purengera kr.*); and (3) the men's alphabet (*rumengera kr.*). One can well imagine from this hypo-thetical differentiation that the 'old men' or elders, that is, the chiefs of tribes, used a secret (hand)writing that would be incomprehens-ible to the ordinary men of the tribe. And that the latter, in turn, would not like the women and children to understand the meaning of their messages. But, however curious it may seem, it is the child-ren's alphabet which derives from the others.

This Gypsy writing is hieroglyphic. The vowels, which represent

1. *Grammaire du Tchingané ou langue des Bohémiens errants* (1908).
2. *Le Déchiffrement des écritures* (Arthaud, 1960).

five different genders (A = simple neuter; O = masculine; I = feminine; E = compound neuter; U = absolute neuter) represent sexual elements;

A (simple neuter) is represented by   **l**   single rod, sign of the eunucate;
O (masculine)   by   **b**   phallus;
I (feminine)   by   **ẞ**   vulva;
E (compound neuter)   by   **ᑲ**   rod and vulva joined;
U (absolute neuter)   by   **ᐅ**   absence of sex.

Presented in this way, vertically, these vowels are vocal sounds (that is, vowel-sounds). But, written horizontally they indicate class and, placed before a word, determine its general meaning:

—	(A) :	ground, place, habitation.
ᴕ	(O) :	strength (force), heat, light.
ᴔ	(I) :	mucosity, liquid.
ᴚ	(E) :	being, thing.
ᐁ	(U) :	cry, word, noise.

So much for the basic alphabet, that of children. At the level of the elders and men, the following writing characters are used:

	Elders	Men
(A)	I	ɼ
(O)	ᑮ	⊢
(I)	B	⌐
(E)	ᕱ	⌐
(U)	D	⊢

– and these, placed horizontally, give the derived meaning as shown in the children's alphabet.

As for the consonants, they symbolize very schematically the archetype-object chosen to illustrate a word beginning with this letter, as in our children's A-B-C: A for *apple*, and so on.

Words are written attaching each sign to a common horizontal line, above them, and one can hardly fail to be struck by the resemblance to Indian writing. The (hand)writing of children and that of the elders goes from left to right. That of men is vertical, from the bottom upwards and along an axis, the vowels being 'caught' (or 'hooked') on to the right; and the consonants on the left of an axis running from below upwards.

Here is a table of this Gypsy alphabet, according to Decourde-manche:

VOWELS

	Children		Elders		Men	
A						
O						
I						
E						
U						

CONSONANTS

Equivalents	Names	Children	Elders	Men	Pronounciation
M	muï, *mouth*				m as in English
P	paï, *foot*				p ,, ,, ,,
B	baï, *stick*				b ,, ,, ,,
V	vaï, *traveller*				v ,, ,, ,,
F	faï, *well, fountain*				f ,, ,, ,,
K	ker, *tent*				k ,, ,, ,,
G	gon, *purse, bag*				g as in *go, get*
H	herko, *bow (archery)*				h as in English
T	tem, *earth*				t ,, ,, ,,
D	dom, *house*				d ,, ,, ,,
N	nak, *nose*				n ,, ,, ,,
R	ruk, *tree*				r ,, ,, ,,
L	lir, *pound*				l ,, ,, ,,
S	sin, *star*				ss as in *hissing*
S'	s'on, *moon*				sh as in *shine*
C'	c'ok, *beak*				ch as in *China*
J	jine, *person*				y as in *yes*
K'	k'ando, *sword*				ch as in Scots *loch*

242

If the Gypsies have no system of writing, as we usually understand the word, they nevertheless use a very full list of conventional signs which enable them to communicate visually and in time. This secret code is called the *patrin* (from *patran*, leaf of a tree) and consists at one and the same time of particular items chosen from nature (cock's feathers, pieces of trimmed wood, scraps left over from meals, and so forth) and signs which may be carved or drawn.

Mostly, when a tribe wishes to leave marks of its passage at a camping place and a message for those who come after, it is enough for the Gypsies to place these items in a certain way. And so a birth is discreetly announced by attaching an elder branch to a tree, with red thread if it is a boy, with white if it is a girl. This mark is accompanied by the distinctive sign of the tribe, and sometimes also by that of the tribe to which it is particularly addressed.

Each tribe of Gypsies has, in fact, its own distinctive sign. According to another tradition, it is the chief of the tribe who is the holder of the sign; and this sign is secret. It is zealously carved on the inside of the chief's rod-sceptre which has been split in two. It seems that, at first, the sign reflected the old totemism of the Gypsies. Consequently, some groups in Germany had as their mark the birch-tree, or the maple-tree, or the elder-tree. . . . It is even remarkable that this totemism at first sight seems to be exclusively vegetable; perhaps related to the ancient cult of the tree, which has already been mentioned. However, some tribal signs are from the animal kingdom (the hedgehog), or from astronomy (a star, a comet).

Under the tribal sign the chief puts his own personal sign, which is often more complex. In this are found elements or representations of elements of the most varied kinds: a hazel rod, horse hair (mane or tail), hog's bristles, pips from a gourd, haricot beans, datura seeds, torn cloth, and sometimes simple strokes cut and blackened with charcoal delineating vertical and horizontal notches. These signs serve to make wills. Thus, a tribal chief wishing to leave his belongings, shall we say eight pigs, his horse, his vehicle and his tent, would carefully carve this message:

But the *patrin* especially is in more everyday use. It serves particularly for marking on the outer walls of farms and dwelling-houses such information as may be required by nomads. In fact, mutual aid among the Gypsies requires that, when a tribe has stayed near a village, it should leave a message addressed to other tribes giving the maximum of information that can be used for commercial or provisional purposes. Thus, a Gypsy woman will be the first to go into a farmhouse on the pretext of selling items of linen-drapery, or to tell fortunes. She operates so as to make the owner's wife talk, and she learns about important family matters – the number and ages of the children, recent illnesses and so forth. As she is going away, she will scratch on the wall or mark with chalk or charcoal signs which only her racial brothers will know how to make out. Some time later, when a second Gypsy woman shows up at the farm, she will have every opportunity to tell fortunes and reveal to the utterly amazed and therefore credulous farmer's wife details of their family life.

These signs are obviously very simply heiroglyphs, but in great variety. I have long pledged myself to maintain silence on this subject, but, just as an example, I reproduce *patrin* signs that have already been published in newspapers and magazines. They are not quite accurate but will give a good enough idea of their symbolism.[1]

✝	here they give nothing.
✚	beggars badly received.
○	generous people.
◉	very generous people and friendly to Gypsies.
◎̲	here Gypsies are regarded as thieves.
///	we have already robbed (this place).
△	you can tell fortunes with cards.
≈	the mistress wants a child.
✗	she wants no more children.
✗	old woman died recently.

1. These signs have been published by Jean-Luis Fèvre in his book *Les Fils du Vent* (1954), a work which, in spite of his great sympathy for the Gypsies, is no less suspect in its affirmations.

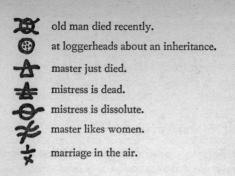

old man died recently.

at loggerheads about an inheritance.

master just died.

mistress is dead.

mistress is dissolute.

master likes women.

marriage in the air.

The signs used in the Gypsy *patrin* may be compared with those of vagabonds in all countries: thus, American tramps (hobos) and German 'travellers' use the same kind of secret language, but obviously the signs differ. The triangle, however, always indicates a difficulty or a refusal; and the circle means a good thing (good business to be done).

7 · Gypsies and society

The Gypsy is primarily and above all else a nomad. His dispersion throughout the world is due less to historical or political necessities than to his own nature. Even among the 'sedentary' Gypsies, some clear signs of ritual nomadism are the indication of a definite characteristic of this racial group. Whether the settled Gypsies be cave-dwellers on the hills of Sacro Monte, or owners of a flat in Paris, they at all times give the impression of camping temporarily. An underground room inhabited by French *Gitans* will always bear a greater resemblance to a prehistoric cave than to a suburban interior. A lodging let to Gypsies in a 'good house' in a big town is first of all invaded by parcels and suitcases. The authentic 'lodger' among them is never known. These ephemeral inhabitants come and go. The family seems to be of utterly astounding elasticity. The beds themselves consist only of blankets and eiderdowns, more rarely of mattresses, piled along by a wall. Cooking is better done on a small portable spirit-stove placed on ground level rather than on a cooker.

There is an important category of semi-sedentary Gypsies, particularly in Eastern and Central Europe. These live in villages or suburbs, sometimes lodging in solid houses, and devote themselves to artisan occupations. But, when the first fine days come, the whole tribe takes to the road. This seasonal nomadism obviously is of a ritual kind (Professor Pittard calls it 'ceremonial nomadization'). In fact, a study of the calendar of these movements reveals shifting differences in the actual time intervening between the pure and simple passage from one season to the other. The sedentary Gypsies are generally 'excluded' people, groups or families or couples who have founded a family and who have been banned from the clans or made *marimé*, that is, 'unclean', because of serious violations of the Tradition (marriages outside the tribe, theft among Gypsies, violation of oath, etc.). Their seasonal nomadism would be nothing other than a psychological clearance of the incurable obsession for moving which characterizes their people.

Yet the great majority of authentic Gypsies are still uncompromising nomads. The courses of their migrations have been noted. On the scale of a man's lifetime, their movements represent impressive distances. Thus, the Kalderash chief Zanko, now eighty years of age, remembers cities as far away as Moscow, Petrograd (now Leningrad), Odessa, Batum, Mexico, Buenos Aires, and the list could be extended. Within a single country such as France, there are regular circuits which would be interesting to map. We know that, to attend the annual pilgrimage at Saintes-Maries-de-la-Mer on 25 May, Gypsies come not only from every region in France but from Belgium, Germany, Spain and England. Some families come from further afield, temporarily leaving the Banat plains and the banks of the Danube.[1] The increasing difficulties experienced by itinerants in obtaining passports and visas must still be considered.

This nomadism in its pure state is one of the oddest examples of human universalism. In fact, when most of the last nomads of this world have perfectly organized areas for expansion, and are reduced to spaces which hardly suit the sedentaries, the Gypsies are the only people who are wanderers in the midst of stable and organized civilization. They seem to regard European countrysides as inhabited steppes, and their passage through towns as though they were the simple and ephemeral stopping places of the caravanserais of Central Asia. Their idea of property has been recorded (think of the thieving of which they are regularly accused) and one sees that in essence it derives from this attitude.

Their relations with non-Gypsies are always tinged with reticence, not to say contempt. Let us remember that the term they use for non-Gypsy – *gadjo* – has a first meaning of 'peasant', 'clod-hopper'. Their catalogue of abusive language is rich in terms, of which the sedentary Gypsy bears the brunt. Their savage obstinacy, which will not allow them to form an alliance with anybody who is not of pure Gypsy blood, is one of the most astonishing findings in the data of contemporary European sociology.

It was inevitable that there should have been many attempts to integrate the Gypsies during periods when they were the object of repressive measures. In our own time, when psychology is at last

1. Occasionally also from the Americas, and occasionally in whole families. *Tr.*

intervening in the establishment of social relations, these are, nevertheless, far from being successful among Gypsies.

But let us first see what is the present situation of the Gypsies in our world.

GYPSIES IN THE WORLD TODAY

The reader has seen that the Gypsies' area of expansion covered practically the whole of Europe. There are many of them in Asia Minor. There are many in North Africa, Egypt, the Sudan, South Africa, in North and South America (mainly in the United States, Chile and Peru), and as far away as Australia. Their presence in China has been reported several times, though never convincingly attested. It is impossible to give an exact number for this moving population. Yet it is certain that the total number of Gypsies in the world can now be estimated, with a small margin of error, at five million.

We shall be satisfied here to consider their situation in the principal European countries.[1]

Spain

It is in Spain that the Gypsies, or rather the *Gitanos*, have found one of their most favourable homes. In fact, and only after centuries of repression, they have gained almost complete freedom which only the Gypsies of Britain (and the United States: *Tr.*) need envy. At a time when, in the rest of Europe, the nomad remains a pariah, subject to coercive and vexatious measures, the Spanish *Gitanos* are perfectly integrated in the Spanish population, especially in Andalusia. The most outcast of them even end by intermingling with the usual fauna of suburbs and outskirts of towns and cities.

Britain

The geographical position of England has resulted in the creation of Gypsy insularism. Having little occasion or desire to cross the sea, the Gypsies have little by little formed here a peculiar group that has

1. For readers of this edition, I have added (pp. 260–67) some notes of my own relating to the Gypsies in Britain (many of whom have gone or may go to Commonwealth countries) and about the Gypsies in the United States of America. These brief notes have been gleaned from reliable sources. *Tr.*

hardly any contacts with continental Gypsies. On the other hand, relations between nomads with the same way of life, although of different origin, seem easier and less formal than elsewhere. Nevertheless, even within the limits of England, the Gypsies continue their unflagging nomadism.

The special areas within which they move are Wales and the outskirts of London, notably Surrey. The latest official figure (1942) recorded 30,000 Gypsies in Britain, of a total population of 45,000 nomads.[1]

The occupations of British Gypsies are more or less the same as those of Gypsies elsewhere. However, two other fields of activity are open to them: the racecourses and seaside resorts. The British Gypsies are, in fact, the only ones who have become jockeys. Their knowledge of horses makes all activities lucrative in which horses are involved. So there is nearly always a great gathering of them at Epsom on the day the Derby is run; and normally lesser numbers attend the less important racecourses. At seaside resorts Gypsy funfair operators rent ground and set up attractions of many kinds for visitors. At Blackpool, for example.

It is normally the case that the English people, who care so much for individual liberty, are not so harsh towards the Gypsies as other Europeans. Laws governing them differ hardly at all from those which apply to any British subject. No special identity card is required of Gypsies. Their movements and activities, so long as they do not contravene the normal order of society, are completely free.[2] It is surprising that, in such circumstances, Gypsies are not more numerous in Britain.[3-4]

Belgium

On the other hand, Belgium is too prosperous a country to be enamoured of nomads, those people whose will it is to live differently from others. According to the terms of a circular sent out by the Ministry of Justice, 'the less we see of them, the healthier the country

1. For a later estimate, see p. 260 of Supplementary Notes. *Tr.*

2. But see also p. 261 of Supplementary Notes. *Tr.*

3. On this subject, see Holleaux, 'Les Tziganes d'Angleterre' in the *Mercure de France*, June 1948.

4. On this subject generally, see Brian Vesey-Fitzgerald's book, noted in the Bibliography, p. 273. *Tr.*

will be'. The prohibition of entry to Belgian territory is the least of the things from which the Gypsies suffer:

The country is generally opposed to the entry on their territory of those bands with customs of their own, whose proximity constitutes a menace to general peace and always causes a great number of complaints on the part of the public. In order to achieve effective action in the interest of all governments, several countries have concluded agreements, or agreed to rules, as safeguards against these nomads. The principle which governs these agreements is the obligation of each State to retain nomads who have been for a long time on its territory, and to refrain from getting rid of them by driving them into adjacent territory.

This does not prevent the Belgian Government itself from driving out as many as possible of these wandering bands. Consequently Belgium is, with Switzerland, one of the European countries least often visited by Gypsies. The gendarmerie modestly recognizes the presence of ... sixty individuals! The 'others' are, however, numerous enough for the problem of their dwelling places to congest whole administrative files.

Some privileged Belgian Gypsies have permit cards as itinerant tradesmen, or have been stall-keepers at fairs for long enough to be less conspicuous. The majority, however, find themselves under the compulsions of the usual forms of servitude: their stay in one place limited to forty-eight hours, and without previous notice being banned by the municipality – and above all, the defamatory identity card of the stateless which automatically records, facing their name and address, the printed formulas: *The self-styled* ... 'X', *allegedly born at* ... 'Y', and this even when the accuracy of the information furnished by the interested person is admitted. Children of nomads are not admitted to primary schools; these systematically refuse to accept a young Gypsy whose attendance may be short-lived. The identity card of the stateless has to be renewed every three months. While awaiting the completion of the officially required formalities, the Gypsies are meanwhile compelled to camp on the spot – under the supervision of the gendarmerie.[1]

Germany

From the advent of Nazism, the Gypsies in Germany have gone

1. See Franz de Ville, 'Les Tsiganes en Belgique' in *Études Tsiganes*, October 1955.

through one of the most tragic periods in their history. In the racialist world of the National Socialists, the Gypsies and the Jews had the sad privilege of again being in the limelight. Long before the outbreak of the Second World War in 1939, when action against the 'asocial' elements of the German population was undertaken, the internment of Gypsies in concentration camps was begun. It was Rudolf Hoess, Commander of Auschwitz camp, who revealed this in the statements he wrote in his cell before being hanged.[1] It is curious to note that Hoess claims that he himself just missed being kidnapped by Gypsies when he was a child. But, at the same time as the Gypsies were being interned and subjected to 'biological research' in a way to make us shudder,

the *Reichsführer* [Hitler] wished at every cost to assure the preservation of the two most important Gypsy tribes. He regarded them as the direct descendants of the primitive Indo-Germanic race whose ways and customs would have been conserved in their original purity. He wanted to have them listed for record without exception. Beneficiaries of the Law for the Protection of Historical Monuments [*sic*], they would be sought for throughout Europe and settled in a region to be defined where scholars would be able to study them at leisure.

It was, therefore, on this pretext that from 1937 to 1938, the nomad Gypsies were parked in 'residence camps' situated near the big cities. But, behind this official façade, the operation had no aim other than their extermination pure and simple. From 1938, with the avowed intention of preserving the purity of Germanic blood (as Greifelt said, Chief of the General Staff of the *Reichskommissar für die Festigung des Deutschen Volkstums*), and to eliminate from the Reich 'sub-human beings' and representatives of the 'lower races', this 'Commissariat for the Consolidation of Germanism' undertook the enslavement and annihilation of the Jews and the Gypsies. Besides the millions of Jews who suffered and died victims of this wave of frantic racism, more than 400,000 Gypsies lost their lives because of their affiliation to an 'impure' ethnic group.

Here is an extract from the letter written by *Gauleiter* Portschy of Steiermark (southern Austria) to the responsible Minister. This letter, I repeat, was written in 1938:

1. Rudolf Hoess, *Le Commandant d'Auschwitz parle* (1958).

Province of Steiermark

To Reichs-Minister,   Graz, 9 January 1938
Dr Lammers,
Berlin W.8.

Very Honoured Reichs-Minister,

I have the honour to send you herewith a clean copy of my memorandum on the Gypsy question.

Signed: PORTSCHY
Gauleiter

ENCLOSED

... ...

(3) The National Socialist solution of the Gypsy question.

(a) Generalities

For reasons of public health and particularly because the Gypsies have manifestly a heavily tainted heredity, and because they are inveterate criminals who constitute parasites in the bosom of our people, and cannot but produce in it immense injuries, subjecting to great peril the blood purity of the German frontiersmen peasantry, their way of life and laws, it is fitting in the first place to watch them closely, to prevent them from reproducing themselves and to subject them to the obligation of forced labour in the labour camps, without however preventing them from choosing voluntary emigration abroad.

It is not possible to achieve this goal fully if the only laws at present in force are taken into consideration or effectively applied. If these laws are conscientiously interpreted, in the strict sense of the term, one would succeed in taking only half-measures in regard to the Gypsy question....

The arguments in favour of sterilizing the Gypsies can in fact *a priori* be tacitly expanded to the point that it can be achieved, by the law alone of prophylaxis against progeniture which carries hereditary diseases, in an effective fight against any increase in the Gypsy population. We must make use of this law fearlessly and unreservedly. This at least would not give rise to outcries on the part of the foreign press, the reason being that one can always and with full justification maintain that this law of prophylaxis against progeny which carries hereditary disease is indeed equally valid for citizens of the German Reich. In the same way, the principle applying in democratic countries, according to which everybody is equal in the sight of the law, is fully respected.

In conformity with the principle by which in a State with morals on a high level, and particularly the Third Reich, only he who works and produces can live, the Gypsies must be liable to compulsory constant labour in accordance with their nature . . . (NG–845).

From that moment onwards, the history of the extermination of the Gypsies follows the same graph as that of the extermination of the Jews. 'A beginning is made with restrictive social measures, trials of sterilization are made, and, to finish, there are the Auschwitz gas-chambers.'[1]

Massive deportations began in 1940 with the removal of 30,000 Gypsies from areas occupied by the Germans in Poland. They were evacuated to territories under the general Government of the Reich.

There were many cases of sterilization of Gypsies. The official text made this clear: 'intelligent sterilization of men and women of foreign blood working in German agriculture in cases where, on the basis of our racial laws – laws which must be applied more strictly in such cases – they have been declared inferior in regard to physical and intellectual traits and to characteristic qualities'. The means employed was by injection or oral administration of the sap of the *caladium sanguinum* plant, whose sterilizing properties were discovered and improved by Dr Madaus.

Finally, in 1945 all Gypsies who were in concentration camps were gassed.[2]

I cannot refrain from quoting the relevant extract from the judgement pronounced by the American Military Tribunal at the trial of the *Einsatzgruppen*:[3]

The *Einsatzgruppen* in addition received instructions to shoot the Gypsies. No explanation has been given of the reason why this inoffensive people, who, in the course of centuries, has given its share of richness in music and song, should be hunted down like wild game. Picturesque in their clothes and customs, they have amused and entertained society, and sometimes annoyed it by their indolence. But nobody has condemned them as a mortal menace to organized Society, that is, nobody except National Socialism which, by the voice of Hitler, Himmler and Heydrich, ordered their liquidation.[4]

1. Billig, *L'Allemagne et le génocide*, published by the *Centre de la Documentation Juive Contemporaine* (1950).
2. Declaration by Ochshorn to the Commission of the United Nations for War Crimes. NO–1934.
3. Session of 8 April 1948. *Einsatzgruppen* = 'action groups' = extermination squads.
4. All these documents are quotations from Billig's book, op. cit. and the archives of the *Centre de la Documentation Juive Contemporaine*.

Since the War, the Gypsies who survived in West Germany have met with greater understanding. Although their situation is far from being adjusted, the Federal Government has tried to assimilate them, and marked improvements have been made in the law of citizenship and in the field of education.

Communist Countries

The present situation of the Gypsies in the Soviet Union and satellite countries is not well known. Few documents on the subject have as yet been published, whether by the authorities or by ethnologists. The most revealing article has been published in the review *Témoignages*,[1] and I rely on it for most of what follows.

The Gypsies behind the 'iron curtain' are one of the four groups of racial minorities important enough to constitute a permanent problem (the other three groups being the Germans, Magyars and Jews).

The number of Gypsies in the satellite countries cannot be accurately given. However, according to information from official sources, here are the latest probable figures for the relevant countries:

Bulgaria: 150,000 (Review *Geografia*, Sofia, 1951).

Czechoslovakia: 150,000 (*Radio Bratislava*, 9 September 1958).

Hungary: from 150,000 to 200,000 (*Nepakarat*, Budapest, 20 October 1957).

Poland: 150,000 (*New York Times*, 6 September 1958).

Romania: 262,501 (*Anuarul Statistics*, Bucarest, 1939–40).

This last figure, one of remarkable precision, no longer has any historical value; tens of thousands of Romanian Gypsies were, in fact, massacred by the Nazis during the War.

No information is available in regard to Albania, but the Gypsy population is insignificant.

As for Russia, a decree issued by the Presidium of the Supreme Soviet, dated 5 October 1956, makes it compulsory for the last nomad Gypsies of the country to lead a settled life. The right to choose a place of residence is granted. Measures have been taken, in accordance with local planning, to facilitate their initiation into agricultural work and work in the towns.[2]

1. Survey of documentation on Central and Eastern Europe, published by Colbert, No. 7, May 1959.
2. *Courrier de l'Unesco*, April 1958.

The Gypsy problem in Russia and the satellite countries is first and foremost one of settlement, for contemporary communist society cannot agree that an ethnic minority, even a small one and little inclined towards collectivization, should continue to wander on the highroads. 'The goal of the authorities is to integrate the Gypsy population in agricultural and industrial communities, and it seems that these efforts have met with some success. It is difficult to determine, in this success, how much of it is due to initiative on the part of the régime and how much to natural historical evolution; for, even before the Communists came to power, there was a tendency among some Gypsies to abandon their nomad existence. This is particularly true of Bulgaria, where the Gypsies had established themselves in various parts of the country, not only as farmers and workmen but also as artisans.'[1-2] The Review *Zemedelske Noviny* of Prague made it clear in 1957 that, in Czechoslovakia, forty per cent of the Gypsy population had settled down to work in agriculture and industry.

Czechoslovakia seems in fact to be the first country to solve this delicate problem of integration in accordance with humane standards. A 'Law of Assimilation' was promulgated on 17 October 1958 with a view to the settlement of 40,000 Gypsies. Official radio emphasized that

the duty of national committees is to separate big concentrations of Gypsies into villages, streets or houses, in order to prevent Gypsy families from bringing pressure on each other, and to make them live on the same cultural level as their non-Gypsy neighbours. National committees must find permanent dwellings for all Gypsy families as well as permanent kinds of employment. All Gypsy children must attend schools, kindergartens and nurseries. We should never be able to proclaim that we had achieved a beneficent cultural revolution if we allowed

1. *Témoignages*, op. cit.
2. See also *Journal of the Gypsy Lore Society*, Vol. XXXVIII, Nos. 3–4, for a most interesting account of the Moscow Gypsy Theatre, based on information supplied to Dr Bertha Malnik. This is a much appreciated and flourishing theatre, in which the Russian Gypsies are encouraged to present their own folk-lore, songs, dances, legends and age-old traditions. It is called *Romen Teatr*. Gypsies have always been popular in Russia, and they have rarely been cruelly treated there. During World War II, they fought bravely, and their knowledge of horses proved very valuable to General Budenny and his Cavalry, especially during the great final offensive which drove the Germans from Soviet territory. *Tr.*

thousands of our fellow-creatures to live in a primitive way and without culture.[1]

In Bulgaria, 'settlement' has taken a somewhat rougher turn. A decree published in *Izvestia* (Sofia) in 1958 made it compulsory for all without regular employment to work in State industries or agricultural undertakings.

In Poland the situation has not yet been officially regularized. The Warsaw *Swiat* of 6 July 1958 complained that 'the years of effort to settle the Gypsies have not produced great results so far. There are from ten to twenty thousand families established at Nowa Huta and at Walbzrych; that is all. The others continue to wander in the open air.'

GYPSIES AND NON-GYPSIES

Nor has the problem of the Gypsies in France been regularized. Nevertheless it is on the agenda of things to be dealt with, and several private bodies – including *La Société des Études Tsiganes*, whose President is M. de Join-Lambert – are doing their utmost to convince the powers-that-be of the urgency for some measures. But, the administrative aspect of the question being disregarded, it must be fully recognized that in France there is racialist feeling against Gypsies, whether they be nomads or sedentaries. The old popular beliefs, the inherited distrust usual to country people and the caste spirit of townspeople and suburbanites condemn the Gypsies to the status of untouchables. They are consulted in secret, people buy some item of trumpery from them, but they are employed only with aversion. Like the North Africans (and I quote this example quite apart from the political fact of the Algerian War), the Gypsies similarly constitute little closed pockets which their fierce independence alone does not create or consolidate. In French towns there are Gypsy quarters, landed properties, cafés, localities and plots of ground, into which the *gadjé* do not go. As for the nomads, their mere appearance almost automatically releases on the part of peasants a reaction which greatly resembles that of a snail. Doors are shut, rabbit-hutches are locked up, and even children are guarded. In the South of France, where French people are much more hospitable, they hardly allow Gypsies to camp in the corner of a field, on the side of a road or at a crossroads.

1. Quoted by *Témoignages*, op. cit.

To settle the Gypsy problem means to settle the problem of the official measures relating to nomad populations. Now these are still governed by a law of 1912, which regards every Gypsy as a nomad, that is, a vagabond. This person, without a domicile, without any recognized occupation, is compelled whenever requested to show an extremely complicated anthropometrical pass-book, giving surname and Christian name and the surname by which the person is known, the name of his (or her) country of origin, the date and place of birth, as well as 'references of a nature to establish identity'. Up to this point one need not grumble. But this little book must likewise give the 'anthropometric' description of the bearer: height, chest measurement, breadth of head, bizygomatic diameter, length of right ear, length of fingers (left middle and little fingers), length from left middle finger to elbow, length of left foot, colour of eyes. It all seems like a bad dream! Furthermore, provisions are made so that fingerprints and two photographs (full face and profile) must be provided.

The use of this 'carnet' limits to the minimum the freedom of the nomad, who 'before staying in a commune (a parish), must on arrival and departure have his personal carnet endorsed by the Police Superintendent, or in default by the commandant of the local Brigade of Gendarmerie, or in default by the mayor of the said commune'. In addition to this document, the head of a family is obliged to show a 'collective' carnet in which are described 'all persons attaching to the family head by bonds of law, or those in actual fact included in the group travelling with the family head'.

It will be agreed that the obligation to be furnished with this document, and to have to show it on request, in fact likens the Gypsies to powerful malefactors. It is ignominious, blundering and . . . useless.

It is probable, fortunately, that this uncouth practical joke will be called off before long. Furthermore, the Church on the one hand, and good-hearted people on the other, for several years have been visiting the poorest Gypsies and alleviating their lot in life. It is not my purpose here to give the results achieved by this effort of the priesthood,[1] but there is one point which I would like to emphasize strongly: that is the essential problem of education. The majority of the Gypsies are still illiterate, their nomadism, like their way of life, not having given them access to schools. Even today, when Gypsy

1. On this subject consult the issues of *Études Tsiganes* to date.

children temporarily attend communal classes, they, like their parents, come up against the hostility of the 'sedentaries'. The families of other pupils do not fail to complain of the 'intolerable promiscuity'. The non-Gypsy children take the little Gypsies as scapegoats, roused by the pejorative comments they hear on all sides. As for the teachers, what it comes to for the most part is that they relegate the nomad children to the bottom of the class, and leave them to shift for themselves, arguing that the ephemeral nature of their presence renders any attempt to educate them impossible.

This question of Gypsy schooling is sufficiently urgent for several countries to be making definite efforts at this moment. These countries have recognized that important factors must be taken into consideration: in France, for example, the fact that the children cannot remain at a school for more than forty-eight hours (the time-limit imposed on nomad Gypsies for their stay at one place), or more than a few days, when local legislation is more generous; next, the natural unadaptability of these children to the discipline of time-tables, impositions, silence and remaining quiet in school; and, finally, their cultural equipment which is based exclusively on tradition, and a kind of life that is fundamentally the opposite of that of Gypsies who have settled down.

Spain has created special schools, under the jurisdiction of the Governor of Granada, for the Gypsy population of Sacro Monte. Of very modern conception, these schools prove an example to be referred to. The courses of instruction take place in the open air, and are adapted to the primitive culture of the little *Gitanos*.

In Sweden an attempt has been made to create travelling schools, but the results are not yet conclusive; the government sees the need for maintaining them during the summer months, because of the seasonal nomadism of the Swedish Gypsies, but is thinking of opening permanent schools near their winter camping grounds. Other travelling schools, but these religious, exist in Morocco where the Gypsy population is comparatively important. In England the Gypsies have been obliged to send their children to primary schools since 1908. But the matter of constant attendance always raises the same problems. In Russia, at last, several big towns have schools specially organized for the young Gypsies. Itinerant monitors regularly proceed to the usual routes of the nomads. Courses of instruction are given at the same time in Russian and *romani*, of which the conservation is from now onwards part of the linguistic patrimony of Soviet countries. Adults may attend all evening courses, primary, secondary and technical.

In France only the Church has attempted some experiments, and they are too recent for the results to be taken into consideration. It may be said that, in practice, everything remains to be done in this field. For a long time to come the Gypsies will camp in their usual places and they will light their fires in corners of our woods, consoling themselves with the nostalgic songs of far-away Asia and oldest Europe.

SUPPLEMENTARY NOTES
ON BRITISH AND AMERICAN GYPSIES
BY THE TRANSLATOR

In the British Isles there are some 50,000 people who are, collectively, spoken and often written of as 'Gypsies'. The generalization is grossly inaccurate, and it is essential from the outset to be quite clear about four main groups which make up this total:

1. Romanies : about 10,000 – these are true *Roms*.
2. *Posh-rats* : about 10,000 – half-bloods.
3. *Didakais* : about 10,000 – mixed, less than half-blood.
4. Travellers : about 20,000 – no Gypsy blood.
   TOTAL: ABOUT 50,000

These are not official figures. They are careful and 'conservative' estimates made by Mr Derek Tipler, who is deeply interested in these people and, failing any official figures, decided to make his own census, which is probably not far wrong. As this book is concerned with true Romanies, and not with Groups 2, 3 and 4, I shall (and *must* because of the nature of the 'Gypsy problem' in Britain) first say a few words about the 40,000 non-Gypsies who are loosely lumped together with the real *Roms* by nearly everybody in Britain.

The reader will remember from Jean-Paul Clébert's text (page 160) that, if a true *Rom* should contract a marriage or conjugal alliance with a non-Gypsy, 'More often than not it brings with it *exclusion from the tribe*, and the outlaw *no longer has the right to the name Gypsy*' (my italics). What mostly happens in Britain is that each group of *posh-rats* and *didakais* keep to themselves and the pure *Roms* also keep fairly strictly to themselves. Nevertheless there have been many marriages between *Roms* and non-Gypsies. Those who are not true Gypsies abandon most of the old traditional practices, though they do not always follow the same occupations as those of the true Gypsies and, to all intents and purposes, follow a way of life that is closer to that of Romanies than to that of British people. The so-called 'travellers' are steadily increasing in numbers. They are mostly caravan-dwellers who go from place to place and make some sort of living as they move about. Many have joined them merely because of the 'free life' and do not seem to have to worry about making a living. Among the 'travellers' one sometimes finds very obvious 'escapists'. *Posh-rats*, *didakais* and 'travellers' often make nuisances of themselves to farmers and townsfolk, for reasons that are not far to seek: unlike the *Roms*, they have no real traditions of their own; and they are not always entirely respectful of the 'Law of the Land' which, everywhere in the British Isles, makes no distinction between any of these groups of wanderers and the true-born English, Welsh or Scottish people. Troubles arise from their inveterate habit of wishing to camp anywhere there seems to be an inviting piece of land, and because they often leave behind them a lot of litter for the landowner to clear away.

The true *Roms* are very different in innumerable ways. No great sociological study has yet been made of the differences, but, for anybody who has read the pages of this book, it may be roughly summed up by saying that most of the British *Roms* follow, in usually less intense forms, traditions observed by Gypsies on the European continent, adapting themselves, when they think fit, to British customs. They are, on the whole, peaceable people who seldom make nuisances of themselves and almost invariably follow law-abiding occupations of their own choice. They have their own taboos, marriage customs, and the usual Gypsies' customs of death and burial. The women are fortune-tellers; many of the men are quite good fiddlers. But they do not often approach some of the continental Gypsies as dancers or musicians; and they are not often so blazingly colourful as some of the continentals. But they, too, have their troubles and some are constantly being 'moved on', which they accept with the fatalism of the true Gypsy.

In August 1962 an historic decision was made by the Minister for Housing and Local Government of the British Government. He granted planning permission for the use for two years of a site at Lodge Lane, Cobham, Kent, as a Gypsy encampment. Kent County Council was already working in conjunction with district councils to provide long-term sites for Gypsies, and the Minister hoped that these would be ready before August 1963. Mr Norman Dodds, M.P., who campaigned indefatigably for the grant of suitable sites for Gypsies, regarded the provisional grant and promise of permanent sites as a great experiment; no doubt it will duly be followed by others.

'English Romanies speak a very corrupt dialect (excepting for a small group surviving mostly in Wales)' – this statement I overheard some time ago at an English university. It is, I think, a half truth. English Romany, as spoken by the majority of British *Roms*, certainly *is* a corrupt dialect; like most Gypsy dialects, it takes advantage of the language of the environment – everyday English, in this case – for a rough kind of accidence, mixing in English words, provincialisms and slang, and conforming to English common usage for the order of words in a sentence. It has abandoned almost entirely the inflexions of the old *romani* language. But in Wales the old 'deep Romany' still survives, I am assured, to a far greater extent than one might imagine. Alas, there are no statistics. John Sampson (see Supplementary Bibliography) made a great discovery in 1894:

... I chanced upon a Welsh harper at Bala, and made the discovery that the ancient Romani tongue, so long extinct in England and Scotland, had been miraculously preserved by the Gypsies of the Principality. As I listened to Edward Wood unconcernedly discoursing in a dialect hardly less pure than that of Paspati's Tchinghianés, I felt almost with a sense of awe that Borrow's dream was fulfilled in my own person, and that this was the very speech of two hundred years ago ... and the dialect so religiously kept intact in the fastnesses of Cambria is thus a survival of the oldest and purest form of British Romani.

Webb, an English writer (whose excellent book *Gypsies: The Secret People*, London, 1960, can be recommended), says this:

There may be a few old Gypsies who can still speak the Romani as a complete grammatical language, but I doubt it. But, of course, you can never be sure about Gypsies. I fancy that no matter how well you may think you know them, they know a great deal about a great many things that they will never admit to a 'gorgio'. And that includes their knowledge of the Romani language.

On this Vesey-Fitzgerald wisely comments:

How very true! How very perceptive! ... I think that there are many who can still speak a complete *Romanes*, grammatical enough, when need arises. I do not believe that the language is dying out. I think that, under the press of modern conditions, it is becoming more secret.

One may say that in Britain we still have true and worthy *Roms*, who, like their continental racial brethren, preserve the old traditions and the old language. In Wales, they may still be found following the old avocations, recorded by Sampson: harpers, fiddlers, horse-dealers, knife-grinders, basket-makers, woodcutters, fortune-tellers, hawkers and, for Gypsies, the rare work of fishermen.

The writer of these notes has had very little practical experience and no long-term close contacts with the Gypsies of the United States of America. What follows is therefore based on the observations of competent and reliable non-Gypsy Americans who have proved themselves to be interested in the subject, and though sympathetic towards Gypsies, are objective in what they have recorded. This field for observation is obviously an extremely rich one; in Britain it has been possible to sort out into four main groups some 50,000 people who have been called 'Gypsies', to find that there are only about 10,000 who really merit the name. But Britain is a compact little island in which it is easy enough for the interested person who is willing and can spare the time to see most of the *Roms* and judge them at close quarters. The geographical nature and size of the U.S. makes this more difficult. Furthermore, the American Gypsy population mostly consists, not of long settled Gypsies like that of Britain, but of *Romanichels* originating in many countries, and arriving in the U.S. at different times, but mostly within a period of at most one hundred years. The true American *Roms* have not yet been fully or very systematically charted. Yet, in spite of the *lacunae* in exact knowledge, it may be said that, broadly speaking, in reading about the American Gypsies, the person who knows as much about Gypsies as is given in this book by M. Clébert will find himself on very familiar ground. It is indeed strikingly remarkable that, in spite of the Atlantic Ocean and the distance of separation between American Gypsies and their roots in Europe, the Near East, or countries of the Communist world, the general pattern of Gypsy life remains fundamentally more or less the same as that of Europe. Of course, one must never forget that, wherever they go and remain for any length of time, the Gypsies will adapt their way of life to suit the environment, compromising in many directions. A very simple example of this is that American Gypsies, like all other Americans, make greater use of the automobile, the telephone, consumer goods and, as one correspondent tells me in reply to a direct question, quite often of the banking system! To those of us accustomed to think in terms of European Gypsies, it is not easy to conjure up the image of a Gypsy flourishing a cheque book.

This adaptability applies, as might be expected, to the impure

Romany dialect spoken by many American Gypsies; others keep more closely, especially the old ones, to their more inflected European dialects. The corrupt Romany follows the same pattern as other corrupt Romany dialects. Many American Gypsies have made a viable speech through American English syntax, plus a vocabulary of Romany and English mixed – the brand of Romany depending upon whatever original dialect the tribe spoke, or the old people still speak. The nearest parallel is corrupt English Romany, which has Welsh, Southern, Eastern and Scottish words added to the almost uninflected simple English that makes it viable. But here again, one must allow for some slight difference and words common in the areas most frequented by the American Gypsies. This transference and adaptation by the Gypsies everywhere resulting in a compound language consisting of *romani*, plus local vernacular to form a 'grammar', plus a mixed practical vocabulary for purposes of everyday life in a given country, is an extremely interesting linguistic phenomenon from which much light could come on the formation and growth of language. It is a possible study for priority in the new science of Linguistics; a vast amount of Gypsy raw material is there awaiting investigation.

Although American Gypsies tend to keep to the old occupations (as workers in metals, tinsmiths, coppersmiths, goldsmiths, silversmiths, platers, musicians, and the women as fortune-tellers, small traders, pedlars, dancers etc., as recorded in this book), they rarely if ever engage in heavy or strenuous work (like, for example, the Irish), and in the United States they often make very good money by their skills. That applies chiefly to Gypsies of East European origin. There is a fair number of American Gypsies who are descendants of English Gypsies and, like English Gypsies, they quite often work in the fields. In the United States, the tribal organization continues as clan or sept (or as the 'family', which may be numerous and elastic) and is the Gypsy unit – as elsewhere. There are tribal chiefs (or 'kings', as formerly 'dukes'), and the chief follows and keeps discipline relating to traditions. He often acts as banker for the tribe, and always has a share of the community's money. What we call the caravan is used as itinerant habitat (but is called a house-trailer or 'house-wagon'); those who move about also use the tent, and form camps. As in other countries (France, for example), many take houses or apartments for the winter; and 'camp' in them, sleeping on the floor. Gypsies as small traders are found in many cities and not far away is the eternal Gypsy woman telling fortunes. It would be possible to extend this note on occupations indefinitely, but such an extension, it seems, would merely amount to recording slight modifications of the general Gypsy pattern.

The majority of American Gypsies are poor, and seem quite content to be so. Many live in cities and, among these, the old men and women are nostalgic for the old way of life on the roads, which becomes more difficult every day – as in Britain and elsewhere. Georgina J. Traverso provides a vivid and lively account of 'Some Gypsies in Boston, Mass.', and particularly interesting is her description of an old Gypsy woman named Mara Miller:

> She wore a long green skirt with a border of coarse yellow lace and a maroon cardigan over a full, Gypsy blouse of brown floral cloth. Her long plaits fell down her back, tied together at the ends and her *diklo* [kerchief], which was of a gaudy yellow, orange and green pattern, was worn in the old style, rather low over the forehead and tied at the back with long ends hanging down.[1]

This might be an old Gypsy woman of Continental Europe. The *New Yorker*[2] has a long article about New York Gypsies with the title *The Beautiful Flower*. This article is important if only for some cogent references to the attitude of the New York police *vis-à-vis* the Gypsies. Georgina Traverso comments:

> Despite the fact that these detectives often had to arrest them, the Gypsies seemed to like and confide in them, undoubtedly because of that very feeling of sympathy. It is highly commendable that a modern, efficient, tough-minded police force should have men who, despite the demands of their work, have the ability to understand and appreciate to some degree these people who refuse to conform to the ways of normal society or to obey the laws of the *gadjo*.[3]

British Gypsies, I mean the pure *Roms*, have been so long in Britain that they call themselves English, Welsh or Scots. To Spanish Gypsies the same applies; they mostly call themselves 'Spaniards'. American Gypsies, possibly because they have not yet taken full root in the country of their adoption, tend to consider themselves first and foremost as Gypsies and then as American nationals, and usually refer to their *gadjé* fellow citizens as 'Americans' or

1. *J.G.L.S.* Vol. XXXVII, Parts 3–4, pp. 126–37.
2. 4 June 1955.
3. *J.G.L.S.* Vol. XXXV, Parts 3–4, pp. 177–80.

'American People', just as the French *Manouches* and *Gitans* usually speak of *les Français*. I cannot comment on this, but can tell what my friend A. F. Tschiffely, the author of *Tschiffely's Ride*, knowing my interest in Gypsies, told me:

We [he always referred to himself and his two horses as 'we'] had had some hard going in the mountains and one day reached a favourable place for a long view ahead. The atmosphere was beautifully clear and there, some miles straight ahead and below in a valley, I saw a covered wagon pulled by two horses with a man leading them and people walking beside and behind the vehicle. We made for them as quickly as my horses could move down the mountain-side. As I approached the group, I saw dark men and women and at first thought they were Peruvians. But, as I approached, I heard English spoken: American English, which surprised me greatly – at the foot of the *cordillera*! I came up to them, got off my horse, and asked them who they were and where they were going. An elderly man in a wonderful get-up with all sorts of silver and even gold ornaments all over him, it seemed, and top-boots, spoke to me in good English and said: 'We are Romanies from the United States and are travelling south to join some friends and relations in Argentina. Is it very far and will it be hard going?'

Tschiffely was quite taken aback. Here he was attempting a most difficult ride, alone with two horses. Here was a group of Gypsies who were doing the same thing; a whole family, with a wagon, women and children! I am unable to complete the story by recording that they reached the Argentine Republic. But there they were, gaily on their way, thinking apparently nothing of it, and treating it as all in the day's work. American Gypsies, yes; but Gypsies first and foremost, emulating their remote ancestors who came from North India to the most westerly parts of Europe. And so these wanderers go on wandering, still happy to wander – as in the past, for over a thousand years.

No official statistics, nor even approximate estimates of the Gypsy population in the United States of America, are available. The reason for this is that immigration statistics and Census Reports list Gypsies simply as 'foreign born' with the name of the country from which they have come. It remains for some foundation or private body to undertake this task, which might produce results of considerable historical interest. Furthermore, there is very little reliable modern literature on the subject, though Irving Brown's *Gypsy Fires in America* (published U.S.A. *c.* 1930) and *A Gypsy in*

New York by Juliette de Bairacli Levy (published London, 1962) go below the surface of the subject. Worthy of mention also is Joseph Mitchell's excellent reportage, long and full of details, in the *New Yorker* magazine of 4 June 1955. It may be said, in general, of these writings that they disclose little that does not come within the patterns of Gypsy life recorded in this book by Clébert, with modifications to be expected springing from the American environment, on lines not very dissimilar from those noted above for British Gypsies. The really comprehensive work on American Gypsies remains to be written.

BIBLIOGRAPHY

This is the author's 'Summary Bibliography' and relates only to works of
gypsiology, especially those quoted in his main text. The translator has
added a 'Supplementary Bibliography' for English-speaking readers
who may wish to know more about British and American Gypsies. See
pages 270–73.

ARNOLD: *Vaganten, Komoedianten, Fieranten u. Briganten.* ...
Stuttgart, 1958.

BATAILLARD: *De l'apparition des Bohémiens en Europe.* 1844. *Nouvelles
recherches sur l'apparition des Bohémiens en Europe.* 1849. *État de
l'ancienneté des Tziganes en Europe.* 1876.

BAUDRIMONT: *Les Bohémiens du Pays Basque.* 1862.

BERCOVICI: *The Story of the Gypsies.* New York, 1928.

BERNARD: *Mœurs des Bohémiens de Moldavie et de Valachie.* 1869.

BLOCH, (J.): *Les Tsiganes.* 1953.

BLOCK, (M.): *Mœurs et coutumes des Tziganes.* 1936.

CHATARD, (Rev. P.): *Zanko; Traditions, coutumes et légendes des
Tziganes Chalderash.* 1959.

CHINA, (O.): *Os Ciganos do Brazil.* São Paulo, 1936.

DECOURDEMANCHE: *Grammaire du Tchingané ou langue des
Bohémiens errants.* 1908.

FEVRE, (J.-L.): *Les Fils du Vent.* 1954.

GRABERG: *Doutes et conjectures sur les Bohémiens et leur première
apparition en Europe.* No date, but before 1817.

GRAFFUNDER: *De la langue des Bohémiens.* 1835.

GRELLMANN: *Histoire des Bohémiens.* Translation dated 1810.

HAESSLER: *Enfants de la grande route.* 1955.

HAMPE: *Die fahrenden Leute in der deutschen Vergangenheit.* Leipzig,
1902.

KOGALTNICHEANU: *Esquisse sur l'histoire, les mœurs et la langue des
Cigains.* 1837.

LAFUENTE: *Los Gitanos, el flamenco y los flamencos.* Barcelona,
1955.

LESPINASSE: *Les Bohémiens du Pays Basque.* 1863.

LISZT, (F.): *Des Bohémiens et leur musique en Hongrie.* 1881.

Maximoff, (M.): *Les Ursitory* (novel). 1945. *Le Prix de la Liberté.* 1947. *Savina* (novel). 1948. *Wanderndes Volk auf endloser Strasse.* Zürich, 1959.

Neukomm: *Les Bohémiens chez eux.* 1898.

Pechon de Ruby: *La Vie généreuse des Gueux, Mercelots et Boesmiens.* 1596.

Pittard, (E.): *Les Tziganes ou Bohémiens dans la péninsule des Balkans.* 1932.

Pott: *Les Tziganes d'Asie et de l'Europe.* 1844.

Sampson: *The Dialect of the Gypsies of Wales.* 1926.

Samuel: *The Gypsies, their origin, continuance and destination.* London, 1836.

Serboianu, (P.): *Les Tziganes.* 1930.

Vaillant: *Les Roms, histoire vraie des vrais Bohémiens.* 1857.

De Ville, (F.): *Tziganes.* Brussels, 1956.

Wolf: *Grosses Wörterbuch der Zigeunersprache, Wortschatz deutscher u. anderer Zigeunerdialekte.* Mannheim, 1961.

Yates, (D.): *A Book of Gypsy Folk-Tales.* London, 1948.

Periodical publications

Journal of the Gypsy Lore Society (founded in 1888). Correspondence to: Miss Dora Yates, M.A., The University Library, Liverpool, England.

Études Tsiganes. Bulletin de la Société des Études Tsiganes, 5, rue Las-Cases, Paris, 7e.

Ciba, Basle, 1939. Nº spécial sur la magie médicale des Tziganes.

Problèmes. Revue de l'Association des étudiants en médecine de Paris, No. 35, 1956.

SUPPLEMENTARY BIBLIOGRAPHY
TO THE ENGLISH EDITION

Note: The inclusion of the items which follow is intended: (1) to serve English language readers as a guide to further reading on British and American Gypsies; (2) as a guide to some important or interesting works on Gypsies in general. It is not intended to be exhaustive.

BERCOVICI: His book *The Story of the Gypsies* contains an interesting chapter on the American Gypsies (U.S.A.). He often writes with feeling rather than objectivity, and is inclined to romanticize.

BLACK, George F.: *A Gypsy Bibliography.* Gypsy Lore Society Monographs No. 1. Printed for the Members of the Gypsy Lore Society, at the Edinburgh University Press, 1914. Published by Bernard Quaritch, 11 Grafton Street, New Bond Street, London. It includes, 'besides separately published books and pamphlets, papers in the proceedings of societies, or periodicals, magazine articles, important references in books dealing principally with other subjects'. The best bibliographical guide up to 1913.

BLOCK, Martin: *Gypsies.* Published London 1938, the English edition of his scholarly book *Die Zigeuner*, an important contribution to the subject.

BORROW, George: No writer about Gypsies in English has been more popular than Borrow, whose works, up to 1913, occupy over four pages of Black's Bibliography. The most important for the general reader are:

The Zincali: or an Account of the Gypsies of Spain. With an original collection of their songs and poetry, and a copious dictionary of their language. First published by John Murray, London, 1841, and many times reprinted.

The Bible in Spain. First published by John Murray, London, 1843, and many times reprinted. The pocket edition, with notes and a glossary by U. R. Burke, serves the general reader.

Lavengro: The Scholar – The Gypsy – The Priest. First published by John Murray, London, 1851, in three volumes. Many times reprinted. In Everyman Library.

Romany Lavo Lil: Word-book of Romany; or, the Gypsy Language. First published by John Murray in 1874, and many times reprinted.

Note: Borrow translated the Gospel of Saint Luke into *caló*, the dialect of the Spanish Gitanos (published in Madrid, 1837). This is both a literary and a linguistic curiosity. It shows that Borrow wrote this interesting dialect with clarity and grace.

CACCINI, G. S.: *L'ultima parola sugli Zincari*. Published in Foligno, 1911. The author was a half-blood Gypsy.

COLOCCI, Adriano Amerigo, Marquis de: *Storia d'un popolo errante*. A general account, with special reference to Italian Gypsies and containing a vocabulary *Italiano-Tchinghiane*. Published in Turin, 1889.

CROFTON – see SMART and CROFTON.

GILLIAT-SMITH, Bernard Joseph: a writer on Gypsies and their dialects, of which his knowledge must be unique. His contributions to the subjects began in the early part of this century, happily continue, and are mostly to be found in the pages of the *Journal of the Gypsy Lore Society*. A great gypsiologist.

GROOME, Francis Hindes: *In Gypsy Tents*. First published by Nimmo & Co., London, 1880.
Gypsy Folk Tales. First published by Hurst & Blackett, London, 1899.

LELAND, Charles Godfrey: *The English Gypsies and their Language*. Published in London and New York, 1873. Several times reprinted.
The Gypsies. Contains accounts of Russian, Austrian, English, Welsh and American Gypsies; Gypsies in the East; Gypsy names and family characteristics; Gypsy stories in Romany, etc. First published in London and Boston, 1882.
Both books are valuable for their linguistic material and folklore.

MAXIMOFF, Matéo: *The Ursitory*. A novel published in French, and in English (1948).
Savina. A novel, not yet published in English but available in French. He is the first full-blooded Gypsy to have written novels, and these are characterized by a stark authenticity and *farouche* realism. Maximoff is a Kalderash Gypsy. His people are noted for their observance of the old traditions of the race.

MIKLOSICH, Franz Xaver von: *Beiträge zur Kenntniss der Zigeunermundarten*. In four parts, published Vienna, 1874–8.
Über die Mundarten und die Wanderungen der Zigeuner Europas. In twelve parts, Vienna, 1872–81.
Two great works of scholarship which provide a mine of information on Gypsy dialects, folk-lore, customs and the wanderings of the Gypsies. Indispensable for serious students.

PASPATI, Alexandre G.: *Études sur les Tchinghianés ou Bohémiens de l'Empire Ottoman*. Published in Constantinople, 1870. An indispensable work for students of *romani* and linguistics. (The Greek name of the author is Alexandros Georgios Paspates, but he is better known as Paspati.)

REBOLLEDO, Tineo: *Diccionario Gitano-Español y Español-Gitano.* Published in Barcelona and Buenos Aires, 1909. Contains what is probably the fullest existing vocabulary of *caló* and some of the grammar, including conjugations of auxiliary and regular verbs. Useful for the interested traveller, though the scholarship is often questionable.

SALES MAYO, Francisco de: *Los Gitanos, su historia, sus costumbres, su dialecto.* With a vocabulary *caló-castellano.* Madrid, 1869. A treatise on Spanish Gypsies.
El Gitanismo. Another (revised) edition of the preceding work. Madrid, 1870.
Note: The author also wrote under the Gypsy form of his name: *Quindalé-Mayo* (English, 'May').

SAMPSON, John: *The Dialect of the Gypsies of Wales: Being the older form of British Romani preserved in the clan of Abram Wood.* Published by Oxford University Press, 1926. This book is a landmark in linguistics and philology. The author devised a practical phonetic alphabet for *romani*, took down in writing the speech of the Wood clan, and from it evolved a very full grammar and vocabulary, here published. Of it the late Augustus John, O.M., wrote: 'There must be many of our members of the Gypsy Lore Society who find it, as I do, the best bedside book in the world.' There are few if any modern books which cover so much ground in the richly inflected *romani* language, preserved by a small 'pocket' of Gypsies in Wales.
Welsh Gypsy Folk Tales. Gregynog Press, 1933.
The Wind on the Heath: A Gypsy Anthology. The compiler's 'attempt to interpret to gentile (and I hope gentle) readers something of the glamour that enwraps the Gypsy race, and their strange choice of ways in their earthly pilgrimage'. The most comprehensive anthology in English on the subject, by a great gypsiologist (himself a writer of poetry in *romani*).

SIMSON, Walter: *History of the Gypsies.* London, 1865.

SINCLAIR, A. T.: American-Romani Vocabulary, edited by G. F. Black. *J.G.L.S.* new series, IX, pp. 185–222. Edinburgh, 1916.

SMART, B. C. and CROFTON, H. T.: *The Dialect of the English Gypsies.* Contains a short descriptive grammar and a Vocabulary. Published London, 1875. It is interesting to compare this corrupted Romany with John Sampson's *romani*.

STARKIE, Walter: *Raggle Taggle – Adventures with a Fiddle in Hungary and Roumania.* London, 1929.
Spanish Raggle-Taggle – Adventures with a Fiddle in North Spain. London, 1934 (and Penguin Edition, 1961).
In Sara's Tents. A book on continental European Gypsies, set round

their annual pilgrimage to the shrine of Saintes-Maries-de-la-Mer. London, 1954.

Walter Starkie, C.M.G., is President of the Gypsy Lore Society, in succession to the late Augustus John, O.M. He has written many contributions to the *J.G.L.S.*, speaks fluent *caló*, and has had much experience of Gypsies and their lore. A fine violinist, he is a magnificent player of Gypsy music. All his works are lively, scholarly and show deep sympathy with the Gypsies, whom he loves and admires.

VAILLANT, J. A.: *Grammaire, dialogues et vocabulaire de la langue des Bohémiens ou Cigains.* Paris, 1868.

VESEY-FITZGERALD, Brian: *Gypsies of Britain, an Introduction to their History.* Published London, 1944. A most unassuming book, nevertheless a very excellent introduction to British Gypsies, whom he knows well.

WEBB, G. E. C.: *Gypsies: The Secret People.* With illustrations by the author. London, 1960.

YATES, Dora E.: *My Gypsy Days.* Autobiography of the veteran Honorary Secretary of the Gypsy Lore Society, which she has helped to grow from modest beginnings. Not only a record of her own almost limitless work for Gypsies and gypsiology, but valuable also for her reminiscences of John Sampson, one of the greatest of gypsiologists.

Note on The Gypsy Lore Society

The Gypsy Lore Society was founded in 1888 with the object of improving the conditions of Gypsy study, promoting the thorough investigation of Gypsy problems from all possible points of view, collating the results obtained by different processes; and publishing such results in a quarterly *Journal*. It was difficult going for the Society in its early days, so much so that, after four years, the *Journal* had to cease publication, thus ending its first Series, now recognized as an indispensable source of knowledge hitherto almost entirely neglected in Britain. It is almost impossible now to buy a copy of the *Journal* in that series. But publication was resumed in 1907, when the Society and *Journal* expanded their scope. The second Series of the *Journal* consists of nine volumes, volume I and part 1 of volume II of which are out of stock, but other volumes and numbers may be purchased from the Society. The third Series began in January 1922. The Society also published some valuable Monographs, of which Black's invaluable *A Gypsy Bibliography* and Sir D. MacAlister's *Romaní Versions* are still available. All requests for sets, volumes or numbers of the Society's *Journal*, and all other communications relating to the work of the Society should be addressed to: Miss D. Yates, M.A., Hon. Secretary, The Gypsy Lore Society, The University Library, Liverpool.

INDEX

The index of the French original has been
enlarged for this English edition – *Tr.*

n. denotes footnote